THE LAST HORSEMAN

DAVID GILMAN enjoyed many careers, including firefighter, soldier and photographer before turning to writing full time. He is an award-winning author and screenwriter.

www.davidgilman.com
www.facebook.com/davidgilman.author
@davidgilmanuk

Also by David Gilman

MASTER OF WAR

DEFIANT UNTO DEATH

GATE OF THE DEAD

DAVID GILMAN

THE LAST HORSEMAN

First published in the UK in 2016 by Head of Zeus Ltd.

9 7 5 3 1 2 4 6 8

A CIP catalogue record for this book is available from the British Library.

ISBN (HB) 9781784974541
ISBN (XTPB) 9781784974558
ISBN (E) 9781784974534

Typeset by Adrian McLaughlin

Printed and bound in Germany by GGP Media GmbH, Pössneck

Head of Zeus Ltd
Clerkenwell House
45–47 Clerkenwell Green
London EC1R 0HT

WWW.HEADOFZEUS.COM

For Suzy, as always

And in memory of my friend James Ambrose Brown,
journalist, author and playwright

A war in South Africa would be one of the most serious wars that could possibly be waged… it would leave behind it the embers of a strife which, I believe, generations would hardly be long enough to extinguish.

Joseph Chamberlain,
British Colonial Secretary in 1896

England must not fall. It would mean an inundation of Russian and German political degradations… a sort of Middle-Age night and slavery which would last until Christ comes again… Even wrong – and she is wrong – England must be upheld.

Mark Twain,
writing in 1900

SOUTH AFRICA
–1900–

DUBLIN, IRELAND

DECEMBER 1899–JANUARY 1900

CHAPTER ONE

It was a foul night to hang a man. The rain swept across the Irish Sea, throwing itself against the grey stone walls of Dublin's Mountjoy Prison. Behind its unyielding façade two prison guards stood outside the condemned man's cell. The number was imprinted on a small metal plaque: D1. It was barely a dozen shuffling steps from the cell across the passage and through the door to the execution chamber. Dermot McCann was twenty-seven years old. He was a thug and a killer, and refused to show these bastard guards his fear. The priest's incantation barely entered his mind, the words pluming in the cold air of the prison's walls as the guards fastened manacles on his wrists. His body stiffened, a moment of resistance, his arm muscles straining. One of the guards, the older man, one of the few who hadn't cursed him for being a Fenian bastard, spoke quietly, his hand squeezing McCann's shoulder. 'Steady, lad. This isn't the time.'

With barely a moment's hesitation they had stepped through the cell door, across the landing, followed by the priest and the small entourage of officials required by law to witness his death. Voices echoed from some of the half-dozen men incarcerated in other cells.

'You took more than they can take from you, Dermot!'

'You're a martyr to the cause, Dermot McCann!'

'It's an Englishman that's hanging ya, my lad! No Irishman would do it!'

But in one of the cells a young man shivered with fear, knees hugged to his chest, back against the cold stone wall. Danny O'Hagan had yet to see his seventeenth birthday, and it would not be long before they moved him into D1. He had neither the courage nor the bravado to face such a cold-blooded death, and every shuffling scuff that echoed from the condemned man's final steps squeezed his heart to near suffocation.

The door to the execution chamber closed behind McCann. Eyes wide, he gazed at the wooden platform, painted black, and the whitewashed stone walls. They called the place of execution the 'hang house' – a narrow covered yard where parallel beams ran along the underside of the roof into the gable walls. The hanging rope was attached to chains affixed to these beams. Below the scaffold, in the flickering half-light of the gas lamps, witnesses to his execution gazed up, eyes shadowed beneath their hat brims. They were all men, a mixture of police officers, lawyers and prison guards joined by other civilians who were there to witness his death. His escort had eased him, almost without him realizing it, to the noose that hung immobile in the dank air. A snare drum's death roll echoed across the yard. He looked up in the direction of the sound, but it was just the rain beating on to the pitched glass roof.

His body trembled as the black-suited executioner stepped forward.

'It's the cold. Nothing more,' McCann said.

There was one man among the witnesses who had already respectfully removed his hat, and who gazed directly at the condemned man. Joseph Radcliffe was a big man with a broken nose. His eyes always gleamed brightly, and his big hands were wrinkled and tough from years on the open plains. He wore his hair short and kept his face clean-shaven. McCann locked on to his eyes, desperately drawing courage from

Radcliffe, who had defended him in court but who had failed to save his life.

McCann's mind found a second of clarity, but the words that formed – *God bless Ireland!* – never reached his lips. The black hood was pulled down across his face, and the words swallowed as he gasped in fear. His panic ended a moment later. The lever was pulled. The trapdoor crashed open. And his final gasp of life went unheard beneath the clattering of the rain.

The Mountjoy Prison bell rang, signalling the successful completion of the execution.

At a first-floor window of a townhouse across the city, a frock-coated man stood looking out at the swirling storm. Broad-shouldered, thickset, hair sprinkled with grey above his dark forehead, Benjamin Pierce had known much hardship and trouble across two continents during his forty-nine years. He half turned as a lanky sixteen-year-old boy entered the room and walked across to stand before the radiant warmth of the fireplace.

'Is my father not back yet?' Edward Radcliffe asked.

Pierce fished the gold hunter watch from his waistcoat pocket, checked it and clicked the cover closed. 'No. It'll be a while.' Pierce knew Radcliffe's son felt the same unease as he did. When a man died at the end of a rope, the spectre of death shadowed Joseph Radcliffe. He would slip into the house quietly, retiring to his study for a brandy that Pierce would have waiting for his friend, along with a made-up fire to ease the chill of death from his bones. Delaying his homecoming allowed the ghosts to stay in the Mountjoy execution yard a little longer.

Chapter Two

The clear dawn brought a crisp bite to the air that now echoed with the bellowing roar of a regimental sergeant major. The Dublin garrison at Royal Barracks was the heart of the British Army in Ireland. A company of infantry marched to the cadence of the RSM's commands. The rhythm of his voice was punctuated by the click of his brass-tipped pace stick, set to the exact marching stride demanded.

'You-are-soldiers of the Royal Irish Regiment of Foot! Not ladies of the night squeezing your arses to stop your drawers falling down! About turn! Lef', lef', lef' right lef'. Thirty inches, ladies! Thirty inches per stride – if-you-please!'

The men were shadowed by their company sergeant as their punishment drill went on unabated. A less than satisfactory kit and weapons inspection had resulted in their having to face the fearsome RSM Herbert Thornton on the parade ground. His reputation was formidable, but, even worse, he was an Englishman. A good proportion of the regiment was made up of English, Welsh and Irish soldiers.

'You're going to South Africa to fight God-fearing Dutchmen in their own back yard and you will die like soldiers not the pox-ridden scum you are!' Mr Thornton's voice boomed.

In the heaving ranks a private soldier whispered to his mate. 'Give me the pox any day, at least I'd have some pleasure gettin' it.'

Nothing in God's creation escaped the attention of a regimental sergeant major.

'That man! Mulraney!' The pace stick pointed unerringly at the marching mass of men. 'Sergeant McCory!'

The company sergeant followed the direction indicated by the most feared man in the regiment. 'Company! Halt!' he commanded.

Hobnailed boots smashed into the ground. Mulraney stood rigid: sweat dripped from his nose, the rough cloth uniform chafed, and he wished to God he had never been tempted to take up the Queen's shilling.

Inside the Dublin garrison stables, a soldier, stripped to his undershirt, had been watching the rigid discipline imposed on those outside. He turned away, hawked and spat into the steaming straw. Mulraney would never learn, the daft peasant. Sweet Jesus, who'd be idiotic enough to tug the corner of his mouth down and make any kind of utterance when the RSM took the parade? Thornton had a Friday-face on him that'd stop a tram in its tracks. And the man could see a fly twitch its arse at a thousand yards.

He forked away soiled straw from the horse's stall. 'I'm an infantryman, in an infantry regiment, and I'm here cleaning out your shit and piss,' he said to the bay mare as he nudged her with his shoulder so he could clear the soggy mess. 'The colonel gets to ride you and I get to follow in the ranks looking at your tail-swishing rump. Now, is there any justice in the world? Move yourself, girl, or there's no apple for you t'day.'

The mare snickered and nuzzled his pocket.

Further back in the darkened area of another stall, Edward Radcliffe waited as a groom saddled a chestnut gelding for him. As the lad tightened the girth, Edward looked across the horse's withers to his friend. Older by several years, Lawrence Baxter waited patiently for the horses to be readied.

'You steal apples from the kitchen do you, Flynn?' said Baxter.

The stall cleaner never broke the rhythm of his task, the pronged fork swishing and gathering. 'That I do, lieutenant. She's a demanding mare, is she not? Like all beautiful women.'

'And my father condones such thievery? It's a disciplinary offence.'

'Aye, that it is, sir. But I think the colonel has a bit of a problem with his left eye. Doesn't focus too well since he took that knock to his noggin in India.'

The groom led Edward's horse along the cobbled passage.

'There's a wager to be had today is there, lieutenant?' Flynn dared to ask.

'You're a cheeky blighter, Flynn. I don't know how you've kept the colonel's favour over these years. It's against Queen's Regs for officers to gamble with other ranks. You know that.'

Flynn bowed his head in acknowledgement. 'But you're off duty, sir, not so?'

Baxter smiled at Edward. 'You'd care for a sixpenny bet?'

'I would, sir,' Flynn answered. 'The colonel grants me the privilege of looking after his horse because he knows there's no one in the regiment who loves her more dearly than his good self. I'll take sixpence on Mr Radcliffe, thank you kindly, lieutenant.'

Edward couldn't help the guffaw that escaped from his lips but quickly set his jaw to a more serious expression when Lawrence Baxter glared at him in mock severity.

'You believe Master Radcliffe has the better horse today, Flynn?' Baxter asked.

Flynn ceased his efforts and kicked the congealed horse shit from his boots. 'It's not the horse, Mr Baxter, sir.' His smile pushed the boundary of what, in the British Army, could be considered dumb insolence. Another offence and one that could have sentenced him to full pack drill at 160 paces a minute on the parade square that was still echoing with the RSM's booming commands. But not with young Mr Baxter. He wasn't just a run-of-the-mill junior officer. He was strict, there was no doubt about that, but the colonel's son hadn't yet been blooded. He was new to the regiment, still finding his way, and the colonel was a wise old bastard, as far as Private Gerald Flynn was concerned. The Old Man must have taken the lad aside, told him to learn the ways of the scum that would be at his side with a twelve-inch shaft of wicked steel on the end of their rifles. And that learning was still going on. Lieutenant Lawrence Baxter was still wet behind the ears. And that gave Flynn some leeway until the day came when he overstepped the mark and took the punishment that would surely be deserved.

Baxter took the reins of his horse from the groom. 'I shall have the pleasure of seeing you forfeit your wager, Flynn. Sixpence will deprive you of ale and a whore from Harcourt Street, and give me the pleasure of knowing it.'

The sergeant's voice carried from the square. 'Mulraney! Your mother must have been standing on Ha'penny Bridge when she dropped you out of her belly on to your numbskull! Extra guard duty over Christmas, you bloody heathen.'

Flynn eased back into the stall. Out of sight was out of mind if extra duties were being handed out, and those with stripes on their arms knew Flynn to be a malingerer. Baxter and Edward eased the horses down the cobbled passage. They waited as the company was turned and marched to the far side of the square. To Edward's eye their steady pace and perfect turns made them look to be the best soldiers in the world.

'I wish I was going with you to South Africa,' he said.

'To fight a bunch of farmers?' Baxter replied, his hand fussing his horse's bridle.

Any thoughts of heroic deeds were deflated by his friend's unenthusiastic response. 'There are more than fifty thousand of them, Lawrence. They slaughtered five hundred of Hart's Brigade at Colenso last week!'

'And that was the only black week we shall have. Hart's a courageous man but he was a fool, he committed his men badly. Trust me, Edward, the country's so vast it'll swallow those fifty thousand like ants in a desert. It's a fool's war, and I fear we will be too late to see any action at all.'

'Still... it's an adventure,' Edward said hopefully.

Baxter gathered the reins. 'There'll be greater battles than this. Give it another couple of years, finish your schooling and then ask your father to use his influence to get you into the Royal Irish.'

'My father would never use his influence.'

'Then when the time comes I will ask mine to use his. We'll serve together. Brothers in arms. How about that?'

Outside the gates two soldiers stood on guard duty, their eyes glancing back and forth across the busy street traders and beggars. Swarms of children worked the streets, selling whatever they could. Orphans mostly, or children whose parents were serving time in prison. Dishevelled and malnourished, they'd take whatever they could get to survive another day in the fetid tenements. The sentries knew that Fenian terrorists could infiltrate street crowds like these with ease. A muzzled black bear reared on to its hind legs as a street entertainer tapped it with his cane – a flicking, stinging hit, a foretaste of the bear's usual beating back in its cage. The man held the chain that ran through the ring in the creature's nose while a ragamuffin boy went among the crowd collecting whatever donation could be prised from the gawping onlookers. The entertainer flicked his cane, and the bear danced awkwardly as it tried to stay balanced on its rear legs. Failing to do so would bring another painful blow. A ripple of applause and gasps of appreciation loosened the onlookers' purse strings. At each tortured trick the crowd clapped and cheered until the sound of their enthusiasm was drowned out by the clattering rhythm of iron-shod horses.

The cavalry troop yielded for no one, forcing the crowd and the dancing bear to move aside. The officer who led them, Captain Claude Belmont, looked neither right nor left as he ploughed his horse through the protesting crowd without breaking formation, leading two columns of men abreast behind him. By the time they had passed the sentries and ridden into the garrison, and the great doors had swung closed behind them, the civilians had filtered away, spitting out a curse here and there for the arrogant Englishmen.

The showman tugged and tormented the abused beast to another, more profitable location.

The sudden flurry of the cavalrymen's arrival stopped Edward and Lawrence from leaving the stables. As Belmont and his troops dismounted Edward held his breath. The jangle of bridles and the creaking of leather mingled with the rattle of sabres and scabbards seemed to make the men bristle with menace. Belmont dismounted lithely, his muscled body showing no sign of fatigue from what must have been a long ride. His weather-beaten face sported a moustache in compliance with army regulations for all officers these past three years, but unlike the majority who prided themselves on trimmed whiskers, Belmont let his grow thick, a confident rejection of the more effete look of some junior officers. He brushed off any gibes about it by saying that he followed the sentiments of the chief of staff, Lord Kitchener, in both facial hair and robust use of force against an enemy.

Lawrence Baxter raised his hand, turned to Edward and whispered, 'Wait a moment until they've all dismounted. I don't want to be drawn into any explanations as to why I am out of uniform and with you.'

Edward deferred to his friend's request and waited quietly. Belmont was half in shadow and gazed down the length of the dimly lit stables. For a chilling moment Edward felt his eyes settle upon them, but then, as if their presence was of no importance, Belmont turned back and strode towards the officers' mess. The cavalry sergeant shouted commands and troopers led in their mounts. Lawrence Baxter let out a sigh of relief. And for the first time Edward sensed his friend's apprehension, his anxiety at the close proximity of the hardened soldiers. Edward, though, felt a ripple of excitement. He could imagine these men galloping knee to knee in extended formation against a formidable enemy and careering through their lines, sabres swishing and slashing. As he led his horse out on to the parade ground not one of the troopers gave the two young men a second glance. They didn't have to. One dismissive look was enough to make Edward feel that he meant less to the cavalrymen than a fly swished by a horse's tail. The vast parade ground had been suddenly vanquished by these bold men and he was glad to ride through the gates towards the open hills that lay beyond – as the mixture of trepidation and admiration mingled with an inexplicable fizz of excitement.

CHAPTER THREE

A few miles north of the city Joseph Radcliffe stood in front of a gravestone. By the time he had left the house to ride out to the small hillside country cemetery, Dermot McCann was already buried in an unmarked grave within the prison walls. But it did not take the execution of a man to remind Radcliffe of his own loss, and each week, at this time, he would make the journey to stand before this grave. The words he uttered were always inaudible, but the guilt he felt must, he thought, be apparent to all. There were few among his friends and associates who knew of his personal tragedy, and this weekly act of remembrance on the windswept hill allowed him sufficient privacy to shed his tears. It was an indulgence he always vowed to resist, but the loss he felt continued to torment him.

A shout, a whoop, the sound of hooves broke into his reverie. The folding hills and scattered woodlands obscured the riders whose voices he heard in the distance. With a few strides he cleared the low overhang that sheltered the grave so he could look out over the stretch of valley below. Two riders came in at the gallop, young men hunched low across their horses, arms moving rhythmically, urging their lathered horses on, neither using a whip. Recognizing them he almost called out, an arm already raised, his hat gripped ready to signal his presence. But he faltered and stayed silent, watching Edward lead his friend by at least half a length. The joy of seeing his son ride so beautifully, in perfect harmony with the horse, made him wish his wife could share the moment. Regret squeezed his heart, and he kept silent and let the riders disappear from view. With a final glance at the grave he walked back to where his horse munched lazily on the sweet grass that grew free of the frost beneath the hedgerows where brambles and thorns encircled the field that held the dead. No harm could befall them ever again.

It was a day to rid himself of the stain of the previous night's killing and he had agreed to ride out to meet his friend Lieutenant Colonel Alex Baxter. An hour later his horse clattered across the cobbled courtyard of an Irish landowner, Thomas Kingsley, a man whose roguish charm concealed secrets of value to both the British Army and the Irish Nationalists. But no one could determine on whose side his true allegiance lay. The horse-breeder could sell a donkey to a monkey and enter it as a three-year-old thoroughbred filly in the mile-long Irish Oaks race. And what's more he could no doubt fix the race so the donkey and its chattering jockey would win.

Radcliffe saw Kingsley and Baxter standing at the far side of the stable yard where a groom held an unsaddled horse's halter. Baxter was a lean man, a regular army officer all his life, one of the few in the officer corps who was not from the aristocracy. He took a serious approach to his manner of command, and the discipline he embedded in his soldiers created loyalty that reflected a lifetime of fair treatment. His concern for his troops' welfare had engendered respect in return, and a willingness to follow him into battle, often against savage odds. It was a foolish recruit who took the man's slight physique as an indication of his character. Baxter would punish offenders as strictly as he would show compassion for genuine hardship, which is why Radcliffe and Baxter found common ground and shared their distaste for useless loss of life. Those who knew war despised it for what it was. But such sentiments could blight an officer's career, which was, perhaps, why the forty-eight-year-old Baxter had remained a lieutenant colonel and had neither found favour from the general staff nor been invited to join them. Not, Radcliffe thought, that his friend would wish to do so. Field officers were a breed unto themselves.

The two men were deep in conversation and their somewhat furtive glance towards him made Radcliffe wonder if he was intruding on a personal exchange. A stable lad ran forward and took Radcliffe's reins. He slipped a coin into the boy's grubby hand.

'Mr Radcliffe, you'll not be spoiling my lads again, I trust. They'll be pressing me for higher wages,' Kingsley said. Whatever they had been discussing had been quickly put aside on Radcliffe's approach.

Radcliffe shook Kingsley's extended hand, and then took his friend's. 'Kingsley. Alex. I'm sorry I'm late.'

Kingsley's skin was as rough as a farrier's file and a half-closed eye showed the scar from eyebrow to cheekbone that some said came from a knife fight in his youth. Others knew, or so they claimed, that it was the result of a drunken assault on a prostitute who broke a chamber pot across his head and laid him low, so that he dashed his head on the whore's metal bed frame. Either way it gave the big man an appearance of someone who could cause violence – despite all his lilting charm.

'We Irish landowners like to keep in step with our English cousins. Modest wages keep a man temperate in his desires.'

'But intemperate in his despair,' Radcliffe answered.

'Quite so, quite so. Now, you'll be staying and having a drink when the colonel here and I have completed the business at hand?'

'No, thank you. I've work to do,' replied Radcliffe.

Kingsley grunted. 'One of the Fenian bastards was hanged last night then? Did he squeal? Most of those murdering scum do when it comes to it. They shit their pants and cry for their mothers.'

'You think there's any dignity in dying like that?' challenged Radcliffe.

'Ah, come on now, you've been a soldier, we're all meat on bone. No one dies with dignity. Better for us all if we rid society of murderous scum and be done with it.'

Radcliffe and Baxter exchanged a brief glance. Was it worth engaging the bluff Irishman in argument?

Kingsley hesitated a moment and then added thoughtfully, 'And this other fella they're hanging, O'Hagan, wouldn't be much older than your own son, would he?'

'I have made an appeal for clemency,' Radcliffe told him.

'There's a chance the murdering little shite will get off?'

'He's a boy,' said Radcliffe.

'Didn't a decent man die at their hands!' Kingsley blustered; then he turned and spat on to the cobbles.

'He's a boy,' Radcliffe repeated evenly.

Baxter could see the rancour would soon escalate and interrupted. 'Joseph, as you know I want to buy horses for the campaign. I've not yet made any decisions, but this one seems to be a beauty,' he said, turning to the horse.

Most of the British horses were supplied by the Irish and this gelding looked to be a fine example. Radcliffe nodded to the groom, who walked the horse around the yard. Radcliffe's eyes studied the horse's gait and watched as it shifted its weight.

'He's taken a fall at some time; he'll weaken under you, Alex.'

'And wasn't I about to tell Colonel Baxter that myself,' Kingsley said with a smile.

Baxter extended his hand to Radcliffe. It was a gesture of silent thanks. 'Then we'll talk again, Kingsley, I'm sure I'll find what I want in your stables,' he said, and added, 'with due care and consideration, when I have more time.'

Kingsley gestured for a stable lad to bring Baxter's horse across the yard.

'And I'll be sure to have your best interests at heart, colonel.'

'And at a price that befits the quality of the horse,' Baxter answered. He turned to Radcliffe. 'You'll ride back with me?'

'Not today, Alex,' Radcliffe answered without further explanation.

Baxter eased into the saddle and gathered the reins. 'You and Mr Pierce will be at the regimental dinner? I expect you.'

Radcliffe didn't answer. Baxter was aware of his reluctance. 'No excuses, Joseph.' He pressed his heels into the horse's flanks and nodded his farewell.

Kingsley walked across the yard with Radcliffe and held the bridle as Radcliffe pulled himself into the saddle. 'You're a strange fish, Radcliffe. A widow man from America with a black fella for a secretary and a son who rides like the devil's burning his arse while his daddy defends murdering Fenians. We get some strange people in these parts. A man has to ask himself if much good would come from it.' He released his grip. 'Be careful how you go.'

Radcliffe wondered if the benign comment was a threat. He eased the horse forward and knew, without looking back, that the man would watch him depart until he was out of sight.

CHAPTER FOUR

Benjamin Pierce sat at a fine old oak desk mellowed to a warm honey patina from a hundred years of use. Radcliffe had bought it at some expense when they first arrived in Dublin. How long ago had that been? Damned near half his life if he remembered correctly. He and Radcliffe were still young men when they turned their backs on a war against the American Plains Indians and searched out a new life. A year in London had given Radcliffe the qualifications to practise law and they would have stayed in that cosmopolitan city had Radcliffe not met a woman there who seized his heart. Kathleen was beautiful, Pierce had to admit that. He had argued with his friend that London offered them more opportunity. That and more. It was the British who had abolished the slave trade and, being a black man, Pierce drew fewer stares in London than when they first arrived in Dublin. But Radcliffe followed his heart and Pierce, as always, followed his friend.

The scratches and chipped corners devalued the oak desk in the eyes of the auctioneer but Radcliffe had bought it anyway, paying too much and ignoring Pierce's admonishments that he was a damned fool. They had little money to set up the practice, let alone for squandering on a desk big enough to sleep on. But within a year that broad expanse of sawn, hand-polished oak was covered in documents tied with red ribbon. Injustice knew no boundaries and Radcliffe took the cases that were most pressing, and which usually offered little payment, if any at all. Landowners and shopkeepers were charged more to fund the truly needy. But, now that he had defended Fenians, clients had drifted away. It was only by good fortune that they had paid their rent on the townhouse six months in advance. Pierce and Radcliffe had once endured the harsh life of soldiering but the chill that hung forever in the Irish house, and the sky that seemed constantly grey and frequently deluged them, made the house unwelcoming and cold. As the months had gone by they determined to save money, and in order to pay the coal merchant's account they burned only one fire in the drawing room, and the other in Radcliffe's study.

Pierce's fingers protruded through woollen mittens as he held the document; it was Radcliffe's appeal for clemency for the young Daniel Fitzpatrick O'Hagan. Its articulate request for mercy had to break through a judicial system renowned for its harsh penalties for crimes against the Crown.

A door slammed below. There was no need for Pierce to move to the window, he knew it was their housekeeper punctuating her resignation with a bang. And who could blame her? The daubed front door bore a message of hate: *Death to the Finians.*

Pierce understood hatred, but having been educated by a God-fearing Presbyterian abolitionist he did not appreciate an incorrectly spelled death threat.

Cell D1 was on the ground floor at the end of D wing; the hang house was immediately across the landing. So short a distance between life and death. The condemned cell had once been two cells until it was knocked into one but offered no comfort despite there being a fireplace at each end. Two guards sat at their posts, part of a rotating eight-hour shift, ever watchful so that the condemned could not commit suicide – and cheat society of its revenge. It was their duty to report anything said by the prisoner to the governor but Daniel O'Hagan had not spoken since they had moved him there. His mind had gone blank, lost in the silence of crippling fear. He could not even remember the Our Father. But the Catholic chaplain would come when it was time and confession would be heard, and then the two guards would move to the far side of the cell, and catch only the numb whispering of a boy unable to imagine his own death was now upon him.

The prison governor's office had the same cream-painted bricks as the rest of the prison. The small ornate fireplace glowed with a meagre heap of coal and the sparseness of the room reflected the man's austere attitude to personal comfort and anything not entirely essential. No feminine touches, no softening of the stark lines – no rug on the floor, no cushions on the two hard-seated chairs that visitors were obliged to use. The governor had no wish to encourage outsiders to stay long.

Radcliffe could barely contain his anger. The frock-coated and bewhiskered Governor Havelock had barely responded to the American's impassioned plea that O'Hagan be returned to the juvenile wing of the prison.

'You have no right to place him in the condemned cell. His sentence is under appeal.'

The governor was known to be a fair-minded but unyielding man. 'He is under sentence of death.'

'But the lad shouldn't be put in there. It's for those men who are to be hanged within days.'

Havelock showed no sign of displeasure or irritation;

Radcliffe's well-intentioned plea was reasonable. 'His stay of execution has already given him extra time. I will have the matter in hand; I will not allow any last-minute bundling with a condemned man. It's a stay, Mr Radcliffe, not a reprieve. We're not inhumane. Do I make myself clear?' the governor said, not unkindly.

Radcliffe's sense of standing alone against the might of British bureaucracy had, he realized, allowed his emotions to get the better of him. He lowered his voice. It was important not to antagonize a man who could deny him access to the condemned boy.

'I apologize, governor. I too seek only the best for O'Hagan's welfare.'

'I understand your concern, Mr Radcliffe, as I hope you will appreciate mine.' He straightened a square nib pen, and tweaked the angle of his blotter pad. 'Very well. You shall see the boy.'

Radcliffe was escorted through the prison, past the sweeping curved iron staircase that brought prisoners down from the three upper tiers of cells. Each cell had a bucket for a toilet which the prisoners would empty each day. This 'slopping out', as the prisoners called it, added to the ever-present stench of urine and excrement that mingled with the clinging odour of carbolic disinfectant. Radcliffe's escort ushered him through the corridor of D Wing, opening the red door that led to the condemned cell.

Daniel O'Hagan was not a bright lad and Radcliffe was under no illusion as to how easy it had been for Dermot McCann to dupe him into hiding their weapons.

'I don't think they can hang me for somethin' I didn' do,'

he said, hunching his body across the table, as close to Radcliffe as the guards would allow.

'You were there when McCann killed the police officer. An Irishman like yourself,' Radcliffe said.

'I didn' pull the trigger or nuthin',' the boy answered. 'Honest to God, as He is my witness, I didn'. McCann shot the poor fella and then put a bullet in his head for good measure. Take this, Daniel, he said, take this and hide it in your lodging. So I did. I took the revolver and hid it. That's all I done, honest, Mr Radcliffe.'

O'Hagan glanced over his shoulder at the door that led to the hangman's rope. 'I'm so scared, sir. I look at that door every minute of the day and I wish I were a blind beggar who could see nuthin'.'

O'Hagan reached out for the tin cup of water that stood on the table between himself and Radcliffe. The boy glanced at one of his guards who nodded his permission. O'Hagan needed two hands to steady the cup to his lips. Water spilled. Radcliffe reached out without permission and steadied the lad's trembling. He swallowed what water there was.

'Jesus, I've a thirst on me,' he muttered. He couldn't keep the desperation from his voice. 'They can't do it, Mr Radcliffe... it's not right.'

Radcliffe would never give up hope, but truth could have a way of strangling a man's faith. 'You were an accomplice in a cold-blooded murder. Do you not understand that?' he said quietly.

For a moment it seemed a glimmer of reality had seeped into the boy's dull mind. There was a jangle of keys and Radcliffe's escort stood ready at the door. Radcliffe reached out and touched the boy's shoulder. O'Hagan's eyes stared down at the table, his hands palm down on the scrubbed surface.

As Radcliffe stepped away the boy raised his head and said with genuine affection, 'Mr Radcliffe, sir, happy Christmas to you and yours.'

Radcliffe stood over his desk, searching the trial notes for anything he might have missed in his defence of the sixteen-year-old. It was a fruitless search and he knew it.

Pierce folded a sheet of paper from the desk and wedged it between the sash and its frame to stop the window's constant rattling. The wind had veered from the south-east; black clouds tumbled across Dublin roofs. Rain began to splatter against the glass.

'We'll need a bucket upstairs again for that damned roof,' he said.

Edward was slumped in a chair by the dull embers of the coal fire. There was a question he had to ask his father and Pierce had already given his own opinion on what the answer would be.

'Mrs Dalton left. She didn't even hand in her notice,' Pierce said.

'We'll get another housekeeper,' Radcliffe answered.

'That's three this year,' Edward said.

'Cook's still here, so we won't starve,' Pierce said, 'at least for another couple of days. Says she can't take the unpleasantness any longer. Good news is I'm interviewing another woman tomorrow. She cooks and keeps house, so that will save on one salary. She'd heard we needed someone. Times are hard so these women don't waste time. She banged so damned hard on the door I thought it was the bailiffs. Her name's Mrs Lachlan and she has a face like a bulldog that's just sat on a thorn bush.'

'If she gets past you then that's good enough,' said Radcliffe.

Pierce shrugged. 'Said she thought I'd been touched by the sun. Don't know whether she was referring to my state of mind or the colour of my skin. Either way she got it right, I reckon.'

He fingered one sheet of paper from the many on the desk. He handed it to Radcliffe. 'There is another letter from the Charteris woman at the South African Women and Children's Distress Fund.'

Radcliffe took it from him and glanced at it.

'How are we to get anyone to work here when you defend the Fenians?' Edward asked.

'Due process of law takes precedence over bigoted housekeepers,' Radcliffe answered, keeping his attention on the begging letter from an Englishwoman in South Africa who was asking for help in her ongoing endeavours to help Boer women and children during the conflict. 'How do these people hear about me?' Radcliffe asked Pierce, who plucked the letter from his hand.

'Newspapers, where else?' Pierce said.

'The papers say you're against this war,' Edward said.

'Some of the papers say I'm against it,' Radcliffe told him, and gently pushed the boy's legs from straddling the chair's arms.'

'But you support this distress fund,' said Edward.

'British women helping other women and their children in a war that shouldn't be hurting them. You think that's unpatriotic?' Radcliffe said to his son. He gestured to the letter in Pierce's hand. 'Get it off to any newspaper who might print it.'

'But still,' said Edward, in a vain attempt to show his father that he was mature enough to take a keen interest in world affairs, 'the Boers declared war on us.'

Radcliffe poured himself a small glass of sherry, and offered the decanter to Pierce, who shook his head.

'Not the brightest of moves I'll grant you – not that I think they had much choice. Bankers, financiers and underhand politicians have caused this war. Best you remember that. This is how empires are made, son, and fortunes.' He threw a few pieces of kindling on the embers and watched as their smouldering veil created less of a smokescreen than Edward's seeming interest in politics. He pre-empted his son's expected question. 'And while I'm busy upsetting the world in general, I might as well tell you that you're not riding in the race,' he said.

Pierce gave Edward a look that barely managed to conceal a smile of *I told you so*. 'I got my own cross to bear,' Pierce said and left the room before Edward could ask for his support.

'It's a hundred guineas prize money!' Edward said, exasperated that the subject had ended before he had even asked the question.

'And every man who thinks it easy money will be riding,' Radcliffe answered.

'Lawrence Baxter says I can have one of his horses.'

'Son, you're a good rider, in fact you're one of the best –'

'Then let me try,' Edward interrupted.

Radcliffe shook his head and sipped the sherry. 'No. The race is brutal on man and horse. And you're not riding. There's the end to it: don't ask me again.'

Edward was on his feet. 'You've done far more dangerous things,' he pleaded.

Radcliffe watched as the wood finally caught and flickered into flame. 'And I promised your mother I'd see that you didn't.'

'I can do this!'

'No you can't! I'm not doubting you're tough enough but these men have the taste for violence.'

'I can hold my own,' Edward said in a final attempt to convince his father.

Radcliffe held his gaze, and said with quiet authority: 'No.'

It was an impasse. The raw energy of a boy colliding with the entrenched love and concern of a parent. Edward fought back the words that he knew could wound his father. Without any further attempt to persuade him, he left the room.

Radcliffe knew only too well what drove the boy. Wearily he went back to his desk and began to look through the various letters and documents, laid out next to the accounts-to-be-paid, all neatly ordered from Pierce's soldierly administration. Radcliffe was about to tease out one of the more interesting pieces of correspondence in a vain attempt to lift his sense of despair when he heard a crash from the room above.

He pushed open the attic door and saw Pierce picking himself up. A steamer trunk that used to be on top of the old wardrobe lay on the floor, its lid now open. To one side of the room an enamelled bucket caught an incessant drip.

'This is a stupid idea,' Pierce said.

'You should have asked for help,' Radcliffe told him as he dragged the heavy trunk into the middle of the room.

'I don't mean me busting a gut,' Pierce said and pulled out two neatly folded Union Army uniforms. Pierce let the folds drop free and passed it to his friend.

'I've had worse ideas, I guess,' Radcliffe said, holding the uniform against his chest and trying to see how it looked in the mottled mirror of the wardrobe door.

'Not in the damned near thirty years I've known you,' Pierce answered.

'Oh, I don't know. I've had a few.'

'They were only stupid ideas 'cause you could've got us killed; this is a dumb idea 'cause you're gonna make us look like idiots. I'm not a kid any more and neither are you.' Pierce tried to button his uniform jacket, but too many years had passed since the last time they were worn. Radcliffe sucked in his midriff.

'I reckon I could manage.'

'Cinderella's sisters had a better chance of squeezing their ass into the glass slipper,' Pierce told him disdainfully and threw his jacket back into the trunk.

'So we don't go,' Radcliffe said, surrendering to the inevitable.

'And insult them? This invitation is a damn privilege and we have got to go now you've gone and gotten us all signed up for it! You'd better go and see O'Rourke.'

'Which one?'

'The tailor. He owes you. Damn. Never could abide regimental shindigs in my own army let alone anyone else's.'

Radcliffe folded the jacket. 'You know, you are becoming a cantankerous man of indeterminate age.'

'If I saw the sun once in a blue moon I'd be happier.' Pierce pulled a dusty old chamber pot from among the attic's detritus and settled it beneath a new drip. 'And another thing – let the boy ride.'

'Don't you two gang up on me,' Radcliffe said.

'You had him in the saddle before he could walk!'

'And she gave me hell for it!'

Pierce took a deep breath. Their friendship had often led them into disagreement, and when it came to Radcliffe's family Pierce was often the peacemaker. 'He's a young man – he wants to show you, for God's sake. Don't smother him, Joseph. Damned if the world won't do that soon enough.'

Radcliffe stubbornly refused to be drawn. 'It's not up for discussion, Ben.'

Pierce fingered the gold braid on the dress uniform and then tossed it aside. 'And how long do you think either of us can keep the lie going about his mother?' he said carefully.

It was a question that had been discussed on rare occasions, but one that would never be satisfactorily answered.

'As long as it takes,' Radcliffe acknowledged. 'I don't know is the answer. Maybe I'll be dead when he eventually finds out the truth.'

They fell silent. Pierce picked up the old blue uniform. It would be fruitless to keep worrying the emotional wound that Radcliffe bore. He sighed. 'Maybe I'll die of embarrassment at this damned ball and that'll save me from ever explaining myself.'

Three nights later, as the light rain filtered through the gas lamps' yellowing haze, a roughly dressed man made his way through the streets of tenements. He made no attempt to pull the collar of his near threadbare coat tighter. The dribble of rain would run down his neck no matter what he did. Being poor meant being hardy, but being poor and under the British heel was worse than being buried alive as far as Cavan Leahy was concerned.

He took pains to evade the policemen who were obliged to patrol the streets, their lives as much at risk now as they ever had been over a hundred years of violence from cut-throats and those with a plain hatred for authority. Gas lamps gave poor illumination in the mist-laden thoroughfares where rain could obscure the feeble light from a policeman's bull's-eye lantern. They made the rounds of the main streets each night from nine o'clock. By eleven, when the public houses closed and the horse-drawn omnibuses no longer ran, the streets would usually fall into an eerie silence. As he skirted the streets where the policemen walked Leahy thankfully acknowledged that the Fenians knew where the police would be. Each constable carried a book that instructed him what route his particular beat should take. There were enough patriots in the force to pass on such information.

Within the half-hour he was alone in a room in one of the slum houses. Each room he had passed along the corridor was no bigger than ten feet wide and twelve feet long yet gave shelter to half a dozen people, adults and children sharing the tenement in rank squalor. The sour stench of boiled cabbage and potatoes mingled with the sickening odour from the vacant room that everyone used as a toilet. Leahy sat at a ramshackle table dipping a crust of rock-hard bread into watery gruel. Within reach was a stolen British Army Webley .45 revolver. Despite the fact that the frugal meal was his only one that day he hurried it down and tossed the tin plate on to the floor. There were more pressing things to do than eat. Lying next to the revolver were half a dozen sticks of dynamite. Leahy retrieved the stub of a hand-rolled cigarette, lit it and let it smoulder in his lips. There was nothing else on the table except what dregs remained in the half-bottle of Irish whiskey.

A footfall on the stairs made him snatch the revolver and thumb back its hammer. The door opened, and another man halted, a hand quickly raised to shield himself. 'Jesus, Cavan!' the man – Pat Malone – said. Heavy-set, he loomed over the frail-looking Leahy.

Leahy lowered the gun as Malone thumped down a coil of detonation fuse.

'Stupid bastard. Ya scared the shit outa me,' said Malone. 'I thought you wasn't here till later. Is this the stuff you wanted?'

The dynamiter grinned at Malone, snatching at the gift.

He quickly cut a piece and touched the end of the damp cigarette to it, tossing the short piece of fuse on to the floor. It burned rapidly. He nodded in satisfaction. Fast-burning detonation fuse was exactly what he had asked for.

Malone drained the bottle as Leahy watched him. He swallowed the liquor and dragged a cuff across his mouth. It would have made no difference had it been a full bottle; it would still not have been enough to quell his fear. There hadn't been a serious and sustained attack by the Irish Republican Brotherhood for thirty years. Time to make amends. He lowered his voice. 'Regimental officers and a company to guard the garrison. Replacement battalion's not off the boats yet. The fog's settling in and will stay for the next couple of days. We'll have 'em like rats in a sack. It's now or never. Tomorrow night. The others are ready.'

'You're certain we can reach the armoury? Your informer can be trusted?' Leahy asked.

'Aye. Like the Bank of England.'

The brothel consisted of the two floors above the small music hall. It was a place where the common soldier was banned. Men who traded on the black market and dealt with cash mingled with junior officers and those who aspired to positions of power in government. For many British rule was profitable and although their hearts were passionate for self-governance, business went on as normal and the music hall and whorehouse was a good place to conduct it. Thirty-odd years earlier Nellie Clifden had seduced the Prince of Wales when he served with the Grenadier Guards at Curragh Camp. Young officers and prostitutes. What was new in the world?

To the muted thumping of girls stamping their boots on

the small wooden stage, accompanied by a fiddle player and a piano, Sheenagh O'Connor clattered her way down the bare wooden stairs from her draughty attic room. Like many of the other prostitutes she had been a country girl who had fallen on hard times and was left with no choice but to strike out for Dublin and earn whatever she could by whatever means possible. Poverty tore away what decency had been beaten into her as a child. An illiterate but pretty eighteen-year-old, she soon learned that a smile and a willingness brought in more money than selling flowers on Sackville Street or at the gates of Phoenix Park. Local women set up brothels and enticed country girls like Sheenagh with a room and a meal; and Mrs Sullivan's establishment, down here in the Monto district, Gloucester Road, was a favourite for those officers stationed in the various barracks around Dublin. For three years she had plied her trade under Mrs Sullivan's roof and learned enough to make better use of what she saw and heard.

Whores were as invisible as servants to most of these young smart officer fellows, and they assumed idle chat about who was doing what and where meant nothing to the girl they fondled while the music played and the sour whiskey loosened tongues into indiscretions. But information was worth something to the foolhardy and desperate men caught up in their own subversive plans for some kind of utopia. Let them have the gossip, let them be the fools they were; sooner or later enough of them would find that utopia lay at the end of a rope.

Yet Sheenagh knew that she had strayed into dangerous territory and if anyone blabbed then she'd be the one facing the hangman's noose or a Fenian's knife. A man had paid her – a man who had been more than generous in the past – and whispered what it was he needed her to say to the 'dynamiters and boys with the guns'. She'd gambled that those desperate men would never be caught when they attacked the garrison. More fool her. Sooner or later one side or the other would trace the information back to a common whore. Time to make a run for it, she had told herself after a cold night of regret counting her money, shoving as many clothes and shoes as she could into a carpet bag. The Royal Irish were shipping out, and so would she.

'Sheenagh!' one of the girls called down the stairs after her. 'Where the devil d'ya think ya goin'? Get yourself back up here before Mrs Sullivan finds out. She'll set her lads on ya.'

Sheenagh turned to her friend. 'No money to be made here, Kath. The soldiers is where it's at and they're all going far from home.'

The girl looked nervously over her shoulder: the music and singing would only muffle their voices for a while longer. 'You're not goin' to bloody Africa? Sheenagh, they're feckin' heathens out there.'

But her friend was through the back door and gone.

'Sheenagh!'

The music stopped; the applause and cheers rose up the staircase. Kathleen O'Riordan had a night's work ahead of her, but in the instant of seeing her friend escape she wondered where she'd got the kind of money needed for a steamer ticket.

Chapter Five

In the officers' quarters of the Royal Barracks the cavalry men's rooms were spartan but comfortable enough. The wooden floors and panelled walls barely reflected the light from the oil lamp on the small table by the window that overlooked the parade ground. Beside the single cot where Claude Belmont's mess dress of the 21st Dragoons was laid out, a pair of polished riding boots stood next to the wall hook from which a cavalry sabre hung in its scabbard. Upside down on the floor lay a gleaming saddle, its leather buffed to a rich sheen. Behind it, standing rigidly to attention, was an orderly, thumbs pressed down the seams of his trousers, chin slightly raised, ensuring his eyes did not fall on Belmont's face. Belmont, half-dressed, braces over undershirt, sipped brandy from a silver hip flask. Moments earlier he had thrown the saddle to the floor. He looked at the orderly. Sweat stains marked his armpits; his hair spiked at the crown of his head from an army barber's shears. There was no doubt in Belmont's mind that the rank and file, with their lack of ambition or desire to improve their lot in life, were worth little more than peasant labour.

'Not good enough. Clean it again,' he said without looking at the wretched private soldier.

For the third time that night the man bent and lugged the captain's saddle away to be cleaned to a higher standard than previously offered. Though he did not know what more he could do. There was no doubt in *his* mind that officers like Belmont were belligerent simply to exert their status. God willing a Dutchy's bullet, or a British one, would soon bring such arrogance to an end.

Belmont took another pull on the flask. The room's confinement weighed heavily on him. Cavalrymen were not like other soldiers. There was an innate elan that gave men like Belmont dash and daring, and he admitted to himself even his common troopers had it. Many of his men had signed on again after their term of service had ended. Signed on to ride down the enemy and use carbine and sabre to inflict terror upon them.

He had taken a cold supper in his quarters but the food remained barely touched. He had no stomach for garrison duties. He was hungry for war.

Benjamin Pierce had never lost the breadth of his chest and shoulders. He had been born nine years after the American ship USS *Creole* had been taken over by slaves carrying them from Virginia to Louisiana. Those slaves sailed the ship to the British port of Nassau and became free. He had been told that story when he was a child and the thirst for deliverance from the cotton plantation where he was born had guided him like the star that navigated that ship to freedom. As a boy he had worked lifting bales of cotton and sacks of corn, and by the time he was fourteen he was a tall strapping youth nearly six feet tall with a conditioned strength greater than many older men. His escape from slavery came months before the Civil War ended when the embittered plantation owner's wife sent him to work at a bible-thumping mission school where the missionary teachers saw to it that the quiet boy's energy was channelled into reading and writing and learning scripture. Falling in love with the preacher's young daughter and the whipping it earned was a biting reminder of the slave owner's belligerent hand. That was when young Benjamin Pierce lied about his age and joined the Union Army. In the April of 1865 the boy, now fifteen years old, gripped the heavy wooden stock of his rifle and charged the Confederate lines at the Third Battle of Petersburg, the last great slaughter of the war.

Thirty-four years later he stood gazing at his reflection from the darkened windows in the Dublin townhouse. He wore his old officer's double-breasted dress frock coat, now neatly tailored to adjust to an expanded girth. Age may have thickened his waist but that still did not detract from the width of his shoulders. The dark blue wool had a polished cotton black lining and each of the fourteen brass buttons now gleamed. The gold shoulder knots bore his regiment's designation and the two silver bars of his rank. Pierce sipped a glass of port, the fire's warmth easing some of the hard-won memories into a more nostalgic account of what had really gone on during those savage days of warfare.

Edward stepped into the room and hesitated at the sight of his father's closest friend in full military uniform.

'Ben, Father says the cab will be here in a couple of minutes.' He moved closer to the sombre man and saw an old tin-framed photograph of a cavalry trooper. 'Is this you?'

'Uh-huh. Found it in an old box a couple of days ago.'

'Is it from the Civil War?' Edward asked, gazing at the young black man who stared back at him, dusty and dishevelled, in front of what seemed to be a western fort.

'Now I may look older than Methuselah to you, but I was too young for most of that war. But it wasn't long after.' He poured a small glass of port and handed it to Edward. 'August sixth, 1866, General William T. Sherman, Commanding Military

Division of the Mississippi, issued a general order establishing the 10th Cavalry.' He clinked his glass against the boy's.

'You and my father.'

'Soon afterwards, yes. Not too many white officers wanted to serve with the coloured regiments.'

'He's never told me anything about his time in the army, do you realize that?'

Pierce took the picture from him and placed it back on the mantelpiece. 'Some men endure and survive war and learn humility because of it. Words don't serve much purpose. Most of the time it's not something you want to remember,' he said.

The old soldier topped up his glass.

'Did you ask him if I could ride in the race?' Edward asked.

Pierce nodded and that was all Edward needed as an answer. He put a brave face on it and swallowed the port.

'You have to understand, he loves you too much,' Pierce said and raised his eyebrows as the boy offered the empty glass. Pierce relented and half filled it again.

'He's scared for me. Ben, he can't protect me forever. I'm strong, I can take the rough and tumble.'

'Your brother was strong. It didn't help him when he needed it. It nearly broke your father when he died.' Pierce held back what he knew was not his right to tell the boy. He covered his hesitation by opening a drawer and handing the boy a gift wrapped in brown paper. Perhaps it would serve to soften the lad's disappointment. 'Couple of days to go before I should be giving you this,' he said.

Radcliffe stepped into the room. He too wore a dress uniform, the only difference being the extra two brass buttons and the insignia of a major on the shoulder knots. He and Edward had barely spoken since their argument about the horse race. 'You coming?' he said to Pierce. 'It's not Christmas, yet,' he told

Edward, who had torn free the paper from his gift. Radcliffe ignored the disapproving look on Pierce's face. Mending bridges was not such an easy feat of emotional engineering for Radcliffe as it was for his friend. 'Still…' he said, relenting, 'I suppose a day or so doesn't matter.' He accepted a drink from Pierce. Edward held every boy's dream knife. The bone-handled hunting knife felt beautifully weighted in his hand. The steel blade was pitted but it reflected back a time when his father and Pierce fought a brutal war in the American West. It was a blade honed by legends.

'Benjamin?' Edward said with a note of uncertainty, as if the gift might only be on loan.

'From the Indian wars,' Pierce told him. 'One day your father will tell you what we did together. That knife's a part of it.' He glanced at Radcliffe as the boy could not take his eyes from the knife that he turned and weighed in his hands. Radcliffe needed little reminder of the savage times he and Pierce had shared. There were nights when the wind coming off the Irish Sea howled against the rafters, a curdling scream that cut into the old soldiers' nerves. It prompted murmured conversations as they sat in the firelight, reminiscing about the Comanche and Sioux braves they had fought. It had been a vicious, murderous war with no quarter given. Those braves curdled a man's blood with their war cries. And then the killing would start…

And something else,' Pierce said, breaking Radcliffe's reverie as he handed the boy a small pocket book. 'To live without poetry is to live in an uncivilized world.'

Edward felt the flush reach his face, uncertain whether it was the drink, the fire or the warmth of friendship. He raised his glass. 'Happy Christmas, Benjamin. Father.'

Radcliffe returned the toast and felt a stab of fear. His son was no more a boy than he had been at that age. The strength of his love for Edward frightened him.

Radcliffe and Pierce stepped away from the cab at the barrack gates. Their capes and headgear and white dress gloves were different from any other uniform Mulraney had ever seen before, and they surely were not officers in this man's army, but he'd seen the American and the black fella before with Colonel Baxter and they were going to the colonel's party, and that was all the defaulting soldier needed to know. He and the other sentry brought their rifles to bear in salute.

Old habits died hard and the two cavalrymen saluted, returning the soldier's acknowledgement. As they approached the officers' mess Radcliffe asked the question he had previously preferred not to ask. But it had become a Christmas ritual these past few years.

'Did he ask about his mother?'

Pierce shook his head. 'But the time's coming he'll have to know the truth.'

'Not yet,' said Radcliffe.

They stepped through the entrance, hearing the restrained skirl of the Irish regiment's pipes and drums from behind oak doors, the instruments unleashed into their full passion as Radcliffe and Pierce entered the room. The hall was decorated for Christmas, its panelled walls rich in wood and history, hung with battle flags. Officers from all units of the brigade were there, in braided tunics of reds and blues, while their wives, in all their finery, twirled with their men. The blood-pounding music reached its crescendo and ended to cheers and applause. A Royal Irish officer saw his colonel's guests arrive and quickly extended a warm welcome to them.

'Gentlemen, good evening. I am Major Henry Drew, the Colonel's second in command.' No sooner had he introduced himself than he guided them quickly to where Colonel Baxter stood in conversation. As soon as he saw Radcliffe and Pierce he quickly excused himself. The music surged again.

'It takes an Irishman to play the pipes, Joseph! Ben! Welcome, come along. I'll introduce you.'

An orderly with a tray of drinks was at Radcliffe's shoulder. Pierce declined the offer and leaned closer to his friend. 'Irish whiskey makes me cantankerous.'

'No one will notice the difference,' Radcliffe said, po-faced, then followed in Baxter's wake.

Conversations were interrupted while the colonel introduced his guests, and as they moved through the crowded room there were stares at the unusual sight of the retired United States Army officers, especially an old Buffalo Soldier like Pierce. But good manners prevailed, especially as Pierce's dignity and bearing demanded it. To one side of the room Belmont stood with two other officers who had arrived that afternoon with their cavalry troops. Captain Taylor and Lieutenant Marsh were from quite different backgrounds to Belmont's. They were well connected, privately educated men whose commissions were bought with wealth and secured by patronage. If Belmont had a weakness it was that he knew Taylor and Marsh were his social superiors, though neither would ever allow the man whose father had been a shopkeeper to think that he was anything but their equal. The fact was that thirty-eight-year-old Belmont had fought in every imperial war for the last twenty years and his battlefield experience and tenacious belligerence against an enemy was something they admired. They acknowledged his superiority in the field which had led to his climb through the ranks. Belmont was fearless. So, despite their inbred disdain for anyone from a lesser regiment or a lower social class, Belmont was tolerated.

Colonel Baxter eased Radcliffe and Pierce towards the cavalrymen. Baxter immediately saw the barely hidden contempt in Taylor and Marsh's eyes when they looked at Pierce, but he saw something else in Belmont's. The man had focused his attention on Radcliffe, and despite the lack of any expression Baxter sensed an unyielding hostility. The two men had silently locked horns.

The colonel's presence demanded restraint and Marsh and Taylor accepted the white-gloved handshake offered to them by the Americans.

'Our cavalry came up from the Curragh. Lieutenant Marsh arrived this afternoon with his troops; Captain Taylor is the squadron's intelligence officer,' the colonel said.

'Which some might consider a contradiction,' said Belmont, and then smiled at Taylor. 'Just kidding, Freddie.' Belmont made his own introductions. He extended his hand to Radcliffe.

'Belmont, 21st Dragoons,' he said. His own disdain for the foreign soldiers was barely disguised. 'My friend Taylor might sit behind a desk these days but he's a crack shot. Probably the best, eh, Freddie? Silver Medal winner at Bisley in '97.'

The newcomers could not help but see Taylor straighten as Belmont's compliment stroked his ego.

'Congratulations,' said Pierce.

'You shoot, do you?' Taylor asked.

'Not at paper targets, no,' said Pierce. And then, realizing that his comment could be construed as sarcasm, quickly added, 'By that I meant that I haven't shot for a long time, captain.'

'But when you did,' said Marsh, eager to bear-bait the conversation.

Pierce held the man's gaze. 'I shot at my enemy,' he answered.

'I suppose… *in your day*…' He sipped his drink to deliberately let the insult settle. '… you would have used muzzle-loading rifles?' His question seemed innocent but Colonel Baxter knew the cavalrymen were having sport with Pierce.

'I've shot with Captain Pierce's rifle. It's a fine weapon. It can kill at fifteen hundred yards. It was used by buffalo-hunters in the American West. Incredible stopping power. Its rear sight gives elevation and windage, in the right hands of course.'

'Not much big game roaming the hills of Dublin, though,' said Taylor. 'Perhaps too much gun to be carrying around?' He smiled indulgently.

Radcliffe caught Belmont's glance. His friends were baiting Pierce. It was like a schoolboy game, and Colonel Baxter's attempt to break it up had little effect.

Pierce was no fool; he knew what they were doing. 'It's an 1875, fifty-calibre Sharps,' he told them.

'Ah,' said Taylor, 'near enough twenty-five years old. Can't have bagged that many, I suppose, with a single-shot rifle.'

Baxter was suddenly wary of the three cavalrymen facing his guests and he bristled at the implied insult, though he saw that Pierce and Radcliffe showed no sign of rising to the bait.

Pierce shrugged. 'You're right, it's an old weapon, but *in my day* I could load and fire fast enough.'

'It is an excellent rifle,' said Baxter. 'Double trigger and elevated rear sights. And with a thirty-four-inch barrel it's accurate at that distance. Providing of course the man firing it is skilled in its use. And I can assure you gentlemen that Captain Pierce is such a man.' The music had stopped and the buzz of conversation and laughter around them did not seem to penetrate the circle of these six men. Colonel Baxter attempted to move the conversation on to common ground. 'Captain Belmont is to command a raiding party to strike the enemy exactly as they strike us. Fast mounted troops who can move behind enemy lines. Major Radcliffe and Captain Pierce are retired Union cavalry officers; I thought, gentlemen, that you might be interested to hear of the guerrilla war they once fought.'

'It was a long time ago,' Radcliffe conceded.

Baxter ignored the self-effacing comment. 'And Captain Pierce was a Buffalo Soldier in the American West in their fight against Indians.'

'Indians? What kind?' asked Marsh.

'Sioux, Kiowa, Comanche,' said Pierce, sensing he was being drawn into a conversational alley where unseen danger lurked.

'A worthy foe?' said Marsh.

'The best.'

Taylor scoffed. 'Hardly.'

He and Marsh exchanged a knowing smile, but Radcliffe noticed that Belmont was watching them.

'I had a bash at the fuzzy-wuzzies. In the Sudan. They're not much good against cavalry,' Taylor said.

'Not when they're lightly armed and on foot,' suggested Radcliffe.

Belmont took another glass of whiskey from an orderly. 'Still, good sport,' he said.

'You might feel different facing a Sioux brave at the charge. Best horse soldiers I ever saw. There are plenty of our cavalry lying dead on the plains because they thought they were fighting an ignorant savage,' Radcliffe said.

'But you beat them,' said Belmont.

'Eventually,' Radcliffe admitted.

'Well. There you are then. You were the better soldiers.'

Colonel Baxter's expectation of cavalrymen sharing their experiences began to quickly fade and he regretted introducing them. The three English dragoons had been steadily drinking and now the conversation became more pointed.

'Your government, sir, is neutral in the South African War yet they refuse to extradite Fenian dynamiters who have sought refuge in America,' said Marsh, looking at Radcliffe.

'Neutrality. The unmistakable stench of moral decay,' Belmont added.

'Watch your manners, sir,' Baxter warned.

'Colonel, I'm a field soldier; bantering with civilians is not my chosen profession,' Belmont answered. 'Even those in fancy dress.'

'I won't have my guests insulted, captain. Tread carefully. I shall only make a slender allowance for the occasion.'

'Is it a coincidence I wonder, Radcliffe, that you defend Fenians?' asked Belmont.

Baxter was about to object, but Radcliffe stopped him with a small gesture. 'I defend anyone I am asked to defend as the law demands,' Radcliffe said.

'I thought you Americans had a different law than us. Seems you shouldn't be allowed anywhere near the murdering scum,' said Marsh knowingly.

Radcliffe smiled and nodded. 'It's not my job to pass judgement, Captain Marsh, but our legal systems are very similar; in fact many jurisdictions in America maintain the use of English common law. I was admitted advocate there some years ago.'

'And your late wife was Irish?' Taylor queried, which sounded more of a taunt than a question.

'Captain Taylor, that's quite enough.'

Baxter's voice was sufficiently raised to draw attention from other officers nearby. As tempted as they were to watch their colonel rip into the cavalry, they averted their gaze. The arrogant horsemen needed to be brought down a few pegs and

Baxter was no soft touch of a commanding officer who could be intimidated by others of higher social rank.

But the younger men were running in a pack.

'My question, Colonel Baxter, is why an American with such obvious republican sentiments, and I mean Irish Republican, is here at all,' said Belmont. He placed his empty glass down. 'My squadron serves within the same brigade as yours, sir, but until I am placed directly under your command I choose not to share my evening with a man of questionable loyalty. Goodnight, sir.'

Belmont nodded at the colonel and turned away, an act of gross bad manners but which fell marginally short of insubordination. Taylor and Marsh followed him.

Baxter took an involuntary step forward. Had he barked out the command that was on his lips the whole room would have fallen silent, but Radcliffe had moved between him and the retreating officers.

'Alex. It doesn't matter,' he said quietly. 'All cavalry officers think the sun shines out their backsides.'

'Which is about the only time you see it around here,' Pierce added. 'Excuse me, colonel.' He stepped away from Radcliffe, who was already being turned by his embarrassed and apologetic friend towards another group of officers and their wives.

Pierce made his way through the crowds, nodding occasionally and smiling at those who cast a curious glance his way. Belmont was drinking with his cronies near the fireplace. The black man's approach stopped their conversation. Pierce made no apology for interrupting them.

'Major Radcliffe is Anglo-American. His father was English, a lawyer and a great philanthropist. Built churches, houses for the poor. A good family. Better bred than most.' He paused, the implication of the final words quite clear. 'I suggest you owe him an apology. A public apology.'

'I've served here before and rumour was that your friend sired a bastard son then married the Irish whore. Least, that's how I heard it,' Taylor said evenly.

One of the orderlies eased his way past Pierce, who reached out and took a glass of Irish whiskey. He swallowed it down.

'Do you fight, Captain Taylor?' he asked.

'Fight?' Taylor queried, but then quickly understood. 'I'm a British officer, I don't brawl like a common soldier.' Without thinking he glanced at Belmont, foolishly letting his true feelings be seen.

Pierce peeled off his white dress gloves. 'Well, I'm a retired captain in the United States Army and a common soldier taught me how to brawl.'

Private Flynn had won his sixpence when a mud-splattered Lieutenant Baxter had returned from his cross-country race with Edward. The illicitly distilled poteen he'd purchased could strip the polish from a saddle but gave Flynn a drunken slumber on this night of the officers' party. He was off duty and the bottle and the warm straw bedding allowed him dreams of being someplace else. And then voices penetrated the joy of a life without orders, and brought him groggily back to reality. He rolled out of his blanket in one of the empty stalls. He grabbed the pitchfork, but soon realized when he blearily peeped through the cracks in the slatted wood that he wouldn't need it. He saw three cavalry officers carrying lanterns, with a tall broad-shouldered black man who was pulling off his blue uniform coat. Within moments Captain Taylor and this man were stripped down to undershirt and braces. Flynn stayed silent. Officers measuring up against each other was a sight he'd never witnessed before, and he'd seen plenty of bar-room brawls in his time. Recounting this spectacle would be worth a few jars of ale in any public house or canteen.

Taylor would be no pushover but Pierce's bulky frame helped absorb the quick blows that Taylor delivered. He jabbed like a boxer and swung low, head down, shoulders rounded, like a fairground pugilist. He felt his fists connect with an old man's body that was still packed with layered muscle beneath his bulk. He was quicker on his feet and caught Pierce two stinging blows on the forehead, but the old man didn't even flinch, simply ducked and weaved his shoulders and head, his eyes watching, anticipating Taylor's style and attack.

'I boxed for my house, old man,' said Taylor, sensing he already had the better of Pierce.

It was only a brief moment of victory. Pierce snapped out a straight left. Short and sharp, the jab bloodied Taylor's nose, who fell back into the arms of his cronies. There may have been a twenty years' age disadvantage but Pierce had fought tougher men than him. Belmont, cheroot clamped between his teeth, heaved Taylor back into the fight. 'Come on, Freddie, low and hard, man. He'll go down. Come on now!'

Taylor ignored the pain and paced himself carefully, prowling around his opponent, throwing a punch, feeling it blocked and then the impact of Pierce's fist slamming into his shoulder, a near miss from his jaw. His body crashed against the stable wall, dislodging bridles from their hooks. Pain streaked across his chest and into his shoulder and the horse snaffles he had slammed his head against stung him into an angry, ill-considered lunge. With two more blows Taylor was on one knee, spitting blood. Horses whinnied, Marsh stepped forward ready to strike Pierce but Belmont grabbed him and held him back. Taylor was back on his feet and landed two fast strikes; one breaking skin on Pierce's cheek. Belmont and Marsh cried out encouragement, but the black man had barely registered the blow. Pierce recovered and slammed an uppercut into Taylor's midriff. It was a hard punch into trained muscle, and Taylor took it well, but he faltered, his lungs gasping for air. Then Pierce put him down with a right cross.

'The fuzzy-wuzzies send their regards,' Pierce said as Taylor struggled to get to his knees.

The cold air chilled the sentries who stood at their posts, limbs stiff, wind stinging their eyes and muffling any sound made by the dozen or more men who had filtered from the night into the streets around the barracks. The anticipated fog had been blown away from the estuary by the onshore wind but the rain's mist gave confidence to those who crept into the night to kill. One of the sentries stamped his feet, completed his turn at the corner of the wall and walked back along the perimeter of his assigned route. He'd be glad to get to the warmth of Africa. The garrison's high walls offered little respite from the rain that swirled on the wind – if anything it seemed to funnel it more fiercely down the wheel-rutted street. He guessed he had less than an hour until he was relieved and then, while the officers supped their brandy and smoked their cigars, he would sip a beef broth and pack a welcome pipe with rough-cut tobacco that caught the throat and cleared the nostrils.

One of the streetlights at the end of his post flickered, then its rainbow glow in the mist snuffed out. That must be the storm. He hoped the duty sergeant had made sure they had enough oil for their lamps in the guardroom. He hunched his shoulders against the cold, soaked greatcoat and did not hear the footsteps approaching downwind. He blinked the rain from his eyes and sudden light shattered his vision: the last moment of his life as Pat Malone's knife plunged into his neck. Now, as others scurried from the alleyways, they had gained another weapon. There was no need to move the dead soldier's body; the attack would soon be launched. And they knew the guard relief was still an hour away.

Mulraney called across to the other sentry who shared his post at the main gate. 'Jimmy, did you hear that? There's someone out there scuttling around.'

The other man gazed into the half-light. He shook his head. 'No, nothing.'

'There's someone out there, I'm telling you,' Mulraney insisted, and edged away from his post, his rifle brought down to the ready.

'Jesus, Mulraney! Get your arse back here!' the other sentry hissed. But Mulraney was already ten paces from where he should have been.

And then the shadows moved.

Mulraney challenged the running figures but the only response was the rising clatter of boots running across cobbles. 'Call out the guard!' he cried to the other sentry. Pat Malone had brought a half-dozen men from the other side of the street and used the others to hold the sentries' attention. Before the guard could do as Mulraney ordered one of Malone's men clubbed him down with a pick handle as another levelled a pistol at Mulraney. But Mulraney smashed it from his hand, calling out for help. He rammed the rifle's stock into one of his attackers and the metal-edged butt of his Lee–Enfield shattered bone. His fingers gripped the cocking lever, but before a cartridge could be loaded into the breech another man struck him from behind. Mulraney tumbled on to the cobbles.

Cavan Leahy placed the dynamite against the gates and as the other men turned to watch the burning fuse Mulraney scrambled to his feet, picked up his rifle, rammed the bolt action back and forth, then his finger found the trigger.

Belmont and Marsh had grabbed Pierce's arms and were too strong for Pierce to throw off. They shouted at Taylor: 'Get up! Come on, man!'

Taylor stood and looked at the helpless Pierce; then he landed two heavy blows into his stomach. Pierce collapsed on to his knees, doubled in pain. Marsh punched down into Pierce's face, sending him sprawling, and then Taylor kicked hard as Pierce tried to protect himself from the flurry of blows.

'Learn to know your place, nigger,' Taylor spat at him. 'Next time I'll break your neck.'

Pierce couldn't move. He was curled up, his brain trying to isolate the agony so he could get to his feet. But the strength was sapped from his muscles, the darkness sucking him under.

It was Belmont who dragged Taylor away from Pierce. 'Leave him be!' he demanded, with enough derision in his voice to insult Taylor. Before Taylor could land any more blows, gunshots echoed across the parade ground. Belmont turned and ran towards the sounds as an explosion flared into the night sky. Taylor and Marsh were at his heels.

The duty officer's whistle shrilled briefly against the sounds of gunshots and men's raised voices. Mulraney had shot at two men, not knowing if the bullets had found their target. He didn't want to be caught outside the walls and ran into the garrison through the swirling smoke and flame of the shattered gates. More explosions followed and he saw soldiers taking up firing positions across the parade ground. Darkness shrouded men's ghostly images; the rain squall and smoke mingled, swallowing friend and foe. Gusts of wind would clear fifty yards and then sweep the curtain of rain closed again.

It was the chaos the Fenians wanted.

That and the armoury.

Radcliffe and Baxter burst from the officers' mess into the conflagration. Bullets ricocheted across the stone walls and Radcliffe saw Mulraney clipped by a bullet in his arm. As Baxter shouted commands to his men Radcliffe ran forward and helped the fallen soldier into the cover of the barracks' archways. But Malone and Leahy with half a dozen others had escaped from the turmoil and were running into the heart of the barrack complex. Leahy carried the Webley in one hand and his satchel of dynamite in the other. As the attackers dashed towards the armoury they turned a corner and faced a squad of Fusiliers whose rifles were already at their shoulders. The attackers stumbled to a halt. They were boxed in, confined to the passageway between the buildings.

'Sweet Christ. They're waiting for us!' Leahy cursed and threw himself aside as the detachment's officer gave the order to fire. The deafening volley smashed into the Fenians. Breathless and terrified, Malone dragged Leahy back a dozen paces to the safety of another building as a second volley shattered the air in the killing ground. A bullet had ripped through the arm of Malone's coat and snagged flesh, which bled. There was no time to be concerned about a flesh wound. The others were dead. It was a miracle he and the dynamiter weren't lying in the passageway. The two men made another fifty yards, desperately seeking out the others, whom they found fighting a ramshackle pitched battle against the soldiers, who had quickly reorganized themselves. There was little doubt the attack had failed.

'Get yourself out of here! We've been betrayed,' said Leahy, shoving Malone away into the darkness. 'Find who it was and finish it!' He turned to run into the darkness, but Malone grabbed his arm.

'Cavan! Come on, man, for God's sake!'

The dynamiter pulled free. 'Get away with you. I'm for taking care of the bastards' horses. At least that!' And then he ran towards the stables.

Isolated pockets of intense fighting went on within the barracks' grounds. Radcliffe stood over the wounded Mulraney, protecting him as attackers dodged in and out of the entwined smoke, mist and rain, wraiths swirling through the colonnade. Radcliffe levered the rounds into Mulraney's rifle and brought down two of the Fenians. His other shots ricocheted into the stone walls. He fired the last of his rounds and brought down another attacker as he saw Belmont, his unbuttoned tunic exposing splashes of blood on his undershirt, pick up the duty officer's revolver that lay next to the wounded man. Despite the mayhem and the bullets that still crackled through the air, Belmont calmly stood his ground, levelled the pistol and brought down an intruder who broke cover in an attempt to escape. But then the hammer fell on to empty chambers. Belmont was isolated and another of the attackers ran forward, knife and pistol in hand. He fired two shots, both missed and then he too held an empty gun in his hand.

Radcliffe worked the rifle's bolt action as he heard the man scream a curse. He had no time to take aim as Belmont took the brunt of the man's charge. They struggled, the man kicked away Belmont's legs, but the cavalryman rolled, recovered quickly and snatched a fallen soldier's bayonet.

In the shifting mist it seemed to Radcliffe that the violence slowed to a mesmerizing dream. Belmont angled his body for the man's lunge and like a swordsman slashed the twelve-inch blade across the man's face. The suddenly defenceless man screamed, hands raised to the horrific wound, and stumbled blindly into his adversary. Belmont grappled him briefly and, instead of allowing the man to surrender, plunged the bayonet beneath his armpit. He pushed the corpse away and sprinted towards the flames that silhouetted soldiers fighting to secure their ground. A flurry of bullets snapped in the air. Radcliffe huddled down next to the wounded Mulraney.

Half a dozen men led by Regimental Sergeant Major Thornton ran into view. As the soldiers sought refuge behind the walls, Thornton stood his ground, upright, casting his eyes across the conflict, prepared for a rush from the enemy.

'Mr Radcliffe, sir, this is no place for a gentleman like yourself,' he said evenly and without any sense of urgency. 'Mulraney, I might have known it'd be you getting shot and causing all this trouble.'

Mulraney shivered from the shock of his wound. 'It's sorry I am to be a bother, sergeant major, but I did raise the alarm.'

'That's as it should be, lad. Now, get yourself off to the infirmary. Can you do that?'

'Yes, sergeant major.'

'Very well, then. Off you go.' The wall above their head was peppered with gunfire, which Thornton seemed to take as a personal assault on his presence. 'All right then! Can't have this gentleman doing your work for you! Rout those murdering bastards out,' he commanded the squad of soldiers, who promptly ran towards the beleaguered enemy.

The sergeant major looked down at Radcliffe. 'Are you hurt, sir?'

Radcliffe got stiffly to his feet. 'No, I'm OK, thank you, Mr Thornton.'

'Very good, sir.' He extended his hand for the rifle. 'I think we can manage now, thank you, Mr Radcliffe.'

Radcliffe handed over Mulraney's rifle and Thornton strode off into the rain.

Colonel Baxter appeared, his clothes and face rain-streaked and smudged with soot. Radcliffe squinted into the shifting light from the diminishing flames.

'Have you seen Ben?'

Horses whinnied; the high walls of their stalls prevented them from seeing the frenetic firefight outside but, despite being trained warhorses, their confinement and the explosions had spooked them.

Flynn had helped Pierce up after his beating and the two men had moved through the darkened stables to calm the horses. Pierce was a dozen stalls away from the entrance when he saw the roughly dressed man with a bundle of dynamite in his hand strike Flynn down with a pistol butt. The man, who hadn't seen Pierce in the shadows, lit the fuse, tossing it towards those stalls that lay further away. There was little time to stop the impending carnage. Pierce ran at him; the dynamiter spun round and fired his pistol twice at the approaching shadow. Pierce instinctively raised a protective arm as wood splinters spiked the air but kept going. Pierce's weight floored the wiry man, but he wriggled like an eel, squirming out of Pierce's grasp. The Fenian was already on his feet, and levelled the revolver at Pierce's face. The old Buffalo Soldier had expended too much of his strength in the fight against Belmont and his cronies.

Beyond the gunmen Pierce could see the fuse burning. There was no time left: the man had a clear shot. Pierce flinched, turning away at the gun's deafening roar, but the bullet went high into the roof. Pierce hardly dared believe his luck. By the time he turned to face the dynamiter again the gunman was gasping through the blood that gurgled in his throat and spilled down across his threadbare coat where the pitchfork's tines jutted through his body.

Pierce snatched the fuse from the bundled dynamite. Flynn let the weight of the dead man fall forward.

Neither man spoke. And then Flynn said, as if excusing his actions: 'Bastard was gonna hurt my horses.'

By first light the surviving Fenians were being led away, arms raised, grim acceptance of the fate that would surely await them etched on their faces. It had been the most daring raid they had mounted. The acrid smell of smouldering timber lingered across the parade ground, the stench heightened by the damp air, clear now of rain. Fusiliers, still half- dressed after being roused from their beds to fight the intruders, began clearing away debris.

Soldiers laid out the bodies of those intruders who died in the attack. Neat rows overseen by RSM Thornton.

Radcliffe shivered in the chill dawn. Belmont turned one of the dead men over with the toe of his boot, and threw the remains of the cheroot he was smoking on to the cobbles.

As the prisoners were taken he glanced across to where Radcliffe, Pierce and Baxter stood.

'More defendants for you, Radcliffe,' he called. 'Though I'll wager you won't save these from the rope.' He turned away.

Baxter was as grime-laden as any other man. He had fought on the ground, commanding disparate groups of his fusiliers. 'If Belmont's squadron hadn't been in station we might have had a rougher time of it,' he said. 'We had been warned. God's grace.'

'An informer?'

'Luckily, yes.'

'You always need luck in a fight, Alex, you know that. How many dead?'

'Roll call's at oh-six-hundred. Men are on stand-to until then. So far we have three dead. A dozen or so wounded. Nothing more serious than that.'

'And the gunmen?' Pierce asked, taking his attention from where Marsh and Taylor met with Belmont at the far end of the square.

'As far as we can tell nigh on thirty of them launched their attack on the barracks while another ten besieged the Royal Irish Constabulary to ensure no help was given to us. It was co-ordinated and long in the planning by the sound of it. We killed seventeen, and there are those nine walking wounded,' he said, nodding towards the ragtag survivors. 'I dare say a couple of them must have escaped.'

'Were the Fenians after the armoury or the brigade officers?' Radcliffe said.

'The officers' mess is stronger than a fortress.'

'You can't be sure, though, Alex. They could have struck a massive blow a few days before you sail.'

'The informer warned us it was the armoury. We weren't sure exactly when the attack would come so I had squads at strategic points. Other than that, we just had to carry on as normal. Didn't think they'd take the gates off its hinges though.'

He touched Radcliffe's shoulder. 'I'd best see to things.' Colonel Baxter pushed the hair from his face, buttoned his tunic and moved off to where his officers were reorganizing their men.

Radcliffe and Pierce walked across the parade ground as the fires were damped down and the garrison was brought back under control. Pierce carried his frock coat across his arm, his shirt blood-splattered and dirty.

'Damned if these Irish don't know how to throw a party,' he said tiredly.

Radcliffe studied his friend for a moment. He was uninjured except for the cut and bruising on his face.

'Damned if I can stay up this late any more,' Radcliffe answered.

Pat Malone pushed his way up the brothel's stairs. No one tried to stop him, not with the snarl on his face and the knife gripped in his grubby bloodstained fist. Kathleen O'Riordan saw him coming and slammed closed the door, but it yielded to his boot. She screamed as he snatched her hair and laid the blade across her face with enough pressure to draw blood.

'Where is she? Where!'

The girl had known rough treatment in her trade, but Malone was a known man of violence, like those he ran with. Still, she tried to protect her friend. 'I don't know, Jesus, she said she was going down to Cork... to see her mother... for Christmas!'

'I'll cut your face off and then see who'll pay you to spread your legs!'

She felt the blade move and knew that Malone would think nothing of fulfilling his threat. 'All right, all right,' she pleaded, the sobs already rising from her chest. 'She's on the boat... for Liverpool, said she was following the soldiers. Jesus, don't cut me, mister, don't.'

Malone threw her to one side and stormed out of the room. Kath felt the moistness on her cheek as tears mingled with the small cut. It was nothing. Nothing to what Malone and others would do to Sheenagh if they found her.

Radcliffe stood stripped to the waist in front of the washbasin in his room as he sluiced the grime and blood from his face and hands. After all the years of being away from the conflict of war the assault had sapped his muscles, but the night's killing had brought home the reluctant truth that in the heat of the moment he had responded like the soldier he had once been. A man can change, he had always told himself, but once learned, the capacity to inflict violence could never be discarded.

He had not seen Edward step into the room. The boy gazed at the old ugly scar that ran across his father's back. Radcliffe caught his look in the mirror. He turned and took a clean shirt from a chair.

'Were you hurt tonight?' Edward said, trying to pretend that he had not seen the puckered slash mark.

Radcliffe shook his head and turned the gas lamp down, hoping perhaps to subdue the boy's unease that he could have lost his only parent in the attack.

'What about Benjamin?'

'He's all right.'

Edward was holding on to his emotions – and a letter. Neither of them knew what to say in that moment. Then, as if remembering the excuse he'd needed for visiting his father's room, he handed Radcliffe the envelope.

'This came. By hand. From Mr Kingsley.'

Radcliffe took the letter and propped it on the chest of drawers. The message could wait; his son could not.

'It was a knife wound,' Radcliffe said, wanting to bring the boy into his life. Edward said nothing. 'The scar. On my back. A knife wound. It was a Comanche,' he added, knowing the explanation sounded lame.

'Did my mother know about things you did... the wars you fought?' Edward asked.

'Only some of it.' He paused and finished dressing. 'It's not something that bears discussing. It's ugly. And you and your mother brought beauty into my life. Why risk blemishing that?'

'Do you still think of her?'

'Every day,' Radcliffe said quietly. And in the moment willed himself to tell his son the truth about his mother. But he denied himself the confession.

Edward nodded. 'I miss her too.' He fussed with his father's cufflinks on the dresser. 'Why did you fight tonight? Couldn't you have kept out of it?'

Radcliffe's lie came without hesitation. 'No,' he answered.

'Did you want to stay out of it?'

Radcliffe's eyes flicked away from his son's. Was it so obvious to the boy?

Edward turned for the door, but then hesitated and looked back. 'Father... I may never be as brave as you or as strong as my brother... but don't be a hypocrite. Please.'

He waited a moment and then opened the door.

'Edward... wait,' Radcliffe said gently, his words holding the boy in the room. 'My horse is stronger than Lawrence Baxter's. Ride him in the race.'

CHAPTER SIX

Christmas Day and the week that followed passed in a sombre, though expectant, mood. Colonel Baxter had refused to cancel the New Year's Eve One Hundred Guineas horse race. He was damned if he was going to allow the Irish nationalists any sense of victory in disrupting what had become an institution that gathered horsemen from across the county. Wealthy landowners and sons of aristocracy who had the quality of horse to race the five miles across broken countryside were the main competitors, but this year the newly arrived cavalrymen were invited to submit a contender for the purse. No one within the squadron opposed Claude Belmont.

The letter that had been delivered several days earlier beckoned Radcliffe to Kingsley's stables. It was barely first light and Radcliffe knew the race could not start until the burly Irishman took himself off to the starters' line. Kingsley was a man of influence and wealth, and it was he who posted the hundred guineas' prize money. The meeting he had requested in the letter had nothing to do with the morning's race.

Kingsley and Radcliffe strode towards the stables across the yard as a stable lad opened the big doors for them. At the end of the stalls was a special enclosure that at first glance seemed to Radcliffe's eyes, in the dim light, to be a small show ring, and, set aside from the others, another stall that was almost in darkness. The wooden slatted building creaked in the wind and something moved in that darkness. Kingsley gave a curt nod to the stable lad, who hoisted a couple of oil lamps on to wall hooks and then he made himself scarce. The big doors closed behind the two men.

For a moment Radcliffe thought he might have walked into a trap. It was well known that Kingsley spoke out against the Fenians, and should there be any animosity towards Radcliffe it would not be difficult to have a man killed and his body disappear. He quickly dismissed the wild imaginings. When Kingsley offered the flask of brandy, Radcliffe took it and let the warmth from the liquid seep into his chest. Kingsley nodded, pleased that the man had not kept him at arm's length. He did not wipe the silver flask's spout when he put it to his lips.

Kingsley's attention had wandered across that darkened ring. 'In my father's time there was only one registered thoroughbred saddle horse in America. My daddy bought from that stock and bred from it. There's limestone under the grass here, it gave the offspring bones like iron and the constitution of a steam train.'

It seemed the burly Irishman nourished himself with the pride of what his father had achieved in the Irish stud business. Radcliffe stayed silent, letting his eyes adjust to the darkness of his surroundings. There was that movement again. He concentrated and the shadow seemed to quiver. A sliver of light caught the reflection of a horse's eye.

Kingsley barely moved his head as he checked whether Radcliffe had seen it or not. The horse stood stock-still. It was watching them. Kingsley made a barely audible sound and out of the darkened stall stepped the most magnificent horse Radcliffe had ever seen.

'Now this is the fella I was talking about. He's stronger, faster and tougher than your American saddle horse. He'll burst his heart for a good horseman. There isn't a man with enough money to buy this horse, and my God they've tried.'

Radcliffe watched as the uncouth Irishman reached out his hand and the horse stepped forward to nuzzle it. It was obvious to Radcliffe that there was a bond of love between the sharp businessman and his pride and joy.

'This is a horse that only a Valkyrie could ride,' Kingsley said. And looked at Radcliffe, waiting for the obvious question to be asked.

'What do you want, Kingsley? You're no friend of mine.'

'It's not what I want, it's what I can offer,' Kingsley said. This time Radcliffe refused the offered flask. 'When Colonel Baxter and his glorious Royal Irish Regiment of Foot get on that boat to go and fight in this damned silly war, you will not have the friendship of anyone in authority or influence.'

'And you are offering yours?'

'Why not?'

'In your pocket, you mean. Evidence in a case I'm defending goes missing. A mistrial here or there. All to make the way clear for you to do whatever scheme you're wallowing in.'

'Listen, Radcliffe, the world is what you make of it. The English Queen is coming to these very shores in April, and I've got the contract for building the pier at Kingston for the royal yacht. I'm making a small fortune out of the Office of Public Works. I'm a man of influence and I pay people for information. Scraps turn into banquets, Radcliffe. You get to hear things in your line of work. Just a snippet here and there.'

'I'm not for sale, Kingsley. Now if you'll excuse me, my son's riding this morning.'

'I could give your boy this race. I could buy off every one of those adventuring bastards. He would win and you would have my horse.'

As if on cue, the horse snuffled Radcliffe's hand. Radcliffe ran his hand along the silky black cheek and down on to the muscled shoulder. There was no denying the strength and beauty of the horse that towered above both men.

Radcliffe patted it one more time. 'You have nothing I want,' he said.

'Oh, you want him – it's just that you're not prepared to pay the asking price. It's a pity. I thought we could do business. It would have benefited us both. But there it is. No harm in my offering, Radcliffe.'

'And none, I hope, in my refusing.'

'Agh. Honourable men.' Kingsley laughed. 'Jesus, what a pain in the arse you are. Still... someone has to be. Right, let's be off and see who's going to take my hundred guineas today.'

Traces of intermittent rain whipped across the low hills, making the couple of dozen horsemen steady their mounts as bookmakers shouted their odds over the wind. The chilled weather would never stop money changing hands as rich and poor vied to gamble. Horse racing was the great leveller. Those from the poverty-stricken areas would never use a racquet on the Rathgar courts, or clutch the leather of a rugby ball. Those sports were for the wealthy young men who visited the illegal cockfights in the working-class area of Blackpitts. But horseflesh at the gallop was as free as the soot-clogged air they all breathed.

The riders fussed about their horses, mostly hunters used for pursuing a wily fox or inexhaustible stag. A snaffle tweak here, a stirrup length pulled and checked. Saddles were rocked back and forth. Last-minute fidgeting before the riders hoisted themselves into the leather. Most wore shirt and jodhpurs;

the sweat of exertion would soon cling anything heavier to their skin. Belmont was on the far side of the riders, relaxed, smoking a cheroot, his horse nibbling the cropped grass. Captain Taylor and Lieutenant Marsh shared a silver flask with him. None of them sought out the black man standing with the boy.

'You wearing an undershirt like I told you?' Pierce asked Edward, who shivered as he held the reins. The boy nodded. The New Year weather added to his nerves.

'I'm not really cold. Well, a little.'

'It's not for the cold. Someone lays a whip across your back, and they will, you want to take the sting out of it.'

'Where is he?' Edward asked.

'He'll be here,' Pierce answered as Edward scanned the crowd for his father. 'Edward, if you don't want to ride, that's OK. You understand? There's no shame in changing your mind. Hell, wish I'd have done so plenty of times.'

'I'm not scared, Ben. I want it to start. That's all. Where is he?'

Edward grinned as his father pushed his way through the riders and horses.

'I knew you'd come, Father.'

'I said I would, didn't I? But I had business to attend to. You ready?'

'Yes,' Edward said, and nodded enthusiastically. Radcliffe glanced at Pierce, who gave an almost imperceptible shrug. Who knew if the lad could stay the course?

Pierce gave the boy a hoist into the saddle. The riders were making their way to the start line.

'They'll use the whip on their horses and on you,' Pierce reminded him.

'You don't need a whip on this horse. He'll run for you without one. Remember what I told you,' said Radcliffe.

The boy had already done as Pierce and his father had coached him. He held a handful of mane and then wrapped the reins around wrist and hand. Nothing would dislodge his grip, and he had a free arm to ward off any blows struck against him.

Radcliffe covered his son's hand with his own. 'Stay away from the pack. Don't mix in with them. You hold back and choose your moment. Once they break through the valley you'll be out of sight. That's when it's dangerous. You'll get to the farm walls; they'll jostle and make mistakes. Those walls are high: you need to get through the open gate.' He could feel the concern creeping into his voice. He smiled and patted his son's leg. 'Five miles and you're home.'

Kingsley's voice bellowed over the hubbub of bookmakers and gamblers. The betting was fierce but Kingsley's presence on the back of a trap gathered their attention. 'To the line! To the line!'

'You'll be here, Father? At the finish? I'm going to win for you!' said Edward as he controlled the skittish horse that sensed the excitement of the moment.

'Of course!' Radcliffe said, but saw the look of doubt on Edward's face. 'I promise, son. I'll be here.'

Pierce had the last word. 'Stay away from that man,' he said, nodding towards Belmont. 'He doesn't like poetry.'

Outside Radcliffe's house a horse-drawn cab pulled up and a neatly dressed man hurried to the front door, instructing the cab driver to wait. The man banged hard with his fist and pulled the bell chime with unmistakable urgency. The cab driver watched as he repeated his actions until a flustered woman opened the door, causing the man to doff his bowler hat. The scowling woman looked to be the housekeeper and vigorously shook her head at his questioning. Without bidding the woman farewell the fare climbed back into the cab and instructed the driver to proceed with all haste to the hundred guineas race.

Kingsley held a large patterned red handkerchief above his head. He teased the moment, watching the line of snorting sweating horses straining for the off, their veins pumping with blood. Edward Radcliffe looked across the tense men to his friend Lawrence Baxter, but that young man only gave him a brief nod and a worried smile and then, like the others, fixed his eyes on Kingsley's lifted handkerchief.

His arm swung down. 'Go on with you then!'

The horses lunged into the wind and stinging rain.

For the first half-mile the pack nudged and barged their way forward, each rider finding the space he needed. It didn't take long for the first whippings to take place and Edward steered his father's hunter into open space. The horse wanted to surge ahead but the boy kept it on a tight rein and a steady rhythm with his hands and body, controlling its urgent energy, letting the horse feel his mastery. Other riders' aggression caused their horses to veer away and two men had already been unseated, their horses barging and getting in the way. He saw Lawrence Baxter take a whip across his shoulders which made him heave on the reins. Had his friend not been such a good horseman he would have surely fallen beneath the pounding hooves.

At the mile-and-a-half turn there were only eight riders still in the saddle and Edward's strategy had kept him on the flank in fourth place. He saw Lawrence pull up his horse; it had gone lame. The desperation on his friend's face said it all, but he saw Edward looking back over his shoulder and pumped a fist in the air, urging the sixteen-year-old boy on.

Two riders boxed Belmont in. It was obviously a strategy they had decided upon, knowing the cavalryman was the better rider. As one laid his whip across Belmont's neck, the other barged his horse. Through the tears that streamed from the cold, Edward saw that Belmont barely flinched. He let the man strike twice more, then, allowing him to raise his arm a third time, Belmont snatched the whip before it struck again. He laid its grip across the man's face in a wicked slash that yielded a scream of pain as the man's cheek was split open. Unable to control the horse he veered away.

Those riders had slowed Belmont's progress. Edward lengthened his horse's stride. They were at the farm turn where the surviving riders would want to be the first through the open gate. The horse gathered pace. Edward knew his father's horse had not yet reached its full stride. He was closing in on Belmont, watching as he let his second attacker move slightly ahead. The cavalryman leaned in the saddle and reached down, his hand slipping beneath the saddle flap. His fingers found the slide bar that held the stirrup leather and a moment later the straps had fallen free and the man's unbalanced weight nearly threw him from the horse. His skill kept him in the saddle a moment longer but the vicious beating he took from Belmont's whip couldn't be avoided. He fell from the horse.

Belmont's horse's rear hooves nearly took the man's head off as he tumbled on the ground, arms thrown across his face. Edward sucked in the cold air, felt the raw bite in his lungs. Fear and excitement surged through him. He was fifteen feet to one side of Belmont. And then they were level.

Pierce and Radcliffe clambered on to rising ground. Breathless, they both held binoculars to their eyes.

'Five riders in the front! Where is he?' Radcliffe gasped. The exertion to get to the vantage point caused their hands to tremble: both men calmed their breathing and kept track of the distant specks that were the horsemen.

'There he is! See him? They're heading for the farm. He's level with Belmont!' Pierce said.

Radcliffe concentrated on the distant figure of his son. 'No... He's taken the lead.'

'I'll be damned, said Pierce, 'he can win this thing.'

And then the riders disappeared from view.

But Radcliffe's attention was elsewhere. He watched the perspiring man in the bowler hat clamber out of the cab and bend into the hillside as he scrambled up to reach him.

Edward had gained a horse's length on Belmont, but he could sense the cavalryman's horse was likely to out-pace even his father's strong hunter. Out of the corner of his eye he could see the snorting beast was drawing level, its pounding hooves tearing up the ground. Belmont's shirt was flecked with blood and, like Edward, tears smeared his cheeks.

Edward was determined to keep his line. Three hundred yards ahead stone walls, six feet high, barred their way, but it was the open gate they wanted.

Belmont yelled something at him. Edward turned his head slightly, wanting to hear.

'All right, boy! ALL RIGHT!' Belmont cried, a smile creasing his face, loving the madness of it all. Wanting the boy to be in contention.

He whipped his horse and then barged into Edward. A hard

swerve that might have knocked a heavier man free of stirrup and saddle. But Edward was half-raised, beautifully balanced, arms pumping, giving his horse its rhythm. He was lighter and more agile than the other riders and it was Belmont whose body swayed, causing his horse to fall back a pace or two, and veer a couple of feet away.

The gate. Edward needed the open gate. With a hundred yards to go he saw that it was closed. They'd failed to open it. The five cross-bar struts denying him the chance to block Belmont and pull further ahead. His brief hesitation communicated itself to the horse, which momentarily missed a beat in its stride. Belmont pulled level.

'Come on, boy! Come on! Use your spurs! Come on!' he spat. And then he was two strides ahead. And then three, the snap of the whip on his horse.

Edward held his nerve, and eased the reins. The horse surged. Belmont had the line for jumping the gate; Edward nudged a knee into the horse's side and it angled away. Even from the saddle the wall seemed massive, but if he could be the first to jump he would gain a half-dozen strides on Belmont.

There was no time to control the horse, no chance of measuring its stride to take the wall at the right distance. Everything depended on the horse. Without conscious thought he realized his body had found the perfect position for the forward momentum; and then the pounding hooves were quiet. No more grunting exertion, just a long, soaring silence broken only by his gasp of exhilaration and the rush of air against his face.

And then the bone-jarring thud as hooves hit the ground. The horse stumbled; Edward nearly fell sideways from the saddle, but his bound wrist gave him purchase on the coarse mane and he steadied himself. He had beaten Belmont across the other side. Three other riders laboured behind them.

One fell at the wall. Two others cleared the gate. But the race was down to these two horses.

A straight half-mile lay ahead, then a long curving quarter-mile bend below the hills, and then only another half-mile to the tape. Belmont had unexpectedly made up ground by cutting across a corner, ignoring the track, and when he rejoined it he was ahead. The cavalryman sat less hunched than Edward, his torso easily moving with the horse. The half-mile was soon taken and Edward realized before they reached the curve of the hills that he had gained on Belmont, who seemed to have slowed. Had the man's arrogance let him think his nearest rival couldn't challenge him any longer?

Edward's horse grunted, its nostrils flared with blood. Sweat glistened on its shoulder and chest, but its snorting breath was even and steady. They were closer. Belmont glanced back; Edward looked beyond him to the turn. He needed to be on the inside line. As he steered the horse Belmont nudged his horse the same way. He had read the ground and was taking control of the race. Edward had no choice: he couldn't veer back. Urging the horse on he drew closer to Belmont, and was then level. An outstretched arm's distance between them. Belmont smiled. Then shouted: 'You did well, boy! Good sport. I had good sport!'

Before Edward grasped the meaning of the words Belmont lashed out with his whip, catching Edward across the neck and shoulder. His undershirt took the sting from the blow, but his neck felt as though it had been ripped with a sawtoothed blade. Belmont came closer, forcing Edward on to steeper, more uneven ground. The constant lash of his whip meant the boy had to raise his free arm from the reins to protect his face.

It was then that Belmont blinded Edward's horse.

The horse whinnied in agony, the pain sending it surging out of control. It barrelled into undergrowth and trees, the low branches sweeping its rider out of the saddle. A fleeting moment of realization allowed Edward to unfurl his hand from the mane, and then he thumped into the earth as the horse tumbled over stone-laden ground.

The last thing he heard before the fall knocked the wind from his lungs and sent him into a dark sea was the sharp crack of his horse's leg breaking.

Elsewhere, another boy fell. An instant of pain shot through his mind like a searing fire. The pool of blackness that swept away his soul closed rapidly and whatever breath there had been was gone long before the statutory hour of leaving his hooded body at the end of the creaking rope in the hang house.

The prison guards pushed the black-painted wooden steps up to the body and eased it down on to the waiting trolley. The prison doctor examined the corpse, removed the hood, and declared Daniel Fitzpatrick O'Hagan to be dead.

The clerk of the court who had beaten on Radcliffe's door and raced out to the windswept countryside waited in the corridor outside the prison governor's office. He heard the dull murmur of indistinct words from within the office.

Inside the room the governor handed a distraught Radcliffe the official document of execution.

'The Home Secretary signed the order early this morning. Your appeal for clemency was dismissed. It was felt by Her Majesty's Government that the Fenian attack on the barracks needed a forthright response. O'Hagan's execution was carried out with immediate effect.' The governor laid his fingertips on the desk blotter, and then brought them together, as if about to pray. 'Had it not been for the attack... I believe your efforts on his behalf would have been rewarded.'

Radcliffe placed the document on the desk and turned away.

Pierce had waited as the riders crossed the line. When Belmont cantered effortlessly across the tape he saw that streaks of blood mingled with the mud on his splattered clothes. Welts were visible where his shirt fell back from his neck and chest. There was no doubt it had been a brutal race. He waited anxiously for any sign of Edward. When last seen he had been leading the race before the farmyard turn. As the stragglers rode in on exhausted horses Pierce's anxiety increased.

He made his way among the latecomers asking for news of the boy. Most rode past him. A black man's interest easily ignored. One rider was walking his horse in, and Pierce made the same appeal. The man pointed back along the valley. 'There's a horse down,' he said.

Pierce began to run and then waved down a trap carrying two race officials heading in the same direction. One of the men recognized him and helped him clamber aboard the rig. Within ten minutes they were at the place where Edward's horse had fallen. The boy was scratched, bruised and cut. His face was peppered with mud; tears had etched channels across his cheeks. He was trying to comfort the injured horse. Pierce called his name, unable to keep the concern from his voice. When Edward turned, his deep distress was apparent and made Pierce groan with compassion. The boy looked beyond Pierce for any sign of his father. Others had gathered around the stricken horse, each voicing their own opinion on what to do next. Despite his desire to reach out and hold the boy to him, he did not for fear of humiliating him further.

One of the race officials laid a pistol against the horse's head.

The boy walked past Pierce without another glance; he flinched at the gunshot, but did not look back.

CHAPTER SEVEN

Edward allowed their new housekeeper, Mrs Lachlan, to dress the cuts on his arms and neck. The raised welt across his neck would discolour and then fade. The bruising would take its own time, and the stiffness in his muscles from the fall would pass quickly thanks to his youth and fitness. But the sullen ache that buried itself within him would take longer to heal. Radcliffe and Pierce had tried to choose their words carefully when Radcliffe returned home, but little was said for Edward refused to stay in the room long enough for a conversation to begin. Mrs Lachlan had admonished Radcliffe for allowing the boy to ride.

Radcliffe had explained to Pierce what had happened at the prison. Neither expressed their feelings other than to condemn the execution of a boy the same age as Edward. Later, when Pierce came downstairs, he told Radcliffe that Edward was in his room packing his suitcase. School vacation still had two weeks to run. Radcliffe acknowledged that the divide between father and son was widening, and his sense of helplessness accompanied him when he went up to Edward's room. The boy was calm, almost matter-of-fact.

'I thought I'd go back to school early... The dorm's open... there'll be other boys there. I'm sorry about your horse, Father. Captain Belmont blinded him.' The boy folded the last of his clothes, his back still to his father. Radcliffe reached out and touched his shoulder, turning him.

'Belmont is a war soldier. That's what he lives for.'

Edward's face couldn't disguise his anguish. 'I couldn't do anything,' he said quietly, head bowed.

The boy was almost as tall as Radcliffe himself. There was still some way to go before he had his father's layered muscle from the years he had spent on horseback, but he was nearly a grown man and too big to embrace. More than anything else, at that moment, Radcliffe wanted to pull the boy to him.

'I don't care about the horse. I wasn't there for you and for that I'm truly sorry.'

Edward met his father's gaze. 'I didn't win anyway.'

'That wasn't the point.'

'It was to me,' said Edward, an edge to his voice.

'You think I missed the race through choice? They hanged a boy not much older than you.'

Edward moved further away from his father. 'He was a murderer.'

'They hanged a boy!'

'A killer!' Edward shouted, his face flushed with anger. 'I'm your son. Where do I fit in? Where?'

Radcliffe strode across the room and stopped Edward from packing. 'For God's sake! What am I supposed to do?'

Edward snatched his arm away from his father's restraining hand. 'Be my father!'

'I have tried to be that and more. You can ask anything of me. Anything, and I'll give it.'

'I've already asked. I want to be as good as you and do things without having to beg for it.'

'I want you to be better than me! And I want to protect you.'

Edward sensed his father's vulnerability; and as in any father and son conflict the young knew how to cause the other pain.

'Like you protected my brother? Protected him so well my mother died of grief!'

As if struck by a vicious blow Radcliffe recoiled. 'Don't... Edward... please.'

But his son had him on the defensive, his insistent words beating his father into a corner.

'You let him do anything he wanted. Isn't that right? Isn't that why he died?'

Radcliffe tried to soothe the boy's inflamed accusation. 'I was in the water with him. I couldn't save him. You think I don't carry that every day of my life?'

'I was a small boy. I barely remember him. I don't want his death pulling my life down. I need to take my own risks. You were right, Father: they were hard men and I wasn't tough enough for the race. Just as well you were not there after all,' he said, his anger slipping into self-pity.

'Don't whine!' Radcliffe ordered him. Better for the boy to be angry than feeble.

'I thought I could do it!' Edward shouted back, stung by his father's seeming lack of understanding.

'Grow up! Ben was right: I've treated you like a child for too long.'

'Why? I didn't ask you to.'

Radcliffe took a step towards him. The boy backed off, suddenly scared of his father's physical presence. Radcliffe held himself in check.

'Because I was scared for you! Scared I had let your mother down, scared I'd give you a free rein and lose you! Those horsemen were better, tougher, meaner. That's life, and it's unpleasant and it's hard and there are moments when you think you can't take the pain any more but you do. You learn from it and you grow up!'

There were too many feelings still buried too deeply. They fell silent, and then Edward pushed past his father.

Pierce heard the heavy footfalls on the stairs. Radcliffe called his son's name but the front door slammed. Pierce looked through the sash window to the street where Edward climbed into a cab. The house had fallen silent except for the sibilant hiss of the gas lamps. The grey day was already darkening into winter's night. Pierce took a pinch of tobacco from its pouch and with a slow, considered process he packed the pipe's bowl, then he laid a taper's flame across its crown. By the time he exhaled the first plume of blue smoke, the cab was turning the corner, out of sight. Edward was gone.

The New Year had begun badly with the burden of sorrow and misunderstanding, and the pain of a loved one running in anger without saying goodbye.

Within days of the race Colonel Baxter led his troops out of the barracks and down to the Kingstown quayside for their three-week voyage to Cape Town and the war that was claiming many young men. The staccato drums tapped out the rhythm of a battalion on the move. Formations of stamping infantry and their mounted officers were followed by Belmont and the dragoons. Locals lined the route, cheering and waving, bidding the garrison farewell, some wishing them good riddance. This was no colourful parade. The traditional bright uniforms of bygone wars had been replaced with khaki for both officers and men. Belmont and the dragoons wore slouch hats, their chests crossed with bandoliers, their carbines tucked into a saddle sleeve. As Pierce watched the men who had given him a beating an image came into his mind of other soldiers in another war, one in which he and Radcliffe had fought. A war where they hadn't looked too different from Belmont's men. Horse soldiers spoiling for a fight. Damned if he didn't feel that pull of youthful adventure. His feelings subsided when he remembered the hardship of it all, and his knees reminded him of how stiff his joints had become on this interminably wet island.

'You were born in a barn, were you, Mr Pierce?' said Mrs Lachlan from the open doorway, looking down at Pierce who stood on the front steps.

He turned to the stern-faced housekeeper. 'The British are taking a shellacking in South Africa and they can't see why and we have friends going over there who deserve better. Goddammit, it doesn't take a genius to see that they're up against a robust enemy on sure-footed ponies who know the ground,' Pierce said to her. 'They need to fight a different kind of war.'

'And if I had the foggiest idea what it was you was talking about I'd be able to give you an answer, not that I'm sure it was a question in the first place, mind. I'd like to close the front door and try and keep some heat in this draught-ridden place. Will you be taking your tea in the front parlour, or should I just chuck it down the sink and not bother myself to try and look after you and Mr Radcliffe?'

Pierce turned his back on the passing troops and yielded to the no-nonsense woman. 'Mrs Lachlan, they need you out in South Africa, they surely do.'

'I don't know about that, I've enough on my plate in this place without goin' off to win some Englishman's war for him. That's all you men think about. Killin' one another!'

'The parlour would be fine, thank you,' Pierce told her as she ushered him inside the house.

'Right. Then wipe your boots, and I've told you before,

you may be an American gentleman of colour, not that I hold that against ya, God made us in all shapes and sizes and you can't be blamed for being dabbed with the tar brush, but I'll not have rough language that touches on blasphemy while I'm working here. I've mentioned it once and I don't wish to mention it again.'

Duly chastised, Pierce nodded in acknowledgement. 'I apologize.'

'Right you are. And it would be a help if the master of the house could let me know when he might be home. We can't be wasting food 'cause he's off gallivanting.'

Despite her hands being dry she wiped them on her apron as she turned back to her kitchen, a slow, worried hand-wringing that let the household know she was a woman who carried the burden of the house on her shoulders – and that they should never forget it.

Since Edward had left several weeks earlier the house had been almost desolate in its silence. Reminders of the young man were everywhere and Pierce was tempted to write a letter of his own to the boy. The boarding school was miles to the south in Cork and by now he would have been unpacked and settling back in. He toyed with the pen, dipped it in the inkwell, steadied the sheet of paper beneath his hand and waited for the words to come. But they never did. He had tried each day since the boy had left and each of those times he failed.

Instead he spread open the *Manchester Guardian*, an English newspaper that was despatched weekly to Radcliffe on the Liverpool mail boat. It was a newspaper firmly against the Boer War and stood its ground against fierce opposition from the more jingoistic press. He let the broadsheet cover the desk and turned the pages in a slow, deliberate manner. His eyes scanned them for a column headline that might entice him to put on his bifocals. It was always a struggle to read the small typeface in the soft light from the gas lamp. War reports and casualty lists, columns of news, advertisements, obituaries and a faded photograph of a woman with a caption: *Evelyn Charteris – the thorn in the British government's side.*

Pierce held his spectacles inches from the newspaper like a magnifying glass. The smudged print was of poor quality, but it was the same Evelyn Charteris he knew was trying to help the women and children caught in the conflict of the war.

'Well, I'll be goddamned,' Pierce muttered to himself, then glanced across the newspaper in case Mrs Lachlan was in earshot. Which she wasn't. Pierce harrumphed in quiet disbelief as he scanned the text. This had been the letter he had sent out to the various newspapers and the *Manchester Guardian* had given it some column inches and written an article about her. Charteris, the well-to-do woman who had set up a charity for those women and children, might now get some support from the paper's readers. The British and their colonial troops fought not only the Boers but a Foreign Brigade of volunteers from America, Europe and Ireland. And this woman was right in the middle of it. The newspaper had got hold of a photograph from somewhere. Pierce had always imagined she would be a robust woman who looked like a beef farmer's wife, not this delicately featured woman with her hair tied up, a small wisp falling from its confining hairpin. He was already impatient to show Radcliffe. Such a woman could match Radcliffe's sense of justice. It's what his friend needed – the kind of woman who would – He stopped the thought in its tracks and gave a mental shrug. It was time for Radcliffe to abandon his wife's memory.

He closed the paper, cursing himself for even thinking the thoughts. Matchmaking should not be something considered by a man who'd had enough grief with women over the years to know he was unsuited to waking every day to the same face on the pillow next to him.

It took a couple of weeks before the first alarm was raised.

It was not another dispatch from the war with its ongoing news of defeats and casualties that caused trepidation but the letter sent by Edward's headmaster querying why the boy had not returned for the start of the new term. The Dublin Metropolitan Police were not in the business of trying to find runaway boys, and the County Cork police made only rudimentary inquiries. Radcliffe seemed trapped in a cage of bureaucratic apathy. He reached out to those he had helped over the years in court and it seemed for a week or so that there was a chance the boy had been seen back in the city. The fleeting moment of hope proved as false as those sightings. Edward Radcliffe could be anywhere in the country or, worse, have become a victim of his father's reputation for defending Fenians. Fear clawed at Radcliffe and Pierce every day. It was the threat of political repercussions should this fear bear any truth that finally made the Dublin police begin an investigation.

Pierce entered Radcliffe's study and saw him gazing through the window. It took a moment for him to turn, realizing that Pierce had entered the room. Pierce laid the day's mail delivery on the desk as Radcliffe fingered through the envelopes.

'I should never have taken Fenian cases. What if those who see me as being a sympathizer have hurt Edward because of it?'

'Damned right, Joseph. We'll burn every damned begging letter and decline every case desperate for a defence,' agreed Pierce.

Radcliffe raised his head and stared at his friend. Did Pierce actually believe that?

Pierce gave his friend a questioning look.

Radcliffe knew his moment of self-pity was being mocked. 'OK, but you know, Ben, if they have hurt the boy because of me then we're heading back to America. The British and the Irish can scratch the scabs off their own self-inflicted wounds without me trying to heal them.'

'Edward is a resourceful kid. He's tougher than you think. Wherever he is he's blowin' off steam. I'll put money on it. He's giving us a fright is all. Just letting us know that he can manage this big wide world on his own.' Pierce tapped the sheaf of envelopes. 'Put your mind where it's of use.'

Radcliffe slipped the letter opener into an envelope. 'You and Mrs Lachlan, you make a fine show of ganging up on me. If I didn't know better I'd say you two are closer than you admit.'

'I'll make allowances for the trouble that's going on in your head, but if *I* didn't know better I'd say you need to see a doctor. Damned if that woman couldn't turn a Comanche war party back to their camp with their tails between their legs.' He shook his head at the thought of the formidable housekeeper. Mrs Lachlan had the measure of them both.

Out in the blackness of the countryside coach lanterns at Kingsley's stables flickered behind their soot-stained glass. The man's bulk filled the archway to his yard. He was drenched from the cold night's rain, and the cigar he smoked smouldered like peat, but he was impervious to the weather. Steam rose from his wool coat as from a beast of the field. A coatless urchin stood shivering before him: he had run from the city until he was almost on his knees with exhaustion. Kingsley had listened to the boy's stumbling speech. Questioned him once and then again, making certain of the message being delivered.

'Fergal!' he called and a moment later the stable lad who had gratefully accepted Radcliffe's coin that day came out of the stables, pulling on his coat and turning up the collar against the cold night air that bit hard after the rain. There would be a frost by morning when he exercised the horses and it seemed there would be little chance of returning to the comfort of his bed, as crude as the sacking and straw was. He stood next to Kingsley awaiting his orders. For some reason there was a slum kid standing there, shivering like a fish out of water. His master puffed hard on the cigar until it glowed and only then, as if he had made a decision, did he turn to the stable lad.

'You see this boy here? You take him into the kitchens and give him a bowl of Cook's fine stew, and a loaf of bread for him to take away with him. And then you find a coat from one of the lads and let him sleep in an empty stall.'

'Yes, Mr Kingsley,' the stable lad said, and tugged the urchin towards him.

Kingsley reached out to the bedraggled child, a silver coin held between finger and thumb. 'I reward those who help me,' he said as the wide-eyed boy reached out hesitantly to take the money. 'You see to it this child gets back to town tomorrow morning,' Kingsley told the stable lad, 'and then you fetch Mr Radcliffe here.'

Kingsley watched the older boy run with the child across the courtyard to the kitchen door.

The stubborn lawyer's pride was always something that couldn't be bought, but when it came to the fate of one's own child, what price wouldn't a man pay?

The cigar tasted sour on his tongue and he tossed it into the puddles. The scattering clouds fled past the moon and as the rain eased the crystal stars shone with a clarity he had not witnessed for as long as he could remember.

The following day a mantle of frost cloaked the grassland hills. Trees, stiff as angels with frostbitten wings, hovered over the graveyard as Radcliffe stood before the memorial stone. His weekly ritual of visiting the cemetery had been delayed by Kingsley's summons and the slow cold journey on horseback. Splashes of blood and a fox's tracks told him a rabbit had been trapped and killed in the confines of the cemetery. The blue sky and white birches roused memories that haunted him: memories of another country when he and the Buffalo Soldiers had trekked across snow-capped hills and laid waste their enemy's village. Blood on snow was a common theme in Radcliffe's bad dreams.

He stooped over the gravestone and brushed the frost clear from the name etched into the granite; as he did so his breath plumed, caressing the cold surface in a ghostly kiss. He took a pace back and wiped away the morning's tears. Grief had long drained such emotion from him – these were from the cold air – but the blurred name was as fresh in his mind as it always had been.

JOHN MICHAEL RADCLIFFE
1874–1891

BELOVED SON OF JOSEPH AND EILEEN
BROTHER TO EDWARD
IN GOD'S CARING HANDS

One son had been taken; another was missing. Now nothing mattered more than finding him.

CHAPTER EIGHT

Kingsley leaned on the wooden wall surrounding the show ring. The horse, free of its box, kicked and scuffed the sawdust. It snorted and pranced and then raised its head, nostrils flaring, gazing at the man who loved and cherished him. Kingsley allowed a smile and sipped from a hip flask. The horse whinnied and trotted around the ring, the shallow light painting a silver line from withers to tail across its black sheen.

'Is that you, Radcliffe?' Kingsley asked without turning.

Radcliffe had stood for a moment inside the huge doors behind the hunched shoulders of the Irishman as the horse moved in and out of shadow. The barn's stone walls held the chill, and the horse's snorting breath made him seem as Kingsley had said: a horse for unearthly warriors.

Neither man moved for a moment, and then Kingsley half turned. It seemed to Radcliffe that the Irishman had barely slept. Cold whiskers of frost clung to his wool coat. 'You and your boy… there's misery between you, is there not?' He waited, but there was no answer from Radcliffe. Kingsley shrugged: 'Your son. He ran off to war.'

He watched Radcliffe's reaction. There was barely a flicker of the fear that information must have driven into the man. He knew the lawyer was waiting to find out what Kingsley was after. Valuable news had a price.

'Aye, I'm certain,' Kingsley said in answer to Radcliffe's

silent doubt. 'People like to be in my debt – they tell me things. Seems he caught a steamer the night of the race.'

Radcliffe walked to where the man stood. 'No. I checked. And so did the police.'

Kingsley snorted and spat into the sawdust. 'The police. Jesus, Radcliffe. You know as well as I do those clowns couldn't find a whore in a brothel. Your boy used a false name. Give the lad credit. Probably going off to find that chum of his, Lieutenant Baxter. He went to South Africa all right. Guaranteed. You should've let me fix that race like I said. Saved yourself this grief.'

Radcliffe nodded, resisting the fact he was in the man's debt. 'Thank you.'

Kingsley clicked his tongue at the horse, and it responded with a sudden flurry that caught Radcliffe by surprise. It surged forward and then braced its legs into the sawdust, stretching its head towards Kingsley's open hand.

'You'll be going after him, so you'll need a horse that'll take you to the ends of the earth, through shot and shell and bring you back again... He's yours. And I want nothing in return.'

The impact of the man's offer was not lost on Radcliffe. 'Why give me that which you prize the most?'

Kingsley looked at him. He had no need to give Radcliffe any reasons but he had already made his decision. 'Seventeen years ago I had a bit of fun with a girl... down in Wexford. I was going off to war m'self. She had a baby... I couldn't own up to it. Over the years the lad went adrift. His mother, she was trash anyway and the boy didn't turn out well. I tried to keep my eye on him best I could – he never knew me – but he got himself caught up in the wrong business... Do I have to spell it out to you?'

Radcliffe still couldn't grasp what the man was trying to tell him in his stumbling fashion.

'For a lawyer you're not very illuminated in the upper regions,' Kingsley said. And waited, because he saw the realization dawn in Radcliffe's eyes.

'The boy they hanged? O'Hagan? Your son?'

Kingsley nodded, took a swig from the flask, wiped it off and offered it to Radcliffe, who accepted and took a swallow.

'You tried to save him, you fought for him, and you made no judgements against him. I feel I owe you a debt,' Kingsley said.

'You're a Fenian?'

'When I have to be. Those stupid bastards think it'll be solved with a gun. It's the politicians that'll make the deals and sell us all downriver.'

Radcliffe saw the pattern of events more clearly. 'It was you who warned Colonel Baxter about the attack on the garrison.'

'I knew an attack would make the English spit blood. That they might hang my boy without another thought. And I couldn't let on; I couldn't show what I felt. Y'get it, d'you?'

'If they discover who betrayed them, they'll be coming for you,' Radcliffe said.

'Ah... mebbe not. I made certain they got their information from a whore.'

'They'll kill her then.'

Kingsley shook his head. The flask was empty. 'I warned her off, gave her money. There's the stupidity of it. By saving her someone sooner or later might find out it was m'self. If they get to her. Thing is, Radcliffe, they'd kill the horse first to spite me.' He stroked the horse's face. 'You spend a few days out here, get to know him, make sure he knows you. You're a kindly rider, I know that.'

Kingsley turned away and made for the fresh air. 'So – there it is. Go on with you, then. I've done all I can do for you and your son. You find him and you tell him about his mother.'

Radcliffe stopped mid stride.

'I know what you did. Using her maiden name and all that,' said Kingsley.

'How long have you known about my wife?'

'A while. And he must think his mother's buried elsewhere,' Kingsley added.

Radcliffe nodded.

'How did you keep the lie going for so long?'

'Edward was in boarding school. I couldn't tell him what happened to her. A boy grows into a man and the stigma would never leave him. At every turn his life would be blighted.'

'Jesus, Radcliffe, you've less faith in humanity, though I use the word lightly, than m'self.'

'It served no purpose to tell him. She was as good as dead. Like you and your son. Circumstances dictate our actions. You do what you think is best at the time.'

Both men fell silent for a moment, the dim light a welcome camouflage disguising their regret.

'Don't worry, no one knows the truth. Only me. You tell him. He has a right,' said Kingsley.

There was little more that could be said between the two men; anything further might lead them both into emotion they'd rather not express. Radcliffe extended his hand in gratitude and Kingsley took it.

'You bring that boy home. We need our sons, Radcliffe... but this country needs them more.'

To the north of Dublin, through the country lanes, an imposing group of Victorian buildings rose up behind their cast-iron gates. These three- and four-storey buildings were not far from the Dublin Workhouse. Inside one of the wings, in a room that overlooked the walled gardens, Radcliffe stood at the doorway and gazed at the imposing room, twenty feet square, high-ceilinged and rich in furnishings. The large, richly patterned carpet was soft underfoot; heavy drapes defied the cold air that seeped through the sash windows. Bookshelves ran across one wall and the wingback chairs offered a place to sit, away from the draught, in front of the glowing coals. It was a room richer in its welcome than Radcliffe's own house, and was meant for someone who needed such cosseting comfort. The landscape paintings on the wall suggested it might belong to a country gentleman and his family. But no dogs barked and raised themselves from the front of the fire, no tails wagged in welcome. Except for the crackling coals and whisper of gas lamps it was quiet. Above the roaring fire on the marble mantelpiece were photographs showing a young family. Parents and sons. A faded picture of Joseph and Eileen Radcliffe with two young boys.

There were two women in the room. One, the more matronly, had given up her fireside chair when Radcliffe entered. She had whispered a brief greeting, and retired to the other side of the room to afford Radcliffe privacy. The woman who sat in front of the fire was in her mid-forties, simply but elegantly dressed, her raven hair pulled back and gathered in a tidy bun held by a tortoiseshell hair comb. She lowered the book she was reading on to her lap as Radcliffe sat down in the vacated chair.

There was a sculptured beauty to the woman's face that Radcliffe had always loved.

'I'm going away. I won't be able to see you for a while,' he said gently, gazing into her eyes.

The woman smiled. 'That's all right. It has been very kind

of you to visit me. Very thoughtful. Thank you,' she said, the soft lilt of her voice as delicate as it always had been.

Radcliffe slowly reached out his hand, pausing before he reached hers. For a moment she looked at the open palm and the half-curled fingers waiting to embrace her own, then she reached out and laid her fingers into his hand, and looked at him expectantly.

'Eileen... I'm going to find our son,' he said.

A brief shadow of uncertainty crossed her face.

Radcliffe laid his other hand across hers, reassuringly. 'Edward. I'm going to bring Edward home... and then I'll tell him about you and hope he will forgive me.'

Uncertainty crossed her face again, and she turned her gaze to the flames, her hand slipping from his and returning to her lap, fingers twisting her wedding band. Radcliffe stood and was about to lean forward to kiss her forehead when he sensed her stiffen. He looked at his wife's companion. The woman's kindly face creased with a smile of pity as she shook her head.

The room's double doors closed behind him; the woman locked them.

'As you heard I'm going away,' said Radcliffe. 'I have made full provision for her ongoing care. Has anything changed?' he added hopefully, but knowing it was a question that would never have a satisfactory answer.

'She still does not know anything, she knows no one. She sits, she reads and she gazes out of the window at the gardens. She remembers nothing. Nothing. Grief destroyed her mind.'

Much of what Radcliffe earned came each month to this private wing in the place of sanctuary. He thanked the woman and made his way to the coachman who had brought him from the city. As they drove through the gates he turned and looked back, hoping his wife might have gone to the window to watch her visitor leave. There was no one there. Arching across the gates' pillars the sign – *Richmond District Lunatic Asylum* – seemed even starker than usual.

Over the next days a new impetus seized Radcliffe. There was much to do in a short time if he were to arrange the shipment of Kingsley's horse and catch the next steamer to Cape Town. Pierce made all the arrangements while Radcliffe briefed other lawyers to take his upcoming cases.

Their brief respite of clear bright days was overtaken by stormy weather, thrashing rain, and it was on such an inclement day that Radcliffe returned home to find Mrs Lachlan clattering the kitchen pots more animatedly than usual as she dried and hung them in their places.

'This house has an air of impending doom that no sane person should ignore, Mr Radcliffe. I hope prayers are said and confessions made. A good Catholic house should be on its knees three times a day, five on a Sunday.'

'Not exactly the house, Mrs Lachlan, more perhaps the people in it,' Radcliffe said gently in an attempt to soothe the woman's obvious anxiety.

'Mother of God, it's not the time for cleverness with words, Mr Radcliffe. Your lad's away in a heathen land and I pray strongly for his safe return but Mr Pierce needs a lesson or two in devout prayer himself. All that bangin' and cursin' at the top of the house and him thinking I don't hear down in the kitchen. The attic is closer to heaven and blaspheming that close to the Lord will bring even more misfortune on us all. And another thing: what am I expected to do rattling around here on my own while you two gentlemen go off on this hare-brained adventure? And you'll forgive me for saying this, Mr Radcliffe, but you're both of an age when going off to war should not be a consideration. Old age has its limitations.'

She had not taken a breath as she berated him and punctuated her final exasperated comment with a bang of a pot on the kitchen table.

Radcliffe climbed the stairs to the attic.

Pierce was packing his travel bag, but old chests of clothes and boots had been turned out as he chose the most suitable. The look on Radcliffe's face pre-empted the question. Pierce gave him a warning look in return.

'You know the boy's as close to me as my own kin, if it was I had any. Don't tell me I ain't going.'

Radcliffe said nothing for a moment and moved one of the buckets more squarely under one of the leaks from the roof. 'I've arranged to have the roof fixed while I'm away. And I told them you'd be here to oversee the work.'

'Then you can untell them, and have Mrs Lachlan stand over them. She's a damn sight more difficult to please than me.' Pierce eased down a bedroll and as he laid it out two US cavalry sabres, their curved blades snug in their scabbards, clattered to the floor.

Both men looked at the weapons neither had held for many years.

Radcliffe picked his sabre up from the floor and slid the curved blade halfway clear of its sleeve. 'They're calling this a white man's war. Dammit, Ben, you're gonna complicate things.'

Pierce hefted the weight of the weapon in his hands. 'We people of colour have a tendency to do that,' he said.

The drips of rain from the leaking roof dribbled down a rafter, forcing him to find another receptacle. Radcliffe handed him an old storage tin. 'Neither side is arming the Africans and if you step off the boat you're likely to start a whole new war of your own. You don't know anything about the country,' he said.

'I'm taking it for granted that the sun shines,' Pierce said hopefully.

SOUTH AFRICA

FEBRUARY–MARCH 1900

CHAPTER NINE

Young, bareheaded, his khaki uniform bloodstained, the British officer crawled through the low dry grass, his .45 Webley revolver dragged along behind him by its lanyard. He was dying, but valiantly attempted to reach his horse, which grazed nonchalantly twenty yards away.

As each movement sent agonizing pain through his body, a sense of confused wonderment struck him: he marvelled at how a perfect blue sky embraced the majestic beauty of the mountains. It was a breath-taking amphitheatre of the gods, now tinged with the blood light of the setting sun. The gods must be watching him die, he thought.

The might of the British Army had engaged in what they hoped would be a short imperial war against a citizen army consisting mostly of farmers, clerks from the city and miners from the gold- and diamond fields. The Afrikaners were Dutch-speaking farmers, Boers who often operated in small, self-reliant groups. They were expert riders and marksmen who struck hard and fast and they called themselves by a name the world had not heard before: commandos.

The nineteen-year-old British officer carried not only the burden of his wounds but that of being the son of an aristocratic family. Surrender was not an option; the Dutchies would shoot him anyway. They had no means to care for a wounded enemy. All this young man from the gentle landscape of the English countryside could do was uphold the honour of his regiment and his family. That he should die well had been ingrained in him since he was a boy. But he wept from the pain of his efforts and the knowledge that he would be dead before the final rays of the sun speared the mountain peaks.

It was not only the gods who watched him crawl away from the ambush site. Behind him a ragged group of men wearing homespun clothes, felt hats and bandoliers picked their way across the killing ground where a dozen or more khaki-clad soldiers lay scattered in the grass. The fifty-strong commando ransacked the ambushed supply wagon. One of the men, older than the others, had fought the British in their first war twenty years earlier. With his tobacco-stained beard and his limp from an old wound he looked as if he should be sitting on a rocking chair on the stoep of his dirt-poor farm, gazing out across his beloved land. Piet Van Heerden, Oom Piet, might have been the oldest man in the commando but those who rode with him knew the sixty-three-year-old was a crack shot and horseman. And his age tempered the sense of injustice that had been inflicted on him and his kind. His was a stoic understanding that this war would be vicious and bloody and that independence was the prize. He was glad, though, for the younger men who rode with him. They were mostly from the northern city of Johannesburg and the goldfields, men who had escaped the poverty of Europe to seek out their fortune. These men of the Foreign Brigade were there to fight the cartel of bankers and industrialists who craved the mineral wealth that lay beneath the African soil. It was a war of defiance.

At first these ragged-arsed volunteers had made fun of Oom Piet's guttural speech but the Afrikaners in the group had tolerated their jibes, and the men soon realized that they were all moulded from the same clay, labouring men from peasant stock who only wanted freedom from what they saw to be tyranny.

Oom Piet called out to his twelve-year-old grandson, whose father had died in one of the first engagements two months ago: 'Boy, take their boots and jackets. We'll be needing them.' The old man's years meant his seniority gave him honorary command of the group of horsemen, but the commando was actually led by Liam Maguire, an Irishman, chosen by common consent for his strength and intelligence, who had outfought the British since the war began. A man who had fled from Ireland to the Transvaal goldfields, who could think of no better way to strike back at his imperial enemy than to join forces with the Boers. He stayed in the saddle as the others pulled sacks from the wagon. Maguire's brother, Corin, five years younger than Maguire's twenty-seven, called out, 'Liam! There's salt! Flour! And sugar! Sacks of the stuff.'

'Take only what you can carry on the pack mules. Burn the rest,' Maguire instructed the men. His eyes had not strayed from the grass and the wounded man fifty yards away who was close to reaching his horse. He muttered to himself: 'Don't be a brave officer gentleman now, my lad...'

The young lieutenant had reached his mount and grabbed the stirrup to haul himself upright. Half-blinded by the pain he fumbled for his revolver at the end of its lanyard. Maguire eased the Mauser rifle into both hands and watched as the soldier's pistol wavered. The booming shots made everybody duck and seek cover, but the lieutenant's shots went wild, a desperate and futile act of defiance. Maguire hadn't moved. He calmed the horse and then, without haste, raised the rifle and shot the young officer dead. His body slammed back into the horse and then tumbled into the dirt. The gods' cruel laughter echoed and faded across the mountains.

The men quickly recovered, laughing among themselves at their fear. Corin unhooked his fiddle from his saddle strap and played a few bars of a jaunty jig in celebration.

'Put it away, Corin,' Maguire told him. 'There's men lying dead on the ground. Do ya think it matters that they're British? Their womenfolk'll be grieving as much as ours would grieve for us. Let's not forget that.'

Chastised, the younger man secured the fiddle, then followed the others from the killing ground.

He would never admit it to the brother who had cared for him for most of his life, but this unyielding land, an anvil beaten by the sun, made his heart yearn for the mist-laden hills and green fields of Ireland.

This was a war that would snatch even more men into its madness and inflict its pain and suffering without favour.

Ireland was a very long way away.

Since the war began the British had suffered defeats that had shocked those at home. The so-called ragtag army of Boers had been underestimated. These were superb horsemen and marksmen, fast and manoeuvrable, whose German weapons made them even more deadly. The Mauser rifles and Krupp artillery slew many a British soldier sent into a damnable battle by generals who had not yet rid themselves of outdated formations used against a lightly armed indigenous population across the Empire.

Infighting and rivalry among the generals fuelled the British defeats. Napoleon had believed that no one general should lead an army and after the British were slaughtered at Spion Kop, Colenso and Magersfontein there were those in the British Cabinet Defence Committee who agreed. The British sent Field

Marshal Lord Roberts as General Officer Commanding South Africa. 'Uncle Bob' had saved India for the Empire, had lost a son at Colenso and was determined that his generals should reverse their failures. Roberts gave himself a fighting force greater than those of his generals who faced tougher odds. Forty thousand men, a hundred artillery pieces and a cavalry division struck into the Orange Free State, sister republic to the Transvaal – the spiritual homes of the Boers. At a cost. The British were exhausted. Poor planning and Roberts's lack of understanding of how his supply lines could remain intact meant his troops suffered twenty-four hours without food or water and officers and men bravely cast away their lives to even more reckless plans. The Boers, vastly outnumbered, dug in tenaciously on the east and north-west of the Modder River and launched an audacious attack, seizing the whole south-east line from the British. Roberts almost ordered his men to retire from the field, a fatal mistake that would have allowed thousands of Boers to escape. The cost had been too high, but the gods of war saved him when the Boers surrendered. The British artillery had slaughtered most of their horses, and without them the commandos lost their fighting strength. Nigh on four thousand Boers surrendered.

What became known as the Battle of Paardeberg was the first great victory of the war. Roberts had won almost by default but the casualties from that battle were in plain sight at Naauwpoort; this was an important railway junction, but it was only a strip of corrugated iron houses on each side of the railway line. It was here that many of the wounded were brought from the battle that had been waged, and served as the principal base hospital of Lord Roberts's advance.

The British dead and the dying were laid to one side of the railway siding. Flies smothered the wounded but the corpses were being buried as quickly as possible to avoid the spread of disease. A forlorn crop of graves rose up from the arid land and men with shattered limbs, pierced lungs and broken bodies clung to life in appalling conditions. Soldiers lay suffering in stoic silence, regional accents from town and country blending into words of comfort for each other until those in greatest need fell silent, and the hard land claimed them.

The distant sound of a steam train reached these men, offering hope of evacuation that lifted their spirits. The Red Cross hospital trains would run from the Cape to the battlefield hospitals and take the wounded on the first leg of their journey home. God's gift, the men thought. Clean sheets and a food sack of fruit, milk and eggs. Linen bags, stencilled in red: the Good Hope and Red Cross Societies had clean clothes and soap, a shaving block and toiletries. It was the human face of war and a welcome relief to the desperate. Walking wounded edged towards the platform's edge. Was the train slowing? No comforting words from the Indian stretcher-bearers were uttered, no orders were received. They cursed. This was a troop train going up the line to help 'Uncle Bob' beat the *boojers*. There was no fucking train for them. Those that could watched the distant speck get larger, its pennant of black plumed smoke heralding its approach. Good luck to those poor bastards then, they muttered. Rather them than us.

The Royal Irish Regiment of Foot had landed in Cape Town days earlier: their first sight of the great curving bay was the three-thousand-foot Table Mountain buttressing a spine of peaks raking back to another coast and another ocean. A formidable symbol that seemed to warn those who disembarked not to venture any further. The Irish came ashore from their ship as did other regiments from theirs.

A dozen ships had unloaded men, supplies and horses. It had been an arduous journey at times on overcrowded ships and insanitary conditions and men died from dysentery. A vicious head wind across the Bay of Biscay had confined soldiers below decks despite their desperation to go topside and suck in the cold air. Anything was better than the stench of vomit below. But rough seas threatened to take men over the side and their lives were cast in misery for another two days.

By the time the ships reached Tenerife where they took on water and coal they had their sea legs. Some foolishness was had four days later when they crossed the equator and Mulraney had been blessed with a ducking by King Neptune, an embarrassed Sergeant McCory wearing a wig – *like a whore on the high seas* – quipped Flynn, which earned him extra duties, but then, as the churning ships ploughed their way southwards to St Helena, the men were obliged to strip and clean weapons with unremitting regularity by their NCOs. Had deck space been sufficient, RSM Thornton would have had them drilling; small mercies were few but that was a blessing, though there was to be no escape from a fitness regime that had groups of men stretching, bending and running on the spot.

With fair winds and mostly clear skies the small flotilla sailed close enough for each regiment's band to be heard. Bagpipes and flutes from the Scots' vessels made the Irish music, with their tin whistles, bugles and paper and comb, seem modest by comparison. Seven days after they lost sight of the island they arrived in Cape Town where hundreds of steamers, brilliantly illuminated with their electric lights, lay at anchor in the bay.

With kitbags slung the men were shuffled into order, squared away as neat and tidy as a soldier's footlocker, and then they were marched off to camp. The three-week voyage was softened by their first night in Green Point Camp, an expanse of flatland a short march from the docks, where bivouacs nestled beneath the heights of the mountain and Signal Hill. Troops were entertained with sentimental songs from home by Cape Aberdonians, which suited the Scottish regiments, but was met with heckling from those Irish who had arrived with the latest contingent. Inter-regimental rivalry was good for morale but insulting the Aberdonians from the Cape was considered bad manners. Regimental Sergeant Major Thornton threatened punishment, which quietened them, but Colonel Baxter and his officers secretly lauded their men's disregard. They would need even greater disdain for their enemy in the following months.

The comfort of camp was short-lived, however. Next morning they were marched to the city, waiting in ranks to cross the broad thoroughfare as electric tramcars rumbled their way between foreshore and city. Cape Town train station was packed with waiting soldiers, who were issued with a hundred rounds of ammunition per man and then herded into cattle trucks. *Welcome to South Africa*, one of the Cape Afrikaner railway workers had shouted in English as their train pulled away. *Now fuck off home.*

The trains lumbered continually from Cape Town station and docks, hauling not only new recruits but also veterans of Indian and Sudanese campaigns across the South African veld. This was yet another war to hold the Empire together, and Great Britain's war machine had swung into its efficient role of supplying men, provisions and equipment to the front line several hundred miles to the north. British troops were already engaged with their enemy in the harsh conditions, learning even harsher lessons from the Mauser rifles of the Boer 'farmers'. It was now widely reported that the British and colonial forces were suffering heavy casualties from battle and illness. But the Irish press concentrated on two elements of the conflict. Irish regiments were beginning to lock horns with the Foreign Brigade, made up of volunteers from Europe and Ireland, but most specifically they were facing Irishmen from the Irish Transvaal Brigade. The Irish Republicans who years earlier had flocked to the goldfields of Johannesburg now gathered themselves into a force to be reckoned with, having seen the ideal opportunity to fight the British Army and, by consequence, the Irishmen who served in it. But the Royal Irish Regiment of Foot was not yet in conflict with the enemy, be they the Foreign Brigade or the thousands-strong Boer Republic's army.

The train carrying Baxter's battalion rolled along its narrow three-gauge track that made the carriages swing and sway across a landscape of dreary sameness. Flat-topped hills and mountains stood bare, treeless, without even scrub bush to soften their rugged outlines. For two days and nights of mind-numbing monotony they travelled towards the border of the Cape Colony whose Afrikaners had yet to decide whether to throw off the British yoke and join the war or to stay neutral. Some had volunteered for the British and thus torn their families apart. As loyalties hardened this wretched war would squeeze blood from stone.

The Royal Irish troop train rattled past Naauwpoort. It was a sobering sight for the Irish as the train slowed. More than eight hundred sick and wounded men were quartered there.

'So they're just sheep farmers, these Dutchies, are they?' quipped Mulraney. 'They've given Uncle Bob a shearing, that's for sure.'

Soot billowed backwards from the engine, and Flynn spat the black grit from his mouth. 'And if I don't start seeing a blade of grass or a tree soon enough I'm transferring to the Mounted Infantry. This is no place for a foot soldier. What the feck is a man supposed to take cover behind?'

'You and you bloody horses,' said O'Mara, a Liverpudlian Irishman. 'Jeezus, you can shovel their shit but you'd break your fucking neck just trying to climb into the saddle.'

'O'Mara's right, Flynn. You'd look like a sack of shite on a nag,' Mulraney added.

'Aye, well, I'd have a better chance of outrunning a *boojer*'s bullet if I was clinging to a nag's neck, not like these poor bastards, blind and lame.'

Mulraney stuck a cigarette between his lips, balanced himself as he lit it and gazed across the bleak horizon. 'One of the fellas at the camp said it doesn't rain for nine months of the year, parched to buggery it is, like this, then it pisses down and all this red soil gets covered with a carpet of grass and flowers.'

Flynn took the cigarette from his fingers and drew in a lungful of smoke. 'Fuck the flowers, that red dirt is probably our lads' blood, that's what brings the buggers into bloom.'

Mulraney took back his cigarette. 'And when you take a bullet up the arse I'll wager a bloody great thorny cactus'll grow.'

They laughed, gripping the sides of the swaying truck, but the shattered bodies of the wounded they passed were a sobering sight. Better to die quick than have yourself ripped apart by shot and shell. Better yet was to kill the bastard enemy first.

Chapter Ten

Craggy mountain ranges and sun-baked plains seared their own peculiar harsh beauty into every soldier's dust-gritted eyes near the border of the Orange Free State and Natal Province. The dust caught the back of Lieutenant Baxter's throat. The damned horizon seemed so distant, though he knew it to be no more than three miles away. Or so his training had always told him. Had anyone ever sent a man to the horizon and measured it? Like many things he expected the information to be vaguely accurate. The best way to judge distance was to locate an enemy and watch his shots fall. How many thousand yards for various guns, how deadly the rapid-fire pom-pom would be. A weapon that the British Army had decided not to purchase, but which the Boers had seized on with glee. When would he ever get to test himself? Jumbled questions flitted through his mind.

He discarded what was left of his cigarette and shifted in the saddle to watch the company of Royal Irish go about their work. He had expected a more glorious war, despite the fact the army was fighting irregular troops who had the advantage of knowing the desolate landscape. And what they were doing now was far from damned glorious. It was downright shameful. The Irish troops in particular carried memories and a history of their own countrymen being forcibly removed from their land. And here they were burning out Boer homesteads and imprisoning their women and children. Baxter sat grim-faced on his horse as his men put the dirt farmer's stone and sod-roofed house to the torch.

'Not exactly giving the enemy a good thrashing, would you say, lieutenant?' Flynn said to Baxter as the wife and four grimy-faced children of various ages were eased away from their burning home and put on a flatbed wagon hitched to oxen. The woman cursed at the men in her guttural language. Their cow was tethered, the family's half-full sack of corn confiscated.

'Our orders are to deny the enemy any safe refuge, no place to rest, nowhere to resupply,' the lieutenant answered, without allowing his true feelings to show. 'Shoot the cow, Flynn.'

Flynn looked back to where the small patrol of half a dozen men with bayonets fixed guarded the poor woman and her children. 'With respect, Mr Baxter, do we honestly think that by killing this poor woman's cow we're gonna help win this war?'

Lieutenant Baxter eased his horse past Flynn, levelled his revolver and shot the cow dead. The woman's scream of abuse and the children's cries echoed across the veld.

A stony-faced Baxter turned on Flynn. 'We have our orders, Flynn. You'd do well to remember that.' He turned his horse and led the men across the rock-strewn ground, black smoke billowing into the stark blueness of the sky testament to the fulfilment of their duty.

The nasty business of war was already changing the young Mr Baxter, Flynn thought to himself as he spat the acrid taste from his mouth.

There were others who found the war more to their taste.

A day's ride away from the burning house, Belmont's troop of dragoons and colonial volunteers pushed hard across the veld. Individual items of clothing distinguished them from other soldiers: drab khaki trousers and jackets, brass buttons dulled to stop the chance of them glinting to a sniper's eye, and slouch hats to keep the sun at bay. Rough and ready, dirt-laden and vicious, they were closing in on a Boer encampment belonging to a commando that had been raiding for months.

Unaware of the impending threat Oom Piet was laying kindling on to the cooking fire. Turning to the tin-roofed house that had once been a farmer's shelter: 'Do we have any salt left?' he called to the boy who had unpacked their bedrolls and found them the best shade. The old man knew they had run out of salt more than two weeks ago but when the question was answered it gave Oom Piet the excuse to complain again about eating freshly cooked food without the essential condiment. The damned English. They were devils who took a man's salt from the table and then burned the table for good measure.

The fifteen commandos had hobbled and fed their horses with what little grain they had, then began to gather in the clearing to spit-roast a goat. Oom Piet raised his head from the smoke and crackling wood when he heard the first gunshot. Its crack bounced around the boulders as the first man fell, muscle and blood torn from his body. Confusion held them in a moment's fatal hesitation as Belmont's men stormed into the clearing. The Boers ran for their horses, trying to find cover and retaliate, but they were too exposed. Some managed to return fire, but they were instinctive shots, not aimed, fired in hope that they would help the escaping men reach the boulders.

The rattle of gunfire created the shock that Belmont wanted. His horsemen went to work with their sabres, slaughtering the men on the ground, while those on the flank shot escaping commandos with carbine and revolver. It was the perfect killing ground and the terror of dying by the sword caused the bravest of fighters to scream for mercy. The old man had stumbled from the fire as a bullet ricocheted and torn into his arm, the pain dropping him to his knees. He watched as the horsemen swung their horses this way and that, slashing through the swirling dust with cruel swords. As if by some miracle the kneeling man remained unharmed. The attack was over in minutes. Torn and bloodied bodies lay where they fell, and the old man saw that four other men survived, wounded but cornered and surrendered. Where was his grandson? He saw one of the riders dismount and drag the crying boy from the shelter of the rocks. Cowed and shaking the boy cried out when the soldier cuffed him across the head and then threw him into the clearing. Oom Piet beckoned the boy to him as the survivors were pushed together and soldiers stripped the bandoliers from them.

The Boers watched as one of the men eased his horse forward, and gazed at those beneath the troopers' rifles.

'Do any of you Dutchies speak English?' Belmont asked.

None of the men answered. Those who were wounded could barely stand, trembling as shock began to take hold of their bodies. The old man's arm felt raw. '*Meneer*, I speak a little.'

Belmont turned his gaze on to the old man. Sixty-five if he was a day, Belmont thought. Was he their leader? The old man was dressed no differently to the others. Patched homespun clothes, worn boots and tobacco-stained beard. 'Where are the others? There are more men than this in your commando.'

'*Asseblief*, we surrender to you, sir. There are no more men.'

Belmont's eyes followed the skyline in case others were watching, but he knew that had there been other commandos they would already have heard the crack of a Mauser and seen men, his men, dying. His scouts had made certain no one else was hiding but it was second nature to let his own eyes confirm it.

'You're wearing a British Army jacket under your own,' Belmont said.

'Sir?' Oom Piet answered.

Belmont tugged his own field jacket. 'British Army.' And pointed again at the old man.

'*Oh ja*. Our clothes they are old. We take this from a supply wagon. We need everything. We have nothing.'

'And slaughtered British troops to get them.' Belmont sighed, almost bored with the obvious. He nodded to the troop sergeant and the bolts of a half-dozen carbines rammed home bullets into their breeches.

The old man stepped forward and pointed at the raiders. 'You come here and attack my country. We are farmers and poor people. We are men who have worked this land with our bare hands. And now you will murder us? In cold blood?'

'Yes, I'm going to kill you. I have no use for prisoners,' said Belmont.

The boy was trembling and a pool of urine seeped through his trousers into the dirt. Oom Piet took another step towards Belmont, his arm raised this time in supplication. 'Sir, the boy. He is only twelve years old. I beg that you let him live. Take him with you. *Meneer*, I beg you.'

'Where's your dignity, Dutchy? No man should ever beg,' Belmont said and shot the old man in the head. The boy cried out; another of the Boers quickly held him, turning his own back to the soldiers who levelled their rifles. The gunfire echoed; the bodies fell. The protector's shielding body was shot through, killing both man and boy.

Far beyond rifle range, Liam and the rest of the commando heard the rattle, like torn lightning, and pulled up their horses. Liam's field glasses showed him the cavalry troop leaving. By the time he and his men rode down through the hills there would be nothing they could do except bury their dead.

Chapter Eleven

The SS *Calabash* had been acquired by the shipping controller and acted as Her Majesty's Transport No. 93. *Calabash*'s twin three-cylinder steam engines gave her a service speed of eleven knots. During the nineteen-day voyage Radcliffe went down each day into the aft well deck where stables had been fitted for the transport of horses. The cramped conditions and the rolling ship meant the livestock were penned in tightly packed stalls. Radcliffe knew its confinement would stiffen and weaken the horse's muscles so he groomed the horse every day, vigorously wielding the brush, hoping his efforts would help keep the beast supple. Once they sailed further south, beyond the north Atlantic gales, and the sea calmed, he would ease the horse into the narrow confines between the stalls, walking him back and forth in the short passageway. And each day the bond between man and horse grew.

The sheltered harbour of Table Bay gathered the ship into its calm waters. The buffeting south-westerly wind had made the passage over the last couple of days very rough. The top of the broad, flat-headed mountain that rose before them was smothered in a billowing cloth of white tumbling cloud beneath which goods trains sat along the dockside, their open boxed carriages waiting to shuffle the human cargo from the troopships to the front line. For some there would be no enjoying the pleasures of Green Point Camp; the war's urgency required their presence now. A hundred vessels cluttered the bay and harbour: not all modern steamers, but a host of tall ships, their masts bristling like a small forest clinging to the shoreline. Wagons laden with sacks and boxed goods vied for position, their African drivers urging the mules and horses on, ready to be checked by their headmen, who acted as intermediaries between their workers and the Harbour Board. Steam cranes landed cargo, lowered into willing hands to empty the nets and pack wagons or boxcars. Coal smoke clung to the air despite the breeze as steam trains shunted back and forth the length of the harbour. War was good for business.

Radcliffe insisted on supervising his horse, which was being winched down from the ship. He eased its bridle on carefully and then walked it along the quayside, sensing its urgent desire to run after its long confinement. Its head raised and nostrils flared as it smelled the air and the first scents of Africa. Troops shuffled to one side, forming into ranks as sergeants bellowed; African levies manhandled the cargo; and the shunting clash of metal couplings from the trains rattled the length of the quay. The bustle of the harbour and the hiss from the steam engines made no impression on the horse. It looked left and right, but made no effort to bolt at unusual sounds or yelling men. It was as if, like Radcliffe himself, it wished to view this new world and all it offered.

An hour later Radcliffe returned to where Pierce, his face tilted to the sun, sat hunched against the wheels of a boxcar with their blanket rolls and saddlebags at his side. Nothing more, they knew, would be needed for where they were going. Radcliffe eased the horse up the ramp and made sure the bridle rope was secured.

The rolling cloud was turning black, gathering the moisture from the cold Atlantic. A smattering of rain swept down the mountain's face, light droplets that briefly interfered with the sheltered warmth.

'I'll be damned,' Pierce said.

'I spoke to some English supply officer down the ways who's organizing this train. He said it happens sometimes. Said it was unseasonal. It blows over.' He smiled at the disgruntled Pierce. 'He didn't say when.'

'You're just a man of pure joy who takes uncommon pleasure in another man's misery.'

'Then you might be happy to know that your presence here has already upset the Cape Colony's bureaucrats, but I've saved you from probably being held at the docks here, and most likely put into forced labour.' He unfolded a sheet of paper that bore an official stamp and handed it to Pierce.

'Native labourers need a Plague Pass to leave the dock area. Alex Baxter organized it along with the military passes when I wrote to him.' Radcliffe picked up his blanket roll as Pierce studied the document.

'So that's me with a clean bill of health,' he said.

'Well, I couldn't see a man of your age humping bales. But there's another problem, Ben, and best we face it up front.' He looked up at the passenger carriage. 'You're the wrong colour to travel in the couple of carriages they have.'

'Now where have I heard that before?' Pierce said.

'Thing is, it's a lot more comfortable on those wooden benches than in the cattle trucks,' Radcliffe told him reluctantly. 'My pass lets me travel in the carriage.'

'Well, you have yourself a fine trip,' said Pierce.

'I thought you might take a less than positive attitude about that, so I spoke to that fine English officer and he said that because you're an American he can give you honorary white status.'

'I'll be damned,' said Pierce again, shaking his head. 'Isn't that something I've always wanted,' he added sarcastically.

'Well, it's convenient. And you being an old man and all, I thought your backside might appreciate being white for a few days.'

'A white ass. You are kidding me?'

'No,' said a straight-faced Radcliffe.

'And what did you say to that English officer of holy miracles?'

'I said you weren't *that* old. And that the black goes all the way through to your white bones.' Radcliffe threw his blanket roll into the cattle truck next to the horses. 'Unfortunately,' he added, and clambered into the wagon to share the hardship with his friend.

'And how long 'til we get to the front line?' said Pierce.

'The British are fighting battles across the north is all I know. Two days by the sound of it,' Radcliffe said, giving his friend a hand up into the boxcar and the rancid smell of the horse stalls next to it. Pierce struck a match and laid its flame across the tobacco in the pipe's bowl.

'The Irish?'

Radcliffe shook his head. 'Not sure. But we're going in the right direction.'

There was grim satisfaction that they were now in the place where they believed Edward was fighting with the Royal Irish and that tempered any tiredness from the voyage or ache in their limbs from the cramped quarters. They had lived rough in the past and would do so again. A soldier's forbearance seldom left him and both men settled down close to the beasts. It would take some hours until the train began to haul its cargo to the campaign and until then the clanking of equipment and the shouted commands of NCOs to their men would go on.

Radcliffe and Pierce would feed themselves and stay out of the army's way as much as they could. Dirt was already ingrained in their hands and their own smell of stale sweat mingled with the horses' pungency. Their situation lacked the niceties of city living where hot water and gas lamps wrapped their comforting veneer. Pierce grunted with pleasure as he settled his head against his saddle. Being this rough and ready, allowing yourself to stink and not caring, was a freedom in itself.

Nearly eight hundred miles north of the windswept docks at Cape Town, a lone rider, lost in the great expanse of the veld, brought his horse to a halt. The heat penetrated every fibre of his clothing, and although he had stripped off jacket and shirt, it was not enough to ease the sweat that clung to his undervest. The wide-brimmed felt hat shielded his face, but could not hide the concern he felt at being so lost. A day and a half ago he'd been told at a railway junction that flying columns of British troops were operating somewhere to the north and that an Irish regiment had passed through a week before. Edward Radcliffe sensed he had dared himself too far. Death would claim him if he didn't find more water soon and the old horse he'd bought with the last of his money was fit only for the slaughterhouse. He'd scrimped and saved every penny of his father's allowance and now it was gone. The steamship ticket, the hand-me-down jacket and trousers and the forty-year-old single-shot Martini–Henry rifle had taken everything. At each step of the journey those he did business with took his money and fleeced him under the guise of helping the stranger.

He squatted beneath the meagre shade of a kopje's outcrop and pulled Pierce's Comanche knife from inside his boot to cut a leathery strip of biltong even though he knew the salty dried beef would soon make him crave more water. As he chewed he looked across the featureless landscape broken only by shadows cast by the outcrops. Beyond the farthest undulating plains, he saw a pancake layer of smoke unable to rise higher than the heat-baked hills. Soldiers or farmstead? It didn't matter; he would have food and water for himself and his horse. With renewed hope he urged the old horse on.

It took him longer than he anticipated: the distances of this vast country were deceptive and the harsh light and shimmering heat distorted perceptions. By the time he reached the elbow of outcrop that sheltered a stone-built one-room farmstead it was well after noon. Dried cowpats were being stacked against the wall by a girl who looked to be a couple of years younger than himself. Edward couldn't determine the age of the older woman whose frayed dress was covered by an equally stained apron and whose face was blinkered by a bonnet. There was no doubt that she was the mother of the half-dozen children, all of them, he guessed, under the age of twelve, except for one older girl. The woman and children looked dishevelled. Dirt streaked their hands and faces and it was obvious they had little in the way of food. Two scrawny cows stood in makeshift pens. Flies buzzed and the unmoving air was heavy and silent. The family said nothing as they went about their chores. A windmill stood over a borehole, its metal-winged blades unmoving, as one of the children carried a bucket of water from the shallow trough at its base. Edward could almost taste the water. He dry-swallowed and curbed the urge to rush forward and dunk his head into the clay-walled pool. His horse smelled the fresh water and whinnied, causing the family to turn, startled at his presence. Within a moment the woman had reached for a shotgun and levelled it at him as the children scurried behind her for safety.

Edward raised his hand, but his horse was skittish, wanting to drink, so he brought it back under control with one hand on the reins, keeping the other in a gesture of submission.

'*Engels?*' the woman said, never once letting her eyes stray from him.

He was uncertain if the word meant what he thought. 'I don't speak your language… I don't mean any harm. I need water.'

His words appeared to mean nothing to the woman. She signalled him away with quick jerk of the barrels and spoke the few words in a fractured, guttural accent. 'Go. Get away. *Voetsek, Engelsman.*' She almost spat the words at him.

He had seen railwaymen in the Cape throw stones at stray dogs on the track, and heard them curse the pejorative warning. *Voetsek* was for feral dogs – and Englishmen.

Edward couldn't take his eyes off the young girl's sun-burnished face. Like many a farm girl her hair, bleached by the sun, was tied back. It wasn't only her blue eyes that captivated him; the shape of her breasts pushed against the cotton dress and the two top buttons were tantalizingly open. Milk-pale skin beneath the sunburned face. A body that had never been exposed to the harsh light. Had probably never been seen naked by any man. The girl allowed him a brief smile, but then turned away in embarrassment. Perhaps, he realized, his thoughts were all too apparent.

The woman took a sharp pace forward and raised the barrels directly at his face.

'English. No. No, not English. *Nee Engels*,' he said, hoping to placate her. 'Ireland. I live in Ireland. Dublin. The Irish? You've heard of the Irish?'

The woman looked doubtful.

'You have food?' Edward asked, putting his fingers between his lips. 'You have any food? Any meat?'

'Nothing! Go!' The woman said.

Edward felt desperation begin to take hold. 'Look... please...' His mind raced, searching for the word. '*Asseblief*. Please. Just some water... for my horse...'

Once again the girl muttered something to her mother; the woman shook her head again and kept the barrels level on Edward's chest.

With more willpower than he knew he possessed, he turned the horse away from the water. 'All right... listen... I will get you food,' he said, patting the rifle butt in its sleeve on the saddle strap. 'There's buck' – he pointed – 'in the hills. I'll get you food.'

The woman made no answer but gave him a long, assessing look, then instructed the boy to place the water bucket in front of the horse. The child ran back to the protection of his mother's skirts as the horse buried its muzzle into the bucket and slurped noisily. Edward was still covered by the shotgun. His lips were parched. Once the horse had drained the bucket, he turned it away.

The woman called after him: 'Irish.'

He turned to look at her.

'You bring us food, I give you water, *ja*?'

He nodded and spurred the horse away.

Chapter Twelve

Once he was beyond the second ridge of hills, Edward weighted the horse's rein with a rock and scrambled further on foot. He tracked the buck, creeping forward in the shadows cast by the boulders as the sun moved further to the west. The buck was part of a small grazing herd, no more than half a dozen animals, but it limped and could not keep up as the others in the herd searched out every morsel that managed to grow in the harsh landscape. Edward wiped the sweat from his eyes and raised the heavy weapon to his shoulder. He had fired shotguns before when his father had taken him and Benjamin Pierce on a shoot with Lawrence Baxter and his father. But now his left arm trembled under the weight of the wooden stock and when he squeezed the trigger the recoil forced the barrel up. The steel-plated butt kicked into his shoulder as the .45 bullet smashed into the rock face seventy-five yards away. He had missed. The herd bounded away, but the injured buck still lagged behind and now stood nervously on the spot, tail twitching, head raised and eyes wide, staring towards the shadow that concealed Edward.

He kept his eyes on the wary animal, forced down the lever to open the breech and fingered in another stubby round. This time he wedged the rifle and his arm against the rock and waited until his impatient breath slowed. As he exhaled, he squeezed the trigger gently and this time, as the boom of the gunshot echoed around the rock's overhang, the buck jumped, then staggered a few paces, and fell. He gaped in amazement.

Excited by the kill, he clambered over stony ground, already seeing the girl's face when he arrived back with the buck laid across the front of his saddle. They would invite him to stay, skin and gut the animal, and then roast it as he told them about where he lived, and why he had run away from home. It wouldn't matter if they didn't understand him.

Edward's first shot sounded like a distant twig being snapped as Liam Maguire's commando led their horses through a narrow pass. The farmhouse was out of sight, and would be until they clambered their way over this range of hills. By the time they heard the second shot, they had remounted and urged their horses on through the difficult terrain. The farmhouse was a refuge, but now, perhaps, they had been warned off by the woman who lived there. Or worse still those damned cavalryman were there.

The Boer commando was not the only group of men on the veld that day.

It took Edward another half-hour to bring his horse down to where the buck lay, eyes glazed in death, flies buzzing around its moist eyes and gunshot wound. By the time he had made it back across the escarpment the sun had almost set and the darkening sky sucked light from the land, turning the veld into a purple haze. He was a mile from the farm, and he could already see smoke from the fire pluming upwards. But there were other darkened shapes moving about the building, and he realized that the smoke was not from any roasting pit, but from the house itself. Fear burst into his chest. He slung the weight of the carcass free and urged the horse on.

*

'Two women and girls in the bed, sir,' said Sergeant McCory. 'Pulled back the coverings and they were hiding these rifles 'neath their skirts.' He nodded to the two soldiers who carried the German rifles. 'Them gunshots we heard back there might mean the men who own them will be coming back to claim their property.' The grizzled sergeant needed the young officer-gentleman to see how vulnerable they were.

Lawrence Baxter had also heard the muted echo of the gunshots. 'Then let's hurry along, Sergeant McCory,' he said, turning back to where his men were clearing the farmhouse. The woman and her children were being ushered towards a mule-drawn wagon. They were joined by the children's grandmother, who was being eased from the darkness of the house by Mulraney and Flynn.

Sergeant McCory lifted the younger children on to the wagon. 'You and the little 'uns will be safe, you see if you're not.'

The children stared blankly at the muscled soldier whose moustache curled down the side of his lips, framing broken and uneven teeth, making his smile of assurance seem more like a snarl of hatred. When he turned to help their grandmother climb on to the flatbed, she snatched away her arm and let her family help her up. The children flinched as two soldiers shot dead the scrawny cattle.

'*Julle Engelse! Julle noem julself mans! Skaam julle!*' the old woman hissed derisively.

McCory stepped away and allowed her to clamber up unassisted: 'Aye, well, whatever it is you're on about, I'm sure you've got a point, but orders is orders.'

'She says you English call yourself men – you should be ashamed,' the woman said, settling her aged mother on to a bedroll – as much comfort as could be had on the hard-planked wagon.

'The old girl's right. And for once in m'life I wish I *were* an Englishman,' said Mulraney as he tossed a burning torch into the house's storeroom.

'Keep those thoughts to yourself, Mulraney,' said the sergeant, glancing towards their English officer. 'And get a bloody move on!' he ordered more severely.

As the last few pieces of pathetic furniture were roped on to the wagon, McCory moved the men out. Mulraney and the others walked each side of the wagon to ensure no child would think of jumping down and making a run for it into the scrubland.

'This is a beautiful country, missus,' said Mulraney. 'Much warmer than where I come from but, still, not much of a place to be fighting over, that's for sure. Mind you, I'd be doing the same myself if I were in your shoes. Which I'm not. But I could be. If you take my point.'

Mulraney's attempt at easing the woman's grief was to no avail. She gazed back stoically at her burning homestead, clutching her tearful youngest to her skirts.

Lawrence Baxter eased his horse alongside. 'I'm sorry this is happening to you, but we have to stop your men from coming home for resupplies. You do understand that, I hope?'

'We have nothing,' she said and spat at him.

The lieutenant remained silent; this was not the war he wanted either. 'Mulraney, make sure they get water when they want it.' He spurred his horse away from her hatred.

Edward's horse would soon be blown, its lungs already heaving beyond its ailing strength. He urged it on relentlessly, one hand on the reins, the other clutching the Martini–Henry. He was shouting, raising the rifle, trying to attract the distant soldiers' attention.

'Hey! No! Don't hurt them!' But his voice was swept back into the bleakness of the empty land. With the skill of an experienced rider he gathered the reins and pointed the rifle into the sky and fired a shot. At last the soldiers stopped and turned his way.

'Stand to!' Sergeant McCory yelled. 'Rider to your front! Seven hundred yards!'

The men took up their firing positions. 'It's a Boer,' Mulraney called.

'*Nee!*' the woman cried, but was held back by one of the soldiers.

'Wait...' Lieutenant Baxter ordered, but his command came too late as one of the men fired, and then the others pulled their triggers; a rippling staccato punctured the air.

Edward saw the puffs of smoke and felt the horse lurch as bullets struck home. He nearly fell, righted himself, tried to steady the horse as the air snapped and whistled around him. The horse was going down. He was barely three hundred yards from the soldiers. Why had they fired? Then a burning crease of pain cut across the side of his head. The blurred image of the veld grass raced upwards; the horse's legs flailed, and with a jarring impact he fell on to the hard ground.

Soldiers ran towards him as a distant voice called out commands.

His last memory was that of the horse's body shuddering in death beside him and the sound of boots running.

Liam's commando had buried those killed by the dragoons as best they could in graves that were little more than scrapes in the hard ground. They covered the bodies with piled-up rocks to stop predators feasting on them. The harsh land seldom offered fresh meat to wild dogs and jackals. They stripped what ammunition they could find, but the killers had taken all the food and had burned everything else. Most of the commando's horses had been shot; only two had run free and were later caught. It was God's grace, Corin had said, that Liam and the others were away on patrol when the cavalry struck. And their good fortune still held. They had missed being at the farmhouse below by less than an hour when the soldiers arrived to clear it. Luck was an Irish blessing, he insisted. Jesus, they'd have been huddled in the old place and caught like rats in a trap. As the commando crested the ridge they saw the distant figures running forward from the burning farmstead. One of the Boers was the first to spot the fallen horse and rider lying smothered in the brush. Liam Maguire raised his rifle.

'They're out of range,' Corin said.

'Keep them off him, though!' he said and fired, working the bolt action, as the others followed his example.

The two soldiers were within thirty yards of Edward's crumpled body. The crackling of gunfire brought them to a halt. Puffs of dirt kicked up in a broad scattered arc well out of range. Lieutenant Baxter's voice carried across the plain ordering them back. There was no telling how soon those guns would be in range.

'Leave him! Back to the wagon!'

'Shall we take 'em on, sir?' McCory said.

'Those are not our orders, sergeant. Get those men back. The Boers won't risk attacking with their women and children here.'

'Get your arses back here! At the double!' Sergeant McCory bellowed.

One of the men turned back, instinctively hunching his shoulders despite the ineffective fire; the other, O'Mara, ran forward, ignoring the commands. His companion yelled: 'Scouse! Come on! Get out of there!'

'Not yet!' he shouted back. There had to be something to loot. He turned the body over, rifled the pockets, but found nothing. The rider wasn't much more than a boy. A dead boy with a head wound. He glanced back – the soldiers were leaving. It had been a long run for nothing. As he got to his feet he saw the boy's exposed boots: they weren't worth having, but the bone-handled knife that protruded was. The man bore a scar from ear to lip from a blade of lesser quality than this knife. Snatching his prize he ran back as fast as he could towards the retreating soldiers and Sergeant McCory's curses.

By the time the commando made their way down from the hills the soldiers were gone.

'We can still get the bastards,' Corin said.

'No. They've women and kids with them. They'll find themselves a defensive position in the rocks and we'll be cut to ribbons. Leave them be,' Liam answered. 'You men check the farm, see if there's anything left we can use,' he told them and rode forward to where Edward lay.

They recovered the boy's body and tied the lad to a horse. By the time Liam's commando found their next safe haven – a one-room barn well away from any British patrols in a ravine whose high boulders would offer a good defensive position should it be needed – there were already a hundred or more horses tethered outside. A dozen Africans squatted around a fire, huddled against the cold, eating from an iron pot nestled in the fire's embers. A young Boer stood guard on a craggy outcrop as the men inside relaxed in the warmth and safety offered by the old stone building. Tobacco smoke fugged the air in the barn as the ragtag Boers drank and ate, mingling with the men from the Foreign Brigade. A couple of the Boers shuffled in a half-hearted dance while one of their men played a squeezebox and another dragged a bow over an old fiddle that had only three strings left on its battered body.

Liam and his commando pushed through the throng of men. 'Jesus, these Boers might believe they're God's chosen people, but the Almighty must've had an off day 'cause these are the most boring bastards who ever tried to squeeze out a tune,' said Corin, clutching his violin case to his chest.

Liam pulled one of the men to him. 'Find Hertzog,' he said. The fighter nodded and pushed his way through the men towards the barn's dark corners. Within minutes he returned with one of the Boer commanders. Now that Oom Piet was dead Hendrick Hertzog was the senior man as far as the Boers were concerned and Liam knew as well as the next foreign fighter that a nod had to be given to those whose land had been invaded. He shook Liam's hand and Liam bent his head towards the man's ear, speaking plainly and slowly so that he might understand what had happened. Hertzog's face registered his shock as he heard of the killings, and then turned to follow Liam outside.

Corin grabbed Liam's arm and pushed his blanket roll at him. 'It's cold out there.'

'You're my brother not my mother,' Liam told him.

'It's not for you,' Corin answered.

'He won't need it,' answered Liam.

Realization dawned on the younger man. 'Jesus, Liam, you can't kill the lad, the English already tried.'

'He's not part of any commando, Corin. If he has information about the British we'll get it from him. It's Hertzog's decision whether he lives or dies.'

The night air polished the crystal stars as Liam led Hertzog to where a fresh-faced young Boer stood guard in the lee of the building. Edward sat slumped in the shadows, his back pressed against the wall, as one of the Africans prepared to put a freshly boiled dressing around his head. The bandage had been used before and would never be rid of the old bloodstains no matter how often it was boiled.

The Afrikaner spoke harshly to the African, words that Edward could not understand, but the man retreated quickly, taking the bandage with him. Edward ached from fatigue and the fall from the horse and the pounding in his head nearly blinded him, but as the African servant moved away he summoned the strength to reach down towards his boot and the knife that should have been there. Liam and Hertzog appeared before him.

'You've taken my coat,' Edward said, with a sense of loss more pressing than the lack of its protection against the night's cold.

'And it's a good one at that. There's a label inside that says it's pure wool and made in Dublin,' said Liam. 'A fine coat that's worth a bob or two. Now where did you get it is what I'm wondering. None of my lads have such finery.'

'My father bought it for me... please... I'm cold,' Edward admitted, the fear and pain from the wound mingling in confusion.

'We've given it to one of the boys who ride with us. He needs it more than you,' Liam said. 'The British have patrols out in the hills; they've learned how to fight. They're raiders like us, they live rough, colonial irregulars mostly, but they don't take prisoners. Get m'drift? So we shoot spies. Tit for tat.'

Hertzog kicked the boy's boot. 'Are you a British spy, boy?'

Edward flinched. The man's beard made him look even more menacing; it skirted his chin but he was clean-shaven around his mouth, which accentuated the lips that curled back in disgust.

'I'm no spy. I tried to help the woman at the farm – that's why I went out and shot the buck. And if I'm a spy why did the patrol shoot me?'

'*Ja*, you're a do-gooder, eh? They shot you because you look like a Boer. Not all these soldiers know who rides as a scout looking for us. Who do you report to? We had men killed, slaughtered by cavalry. Men and boys. One of them younger than you. You know about that?'

'No,' Edward insisted, beginning to think that no matter how he answered, this man was intent on killing him.

'Stand up,' said Liam. 'On your feet.'

Edward pressed against the wall and staggered to his feet. He was dizzy and his head pounded. His knees gave way but he braced himself, determined not to appear weak in front of these violent men.

'How did you get here? Why that farm?' Hertzog demanded.

'I don't understand what you mean. I was lost,' Edward said, stumbling for an explanation, suddenly realizing that he could not confess that he sought out his friend Lawrence Baxter with the Royal Irish.

Hertzog's slap sent him reeling. '*Verdomde rooinek!*'

Edward tasted blood, and the blow nearly knocked him senseless. The night sky swirled.

'You're lying,' Hertzog said. 'My people are dead. You're old enough to fight, boy. Who do you report to? Where are those horsemen camped? On your feet.'

Edward tried but could not find his balance. He was

slipping under a veil of darkness, the man's voice distant, a faint echo. He spat blood, tried to stand again but failed. His head wound throbbed viciously: the calloused hand that had struck him had opened the wound. He heard muted words between the two men who stood over him. The Afrikaner tugged a pistol from his belt and Edward heard the words that confirmed he was about to die.

'If he has no information then he is of no use to us. He will slow us down.'

Edward raised his hand as the man levelled the pistol. There was no mercy to be seen in the older man's face. He desperately tried to stay conscious so he could plead for his life. The Irishman appeared to look regretful at the impending execution.

'I ran... away from home... that's all ... I don't know anything about... anybody being killed... Don't kill me... please... Let me go... or leave me here... I won't say anything... I'm... Irish... Dublin... My name is Edward... Radcliffe... I... ran away...'

Liam Maguire pressed Hertzog's gun hand down.

Chapter Thirteen

The frontier town of Verensberg was made up of a mixture of iron-roofed stone and timber houses, boardwalks and dusty streets that turned to calf-high mud when the rains came. It was a through line for the British Army as they ferried troops to the rail yards, and then on to the battlefields of the north and east. And where there were soldiers there would be camp followers, brothels and a music hall. For those soldiers in the field who were sent back wounded or who sought creature comforts away from the fighting Verensberg was a small oasis of distraction and sin.

The Diamond Hotel was well known among the troops for the number of prostitutes who plied their trade there. The room was packed with junior officers from different regiments who sat in boothed areas with whores on their laps and whiskey on the table. The rest of the audience was a mixture of civilians and black marketeers. A quartet of musicians fought the noise of the raucous soldiers but the musicians were not the main attraction. The crowd waited for that rare sight, a woman of beauty who seemed beyond the reach of them all. And she could sing. That was why the room was packed that night.

A short, frock-coated man waddled on to stage, raising his hands to quieten his audience. Charles Frimley, oiled hair and moustache glistening in the heat from the stage lanterns, had once trodden the boards in some of London's best music halls, but drink and debt and the threat of men sent to recover what he owed had driven him to seek opportunities further afield, and what better place to strike the gold in men's pockets than a music hall with a pretty whore and her enticing song?

'And Now...' the master of ceremonies chirped, his voice rising, building the men's expectations, savouring the emphasis on each word, '...For Your Delec-tation, For Your Tingling Groins and Tinkling Coins, With Breathtaking Bravura to Set Hearts-a-Breaking –'

'Get on with it, you old bugger!' one of the men shouted, which raised a chorus of approval. 'There's a bloody war on!'

As the laughter subsided Frimley acknowledged the heckler. 'I take your point, sir. Your friends mentioned only a short time ago that you had devoted yourself to avoiding it.'

The soldier swore, embarrassed by the attention, and the truth that he was rear echelon. His friends roared with approval; one of them tipped a glass of beer over his head. Frimley knew he had the crowd in the palm of his hand. The audience would love him before the night was out. Drunken soldiers were God's gift to a barroom that overcharged for tampered liquor and gave him his cut of the takings.

Belmont, sitting with half a dozen other officers, wearing their tunics unbuttoned, safe from official censure, stood on his chair, whiskey bottle in one hand, cigar in the other. 'Where is she, Charlie? We know she's here!'

The sweating mass of men howled their approval and drummed their heels on the wooden floor. Once again Frimley raised his arms and made a slight, courteous bow towards Belmont. 'Ah, I thought I smelled a cavalryman!'

Belmont took the laughter and jeers in good grace.

'A high-ranking officer perhaps? I hear, sir, you're in command of the Post Office Hussars.'

Belmont made a mock bow to the laughter. 'Aye, and we've delivered plenty of surprises for Dutchy!'

The room erupted with a furious cheer.

Frimley could hold them no longer: 'Very well, my brave boys: the vivacious, the voluptuous, the wickedly witty and wilful... Miss Sheenagh O'Connor!'

As Frimley backed offstage Sheenagh, the sexiest whore this side of the battlefield, swept on stage in a dress fit for the finest of London ladies, but paid for by their officer husbands. As she swept her eyes across the baying men she settled her gaze on Belmont. He raised his glass to her. A familiar look passed between them. These two knew each other.

On the edge of town, far beyond the uproar that Sheenagh's appearance created and the perimeter pickets that carelessly went about their duties in the belief that they were a long way from their enemy, Corin Maguire and a dozen other commandos lay shivering in the cold dirt, teased by the flickering warmth of the town's lights. They were no more visible than the black shadows of the rocks. Edward sweated, trembling with fever, his hands still bound. One of the American volunteers, Jackson Lee, hunched close to Corin with the wounded boy between them. 'Liam's putting us at risk 'cause of this kid. It'd be a damned grievous thing if he got us shot 'cause of it.'

Corin pulled a half-bottle of whiskey from the man's hands and swallowed a mouthful of the warming liquid. 'Liam's been my brother all my life. So I've known him longer than you have. He's doing what's right.'

The American took back what was left of the liquor. 'I wish I knew why,' he said.

'It's an Irish thing. You wouldn't understand,' Corin answered.

'I had a grandmother from Cork.'

'Jesus, the whole world has a grandmother from Cork. That doesn't count.'

'I don't know why we didn't just shoot the kid or leave him be. It's a grievous thing being put at risk without knowing why,' said Lee. 'What'll we do if he starts to moan or cry out? Sound travels far here.'

'Are you listening to y'self? The music in town would deafen a bloody cavalry charge. The soldier boys are havin' themselves some fun. Just as we would.' He winced as the rough whiskey burned his throat. 'Given half the bloody chance. God, what I wouldn't give for a fat and comfortable woman tonight. Even if she was a heifer.' He sighed and passed the bottle back. 'Give the kid a slug.'

'Waste it on him?' Lee moaned.

'Well, it'd help keep the lad quiet. And look at him, shivering like a cat being dragged from a barrel.'

The American leaned across and tipped the bottle to Edward's lips. He sipped and coughed.

'Now see what you've done? Making more goddamned noise than –' Corin quickly raised an arm in warning. A dozen soldiers were being marched from the town towards them. Lee's hand smothered Edward's mouth. They fell silent, embracing their rifles, but after a dozen more yards the scraping footfalls turned away. The moment had made sweat prickle on Corin's spine. If Liam didn't sort something out by dawn, Corin reckoned, they might be discovered, that or the wounded and feverish lad that he had tucked close to him to offer a scrap of warmth would be dead. Whatever his brother planned, Corin told himself, it would be hard to escape come first light but he feared that Liam couldn't do anything until then. One way or another Sheenagh O'Connor was going to be busy till daybreak.

An arc of steaming brown piss splashed down from the balcony of the room above the music hall into a back alley. Belmont, wearing undershirt and breeches, stood on the first-floor landing and sighed with pleasure as he emptied his bladder from the night's excess. A hangover was a constant companion when he was away from the field of conflict, an excess of alcohol being one of the few pleasures available, other than those skilfully provided by Sheenagh O'Connor.

Tucked below the overhang, their backs pressed between the swill drums from the food hall, Liam Maguire pushed himself further away from the splashing liquid. He heard the man above him turn and go back into the whore's room. It wasn't yet time for the rebel to make his move.

Sheenagh O'Connor had made the bare-board room as comfortable as she could. A thin rug covered the worst of the painted boards. A quilt had been thrown over a tattered chair, and of the three shawls she possessed, two were draped on the walls in an attempt to give the space a semblance of intimacy and warmth. The room was dry and airy, and the glass-paned doors on to the balcony gave her a sense of wellbeing that she had never experienced in her dark Dublin tenement. She lay naked in the bed, half covered by the sheet, allowing the chill dawn air to goosebump her skin and pucker her nipples. It would be hot enough to fry a lizard's skin soon enough. She felt lazy. She had enjoyed Belmont's attentions, and the commander of the dragoons always paid well, ever since they had first slept together back in Dublin. Chance encounters were a wonderful thing, but a frightening thought shadowed the comfort of having money tucked beneath the floorboards. If the dragoon officer and the Royal Irish had been sent to this area might not one of the Fenians she had betrayed find her? Was there a chance of it? she wondered.

Belmont sat on the edge of the bed and lowered his whiskered face to her ear, rubbing his moustache against her exposed neck. She sighed with invitation, and half rolled towards him, stretching the night's sleep from her body, arms above her head. He settled his lips and tongue on to her aroused breast, and then eased his head back, holding her face in his rough palm. 'What are you up to?' he asked gently.

'Just being nice, Claude,' she said, without a hint of the alarm she felt.

Belmont reached down below the bed and pulled out a satchel bearing a red cross. 'This is army issue,' he said without threat. He tumbled the contents on to the bed. 'Someone thieving army medicines for you?' he asked.

Sheenagh showed no sign of panic despite the sudden flutter in her chest. She took the cheroot from his lips, and sipped from the half-glass of whiskey at the side of the bed. She smiled, unconcerned at his interest, and picked up a couple of the brown-glass bottles nonchalantly. 'Not stolen – requisitioned. Surplus to requirements is what he calls it. It's a bit of extra cash I make selling them. Don't deny a girl a living.'

Belmont took the cheroot back from her. 'Not letting a medical corps sergeant get between your legs, are you, Sheenagh? Can't have that. Officers only, preferably only this officer,' he said, pulling on his boots.

'He's a major and that's all I'm saying. He's a nice man. Don't be jealous – captain.'

'A major. Good for you. You be careful where you sell them. I can't help you if you get caught.'

'Then I'd just have to charm m'way through, would I not?'

There was a sudden pounding up the stairs. In an instant Belmont was no longer a lazy, hung-over officer. He held the heavy army-issue revolver steady, the hammer cocked, without the slightest trembling in his hand. Whoever had run up the stairs now pounded on the door. 'Captain Belmont!'

Belmont opened the door to one of his troopers. 'A message from the general, sir.'

He took the folded paper from the man and nodded in dismissal. There was no blaming the young trooper for letting his eyes linger on the naked woman in the captain's bed. She was a thing of rare beauty, and her auburn hair matched top and bottom. The lad'd take pleasure in describing the officer's whore to the other men. Though he would lie when telling them that she had smiled at him.

Belmont grabbed his jacket, sword and carbine. Sheenagh slid from the bed and pushed his slouch hat on to his head. 'And which poor bastard are you off to kill now?' she said, and kissed his lips.

'More than one. We're riding across the Tugela behind the Boer guns.'

'Then don't you get yourself hurt,' she said, and kissed him again, her breasts pushing through his unbuttoned shirt on to his chest. 'Come back safe and sound, y'hear? I'll be waiting for my brave captain of horse.'

'Make sure you are, Sheenagh,' he said, but the lazy warmth had gone from him, and she knew his thoughts were already elsewhere. She watched him clatter down the stairs in case he turned, but he did not. Thankfully, she closed the door behind her, relieved her own moment of danger had passed, and then quickly repacked the medicines into the satchel.

She spilled water into the washbowl and sponged away the night's passion, then slipped into a cotton shift, one of better quality than she could ever afford at home. This war was being good to her. The scuff of boots outside her door made her turn, readying a smile for what she thought was Belmont returning from a false alarm. No mission to go on after all. No men to kill today.

The door opened before her hand reached the handle and Liam Maguire almost fell into the room as he dragged a wounded boy with him, his head wrapped in a bloodied bandage.

'Liam! Mother of God!' she cried, closing and locking the door quickly as Liam dragged the injured boy into the corner of the room, pulled across the curtains and then found what remained of Belmont's whiskey bottle.

'He tried to stop the English moving a family off their farm. They shot him. We can't keep him,' he said, snatching a handful of leftover food from Sheenagh's late-night supper with the cavalry officer. He rammed what he could into his mouth and then offered the plate to Edward, who did the same. Good meat and sweet stuff was a luxury for men living off the land as best they could.

Fear caught her again: it never seemed to let go these days. The Maguire brothers had sought her out once they learned through the black-market grapevine that an Irish whore from Dublin was getting medicines for the women at the Bergfontein concentration camp. Sought her out and offered protection should she need it. From what? Did Maguire know something about what had happened in Dublin? It didn't take long to discover that he was one of the thousands who had fled to the goldfields years ago. Perhaps they'd even help protect her from those who'd like nothing more than seeing an informing whore dead with her throat cut. She reasoned that if a real threat ever came her way she could always get word to Maguire and his boys. So she had taken him up on his offer. It cost her time on her back with the muscular Maguire – the older brother – but in truth it wasn't anything unpleasant. Sheenagh looked at the boy and pulled on a silk dressing gown: 'Jesus on the

Cross, Liam, you shouldna have brought him here. There was an Englishman here not a minute ago and he's a terror, right enough. He'd have put a bullet through the both of ya.'

'I saw him. We waited. Listen, the lad's Irish. If I let him go he could talk. You keep him here awhile, then get to that Englishwoman at the camps; she'll know what to do with him.'

She shook her head. 'I don't want him here.'

'It was Hertzog's idea. We've a battle coming up – he'd be a hindrance.'

'And where do I put him?'

'Anywhere you like.'

Edward pushed himself up against the wall, holding on to the small table for balance. 'I don't have to be here. I can look after myself.'

'Oh aye, we've seen proof of that. A twenty-year-old rifle and a well-thumbed book of poetry won't get you far in these parts,' said Liam.

Sheenagh gnawed at her knuckle, holding her arm across herself. 'Jesus, I don't know…'

But as Edward slumped on to the floor she instinctively stepped towards him to help. Liam grabbed her arm.

'Leave him be for now. Hertzog was going to kill him. I stopped him.'

'And when did you get so soft-hearted and heap misery on to your own and other people's heads?' she said.

'His name's Radcliffe,' he said tiredly.

'The Dublin fella? His father?'

'How many other Radcliffes do you know?'

She looked at Edward slumped back into the corner. Perhaps the boy wouldn't live long enough for her to risk moving him. She nodded in acceptance. 'The English… they're gonna get behind your guns.'

CHAPTER FOURTEEN

Late the following day Colonel Alex Baxter strode out of the Irish Brigade's briefing. He and the half-dozen other officers said little to each other because they knew the task that lay ahead for each of their battalions was going to cost them dearly. Entrenched and rigid views from the high command allowed scant dissent and demanded the enemy see the courage of the British soldier. That would entail sacrifice, and be remembered as glory.

Lawrence Baxter saw his father shake hands with the other officers as each went on their way. He quickly fell in step next to him.

'We are to be the lead regiment. We're going to force a passage through the hills,' the colonel told his son. 'One of the strongest natural positions we've ever seen. Artillery will bombard the Boer gun positions.' Baxter smiled grimly. 'I'll brief company commanders in an hour.'

'They'll let us wait until their artillery is silenced, though?' the young man asked nervously.

Colonel Baxter shook his head. 'There is a limited supply of ammunition and it's going to be dark by the time we get to the Boer positions. They're dug in on the forward slope of the hills. When we advance the artillery will do their best for us.' He hesitated. 'And once we get across the pontoon bridge the approach is along a narrow gorge. There's no opportunity to advance in open order.'

Realization dawned on the young lieutenant. 'Dear God, not closed order? They'll cut us to shreds. Have they learned nothing from Paardeberg? We walk under their guns shoulder to shoulder?' he said. All the men knew that only days before an assault further downriver had caused grievous loss to other regiments. One of Lord Kitchener's commanders had advised that the artillery should lay a creeping barrage down to afford his infantry protection as they attacked. The advice had been ignored and elements of General Hart's Irish Brigade had advanced in closed order and been mown down as they marched into the Boers' rifle range. It was important, Kitchener had said, that the enemy see British courage: one man's vainglory had slaughtered his own troops.

'Yes. I'm afraid so,' Colonel Baxter said. 'Columns of four until we reach our position. The General will allow open order for the advance once we're there. He's under pressure from Kitchener who wants action and results.'

Lawrence was unable to keep the incredulity from his voice. 'How many more men does he want slaughtered? Surely to God he's learned –'

'Lieutenant!' Baxter reprimanded his son, turning his back to where his own officers waited. He placed a hand on his son's arm. 'We have our orders. It's the only way we can attack. Let's thank God for small mercies. At least the men will have a chance when the time comes.'

'Yes, sir,' Lawrence answered. A greater loyalty was being tested than that felt between father and son.

'Lawrence, we keep our fear to ourselves. Don't let the men see it. They depend on us and it's our duty to lead them. Let's at least do what we can when we can – thirty paces between each man when we reach our forward position.'

Lawrence Baxter's mouth was dry. 'Of course, sir.'

The moment passed and father and son gazed across at the men who waited in their companies. 'His argument is that we cannot control the men in open order. Platoon and company commanders are the linchpin but we must have the NCOs to keep them steady. First light is at four; we leave an hour afterwards. There's no time for breakfast – see what you can do for your men. Biscuits, perhaps. Better than nothing. Good luck, my boy.' He shook his son's hand and turned away without another word. Brave lads – his brave lads – being mown down in a so-called glorious act of courage was no more than stubborn stupidity, the commander-in-chief's. They had no choice in the matter – orders would be obeyed. If his part in the attack failed then others might suffer more. They were just a cog in the military machine. And that machine was in need of urgent repair.

The British had suffered a number of defeats over the previous weeks. Their advance had faltered, started again and then in a stumbling fashion had begun to pick up momentum. Under Lieutenant General Sir Redvers Buller, who commanded the forces in Natal, the pace had been slow and agonizing and the heat sapped men's energy. Guns had been dragged up five-hundred-foot-high hills; at least some of the staff officers finally realizing that a creeping barrage could give their infantry the chance to get close to Boer positions, providing the artillery could be well placed and the location of the Boer trenches known. But as always success depended on the infantryman and his ability to kill the enemy. Taking each successive hill, fighting up and down the difficult terrain, would be costly.

Here and there kopjes interrupted the darkened landscape that had once sheltered Boer riflemen who had since been pushed back across the Tugela River. The broad river had to be forded by a pontoon bridge as other troops waded through chest-high water clinging to steel cables strung across by engineers. It would take almost six hours before Baxter's battalion reached their position.

The Lancashire Brigade were across the Tugela and attacked up the rolling hills that curved like ocean swells above them. They and the other brigades had to reach the main Boer force dug in on the distant Pieter's Hill. It was hard going that required grunting effort as the men struggled on carrying equipment and supplies. They had to get across the river and then clamber up the first undulating rock-strewn thousand-foot hill before they could reach the railway embankment that crossed its plateau. Beyond that was another hill, and then another. Wave after wave of them, until they reached the vast plain of Ladysmith fifteen miles beyond, where a beleaguered town waited, impatiently, to be relieved. Across all these heights the Boers were dug in. Gunners from the Royal Horse Artillery cantered their limbered horses across open ground hauling their 12-pounders behind them. They were an easy target as they halted to set their guns. Many had already fallen, smashed by Boer artillery as soon as they had their range. Man and horse were torn apart, often before a shell could be loaded into the breech. Ten thousand yards behind the British lines the Naval Brigade had hauled their 4.7-inch guns overland to hurl their projectiles across the advancing troops. But to what effect no one knew. All that was certain was that the Boers were still firing and that meant that the infantry had only their own courage to rely on.

The Irishmen swore and prayed in equal measure. It had been a two-mile march under fire.

'Come on, come on, for Christ's sake,' Flynn muttered as

the Royal Irish trudged on in closed formation around the base of the first hill. Rifle fire rattled from unseen Boers scattered among the rocks and shrubs; men fell, abandoned in their agony as the close-ordered men were forced to skirt a defile and face more sniper fire.

'I'm fucked if I'm marching to my death,' someone muttered, breath rasping with exertion and fear. 'Come on! Open order. Come on. Jeezus! We're like pigs to the slaughter! What the fuck are they waiting for?'

Men's screams echoed down the line as they fell. An officer tumbled from his horse; the beast bucked free and ran. As each company reached their position they were sent up the hill, too narrow an attack to be effective, but a chance to break free from the lethal formation.

Men ducked as shellfire exploded above them, but kept marching until ordered otherwise. Shell bursts scoured the road ahead, forcing the column to falter; men dived for whatever cover they could find. Officers and NCOs bellowed their commands above the roar of explosions. Behind them a field artillery howitzer suddenly roared and laid shrapnel on to the high ground.

Baxter spurred his horse on at the head of the formation. He drew fire but miraculously was not hit. Whistles blew and trumpet calls finally allowed the men to abandon their suicidal formation. Cries of command echoed up and down the columns. *Open order! Open order! Thirty paces!*

They burst free like pigeons from a cage and quickly ran into a single extended line, each man putting thirty yards' distance between himself and the next man, stumbling and jumping over their dead. Officers ran with them, corporals and sergeants staying with their sections and platoons, urging them to be steady. They were exposed from kopjes on their left and a lethal crossfire tore into them. They were brought down like ducks at a fairground shooting gallery. Then a howitzer found the Boers and their shells bought respite as the Royal Irish advanced. Progress would be agonizingly slow across the harsh landscape and although the morning was wet and cool following a rainstorm, the dusty ground had turned to a boot-hugging clay. Boer artillery had yet to be silenced, their 75-mm guns puffing out a lethal bombardment that had crept to within striking distance of the soldiers. The air hummed with shellfire. Shrapnel burst in all directions. Pockets of men fell as they held their ground; others steeled themselves for the dash across the open before they reached the higher ground of the rising hills that rolled back upon themselves like a gathering tide. No sooner would the men who survived the initial assault claim the first ridge than they would have to press on, fight the entrenched sharpshooters on the reverse slope and then start the process again against the second rising hill. The flanking hills were under siege by other regiments that had greater artillery support, but the Royal Irish were to go down the throat and dig out the Boers with rifle and bayonet.

Officers, pistol in hand, led the assault. Lawrence Baxter craved water, his mouth already dry with fear. But he held his ground and kept his eyes on the broken hills several hundred yards away. He flinched when shells exploded in no man's land, but felt shame each time that he did. Squaring his shoulders to try and show the troops behind him that they could rely on him to lead them forward he watched as Colonel Baxter guided his horse along the line of soldiers, shouting over the increasing noise.

'All right, lads, you wanted a fight, here it is!'

A salvo of British artillery peppered the distant hills.

'We will advance in extended line.' The men's fear of what

seemed to be a hopeless assault rippled like a caterpillar across their backs. Baxter rode to their front and stood in his stirrups, so all could see him, roaring so that all could hear: 'Because those are our orders!'

He beckoned his orderly forward, who took the horse from him. Colonel Alex Baxter would lead his battalion from the front, on foot. 'The battalion will advance!'

The barrage splintered the air as they ran across the exposed plateau. Lung-bursting fear drove them forward. If they could run hard and fast enough they would get beneath the artillery shells before the Boers could adjust their guns. Soldiers fell, their bodies ripped by shrapnel; dying men screamed and squirmed in agony; others lay contorted from the violence inflicted on them. There was no time to stop for those who survived; the rest just had to get through the smoke and terror. Above it all the colonel's voice bellowed back and forth, urging his men on. Lawrence Baxter could barely keep pace as soldiers began to pass him, their hands clasping the wooden stock of their rifles, desperate to plunge the twelve-inch blade of their bayonets into any damned *boojer* that they could find. The urge to kill had overtaken their fear of dying. Men screamed with blood lust. None looked anywhere other than straight ahead; men disappeared in a storm of explosions. Wet shreds of a man splattered Lieutenant Baxter. He gasped in horror and smeared the blood from his face; tears stung his cheeks and he faltered. But then he felt raw hatred flood through him. The banshee wails of attacking men rang in his ears as he added to them his own primal scream.

Liam's men sheltered in the boulder-strewn hillside, huddled with men from other commandos. The British artillery had concentrated on the distant ridges, not on these unseen men well concealed on the forward slopes behind slabs of rocks and shrubbery. Old and young alike waited, shoulder to shoulder, knowing that their own were being killed behind them. Explosions thundered down the hillsides, clouds of grey and black smoke from the impact of the high explosive lyddite shells that killed anything within a hundred yards. Distant figures of men engulfed in flames had fallen from the top of the hills. It would not be long before the Boer artillery fell silent, forced into retreat to save their guns. And that would leave the commandos alone to stop the British assault.

Colonel Baxter's Irish had faltered under the Boer's mind-numbing artillery fire and fallen back. Smashed bodies stained the veld. Men desperately sought cover that wasn't there, pressing their faces into the coarse dirt, hunched behind ant-hills or lying, barely moving, scraping dirt with their mess tins into a shallow sangar in front of their faces. No banter escaped any man's lips, but whispered prayers for God's forgiveness were common enough.

Colonel Baxter clawed the ground.

'Major Drew!' He called for his second in command.

Ten yards behind Baxter's right shoulder a dust-covered khaki-clad figure dared rise from the ground, zigzagged towards the colonel and then threw himself down.

'Guns are falling silent, Henry,' Baxter said. 'We must make up lost ground and push on. Take your company on the flank before the Boers regroup and strengthen their positions. They'll have more men in trenches than we realize and behind every damned boulder. We've got this far. We must not lose momentum again.'

'I have no company commanders left, sir, only junior officers.'

Baxter knew the carnage that lay behind him. He had to ask the question but he dreaded the man's answer: 'My son?'

'Took command of C Company.'

There was no hesitation in Baxter's order: 'Take him.'

Both men knew that survival that day might be nothing short of a miracle. Major Drew nodded, got to his feet and ran back.

Colonel Baxter looked to where his men lay like mounds of dust. The smoke from the artillery shells lingered in the dry, still air. Perhaps the drifting smoke might give them a few precious minutes before the Boer marksmen picked their targets.

He stood and called to his men, turning his back to the hidden enemy, and then pulled the khaki cover from the puggaree on his helmet, exposing the regiment's band of colour.

'All right, the Irish, let's have you. Come on, my boys. Put a brave face on it. We've only to go forward. Who's with me? Who'll race me to the top of that damned hill?'

Frightened, but inspired, the men clambered up from their kneeling and lying positions. Shots began to buzz and crack. Adrenaline-fuelled fear brought them to their feet. Flynn gripped his rifle and shook it at Baxter.

'You're a mad bastard you are, colonel, and so must I be, by God!'

'Flynn! You'll be on field punishment!' shouted Sergeant McCory.

'Damned if I will, hey, colonel?'

Baxter laughed: 'Damned if any of us will, lad. Come on the Irish! Come on!'

He turned and ran for the misshapen hill with the roar of his men's cries bellowing behind him like a storm coming off the wild Irish Sea.

Seven hundred yards, and then six.

As the drifting smoke cleared and the artillery fell silent, the Irish emerged howling for the blood of their enemy. Liam and the others waited until the khaki-clad figures were two hundred yards from their positions and then, from somewhere on the hillside, one of the senior Boer commanders shouted the order to fire.

Barely a few hundred yards from the first line of Boer positions the Royal Irish flattened themselves into the dirt, scrambling to push whatever rocks they could find in front of them to deflect the Mausers' bullets. British artillery boomed again, shells whooshing overhead as the naval guns fired beyond the Royal Irish positions, trying to knock out the Boer guns. The punishing explosions beat at a man's skull, forcing tiredness into exhaustion. As night fell so did the artillery fire. Occasionally shots rang out as Boers listened for men's voices in the darkness and fired in their direction. Cold, stiff and exhausted, the attacking troops took advantage of the darkness and remained on their bellies, pushing more rocks in front of their faces. Scattered groups of men huddled in the drizzle that only added to their misery. They stayed mostly silent and unmoving, thankful for the rest but desperate for water. Twelve hours of hard fighting across the broken ground had taken its toll on them all.

The wounded moaned and cried as they lay in no man's land, abandoned to their torment. Perhaps there was a small mercy in the drizzle: it might ease their thirst and cool their fever. No one could do anything to help them, and silence crept across the ground as they finally succumbed to their hurts.

'They need a truce, for Christ's sake,' muttered Mulraney in little more than a whisper, fearful that his voice might carry and attract a Boer sniper. They could not be seen but the Boers knew roughly where the men had gone to ground. 'Give them poor buggers a chance. It's a heartless place of misery right enough. Not a stretcher-bearer or chaplain to be had for love or money.'

'You're complaining, are you?' said a slightly built Dubliner, hugging his rifle to his chest as he lay crooked behind a few stones he had managed to gather for protection. 'You don't know when you're well off.'

Mulraney raised his face as the first soft rain began to fall. 'Jesus on the Cross, you'd think the day hadn't been bad enough, now the angels are pissing on me.' He sighed. 'Still, it'll be a soft old day tomorrow. Not too hot. If I'm to run up this bloody mountain best to be done with a bit of moisture on m'face.'

'Sweat's not good enough for you, Mulraney?' said another.

'That's all down my back,' he answered.

'Did anyone see the colonel get into cover?' someone asked.

'Cover. As bare-arsed as a billiard table,' one of the men muttered.

'Last I saw of him he was running up there over to the left. Flynn went down, I think, though I can't be sure,' said the Dubliner.

'Flynn?' said Mulraney.

'Aye.'

'Jeezus, he owes me, y'know. We had a bet.'

'On what? A bloody horse race?'

'On who would get killed first,' Mulraney answered. 'I hope he's left the wager in his kitbag down at the camp.'

'He wasn't hit,' one of the men said, 'he tripped. Went arse over tit.'

'Now isn't that just like him?' said Mulraney. 'Still, maybe he broke his neck. There might still be a few bob in it.' He sighed. 'You'd think the Naval Brigade with their great bloody booming guns would've knocked these *boojers* off their perch by now,' he added in barely a whisper.

One of their group coughed, the damp air congealing the dust from the day's efforts into his chest. He hawked and spat and a sudden crack of a rifle shot made them press their faces into the dirt even though the bullet tore harmlessly above their heads. Two more shots came out of the darkness, their bullets striking stone, sparking like a flint.

'Mother of God. Don't even breathe. I swear those bastards have cat's eyes,' whispered Mulraney.

No one spoke for a minute, but it was impossible not to hear the distressing moans from the wounded that haunted the night.

'Some of them Dutchies are hurtin' an' all,' said a man from another section who, like many others, had joined any Royal Irish soldiers found among the scattered troops.

'And I'm supposed to feel for them, am I?' said Mulraney. 'I've seen some of our boys trying to help a wounded Dutchy and the minute they turned their back took a bullet for their trouble. Fucking treacherous bastards, the lot of 'em. Finish 'em off is what I say – bayonet or bullet – if you've a mind to save your own neck. By first light most of 'em will be dead with any luck. Fewer snipers to worry about.'

A sudden scuffling had them snatching at their weapons. 'Quiet!' hissed Sergeant McCory. 'You're like bloody washer-women. Mulraney, is that yourself there?'

'Sergeant,' Mulraney said, happy for once to see the three-striper, 'what's happenin'? Much more of this come first light and we'll be rat food.'

'How many men here?' McCory whispered, unable to see

the bodies that lay scattered around him. They muttered their names. Nine men clinging by their eyelids to the sloping terrace.

'Lancs and Yorks are coming up in support to try and outflank 'em. We're going straight at them, weed the bastards out with the bayonet. Our field guns are fucked, horses and gunners dead where they stood, so between here and the top of that hill we're on our own. Navy will use their long guns to hit the farthest ridge but there's no close support. Sorry, lads, there's not much good news.'

The men said nothing. Their silence was enough for him to know that once again his men were searching within themselves for the strength to carry the fight to their enemy – wherever he was hidden in trenches and behind boulders in the rising ground.

'Well,' one of them finally said, settling his back into the dirt, squirming to find as much comfort as he could. 'That's grand. About time the English got off their arses.'

'It'll be light in an hour. Wait for the command,' McCory said and slithered away on his belly to find others. 'Good luck, lads,' he said quietly.

After a moment one of the men said: 'They can't leave us lying out here, stiff as a board, soaked through, with no grub and then think that Johnny Boer isn't going to pick us off one by one. I'm all for going back to the river and getting us some water. At least that.'

There was a murmuring of assent.

Mulraney sighed. 'You stupid arse. You'd have the scutters the minute you drink it. Have you not seen the shite they tip in there? Dead horses, guts, slops and latrines. If you've a mind to light a fire tonight and boil it, then I'll wish you all goodnight.' He sighed and settled his head against a rock. 'I'll be having m'self a few minutes' kip before the Dutchies give us a wake-up call. Then I fancy we'll get up there and take their breakfast from them.'

The men fell silent. Somewhere in the far distance Boers were singing a hymn. There were women's voices among them. Those in the Boer laager far behind the front lines had said their prayers and praised God. The new day would bring harsh retribution to those who sought to take their land.

Those that could slept that half-waking sleep that soldiers know only too well. Cramped and exhausted, their bodies gave way to the numbing exhaustion but in their slumber a part of them was always listening for any footfall or untoward sound that signalled danger. Survival was bred into them by experience, their instincts sharpened like a hunted animal. The rain lingered and the cold settled in as the first grey light of dawn exposed the hillsides. All across the slopes the British forced aching muscles to be ready for when the order was given to attack. The rain had eased and the morning promised a hot and humid day. Bleary-eyed, the British scoured the ground ahead of them.

The ruptured terrain rose up into hillocks of five hundred to a thousand feet. Slabs of vertical rock smothered in brushwood hid the kopje's defenders. Snipers lay in shadow and artillery still nestled to the rear of the boulder-strewn flattened crowns. The Royal Irish readied themselves – the lack of gunfire giving each man hope. Sergeant McCory ducked and weaved down the line, steadying the men's nerves, gruffly warning them not to falter when they began their advance towards the Boers.

The Boers were used to the heat and the long patient game of waiting for their enemy. Behind the hidden riflemen, Liam's commando walked their horses into position where the advancing infantry could not see them. They joined the

Pretoria commando who were hidden in their trenches. Over to their left flank Pieter's Hill rose up, men from the Bethal commando entrenched on the forward slope.

Corin lowered his binoculars. 'That the Irish across there,' he said. He handed the reins of his horse to one of the Boers and cupped his hands. 'Is it the Dublin boys we're fighting today?' he shouted across the plateau.

Mulraney grunted. 'Well, will you listen to that?'

He raised his helmet on the end of his rifle and shouted back. 'You're no *boojer*! Where're you from?'

'Engine Alley!' Corin called back, waving his slouch hat above the boulders.

'Ah! Then you had a whore for a mother!' Mulraney shouted knowingly.

'Right enough!' Corin answered. 'And yourself?'

'Cook Street!'

'A coffin-maker's son!'

'Aye. And I'll make sure we bury you nice and deep,' Mulraney answered to a rippling cheer from the rest of his company.

Corin's voice came back as fast as a bullet: 'Sure, you'll have to kill me first. Or me you! And if we don't let's meet for a drink after the war. Down at the Wood Quay. The Irish House!'

'Good enough,' Mulraney answered. 'And how will I know you?'

After a brief pause there was the unmistakable sound of a fiddle: a jaunty jig floating across the veld.

The men laughed and cheered. 'Good luck to you, then!' Mulraney yelled.

'And y'self!' came the answer.

Mulraney settled his helmet back on his head. 'It's good to know who it is you're out to kill on such a fine day.'

*

High up on behind the protective cover of the slab rocks Liam Maguire dragged his grinning brother away towards the horses. The last thing he wanted was to be caught in the frontal attack that was about to erupt. They had more important work to do.

'It's grand, isn't it?' said Corin as he strapped the fiddle case to his saddle. 'Dublin lads. Y'know if they believe we're up here they might think twice about sticking a feckin' bayonet into some poor Dutchy. It'll cost 'em, mind.'

'You think that it would stop them for one minute?' said Liam. 'Christ's tears. Corin, they'll fight the harder, you idiot. They took the Queen's shilling and they want to go home. They'll take this hill and the next – best we can hope for is to slow them. That, and save our guns.'

Chastised, Corin Maguire spurred his horse after the others. What harm was there in calling out to the Irish lads? It had been good to hear their voices. It would have caused him some sorrow to have them at the end of his rifle sights. Better to kill the English. As the horsemen galloped away down the reverse slope of the hill to start their ascent on the next he turned back and saw the bearded faces of the old Boers and the young boys who would hold the hill as long as they could. Some of them called out, waved a hand and shouted something he couldn't understand. It was a cheerful farewell for the foreigners who fought on their side and who now rode to ambush the English cavalry. It would be a serious day of killing on the kopje. Part of him felt grateful that he would not be a part of it. He slapped the horse's rein across its neck and chased after the commando that was already in the valley below.

Over the sound of the horse's hooves he heard a low roar as the Irish rose up from the ground, their yell of defiance spurring them upwards into the Boer gunfire that rattled across the hills. He wished he could have at least seen that desperate act of courage. No matter what else, he felt a surge of pride.

Chapter Fifteen

The sun had barely risen as the steam locomotive blazed its way across the veld's muted drabness, sparks and soot forcing the soldiers in the open-topped boxcars to keep their heads low and their backs to the engine. Radcliffe eased his way into the horsebox and petted the looming black shape. The horse showed no fear of the rocking carriage or of the flickering sparks that eventually died in the cold air. It was used to Radcliffe's scent and nuzzled his outstretched hand. Radcliffe watched as the dark purple sky began to tinge with a paler hue in the approaching dawn. As he turned his back on the horse it nudged him, pushing against the boxcar sides.

'You want to play games?' he said. He put his hands into his pockets and then brought them out, fists clenched. 'Which hand? There's something in there for you. You only get one shot at it though.'

The horse snuffled his one hand, which Radcliffe opened to show his empty palm. 'So, you're not so clever after all.' And then he showed the horse the other, which also held nothing. 'See, you can't play games with me. I'm a lawyer. I can fool most of the people most of the time.'

A slight movement behind his shoulder made him turn. Pierce stood on the metal plate over the tracks between the two carriages.

'You been awake long?' he asked Pierce.

'Long enough to recognize a fool when I see one,' Pierce answered, then spat the night's congestion on to the tracks.

The horse snuffled Radcliffe's pocket, pushing him with its head. 'All right, all right...' Radcliffe said, surrendering the half-apple from his pocket.

'Not so dumb after all,' Pierce said. 'And I'm talking about the horse.'

The steam train slowed until it was stationary, its valves gasping like a breathless horse as the engineer directed his fireman to clamber up the water tower and bring the pipe across to resuscitate his beloved engine. The borehole was in the middle of nowhere, once used by a farmer to water sheep until the rail line carved through the meagre grazing and paid for the privilege, releasing him from a life of subsistence.

Radcliffe finished saddling the horse. Neither he nor Pierce spoke. Somewhere in the distant mountains a mirror flashed. There was a muted rumbling from beyond the peaks that sounded like a gathering storm. Pierce looked from one mountain range to the other, the distance between them shortened to little more than a blink of an eye by a second flashing mirror.

'There's artillery somewhere ahead,' he said.

Radcliffe looked up from cinching the horse's girth strap. The mirrors flashed again. 'Army heliographs talking to each other.' He fussed the saddle a moment longer.

'You and me, we never talk much,' said Pierce.

'It's been a fairly quiet twenty-odd years, I'll grant you that. Though I always thought you were something of a chatterbox given half the chance,' Radcliffe said as each of them clasped a hand on the boxcar ramp's release bolt.

'I mean about things that shaped and changed us,' Pierce told him.

'No. Can't see the point. I dare say you have thoughts on the matter which you're probably going to express,' Radcliffe said.

Pierce's hand stayed on the sliding bolt, not yet releasing its tension. 'You've done your best for Eileen. You did what the doctors told you to do. You can't change what happened to her and you can't go on blaming yourself for the rest of your life about the accident that took your firstborn. It ain't natural and it ain't fair on Edward.'

Radcliffe knew that his friend had never been one to offer an opinion just for the sake of hearing his own voice. 'I realize that. But I don't know how matters can be different. And that's the truth.'

'You need to cut it loose, Joseph. You've done more than your duty demanded of you.'

Radcliffe let his hand rest on the horse's face. 'I lied to my son to protect him. Better he thought his mother dead than being in an asylum. Eileen lost her mind. How would a boy deal with that?'

'You should've let him try.'

'You think I don't think on that every day of my life? I did what I had to do. I protected him. Can you imagine the torment he would have gone through at school? Do you think this world would have given him a fair shake, a boy with a mad mother? That's how it would be seen. His life would have been blighted.'

'You tell a lie: it grows with time. No good kidding yourself or him any longer, Joseph. You're an upright man who lives by the truth but you lied to him, pure and simple. Him being at boarding school and you telling him that you were taking his mother away to America when his brother died, that was just a smokescreen that was gonna blow away sooner or later. You think he won't ever want to travel over there and see her grave? The day's coming, you know it and so do I. And when he finds out there'll be a gulf between you and him that no bridge can ever join.' Pierce took a breath and let the burden of the shared deception ease away. 'I'm party to this but if we find Edward alive we have to tell him the truth.' He slid back the bolt.

Radcliffe let his friend's words settle. He nodded. 'I know. And I will.' He climbed into the saddle and wrapped the reins around his fist. 'You think that's it for another twenty years?'

'Most likely,' said Pierce.

'I appreciate your thoughts, but now I have to see how this fella and me get along.'

The horse never flinched as Pierce kicked the ramp down. Radcliffe guided the horse on to the ground as Pierce called for some of the soldiers to push the ramp back up. Pierce walked to the gangway that separated the carriages.

'You make sure you pace him, Joseph. He's too fine a horse to break down just 'cause you want to see him run fast.'

'He needs a pipe-opener. Air in his lungs. He's ready for it,' Radcliffe replied, holding a tight rein on the horse, which seemed ready to explode.

'That he does,' Pierce acknowledged. 'It's twenty miles to the end of the line.'

'We'll get there before you.'

Pierce swung himself out so his words would carry as the train picked up steam. 'Two gold sovereigns say you don't.'

'I hope you've got cash. I don't take markers.'

'Never knew a lawyer who did,' said Pierce.

The engine gushed steam and released power into its wheels. They spun for a moment, finding purchase on the rail, and then eased the train away. Radcliffe held the horse back and Pierce could see that despite Radcliffe's years of experience with horseflesh this was an animal to be prized above all others. Its muscles flexed like twisting clouds in a black storm. Its eyes followed the train, its teeth champed on the bit and Radcliffe had to turn it this way and that until his hands found the right tension in the reins to hold him.

The train gathered more steam and was soon at full throttle. Pierce could see no sign of movement from the great black horse, and fairly soon it and its rider were just a speck on the brown expanse. Pierce held on to his hat as the steam whipped by and the wind battered his back. And then, like a bullet kicking up dust, he saw a smudge of movement as Radcliffe unleashed the horse. Pierce squinted in the glare but there was no doubt that the mote in the eye of the veld was getting bigger.

'Come on, then... come on...' Pierce whispered to himself, imagining the power that his friend controlled. He had long ago overcome the envy he'd once felt that Radcliffe was the better horseman. Steam whipped and died and the horse came closer. Pierce could not believe the strength of the creature as it gave chase. Its head and flanks stretched out, its rider low across its withers, riding the surging rhythm, hands pushing the horse onward. 'Don't give him too much rein... hold him steady,' he muttered. And then an almost devout blasphemy: 'Sweet Jesus.'

It was a horse sent from the devil as surely as the sun came up each morning. Veins bulged, muscles rippled beneath taut skin, bowstring-tight sinews extended its mighty stride. Pierce shed forty years, gripped the handrail, swung out into the slipstream, hat raised, whooping like a nine-year-old child as he waved on horse and rider as they passed the boxcar. Radcliffe was being taken for the ride of his life on a horse whose strength and pace few men could tolerate.

As Radcliffe rode clear, Pierce fell silent. It was seldom a man witnessed such a sight. He was wrong. This horse was no demon. It was one of the most beautiful creatures in God's kingdom: an effortless, mysterious power. A thing of poetry.

Three miles south of the point where the British had crossed the Tugela to assault the killing hills the railway junction teemed with activity. Hat-rack beef cattle were herded in pens, and horses were corralled in makeshift stalls in old sheds. The area had once been a large Boer farm settlement; now it suited the British as a rear echelon field HQ. The area was a staging post where wagons brought in the wounded from the battlefield. Native levies unloaded sacks of supplies and tended fires beneath metal urns boiling bloodstained dressings for reuse. Field hospital orderlies laid aside the dead, carried in the wounded, and shuffled men into the tents and half-ruined buildings that served as makeshift operating theatres.

Radcliffe sat astride the horse, its flanks heaving from the gallop, as five hundred yards behind him the train slowed. Dismounting, he walked the horse towards the tableau of misery, the carnage from a battle still being fought less than a dozen miles away. When the train halted Pierce grabbed their saddlebags and came to his side.

'Jesus, they've taken a shellacking,' he said. Muted gunfire crackled beyond the horizon. 'And still are by the sound of it.'

'I hope to God Edward isn't a part of this,' Radcliffe said, and led the horse towards what looked to be the house used as the field headquarters.

As the two men made their way through the bustle of activity he searched out the patch denoting regimental colours on the men's helmets. Some of the puggarees were still hidden by khaki covers; others were not of the Royal Irish. Leaning in the shade of a cob wall one of the bedraggled men raised his head as they passed by.

'Mr Radcliffe, sir,' the man said.

Radcliffe stared at the bareheaded grimy face and tried to place it. As on all soldiers, the helmet's peak had kept the sun from the top of the man's face, a white half-moon, and the sunburn lay below the eyes. But the gaunt face and blackened hand raised in greeting teased his memory. 'Soldier,' he said uncertainly.

'It's Mulraney, sir. Royal Irish. D'ya not remember me, Mr Radcliffe? At the garrison?'

The memory flooded back, and Radcliffe clasped the man's hand. 'Of course. Mulraney. How are you, man? Are you hurt?'

'No, sir, just catching m'breath. I brought in a few of the lads for the surgeon. You wouldn't have a drop of water in that canteen on your saddle, would you, sir? Most here is kept for them that needs it until they boil down the filth in the river.'

Pierce took the canteen and handed it to Mulraney, who took an appreciative swig and then handed it to a couple of the other men who sheltered with him, and who eagerly shared the precious liquid.

'That's rightly appreciated. Lot of lads are down with enteric fever as well as the *boojers*' bullets. Jesus, if the Dutchies don't get you your guts will, that's right enough. You've a few miles behind you to get here,' he said.

Radcliffe nodded. 'Where are your officers?'

'Ah, dead or out there being potted by the Dutchies.'

'Is Colonel Baxter here?'

'At the front with the lads. My God, Mr Radcliffe, our colonel's got more guts than any other, I swear it.'

Before Radcliffe could question the exhausted soldier any

further, Regimental Sergeant Major Thornton strode towards them. Bloodstains darkened his khaki and it was obvious to Radcliffe and Pierce that his rank had not restrained him from helping with the wounded.

'Major Radcliffe. You're a long way from home, sir. And Captain Pierce with you. Whatever are you gentlemen doing here?'

'I was asking the major that myself, seeing as how it's not the sort of place you'd want to be bringing yourself for an excursion unless it was at Her Majesty's pleasure,' Mulraney said.

RSM Thornton looked at the grimy bloodstained soldier as if seeing him for the first time. 'Mulraney, get yourself back up the line. No malingering, lad. Your mates need you,' he said not unkindly.

'Nice to be wanted, sergeant major.'

'No sarcasm now, son. Off with you.'

Mulraney picked up his rifle and pushed the helmet back on to his head, then clambered aboard a blood-slicked flatbed wagon that was returning to the front line to pick up more casualties.

'It looks desperate here, Mr Thornton,' Radcliffe said as more wounded were brought in.

'More than five hundred dead, sir. Third of our men and two-thirds of our officers have been killed. We're barely managing to hold the line.'

'Mr Thornton, I'm here looking for my son. We think he may have enlisted under a false name. Lieutenant Baxter is his friend.'

The RSM looked across the crowded area, as if searching among the boys and men who lay suffering. 'I'm sorry, sir, I know nothing about your boy. It's bloody chaos out there. That's what I do know.'

Radcliffe followed his gaze, a sight no different than he had seen in other conflicts. Badly wounded and mutilated men lying out under a merciless sun. 'Why are these men out in this heat?' he asked.

'Why, sir? Because they're deemed to be less important than horses.' Thornton barely kept the criticism from his voice

'Show me,' Radcliffe said.

The RSM led them through sheds where hundreds of horses were corralled in the shade. There were water troughs and straw. At the far end of the larger shed a bearded, heavy-set horse-trader was checking a manifest with another man.

'I've seen carpetbaggers and horse-traders who'd take the boots off a dying man to make a dollar,' said Pierce. 'And those two look as though they've done their fair share of boot stealing.'

'They're using more horses than bullets,' said Thornton. 'There's near enough a thousand dead in this area alone. But the Dutchies have tough mountain ponies; we have nothing like them. This war's gobbling up horses. The fighting, the weather, the terrain... They're even sending horses from India and South America.'

'Would you mind, sergeant major?' Radcliffe said, handing the reins to Thornton in an act intended to keep the career soldier out of any argument with the civilians. Then, with Pierce at his side, he walked through the cool, high-roofed shed towards the horse-trader. The broad belt holding in his belly exposed a pistol butt close to his hardened hands. There was no doubt that he was a horse-breaker, and would whip a man as soon as a horse. The man was engrossed in the manifest but suddenly became aware that the stranger who accompanied the sergeant major was walking straight up to him as the black man with him started pulling down the makeshift stall poles that held the horses. The moment of dumbfounded surprise quickly gave way to spittle-flecked anger.

'Hey! Kaffir! Get the hell out of there! These are my horses!'

Without need of command the horse-trader's henchman ignored the white man who was a few paces away and ran towards Pierce. Much good it would do him, Radcliffe thought as he pointed a finger directly at the beefy man's face. 'Your man had better learn some respect, mule-skinner. My friend's a decorated war hero.'

Radcliffe heard the blow, fist on bone, and the sound of the henchman drop to the floor, He didn't look back; what had happened was written in shock on the horse-trader's face. Black men did not assault white men. That was a hanging offence.

Flustered by the assault, the horse-trader reached for the pistol, but Radcliffe poked a finger in his eye and grabbed the pistol. As the man's hand reached up to his injured face, Radcliffe swiped the barrel across his head. The man's hat would take the impact, but the pain would still penetrate the numbskull. The trader fell and was then forced to quickly roll clear as a hundred or more horses surged past him.

'They won't run. They know who's feeding them,' Radcliffe said, seeing the confused horses reach the cattle kraals where they slowed and jostled together nervously now that they were boxed in by the other buildings each side. A quickly erected corral would be enough to restrain them. Spilling the pistol's cartridges into the dirt Radcliffe kicked the man's legs, forcing him to stagger upright. 'And my friend here needs a horse. He'll choose it – send the bill of sale to the general. Any general will do.' Radcliffe threw the pistol at the man, who flinched, recovered the weapon and, having suffered enough humiliation, staggered away.

'Did you kill him?' Radcliffe asked, looking at the fallen henchman.

'God, no. What the hell do you take me for?'

'I'll think on that.' He turned to where the RSM had tied up Radcliffe's horse. 'Mr Thornton, wounded men need shade and water. Be good enough to attend to that while I go and explain things to whoever's in charge here.'

'That would be General Laleham, sir,' Thornton said.

Major General Harold Laleham, veteran of India and Afghanistan, sat behind a makeshift desk, his aide-de-camp hovering at his shoulder, while in the background HQ staff flitted between map tables and ringing field telephones. The general read the document that Radcliffe had presented. In the far distance the rumble of artillery was a constant reminder of a major battle being fought.

'You have friends in high places. Lord Mayberry is an influential Liberal peer. But I can't help you find your son. I'm lucky if I know where half my own troops are,' he said, handing back the letter that asked those reading it to extend all courtesies and help to its bearer, Joseph Radcliffe.

An orderly delivered a tray of tea and placed it in front of Laleham. Hospitality was not extended to Radcliffe, who stood, dust-caked, in front of the man who might be able to help find Edward.

'I think he may have lied about his age and enlisted. Can you give me a pass to move through your lines?'

Laleham sampled the tea. News of the upset with the horses had already reached him: it was apparent that, as well as being a man who wielded some influence with those back in England, Radcliffe felt sufficiently confident to cause a fuss. 'We are fighting an enemy who, in some respects, is better armed than us, and who knows the ground. We are taking heavy losses. Liberal politicians were responsible for stripping the army to the bone: I don't care for any of them. Nor their friends.'

'You don't need to be a liberal to care about men lying on groundsheets, some of them in mud scrapes, others racked with fever, huddled together with only a blanket between them.'

Laleham's blood rose above his collar, his face slowly flushing with anger as he attempted to control his impatience with the critical American. 'This is a field hospital. We have no beds. We have no doctors or surgeons. Six hundred miles of railway line, parts of which are being continually destroyed by our enemy's commandos, halt our supplies, Radcliffe. What we have is a damned battle to win.'

'And every wounded man needs shelter and care if he's to return to the line. A couple of hundred wounded men were baking out there while horses were under shelter.'

Laleham was clearly in no mood to be lectured. 'I have six cavalry regiments and five thousand mounted infantry fifty miles from here and they are desperate for new horses – replacement horses that are poor quality at best! Those men are soldiers. Suffering is what they must endure.' He slammed the palm of his hand on the table. 'My advance is bogged down across those hills because there are regiments who can't find the backbone for a fight.' The teacup had rattled in its saucer and the aide-de-camp barely restrained himself from reaching forward to save the bone-china cup from destruction.

Laleham dipped a pen into the inkwell and scribbled on official notepaper. He slid it to one side and now the aide-de-camp had a task to perform: he blotted the wet ink. The paper was folded and handed to Radcliffe. Perhaps granting the American's request might stop him from sending disparaging reports home to his friends in high places. 'The military cannot be responsible for your safety. Here's your pass. Get yourself killed on your own terms, Mr Radcliffe.'

Pierce moved the horses aside, clearing more space for stretchers as an African levy steadied the horse Pierce had chosen for himself and which was now saddled and tethered next to Radcliffe's mount. The horse became skittish as it smelled the blood from the stretchers and the levy quickly took control of it and eased it to a hitching rail further away from the stench. He glanced uncertainly at the man who stood head and shoulders above him. Such a man would be honoured or feared were he a Zulu. The flecks of grey in his hair and the beard that covered the area below his lips down on to his chin denoted a man of age and wisdom and he looked as strong as a bull. He would be a respected warrior wherever he came from.

'You are African?' asked the levy.

'Well, I'm surely not a fully paid-up member of the Ku Klux Klan.' The comment obviously meant nothing to the levy. Pierce nodded. 'Yeah. I guess I am.'

'You do not sound African,' said the levy.

'Can't help you there. But I'm not from around here.'

'Your *baas* is a good man?'

Pierce wondered how to explain that although the word *baas* carried the same meaning as the term *master* he had once been obliged to use as a boy on the cotton plantation, it had no place between him and the white man who rode at his side.

'He's my friend,' he said simply.

The African considered the answer for a moment. 'And you come to this place and you fight?'

'We're looking for my friend's son. I hope we don't have to fight. Your people don't fight in this war?'

'*Cha*,' he said, shaking his head. 'We are not allowed to fight. It is not our war. We work. That is what we do.'

Pierce extended his hand. 'Ben Pierce.'

The African clasped it, and half turned his grip so that his palm covered Pierce's hand a second time. 'I am Mhlangana.'

Pierce nodded in acknowledgement. Beyond them a constant stream of wounded soldiers were being brought in by Indian stretcher-bearers or by their comrades. Royal Army Medical Corps doctors quickly checked the wounded and indicated where they should be taken. Pierce recognized the voice of one of the men who was pulling a scar-faced soldier from the back of a wagon.

'Keep bloody still, won't you? It's a bullet in your chest not an artillery shell up your arse. Jesus, you're not gonna die or nothin',' Flynn urged his wounded mate. Flynn's arm was bloodied and he was struggling to get the big man on the ground.

'Keep our horses in the shade,' Pierce told Mhlangana and went forward to help.

'So it's yourself,' Flynn said as they lowered the wounded man gently down. 'I saw Mulraney and he said the American major and his darkie was here, begging your pardon on that, captain.'

Pierce ignored him and pressed Flynn's hand on to the sucking wound in the man's chest. 'Hold him like that, stop the air from escaping, while I turn him over. Don't let him choke on his own blood,' he said as he wrapped a dressing around the man and tied it off tightly.

A medical orderly with two African stretcher-bearers pushed Flynn to one side and helped Pierce.

'He's still alive,' the orderly said.

'He'd better be,' Flynn said. 'The bastard owes me money. Why d'you think I broke my back getting him here?'

The scar-faced man was eased on to the stretcher; his eyes fluttered and he weakly gripped Flynn's arm. 'Thanks, Flynn,' he whispered.

'Scouse, you die on me, you bastard, and I swear I'll kill you m'self,' Flynn shouted after him as they carried the wounded man towards the surgeon's marquee. 'He'll be all right. The old *boojers* have Mausers and they use a nice hard-cased bullet. Clean as a whistle. Straight through ya.'

'That's very considerate of them,' Pierce said, eyeing Flynn's bloodied arm.

'Aye, well. Not always. Some of the bastards nip the end of their bullets, and Jesus, don't that make a mess of you?'

'You're hurt yourself,' Pierce said. 'Here, let me take a look.'

'It's nuthin',' Flynn said. 'It'll give me a breather from that bloody slaughter going on.'

Pierce gently inspected the ragged flesh wound congealed with blood. It looked worse than it was. 'Let's get you over to the hospital,' he said, and then saw his old bone-handled knife tucked into Flynn's waistband.

Radcliffe held the knife as Pierce and Flynn, his arm now dressed, accompanied them across the camp.

'Flynn here took it off a wounded man they brought down from the line,' Pierce told him.

'Is he alive?' Radcliffe asked.

'He's breathin' but he won't be needing his tobacco ration for a while,' Flynn answered.

'They operated on him an hour ago,' Pierce said.

The men stood and looked at the hundreds of men laid out

in the old buildings and beneath makeshift marquees. 'Do you know where they took him?' said Radcliffe.

'Aye, he's in one of them horse stalls the captain here broke down.'

Flynn led the way, stepping over men so badly injured they were barely conscious. Radcliffe was amazed that so few cried out or moaned in pain. Laleham was right – these soldiers knew how to suffer. Flies buzzed and settled into blood-soaked dressings; levies removed soldiers who had died, their places immediately taken by more wounded.

There could be no doubt that if Edward Radcliffe had been with any of these men his chances of survival would be slender. Flynn settled next to one of them in the corner of a stall; the others squatted next to him.

'I've come to take you back up the line, Scouse. Sar'nt Major says you're malingering,' Flynn said po-faced.

'Bastard...' the wounded man muttered and then sighed as a grin broke Flynn's face.

'Even so, listen to me, these fellas need some help.'

Radcliffe held the knife: 'Where did you get this?' he asked.

The man's eyes shifted to Flynn.

'Tell the man, Scouse. You're in no trouble, I promise ya.'

The wounded man's breath was ragged: 'A boy...'

'Was he a soldier?' Radcliffe asked.

The man shook his head, and it was obvious that there was little chance of him speaking for long.

'Was he alive?' said Radcliffe.

'Head... Shot... in the head.' A trickle of blood dribbled from the corner of his mouth. Radcliffe could press him no further despite his anxiety. 'Dead... Lad was... a goner...'

Radcliffe suppressed the shock that threatened his composure but he involuntarily stepped back from the wounded man. Pierce said nothing, watching his friend assimilate the news like any lawyer taking information into consideration.

'He's not dead, Ben. I don't believe that.'

'Facts don't look good, Joseph. He said he took the knife off –'

'He's not dead. I'd know if he was. I'd know it,' Radcliffe insisted. 'How many men have we seen that we thought dead?'

'All right,' Pierce acknowledged. 'If he wasn't in uniform then he was probably with the militia and if he survived he might be attached to the Irish,' he suggested.

'Were there any irregulars in this fight for the hill?' Radcliffe asked Flynn.

'They was out on a flank. Dozens of 'em. Most of 'em recruited from towns along the way. They got the chop from what we could see.'

'He might be lying out there,' Pierce said.

Radcliffe turned to Flynn. 'Can you show us on a map where the Royal Irish positions are?'

'You'll need no map, major. Just follow the dead and dying.'

Chapter Sixteen

Stretcher-bearers and levies moved among the scattered bodies to the rear of the distant gunfire. Slaughtered horses and mules lay bloated in the day's heat as walking wounded made their way back to the rail junction ten miles to their rear. It was obvious to both men that most of the badly wounded wouldn't make it alive. The jolting wagons and rough handling from the bearers, scared of still being in enemy range, would add to their misery on their final journey. The front line was a thousand yards ahead but Boer Mauser fire could still reach the dead and dying if they chose to. That they didn't, except for the occasional shot that zipped through the air as a lethal reminder, proved that the Boers were more interested in those soldiers still living and who, with what seemed to be an increasingly unlikely miracle, might still attack their positions. The open plateau offered scant cover; soldiers huddled behind anthills and pressed their bodies as low as they could into any undulation in the hard ground, using the shallow craters from the Boer shells. The kopjes rose up, slabs of rock haphazardly tumbled atop each other. The artillery shelling had lessened and Radcliffe realized the enemy must be moving their guns further back behind the rising ground. The Boer sharpshooters would keep the infantry soldiers at bay. The two men tied off their horses on a wheel of a field gun lying on its side, its mules lying dead in their traces. A few paces away was the crater from the enemy's shell. What remained of the gunners lay scattered. Their officers were experienced men, tough campaign soldiers who'd bought their commissions in the Royal Horse Artillery and fought in the Sudan campaign; they knew what they were doing.

But that meant nothing when you lined up like toy soldiers on a general's campaign table, thought Radcliffe as he and Pierce weaved through the debris. The guns' limbers, and the mules and horses that had pulled them, lay ripped and shattered from the Boer bombardment. The haze that settled over the battlefield shifted slightly, exposing another half-dozen slaughtered men and their guns. With parade-ground precision the British Army liked to set up its artillery in neat rows of six in full view of the enemy lines, just to the rear of its own front-line infantry – an easy target for the pinpoint accuracy of Boer gunners.

Rifle fire pinged across the hard ground as Radcliffe and Pierce crouched and ran zigzagging to where they could see soldiers huddled for safety in what was once an animal trail, and which over the years the seasonal heavy rains had widened into a dried-out and eroded watercourse. The donga was the most immediate cover they could both find and they slithered into it as one of the men crouching there cursed them for bringing fire down on to their position.

'That's enough!' Sergeant McCory told the complaining soldier as he scurried along the line to Radcliffe and Pierce. 'I'll be damned. You're a sight for sore eyes, Mr Radcliffe, sir. I don't suppose you've brought any reinforcements with yourself and Mr Pierce?'

'I doubt there are any to bring, sergeant. You got any men up in the kopje?'

'Aye, the colonel flanked them with a couple of companies

and got into those boulders, among all that undergrowth, but the Boers can see the smoke from their rifles so they're getting hammered – and we can't help 'cause the Boers use smokeless cartridges. Just can't see the buggers.'

'Where are your officers?' Radcliffe asked the hollow-eyed sergeant.

'Dead mostly.'

'And Lieutenant Baxter?' Radcliffe queried, hoping that if he had been fortunate enough to find the Royal Irish, then so too would have Edward.

'I think he's with C Company down the line. I can't get a runner across to him.'

'And the militia?' Radcliffe asked, hoping that the volunteers would have been kept somewhere in reserve.

'God knows. They were supposed to outflank them but I doubt the poor bastards ever got through that gap between the kopjes. We're caught in a crossfire. Our guns to the east are out of range. We were told our cavalry would sort them good and proper. They were supposed to cut the bastards down.'

'Well, they didn't, so they can't help you now. The shooters on that hill can keep you here in this bottleneck for as long as they like unless you root them out of those boulders,' Pierce told him, looking across to where the Boers hid on the broken hillside.

'And every time we try, we make fifty yards and we lose more men than we can afford. The colonel's isolated up there somewhere,' McCory said, nodding towards the kopje, 'and we don't have any field guns left to keep their heads down.' He nodded towards a wounded soldier behind him, his back wedged against the trench wall, a groundsheet covering him. He looked to be barely old enough to enlist and his ghostly pallor told the men he had lost a lot of blood. 'He's all that's left of them gunners.' He lifted the groundsheet to expose the man's shattered leg. 'We did what we could. It won't be enough.'

Radcliffe quickly assessed their chances. 'There's a three-inch twelve-pounder back there on its side. If you could get a few shells on to their flank, you'd buy yourself enough time to get across this open stretch of ground and on to that hill. Then it's down to each man and a bayonet,' he said.

'Aye, the Dutchies shite their breeches when they see the steel coming at 'em. But we tried to get back to that gun. Once they see us trying for it, they pick my lads off. We tried, Mr Radcliffe, I promise you that.'

Radcliffe looked across the killing zone: it was obvious from the sprawled bodies that men had tried to reach the gun. 'You can't stay here and they'll shred you out there, right enough. There's some dead ground back there. You get a gun in position they won't be able to get a shot unless they show themselves.'

As if in answer, a Boer artillery salvo landed less than fifty feet to their front, forcing the men to flinch, crouching into the dirt as the explosion and percussion showered the air with stone and shrapnel.

Radcliffe grabbed McCory's shoulder: 'If we can get rounds on them can you get men up there?'

'If the gun covered our flank we can try,' the seasoned fighter said.

Radcliffe looked at Pierce and then back to the gun where their horses were tethered. Realization hit Pierce. Radcliffe was going to get them killed.

'You can outshoot them,' Radcliffe said. 'Their Mausers have five-round magazines, your Enfields have ten. Lay a steady fire on them – don't matter if you can't see them, just lay it on them. And then get to Lieutenant Baxter. If he's alive, you need his company with you. Send runners down the line, sergeant.'

'Jesus, you're thinking dangerous thoughts,' Pierce hissed at Radcliffe.

'We have to risk it,' Radcliffe answered.

'The hell we do,' Pierce replied.

Radcliffe ignored him. 'Sergeant, rapid independent fire on that hillside for as long as you can. If we make it to that gun we'll put a couple of shells on them and then you get your men on your feet. Understood?'

'Yessir. We'll cover you.' He turned to the men. 'All right, lads, listen up…'

'Do I get a say in this?' Pierce said, grabbing Radcliffe's arm, feeling the cancer of fear creep back into him, as if it had never left. 'Joseph, we're getting too old to hot-foot it back and get that gun working.'

'Let's play the hand we've got,' Radcliffe said.

'No, let's not. Let's wait until dark and then get back to the rail sheds. We can ride our way around this mess.'

A rattle of gunfire splattered close to the donga as if confirming Pierce's fear that to venture back to the upturned gun was to be torn apart by Boer bullets.

'Ben, I have to do this. I need to know if my boy is out there. I would never hold anything against you. I'll do this on my own if I have to.'

'That gun weighs six hundred pounds, for Christ's sake. It's going to take at least half a dozen men to right it. At least. And what do we know about arming the ordnance?'

Radcliffe realized Pierce was right. He shouldered past McCory and held the wounded gunner's face in his hand. 'Son,' he urged him, gently tapping his face. 'Son, can you hear me? Gunner? Come on, man!' He slapped the boy's face harder, and the other soldiers in the trench started to look belligerent at the wounded man's treatment.

The gunner's eyes opened and Radcliffe eased a water canteen to his lips. The man nodded his thanks, eyes focused on the civilian.

'Listen to me, son, I have to get your gun working. What do we do with the ammunition? How do we set it? Can you tell me that?'

The young man's forehead creased, uncertain at the request.

'You arm the shells? Is that right? Son? Listen to me. You understand what I'm asking you?'

Military discipline cut through the dying man's befuddlement and pain. It was a routine that he had practised time and again while bellowed at by his battery sergeant, who now lay blown apart out there near his gun. The instilled drills surfaced in his memory.

'Fifty-seven fuze... set the fuze... rotate the time ring... fuze burn time... turn the ring... until the arrow... set the fuze...'

Radcliffe was losing him. What little strength the lad had he was gathering to force the air through his lungs, willing himself to obey the stranger and answer his questions. Radcliffe cupped the dying man's face in both hands, drawing all his concentration. 'I don't have time to set fuzes, son, I just want the damned thing to explode when it lands. Understand?'

He nodded. 'Leave... one safety pin... leave it... for percussion... it'll... explode ... when it hits.' He gripped Radcliffe's arm in a final effort to emphasize his instructions. Radcliffe pressed his hand against the man's face, a brief moment of comfort for the gunner whose eyes glazed and stared into oblivion. The boy was dead.

'Ready, Mr Radcliffe!' Sergeant McCory called, his men waiting, rifles at the ready.

'Goddammit,' Pierce said.

From the time Belmont had left Verensberg and returned to headquarters for his orders it had taken him and his fifty rough riders the better part of two days to get behind the Boer guns that defended the hills holding up the British advance. Their local guide had taken them over difficult terrain which had slowed their pace and now Belmont cursed that they were hours later than planned and that British troops were dying because of the delay. He had whipped the turncoat Boer with a sjambok, and the yard-long, finger-thick rhino hide whip had cut the man to the bone. He was lucky to escape with only a thrashing. The delay had cost English lives and hurt Belmont's pride. The kopje's jumbled slabs of rock fell back on the reverse of the hills. They gave way to scattered boulders and brush until the hillside levelled out into an uneven plain that would allow the Boers to escape. Belmont drew up the men and put field glasses to his eyes. There were half a dozen Boer field guns at the base of the hillside, and he could see that men and horses were being prepared to move the guns away. They had inflicted terrible punishment on the infantry on the other side of the hills, and those Boers whose rifle fire could still be heard would be on the front slopes sharpshooting the exposed troops that lay pinned down on their advance. He passed the glasses to Lieutenant Marsh.

'Half a dozen guns where the hill bellies out. Further back in those rocks is where the sharpshooters will have their horses held. If we drive straight at them they'll be forced to try and get their guns up the slope. You take half a dozen men behind that rise in case any escape. The Boers can't afford to lose any of their guns. We've got them.'

'Claude, damned if I'm going to let you have all the fun. Sergeant White can take the men on the cut-off,' Marsh said, drawing his sabre. This would be a gallop into the exposed

Boers' flank and they'd put them to the sword. The Boers' fear of lance and blade was well known and Marsh could barely contain his eagerness.

The men readied themselves to advance.

Belmont drew his sabre. 'Do you hear that?' he said quietly.

Marsh steadied his horse. 'The guns?'

Belmont shook his head. 'Thought I heard a fiddle playing.'

Liam Maguire kicked his brother hard. 'Put that thing away, you idiot.'

'Ah, there's enough noise to drown a regimental band,' Corin said, but did as he was told. The riders could be seen in the distance and they were coming straight into the ambush that Liam had set.

Liam looked at his commando as each man prepared himself. There had been shellfire from the English artillery bursting on the hilltop behind them. The Boers on the other side of the hill would be feeling the lash of shrapnel and the violence from the Irish infantry moving beneath its cover. It would soon be Irishman against Irishman when the bayonet charge came over that ridge.

'You'll wait for my command. And when we've taken these bastards, we escort the guns to safety. I don't want none of you staying back here; the other commando has to take care of itself.'

The Boers had almost finished lashing their guns, but turned when they heard the thunder of ironclad hooves. For men on the ground the sight of a cavalry charge and the glint of steel as the horsemen hunkered low across their horses' necks could crush the bravest of hearts. They, like the advancing horsemen, did not know that an ambush was in place. Flustered, even panicking, they tried to complete the task of attaching the limbers to the horses' traces. Some took up a kneeling position and levelled their rifles. Any moment now they would be trampled. Most recognized the inevitable: they would abandon their guns and run for their lives. The English would have the Boers' precious few pieces of artillery.

Liam let the first horsemen gallop through and then opened fire, his own shot followed by a volley that took several men from their saddles. Horses screamed; legs and hooves flailed; roses of blood blossomed on men's tunics.

Belmont wheeled the men around and bellowed the command to retreat. There was no choice. At least half the riders were already whipping the flat of their sabre blades on their horses' rumps. But more of his men fell. Horses careered in the echoing gunfire. Moments before Belmont's men were cut to pieces the dragoons' sergeant and half a dozen men who had ridden to the top of the rise laid down fire on Liam Maguire's position. It bought vital moments. Belmont saw Marsh's horse go down. A soft-nosed bullet had passed through the horse's head into his friend's hand as they gripped the reins; then the ragged bullet had ripped on through his elbow before striking him in the chest. The over-eager lieutenant was badly wounded and the crashing impact of the fall knocked him unconscious. Belmont had already sheathed his sabre and fired his revolver into the hillside as he spurred his horse towards the fallen officer. As he dismounted and ran the last few feet towards Marsh bullets whipped the air around him. Survivors had retreated to the mouth of the gully and added their fire to that of the sergeant and his men. It would have little effect other than to let the Boers know that the fight was not yet over and help redirect fire from Belmont, who now dragged Marsh into cover behind his dead horse.

Belmont seemed to lead a charmed life. Three bullets had ripped his tunic and trousers, but none had drawn blood. It was as if his disregard for the hell fire around him acted as a shield. Coolly, he pulled Marsh upright, tugged at the trailing rein of his own horse, bringing the skittish mount closer to him, and heaved the lighter man across his horse's withers. His actions prompted a couple of the Boers to stand free of cover in an attempt to get a clearer shot at the audacious officer, but Belmont's men's cut them down. He spurred the horse away as the sergeant's men continued their rapid carbine fire. That Belmont was as courageous as he was tough would soon run through the ranks, but the raid to seize the Boer guns had ended in disaster. There were fewer than a dozen men who were not wounded, and fifteen lay dead, shot through more than once.

'Let them go!' Maguire yelled. He had lost two men, one of them a Boer, the other a Frenchman. Their bodies would stay where they lay sprawled across the blood-soaked rocks, the gore already drying to a dark stain in the sun's heat. 'Come on, you men! Get them guns hitched. The Irish are comin' and they'll put the steel through ya! Hurry now!' he shouted as he clambered down from their vantage point to the obvious relief of the Boer gunners, who chorused their gratitude. 'That's enough blabbering,' he told them, slapping one of the elders on the shoulder. 'Ya can buy me a drink later on. Corin, get our horses brought up. We need to be away from this place before them Dublin lads come over that ridge.'

Sergeant McCory was as good as his word. The Irishmen's volley followed by rapid gunfire reverberated across the killing ground, its crackling thunder chasing Radcliffe and Pierce like the devil's hoof beats as they ducked and weaved back towards their horses and the upturned field gun. Neither man could run more than fifty yards without stumbling to his knees and sucking in the dry air. Fear drove them continually back on to their feet, ignoring the pain from strained limbs and rasping lungs. By the time they reached the gun they knew that the Boers would have their field glasses trained on any distant movement.

Pierce retched and vomited what little was in his stomach; then he and Radcliffe pressed their backs against the upturned gun seeking respite and cover. Both drank thirstily from the canteens. There was no need, and little breath, for either to speak. The wheels were shoulder height; they got their arms on the iron rims and heaved. The gun was lying at an angle, and was unstable: with luck they'd be able to rock it over. However, Pierce had been right; the gun was too heavy. It was also caught in a rut.

'Strip them,' Pierce cried, pointing to the dead mules as he ran for the horses tied to the wheel of the other damaged gun. Their luck couldn't hold much longer.

Radcliffe pulled the yokes and traces from two of the dead animals and then slipped them over the horses' heads as Pierce tied the traces on to the gun carriage's wheels. Radcliffe geed the horses up as Pierce steadied the gun. With a crash it settled upright. Shots plucked the air; rocks splintered, startling the horses. They shied and lurched forward, hauling the gun into the shallow cusp of dead ground, enough to offer some meagre shelter.

'Cut the traces!' Radcliffe yelled, throwing the yokes clear and climbing on to his horse, settling the other as bullets struck the gun's barrel. Pierce threw himself flat, the horses reared, Pierce's remount broke free of Radcliffe's hold and then screamed as Mauser rounds found their mark. 'I'll draw them!' Radcliffe shouted and spurred his horse away, bullets whining above his head.

Pierce had no time to argue. He got to his feet, yanked the breech open, and reached for one of the blue-tipped shells that lay scattered from the smashed limber. Despite his riding gloves his sweaty hands fumbled the shell's brass casing, and as he ducked to retrieve it pinging rounds from Boer sharpshooters glanced off the gun's barrel once more.

He cursed, yanked free one of the safety pins from the shell and left the other as the dying gunner had told them. He pulled the lever that opened the breech and then rammed in the shell. The gun could fire over three thousand yards and that was too far. He pushed the lever closed. He didn't aim, hoping that the gun crew had corrected the gun's elevation before they had been slain. The recoil rocked the gun back on to the axle spade that limited its rearward movement, but the gun still jumped from the force of the shot. As it settled he cleared the breech, pushed in another shell from the caisson, and yanked the lanyard again.

Bullets sought him out, forcing him down, but as the explosions erupted on the hillside he heard a great cheer from the infantrymen, who broke cover and ran forward. Blood gutters on bayonets caught the sunlight, the sharpened steel glinting as the second shell hurled shrapnel into the Boer positions. Rattling gunfire plucked the dirt, chasing the lone figure who rode crouched low across his horse's withers. Radcliffe was heading towards the right flank of the hill, aiming for the saddle between the two kopjes. Pierce cursed. His friend would be caught in crossfire if he didn't get the hell off that horse and find some cover. Instinct was making the Boers shoot at him; there was no other reason. He was no threat, just one man who had dared them. Pierce bent to try and lift the gun's trail. If only he could move it a few inches the change in angle over the thousand yards could help his friend: Pierce knew the devastating effect the exploding shells would have on the Boer positions. It was a futile effort; the gun's dead weight defeated him. He saw figures approaching in a crouching run. They were levies carrying stretchers, sent to help the Natal Indian Ambulance Corps. The levies were spread out but two of them fell dead from gunfire; the others hesitated, half ducked, frightened, uncertain what to do. Run or retreat. Pierce yelled at them and waved them on.

'Come on! Run! Here!'

The men recovered and with shoulders hunched ran towards him. Bullets skipped in the dirt but the levies made it to the gun. He recognized Mhlangana.

'This way!' Pierce told them, cutting the air with his hand in the direction he wanted the gun shifted. They put their shoulders to the wheel and with brute force shifted the carriage. Another man fell, a bullet tearing through his chest. He writhed and choked in a spasm of sudden pain. The levies' eyes widened with fear and they froze as they watched him die. 'Ammunition!' Pierce shouted, pointing to the scattered shells. 'Come on! Move it!'

Pierce loaded the one shell that remained in reach and yanked the lanyard. The powerful explosion made the men wince but it broke the spell. A half-dozen cartridges were quickly gathered and Pierce kept feeding the breech and laying the shrapnel on the distant hill.

'Again!' he yelled and bent to lift the gun for a wider field of fire. The grunting effort strained every muscle in his legs and back, but the urgency gave him strength. The men heaved; the gun shifted. Pierce pushed two rocks beneath the wheels to stop the recoil then rammed home a shell and tugged the lanyard. The gunfire on Radcliffe was silenced but he cursed when he saw that his friend was still directing the fast-galloping horse between the kopjes and that two Boers had ridden into the gap and raised their rifles to aim at him.

Pierce tugged his right-hand glove free and quickly calculated the distance. He brought his rifle to his shoulder and set the Sharps' sight. The air was still; no breeze shifted the artillery smoke. He might miss at this range but the crack of the .50-calibre bullet would tell whoever was trying to shoot Radcliffe that someone had them in their sights. He laid his cheek against the curved stock. He sighted along the octagonal barrel and steadied his breathing, letting thirty years of experience take over. He cocked the rear trigger which primed the front trigger. It needed only the gentlest touch to fire the weapon. He squeezed off a shot. The recoil slammed back into his shoulder. It took three seconds for the bullet to fly the thousand yards, by which time Pierce had levered free the empty case and thumbed another finger-thick round into the breech, his thumb cocking back the hammer. One of the men in the distance danced aside as a puff of dust from the first shot spurted close to him. Pierce fired again before the man could decide what to do. The second shot made him flail his arms and tumble backwards from the force of the bullet. The second Boer swerved his horse for cover.

Radcliffe was clear.

Lieutenant Baxter shouted his orders, picked up and carried by NCOs. 'Advance!' This was no time to attack in extended line. If he lived through this he'd take the consequences for disobeying the general's order. 'Come on the Irish!' He was the first to rise up and run with Sergeant McCory at his shoulder.

Pierce watched the magnificent sight of hundreds of men rising from the ground and, like a great flock of birds, swooping forwards towards their enemy, bayonets glinting, a roar suddenly erupting from their chests.

Mulraney ran with them, muttering the prayer of contrition: 'Forgive me my sins, O Lord, forgive me my sins…' he repeated over and over until his words gave way to blasphemy with the urgency of the gunfire and their desperate attack. Battle instinct had taken over: field drills of moving forward in extended line were ignored; instead the men took lung-tearing short runs, kneeling to shoot, moving on under covering fire from the next man, gaining precious ground. They swarmed across the terraced boulders, edging their way into the kopje's crevices and gullies. Soldiers still fell to Boer gunfire, but the artillery rounds that Pierce had laid on the hillside bought the Irish regiment a foothold where they could unleash their savage anger. Boers surrendered but were shot down or bayoneted and as the wounded died their cries quickly spread panic. The Irish pushed, shoved, clambered and clawed their way up slabs of rock that rose twenty feet, driven by the desire to kill those who'd had them at their mercy with their longsighted rifles and artillery.

Radcliffe saw the soldiers advance around the side of the slopes. He was sweeping around the assault's flank and had not yet reached the place where the cavalry had been slaughtered on the reverse slopes, but it was obvious the enemy's guns had been hauled away otherwise they would have bombarded the attack. Screams and full-throated curses filled the air as British and Boer locked in hand-to-hand fighting.

Men gouged and kicked, used their fists, rifle butts and bayonets amid the erratic staccato of gunfire. Entrails spilt from men's bodies and the sickening, cloying taste of death clung to the back of men's throats. Few men cried for mercy because they knew none would be given.

Radcliffe saw Boers beat a soldier to death with their empty rifles, the sound of his skull cracking like dried firewood being splintered, and then they were set upon by soldiers who stabbed and ripped at them repeatedly until the bloodied mass below their blades barely resembled that of a tattered carcass. He could ride no further. He pulled the carbine from its sleeve and ran along the edge of the tide of wild, cursing Irishmen, faces contorted in their own lust for life. He saw Lawrence Baxter in the fray as soldiers swept past him; the lieutenant was running forward, calling for the retreating Boers to surrender, but in their blind panic and determination to escape they fired at him. Radcliffe coolly shot three men and then saw two Boers dragging away a younger man who limped from a wound. His heart pounded. It was Edward. The lad had the same broad shoulders and shock of dark hair.

'Edward!' he yelled. But the three escaping men were swallowed by others swarming down the reverse slope of the hillside with the soldiers at their backs. The mêlée of men fighting hand-to-hand redoubled, as Irishman and Boer grappled each other to the ground. When weapons slid from bloodied hands men snatched at knives and bayonets, fought with fists and rocks, smashing relentlessly into their enemy until their opponent died. Radcliffe chased the three men, emptying his rifle at others who turned to face their attackers. Caught up in the tide of khaki he had to use the empty weapon as a club to ward off the Boers who begrudged every inch of their retreat.

He was closing on the men who carried his son.

One turned, raised a pistol and in that instant Radcliffe realized that Lawrence Baxter had turned his back to yell orders to his men. The Boer could not resist the opportunity to kill a

British officer. Radcliffe shouted a warning and without aiming fired three shots from his revolver; he saw the impact of his bullets shatter the man's head and chest. They had dropped Edward on to the ground. The second man snarled and swore in his own language and lunged, defenceless except for the knife in his hand. There was little to distinguish Radcliffe and the man who faced him; both were blood-splattered and caked with dirt, and each had the desperation to live etched on their faces. Radcliffe killed him at ten paces with two shots and ran forward oblivious to the threat from the random rifle fire that crackled around him. Trembling from exertion he bent over the boy, who lay face down.

'Edward!' he cried, easing the boy's shoulder over.

The fist that held the rock caught Radcliffe a glancing blow. He fell back as the youth pressed his attack. The lad's size and strength belied the youthfulness of his face. He couldn't have been more than fourteen years old. The snarling boy could never have been Edward, who could never have been there in the first place. 'My pa!' he screamed. 'My pa!'

In the seconds before the rock could slam into Radcliffe's face he knew he had just killed the boy's father who had been trying to save his son from the battlefield. That moment of realization seared through him as harshly as the sun blinded his eyes. He raised an arm, trying to protect himself. The boy grunted and Radcliffe heard the thwack of a bullet tearing into bone and heart as the youth spewed blood and fell back. Radcliffe kicked himself free of the shuddering body and rolled clear. Lawrence Baxter, as filthy as the men around him, stood several paces behind him, tunic unbuttoned, bareheaded, revolver in his hand. He allowed himself a nod to Radcliffe and then pursued his men downhill as they mopped up the last resistance.

Radcliffe cradled the boy, waiting for his pulse to finally cease. The young eyes gazed unblinking at the sky that he had known for only a few short years. How long had it been, Radcliffe wondered, since he worked his father's farm, brought the cattle in from the veld and listened to the old men talking of war and their blood enemies and the planned resistance to British imperial ambitions? Young and old alike were fatally bound together in a common history.

He opened the boy's jacket and saw the familiar label. The sight of the bloodied mess clinging to the wool fibres fed the fear that gripped him. There now seemed little doubt that Edward was either a prisoner or had been killed and his body stripped.

Gently, he closed the boy's eyes, and turned him face down so the scavengers would not take them.

With a weariness that was due to more than his years, he walked to where the horse stood. The stallion, ears alert, raised its head and whinnied, stamping on the ground as if trumpeting a call of defiance to the other horses across the kopje.

Chapter Seventeen

The soldiers surrendered to the heat and their exhaustion. The day's killing was over. They sat or sprawled among boulders and brush, slurping what water they had and wiping bayonets free of blood. Alongside them flies swarmed over the congealed wounds of the dead and wounded. Radcliffe picked his way down the re-entrant where the slain cavalry lay scattered. Most had been struck two or three times; some had gaping wounds, proof that some Boers had cut the tips off their bullets. Cruel hatred for a bitter enemy. Thankfully there was no sign of Edward among the fallen riders.

Radcliffe worked his way around the hillside, remembering what Sergeant McCory had told him about the initial attack. If Colonel Baxter had led men into that crossfire of hell he'd have skirted between the boulders and worked upwards for a better firing position. And that's exactly what Colonel Baxter had done, trying to give his men a chance. The colonel had advanced further and higher with half a dozen men at his side even after the main attack had failed. The Irish had scrambled and fought, stabbing and wrestling their opponents into a macabre death embrace. Their colonel had managed to clamber another twenty feet beyond the men who lay dead behind him, and that's where Radcliffe found him, his back against a blood-smeared boulder, one leg twisted underneath him, the empty revolver still gripped in his hand. His head was slumped on his chest. The single shot that had killed him had left a stain on the front of his khaki tunic. Radcliffe carefully straightened his friend's body and sat with him for a moment, easing the pistol from his hand, allowing his fingers to linger on Baxter's.

He rejoined the men on the hillside and told a bedraggled Lawrence Baxter where his father lay. The young man had aged, and his exhaustion was apparent. He appeared numb to the news of his father's death, but nodded in gratitude.

'I must attend to my duties,' he said and turned away, perhaps, Radcliffe thought, to grieve privately or to let the loss of his father take its place amid the sorrow for all those others who had fallen.

Soldiers stirred themselves to gather their dead as the first of the hospital wagons from the railhead arrived. Someone whistled a familiar call. Radcliffe raised his hat and signalled to Pierce, who saw him and jumped down from the wagon.

'Holy God,' Pierce muttered when he saw the carnage. 'Edward?'

'Not here,' Radcliffe told him as he took the offered canteen and spilled water into his hand for the horse, and then drank himself. He took Pierce to where the boy's body still lay, flies buzzing in the bloodied mess of the exit wound. Before long the maggots would hatch and desecrate the boy further.

'Boy had Edward's jacket,' Radcliffe said.

'Then he's a prisoner somewhere,' said Pierce, knowing that there was also an alternative.

His gaze followed the contours of the hills where he had laid his shots. The shrapnel bursts had flayed the impact area and the torn shreds of men's bodies smeared the boulders. Raptors were already pecking at the flesh. All the old memories of another war churned in his stomach. Radcliffe noticed the look of disgust on his friend's face.

'Let's find Edward and go home,' said Radcliffe.

Pierce nodded and the two old soldiers turned their back on the slaughterhouse.

Two hundred and thirty-six British soldiers lay dead on the ground, covered in ground sheets and laid out in neat rows as the regimental sergeant major had instructed. Even death needed to be handled in an orderly fashion. The rail stop seethed with activity as more troops arrived and the dead were taken away to be buried in one of the many war graves that would come to blight the countryside. Stretcher-bearers from the field hospital continued to carry men in from the battle, laying them down in whatever scrap of shade was available next to the open-air operating tables which often consisted of little more than the stretcher balanced across ammunition boxes. As soldiers staggered in, wretched from the fight, Indian water-carriers, turbaned and dressed in their dark blue serge jackets, their legs bound in puttees, carried *puckals*, the canvas bags that cooled water, slung across their shoulders. These *bheesties* were as regimented and disciplined as any soldier, and worked their way diligently through the thirsty men, portioning out a drink for each man desperate for the gut-wrenching cold water.

Radcliffe and Pierce sat hunched in the shade of a barn. The black horse, unsaddled and rubbed down with straw, munched from the nosebag Radcliffe had fastened across its head. Once the horse had been attended to he had squatted down with Pierce, who had cooked a one-pot meal. Pierce dipped the spoon into the meat stew and grimaced. 'Horsemeat isn't beef, that's for sure, but it's better than what most of these men have. Damned pen-pushing logistics can't get field kitchens up here yet; most of the men have only biscuits and tinned meat.'

Radcliffe didn't eat; he was squinting into the sun-baked distance at Lawrence Baxter, who walked towards them with a slovenly Mulraney trying to keep up and stay in step, skipping once or twice as he tried to match his officer's footfall, and to stop his over-sized sun helmet from falling over his nose. Despite his vaguely comical appearance Mulraney's tunic and hands were caked in dried blood, testament to the happy-go-lucky soldier's fighting during the battle.

Radcliffe and Pierce got to their feet.

Lieutenant Baxter half raised a hand. 'Gentlemen, please don't get up. I didn't mean to interrupt. God knows we all need food and rest after what we've been through.'

Neither Radcliffe nor Pierce sat down. Mulraney cast a mournful look at the pot of food. He licked his lips. 'Poor bloody horses give their all. I'm surprised we don't prise off their horseshoes and chuck them at the *boojers*. And they don't smell like proper stew neither. Still –'

'Shut up, Mulraney, no one asked for your opinion,' said Baxter curtly.

Mulraney nodded and took a step back, behind the eyeline of his officer. 'Stay where you are, for God's sake,' Baxter ordered him, the weariness as obvious as his change in character since fighting toe-to-toe with the enemy.

Radcliffe looked at the young man who only weeks earlier had yearned for the excitement of war.

'I was sorry to hear about your father,' Pierce said. 'He extended me every courtesy.'

'Thank you, Captain Pierce,' Baxter said respectfully. 'His body is being brought down with those of his men. He will be buried with them, as it should be.' Baxter paused and addressed

Radcliffe. 'There is no sign of Edward on the battlefield. I personally went and checked the dead in the Boer positions. He was not among them. Thank God.'

'Thank you. I'll move up the line and keep looking,' said Radcliffe.

Baxter hesitated, uncertain how best to continue. 'I may have some news. There's something you should know.'

Radcliffe involuntarily squared his shoulders, as if expecting a blow from an assailant. Baxter's words were tinged with regret.

'The man who had Edward's knife was Private O'Mara. He's since died of his wounds. I've questioned his friend Flynn and can confirm that there were no irregulars fighting near his position where he was wounded. Mulraney, tell Mr Radcliffe what you told me.'

The soldier took off his helmet, as if at a funeral. His sweat-matted hair clung to the white band of unburned skin on his forehead. 'We was on a farm clearance a while back. Shifting a woman and her little ones off to one of the holding camps. There was a Boer who fired at us. Came at us full gallop from the foothills. He must've been the woman's son or something. We put him down. Scouse O'Mara and another lad went out to scavenge, and by the time they got near him, there was a whole bloody horde of riders firing down at us. They was out of range, but we didn't wait until they weren't. We put the devil on our heels and went as fast as we could –'

'That's enough, Mulraney,' Baxter interrupted. 'Return to your section and get yourself some food.' Mulraney nodded and replaced his helmet, but hesitated as he turned away. 'I've missed grub, sir, seeing as how you needed me here.'

'Very well, then tell Corporal Hurly I said you must be given rations.'

'He died up on the hill, sir.'

Baxter barely managed to hide the pained expression at forgetting one of his section commanders had not survived. 'Yes... so he did. Quite right, Mulraney. Very well, tell Sergeant McCory.'

'Yes, sir. Thank you, lieutenant.' He looked at Radcliffe and Pierce. 'Major. Captain.'

Baxter waited until the shambling soldier was far enough away. 'Mr Radcliffe, I was in command of that clearance. We... we thought we were under attack from a Boer. The commandos were all over the place. As Mulraney said, my men shot him. God help me, I never saw the body, you understand. It seems O'Mara looted the knife from the rider.' He shook his head regretfully. 'I had no idea. Why was Edward here?'

'We believe he came here looking for you,' Radcliffe answered.

Baxter nodded; it made sense. 'If that rider was Edward, he couldn't have known it was me. I don't know why he shot at us.'

'I can't guess either. Where was the farm?'

Radcliffe and Pierce followed the rail line as far as they could, the iron tracks leading them across a broad plain before disappearing into the hewn rocks of the low hills. They spurred their horses up through the broken ground until they emerged on to another plateau, a seemingly endless pan of scrub and stony ground. Somewhere beyond the indistinct horizon would be the ruined farmhouse and the possibility of finding Edward's body. A veil of rain obscured the line between earth and sky several miles away, a line that never seemed to get any closer until finally the wind swept the rain away and showed them the uneven crocodile spine of mountains in the distance. It was a two-day ride until they found the abandoned stone farmhouse. It was gutted, its timbers blackened from fire. Radcliffe and Pierce pulled aside the timber ribs and searched the wreckage as best they could. There was nothing to be found of any worth or to tell them anything about the lives of those who had lived there. Scattered pots lay abandoned as if spilled from a burst sack; a torn piece of cloth clung to a rusted nail like a flag of despair. The remains of a cow's carcass, rotten and stinking, ripped apart by predators, sprawled, still tethered by rope to a corral post. The burned-out shell revealed only its forlorn loss of human inhabitation.

Pierce gazed across the veld that stretched to the blue-tinged hills whose shadows clawed down from the ravines. 'Maybe this ain't the place,' he said.

'Maybe not,' Radcliffe answered. 'God knows how many farms they've burned. Irregulars could have been coming through here. Might not be just regular troops burning out the Boer women and children. What if the boy was riding with them?'

'Edward wouldn't have any part of them,' said Pierce.

'You get yourself into a war you break all the promises you make yourself,' said Radcliffe.

Both men had once been caught up in a war of attrition. Both knew the savagery that it spawned. Pierce shielded his eyes and pointed to something that looked like a clump of small boulders a few hundred yards away. They rode forward until they reached the remains of a dead horse, its brown skin drum-tight across its ribs, its eyes, tongue and innards long taken by scavengers.

Radcliffe looked from the farmhouse behind him to the hills in the distance.

'Baxter said the rider came from the hills before he was

brought down.' He looked at the grim remains and then at his friend. 'This tallies.'

Radcliffe tried to imagine his son galloping towards the soldiers. And here at his feet was where he fell.

'Where do we look now?' said Pierce.

Radcliffe shook his head. It was a vast country where thousands of men fought across a dozen fronts.

Pierce slapped the dust from his hat. 'Seems they're burning every farm they come across.'

Radcliffe remounted and gathered the reins. 'Maybe they got the idea from us,' he said.

Pierce walked once more around the dead horse and looked back at the charred skeleton of the farmhouse. 'What? Sherman burning his way down to Atlanta? The English have a lot to learn. Damned if that man didn't know how to start up a fire.'

Radcliffe eased his horse away and Pierce followed. Somewhere beyond the horizon was Edward Radcliffe.

CHAPTER EIGHTEEN

Far from the confounding heat and rain in Natal, South Africa, another struggle for survival had been resolved. The soft Irish rain bore no warmth and its misty cloak sheltered both killers and informers – those who squirmed through the underbelly of Dublin slums, who heard whispers and separated rumour from fact and were well paid for it. Yet it was those who wielded power and influence who would be the ones to come through the conflict to kick the English out of Ireland, and Kingsley was just such a man: he had both. He had used the Dublin whore, Sheenagh O'Connor, to betray the Fenians, and one of their commanders, the gunman Malone, had gone hunting for the girl. Gone all the damned way to South Africa, and if he found her it wouldn't take much for her to confess who had fed her the information about attacking the garrison, about how the armoury was ready to be plucked. She'd spill her guts before the killer cut her throat. Kingsley had learned of Malone's hunt for vengeance and used every channel he could find to betray him to the English. They would be grateful if they snared the Fenian and Kingsley would live, providing the stupid bastards pulled their finger out of their arses and acted like real soldiers instead of in-bred aristos who thought war was a step up from a Boxing Day hunt. He played a dangerous game. Truth was he wanted to live to enjoy it.

Kingsley gazed out into the mist-shrouded darkness. If the

English failed there'd be a dozen men coming to his door. They'd use knives and hatchets on him, taking him apart piece by piece. They'd slaughter his beloved horses and dogs first and probably burn down his stables with his lads still inside. Brutal fucking killers who deserved to be taken behind the wall and shot through the head. An act he would gladly do himself but which he could not. Not when you played both sides. Thank God for the money he had and the influence he enjoyed. So, Malone had taken passage to Durban, had he? Gone looking for the girl. Gone for revenge and information so he could have his bastard friends come at Kingsley in the night. Well, fuck ya, Malone. Kingsley swallowed the whiskey. He'd got to him first.

The field prison was in an old adobe building. It had thick walls to keep the heat from the rooms, but the effect was lost because of the corrugated iron roof which turned one room in particular into a sweatbox. Two big men, both of them sergeants, were stripped to their undervests, their khaki braces stretched taut across their broad backs. A battered man sat tied to an old chair that had fallen over more than once from the severity of their beating, but each time they had picked him up and worked on him again until bones broke and an eye that had been swollen with blood had finally succumbed to complete blindness. They had been careful not to kill him but had inflicted more pain from their flat-knuckled pugilist fists than a man could bear. Their undershirts clung to them, soaked with sweat. One of them stepped back and threw a bucket of water over the beaten man.

In an adjacent room, which was cooler than the prison cell, Freddie Taylor, the intelligence officer, sat at a desk watching cigarette smoke curl towards the slatted reed ceiling that helped keep the heat at bay. The piece of paper in his hand was the confession extracted from their prisoner. He tapped the desk pensively, a hint of anxiety in its rhythm, as he decided how best to proceed. If he was not careful he could be dragged into this mess. The confession gave Taylor vital information about the attack on the Dublin garrison. It would do his career no harm to see Malone tried and hanged, but the damned Fenian had spewed his guts and mentioned a name that caused Taylor's stomach to knot. He knew that what he had discovered could have far-reaching repercussions. What he needed now was someone who would wish to protect his own skin, and was ruthless enough to succeed.

He called out to an orderly: 'Find Captain Belmont.'

Sheenagh O'Connor eased the blood-clotted dressing away from Edward's wound. The discoloured skin seemed less inflamed now and the boy had more strength to him. Some of the dried blood caught the dressing and he winced as she tried to tug it free without hurting him.

'I'm sorry, lad, it's a bugger of a wound, I know, but needs must. A tad to the right and you'd not be in any position to be hurting. Yer brains'd be splattered in the dirt.'

'How long can I stay here?' Edward asked. The curtained-off area was private enough, though the curtain would be little use if anyone came uninvited into the room.

She dabbed his torn scalp with more antiseptic; it must have stung like a bee swarm but the lad held steady. 'Hold that dressing there for a minute,' she told him and put her arms around him to clean the back of his head where the blood had congealed in his hair. The smell of carbolic soap fought the cheap perfume she wore. Her breasts pressed against him and despite the pain he contemplated reaching out and pressing his hand against them. He resisted, the thought of rejection and the possibility of her abandoning him overriding his boyish desire.

'We'll get ourselves off from here to Bergfontein. There's a camp full of women and kids there, and an Englishwoman who can look after you better than m'self.' She finished swabbing away the blood.

'Is that where you sell the medicine?' he asked.

She stood back from the bed and washed her hands in the bowl on the nightstand. 'I give it to them,' she said.

He felt awkward, uncertain of what to say or how to say it. 'I didn't mean to offend you,' he said finally.

She dried her hands, looking at him, as if weighing him up.

'I can make my own way, you know. I don't want to put you in danger, and I swear I won't say anything about Liam,' Edward assured her.

She rummaged in a chest of drawers and chose two shirts, sized one up and replaced the other. 'And when you're picked up? Who'll you say shot ya? The English? In their eyes that makes you a spy. You fired at them first.' She tossed the clean shirt to him.

'Only to draw their attention,' he said defensively.

'Aye, ya did that right enough. So you'd have to lie and tell 'em it was the Boers that'd done the shooting. Then they'll know you have information about them.'

'I can keep my mouth shut,' he insisted.

She involuntarily brushed aside a fringe of his hair. 'But *why* is what everyone will want to know. Now, we have to get out of here. If you get stopped you tell them there was a shooting in town. The provost marshal's office can't keep up with what goes on here.'

Edward steadied himself and pushed the shirt into his trousers. 'I understand,' he said.

'I hope you do. I'm risking my neck for you now as well. Jesus, you play this wrong and they'll have me in front of a firing squad.'

Taylor stubbed out the tenth cigarette he had smoked since sending for Belmont. The cavalryman arrived and he watched as Belmont gave his reins to a soldier. The raider was caked with the fine dust that a man could never seem to wash free from his nose and ears here. It tormented men's eyes and demanded that a soldier adapt quickly and not let it work for the enemy.

Belmont walked past the outer sentry and into the room. It was obvious to Taylor the man was exhausted. Belmont nodded in greeting and bent down to pull open one of the desk's drawers. He took out a bottle of whiskey.

'I need this more than I can tell you. You don't mind?' he said. He went to the water carafe and tossed what water there was in the glass out of the door. Taylor said nothing, just watched him pour a stiff drink and then swallow it in one go. Belmont refilled the glass.

'You sent a runner after me, so I am presuming that you have some sort of vital intelligence that's going to be of help. We had a bad time of it. Marsh is dead, along with a dozen more of my men.'

'I'm sorry to hear that,' said Taylor matter-of-factly. 'He was a good man.'

'As were the others, Freddie. He'd have lived if he'd listened to me but... there it is.' He swallowed another gulp of Jameson's. 'We've raided damned near a thousand miles since we got here and my men are still ready to take on the Boer, so don't keep me away from my duty. What is it you want?'

Taylor's quiet sense of self-satisfaction was obvious. He had reached a position of authority and influence and that meant the likes of Captain Belmont could be reined in.

'We captured an Irishman,' he said, tapping each end of another cigarette on his silver cigarette case. 'Oh, I'm sorry, would you care for one?'

Belmont shook his head. 'Given that half of Ireland seems to serve in the British Army while the other half fights for the Boers I wouldn't have thought that too difficult. Even for you. Why do I sense this one is something special?'

'We were tipped off and we thought him a spy,' said Taylor, blowing the plume of smoke and picking a fleck of tobacco from his tongue.

Belmont pulled a chair back from the desk and propped his feet on it. He sipped the whiskey. 'Not a very good one by the sound of it,' he said.

'He bargained for his life,' said Taylor.

'Ah, a sensible spy at least.'

Taylor fussed the knitted khaki tie at his collar. 'He told us he was part of the raid on the Dublin garrison. He was looking for those who betrayed them.'

Belmont watched him. Taylor had not yet made his point and seemed intent on stringing out the information that he had. Belmont, too, was prepared to wait. The whiskey and the sanctuary the room afforded from the incessant heat outside was worth it. For a while.

'A Fenian prepared to travel halfway round the world to finish what he started in Dublin. That's dedication for you. Freddie, why have I been dragged here? I'm in no mood for playacting.' He dropped his legs from the desk. There was, he realized, only so much respite worth paying for.

Taylor smiled his familiar condescending smile, and slipped

on his tunic from the back of the chair. Belmont saw that the captain's pips had been placed by a major's crown.

'Jesus, Freddie, they promoted you. God help us all now.'

Taylor ignored the insult and handed him the sheet of paper. 'He came here to kill Sheenagh O'Connor.'

Belmont lowered his eyes and glanced at the written confession while Taylor drove home his point. 'She passed information to the Fenians – and they believe she betrayed them. Did you know Sheenagh O'Connor in Dublin?'

Belmont tossed the paper on the desk. 'You know I did.'

'Even when we were stationed at the Curragh you went to Dublin on leave. Is that when you first met her?'

'What is this, your idea of an investigation? You went off chasing foxes while I pursued women. That's the difference between us, Freddie. I fuck and you rub your balls against a saddle for fun.'

Taylor remained impassive. 'You have an…attachment, shall we say, to her. We all know that.'

'Christ, half the officers' mess were *attached* to her.'

'Don't make light of this, old man. If, as I suspect, you have inadvertently told this Irish whore something of value they'll blame you not only for the garrison attack in Dublin but for compromising us in the field.' He ground out the cigarette in the overflowing ashtray. 'You will be in front of a firing squad.'

Belmont smiled. 'All this on the word of a Fenian killer?'

'His word and hers when I arrest her,' said Taylor.

Belmont understood Taylor was now in a position to wield the power that had always been denied him. 'You arrest her and you bring half the regimental officers down with her. You'd all be sitting in the same pile of horseshit as me,' he said.

He went to the window to disguise his concern. The gods had given Taylor an opportunity to climb the slippery slope of ambition even further. If suspicion were cast on him – a serving officer with a known association to a Dublin whore – it would at the very least cost him his rank. For years Belmont had barely disguised his contempt for the preening Taylor: well, now that had come home to roost. Taylor had borne the jocular taunts with tolerance; no man wished to be seen as someone who could not take a ribbing or who fell short of the officers' club's standard of a 'decent chap'. And Belmont knew that his own presence had been tolerated only because of his bravery in the field. He was a common man. An outsider despite his military success.

He gazed out as the day-to-day life of the soldiers went on. That one of their officers could be brought down by an Irish whore would give soldiers enough gin gossip to last a lifetime. Taylor could make up any damned story he pleased and easily implicate him. There was no doubt that when Sheenagh O'Connor was arrested she would agree to anything to save herself. And he didn't blame her. Belmont was a fighting man but he would not be able to conquer the elitism that imbued the officer class with its insufferable self-worth.

Fuck Taylor. He would defend his position and that of every other officer who enjoyed the comfort of whores. It was worth an appeal to Taylor to stave off further investigation, to at least give him time to think and to reach Sheenagh and warn her off. He would pay her enough to get away, perhaps even enough to ensure she never had to return to Ireland.

And then that fickle bitch, Fate, decided to smile on him.

As he turned he saw a canvas satchel nestled next to a cabinet, almost obscured by a chair. It looked just like the army medical bag that he had seen in Sheenagh's room. He grabbed it and threw it on the desk in front of Taylor, spilling some of the supplies.

'Me? Freddie, you're fucking accusing me? Is this how you paid her? With stolen medicines. You always were a tight-arse with your money. I paid for my pleasures and if I've been indiscreet –'

'You admit it then!' said Taylor, feeling the sudden constriction of panic tighten his chest, unable to disguise the guilt etched on his face. The tables had been turned; because of his carelessness his own culpability and foolishness had been established by the man he had accused.

Belmont picked up his bush hat. 'Indiscretion is everyone's curse,' he said. 'She told me a major was giving her medicines. Care to think how you will explain that? Someone in the quartermaster's store take a bribe to slip you a satchel once in a while? Soldiers blab, Freddie. They won't protect an officer. The trail will come back to you. You're fucked. Stealing from your own to give to a whore who's associated with the Fenians. Is your arse pinching yet? Me, Freddie? Me? She'll spill her guts about you before she does me.'

'I could have you arrested now,' said Taylor, desperation tinging his suppressed panic, not wanting Belmont to slip through his fingers.

Belmont took a step towards him. 'And you'd be dead before a guard got in the door. I'd have nothing to lose, would I?'

Taylor knew Belmont was capable of such violence, and that he was not bluffing. He managed to keep his composure but Belmont had seen his fear.

'Freddie, *old man*, you're as fucked as the rest of us. There's no proof she's passing information but those medical supplies put you in the dock more than anyone else. *That's* evidence. You'd go down first.'

Taylor gnawed his moustache. The heat of the room was suddenly oppressive. 'We must do something.'

Belmont watched Taylor squirm. A bead of sweat trickled from his hairline as he looked almost imploringly at the captain.

'Claude… what to do?'

Belmont was back in control. 'Give her a chance to run.'

'What?'

'We should prove she's passing information.'

'And then she should be taken care of,' said Taylor quickly. 'For everyone's sake.'

Belmont turned for the door. 'I don't kill women,' he said, and walked out.

CHAPTER NINETEEN

Edward kept to the rear of the stable, making sure that the stall's wall and the horse he was saddling hid him from the activity on the Verensberg street. The dull, insistent ache in his head seemed worse when he squinted into the sun's glare. He tightened the cinch strap and was about to lead the horse out when he heard a familiar voice bark an order. He stepped quickly away from the horse, pressing his back against the stable wall, peering into the street where Sheenagh's horse was tied to the hitching rail outside the hotel. He saw Belmont dismount and tether his horse alongside hers as his troop filed past with their sergeant and then halted, obeying his command to wait for him.

Panic caught his breath and for a moment the temptation to flee was almost unstoppable. He forced himself to think clearly. Could they have made any connection between himself and Sheenagh? He tried to reason it out. Belmont and his soldiers seemed not to be in any state of alert. The troopers stood idly by their mounts, their weapons slung. He eased away from the entrance and led the horse back to its stall. He would be ready to bolt if they came looking for him. Until then he would watch and wait. Flies buzzed in the heat; horses shifted their weight; riders and pedestrians outside went back and forth. Everything was as it should be. Except the dryness in his mouth told him otherwise. Seeing Belmont had shocked him – and whipped his memory with the man's ruthlessness during the horse race in Ireland. Whatever business had brought Belmont here Edward knew he must not be seen by him. Sheenagh was right; if he was caught and questioned how would he explain his head wound? Who would have treated him? Certainly not an army doctor. And it would soon be revealed that no doctor in Verensberg would have helped him either.

The half-light of the saloon bar caught the rising dust as an African servant swept the wooden floor. Belmont leaned against the bar, one boot resting on the foot rail. He had already drunk half the glass of the pale-coloured beer in front of him, and had swallowed, then refilled, the whiskey in the shot glass. He glanced at the mirror across the bar counter as he heard the rhythmic tap of a woman's heels on the stairs behind him. Sheenagh held his eyes in the mirror until she reached him and then rested her hand against his shoulder, letting her fingers lightly touch the hair on the nape of his neck.

'They said you were here. I thought I wouldn't be seeing you. I heard terrible things about the fighting. I'm pleased you're back, Claude.'

He looked at her, searching for the lies that were camouflaged by the light in her eyes and the tender smile. He took another gulp of beer.

'I have to go away,' he said, pushing the shot glass of whiskey towards her. She toyed with it for a moment as she wiped the damp ring that his beer glass had made on the smooth wooden counter.

'Is that for a while then?' she asked, taking a small sip of the sharp-tasting liquid.

He smiled at the woman whose bed he had shared on every occasion he could find. 'You'll miss me?'

She eased the larger glass from his hand and swallowed

a mouthful of beer. 'God, it's compliments you're wanting now, is it?'

'I've no time for anything else,' he said, the meaning clear.

A look of concern shadowed her face. 'Claude, don't go getting yourself hurt now, will you? I mean it. Where is it you're off to? I'd be heartbroken if I wasn't to see you again.'

He could play the game as well as she did. He was nonchalant, a philosophical shrug. 'Ah, we were pretty beaten up. My men need rest and they'll have to bring us up to strength. They've given me an easy duty. Little more than babysitting a train loaded with the Dutchies' women and children. My troop is riding escort part of the way. As far as the refuelling depot. Then the train's being taken south but I'm going north: we've got the Boers on the run. Mopping up along the way is all we can do now. Until the big push comes, and only God knows when that'll be.'

'You're moving women and kids out of Bergfontein?' she asked.

He nodded. 'The camp's getting too crowded and they want to shift some of those who are sick. I reckon some of them won't make it. I can get you on the train in a separate carriage as far as Swartberg. That's why I came.'

She hesitated, and then shook her head. 'That's thoughtful. And I'm not ungrateful for you thinking of me, it's a fair way right enough, and easier than an arse-aching wagon journey, but no, this is where I belong. I'm a soldier's girl.'

He eased an edge of concern into his voice. 'Listen to me: you'll be safer in Swartberg.' He flicked his head at his surroundings. 'All of this will be there. It would be no different once the troops flood in.' He touched her face.

She took his hand in her own and pressed it to her lips. 'You know how to tempt a girl,' she said. And kissed him gently.

He knew she wouldn't accept the offer. He smiled and nodded, and swallowed the last of his drink. He walked towards the door and called back without turning: 'I'll be warming your bed again, Sheenagh O'Connor.'

'Aye, and my heart,' she answered. But he had already been swallowed by the stark sunlight.

She waited a few moments until she heard his command for his men to mount, and then a minute longer for the sound of the horsemen riding away down the street. She prayed to God that none of Belmont's men had gone into the stable opposite.

Edward squatted on his haunches in one of the rear stalls. He heard Sheenagh calling his name. He peered around the stall's wall and saw her looking frantically. She was carrying the medical bag.

'I'm here,' he called quietly.

Her relief was plain to see. 'Mary and Joseph, I thought they might have taken you,' she said. 'Now, listen, lad, I have to get to the camp at Bergfontein. They're shifting hundreds of women and children. They are so sick it'll be a death train. They'll need these and more,' she said, raising the medicine sack.

Edward's attention was on the street behind. 'Was that Captain Belmont?' he asked, unable to keep the uncertainty from his voice.

'You know him?' she said disbelievingly.

He nodded.

'He's a friend of yours? Or your father?'

'He's no friend of mine.'

'Thank God for that. Right, now, there's work to be done, and you've got to help.'

'With Belmont out there?'

'You listen to me. Liam Maguire saved your life.'

'I know that. But you're the one who said I mustn't be taken. And if Belmont is here then what happens if he sees me?'

Sheenagh kept looking over her shoulder, wary of being seen talking to the boy. A nosey townswoman might think her to be soliciting away from the sanctuary of the hotel. She pressed him back into the stall.

'He won't see you, not if you do as I say. You owe Liam, and you owe yourself to choose to do the right thing. Will you help us save those women and children?'

Edward licked his lips. He was no longer a prisoner of the Boers or the Irish who rode with them. They hadn't killed him, hadn't put him against a wall or left him to die in the veld. 'What do you want me to do?'

'Ride and tell Liam and the Dutchies about that train.'

Captain Belmont and his troop were a mile or so from the dusty streets of Verensberg, waiting on higher ground, using a ruined farmhouse for cover. Their horses were held ready – in the lee of the building, for shade – as Belmont watched the town through his field telescope. A rider had appeared in the distance, head low, the horse already galloping. It was too far to see who the man was, but it made no difference – a rider spurring his horse like that was in a hurry to carry a message.

One of the troopers turned to Belmont. 'We chase him down, captain?'

'No, Marlowe. Leave him be,' Belmont answered, putting the glass back to his eye. A horse-drawn buggy eased from the main street and went in a different direction than that of the horseman. Belmont took no satisfaction in identifying her when she got within half a mile. She wore the same dress as she had when she kissed him in the barroom.

'She's heading towards Bergfontein, sir,' Marlowe said. 'You want us to reel her in?'

Belmont got to his feet and compressed the eyeglass with his palm. 'No. Follow her. Keep your distance; make sure she doesn't see you. Report to General Reece-Sullivan at HQ whatever you see. Understood?'

'Yes, captain.'

Trooper Marlowe eased his horse from the blind side of the building as Belmont hauled himself into the saddle. The captain thumbed open his timepiece. Somewhere in the distance he thought he heard a train's stream whistle carry across the still air. In his mind's eye he saw the old puffer ease away from its siding; a dozen or more boxcars full of Boer women, guarded by a handful of soldiers front and back.

He snapped the inscribed silver watch closed and then looked at the hard-bitten men who rode with him. There were none better for the relentless war he was asked to fight. 'All right, let's kill some Boers.'

Bergfontein was a tin-roofed town of three hundred citizens who benefited from the rail-line junction that pushed north towards the distant mountains and into the Transvaal, the largest of the Boer republics, and then east into Portuguese East Africa. Bergfontein was strategically placed as a refuelling stopover that also allowed wounded British troops to be taken by hospital trains south through the colony of Natal to Durban where the hospital ship *Maine*, financed by generous Americans, was anchored. In this dry wasteland, beyond the battle lines, a thousand large bell tents were laid out in neat formation, the whole area surrounded with barbed wire. The Bergfontein Internee Camp held more than three thousand displaced Boer women and children, guarded by a handful of soldiers who could be easily reinforced by those at Verensberg, thirty-odd miles away, should the need arise. But the rock-strewn plain – a vast expanse that would entrap any attacking force – was no fighting ground for the Boer commandos. Leaving the safety of the mountain ranges and daring to attack would be little more than a futile gesture. How could a mobile army seize and care for thousands of women and children?

At the edge of town a colonial bungalow's wide, shady stoep wrapped itself protectively around the rotting windows and pine front door that had long yielded its resin to the moisture-sucking heat. A subaltern, from the Lancashire Regiment's detachment whose duty it was to guard the camp, knocked decisively on the door.

'Mrs Charteris?' he called.

Two soldiers stood with him. 'Want us to kick it in, sir?'

The lieutenant's hand was on the doorknob. It turned; the door opened. 'I think we can dispense with your boot breaking down the lady's door,' he said and stepped inside the cool, high-ceilinged house. 'All right, she's not here. Get to it.'

The soldiers slung their rifles and followed the subaltern, who reappeared moments later once his orders had been issued, and joined the half-dozen soldiers waiting for him in the red dust street.

'With me,' he commanded the lance corporal in charge of the section, who brought the men to attention, right-turned them, and followed the nineteen-year-old lieutenant whose orders were to find the troublesome Evelyn Charteris and bring her before the Officer Commanding Bergfontein Internee Camp.

The woman they sought was a well-bred middle-class doctor's daughter, calm and considered in her arguments for social justice but inflamed with moral indignation at the camps. She would never grace the social pages of the better-quality magazines back in England, but she was considered by many to be a handsome woman. Widowed by the time she was twenty-three, childless, she had dedicated herself to works of charity on a meagre stipend left in her late husband's will. Vanity, what little she'd had, had been pushed aside when she reached Africa. She had taken scissors to her long auburn hair and wore it unfashionably short at the nape of her neck. It was rumoured this forthright thirty-five-year-old woman had had lovers, but no further knowledge of these relationships had ever come to light, so no smear of scandal remained.

In an effort to help feed some of the more vulnerable children in the camp hospital she had planted vegetables in the depleted soil of her garden, but the yield was poor and disproportionate to her efforts – almost as poor as the responses to her constant letters to anyone in authority who might ease the plight of the women and children being forced from their farms and removed to Bergfontein. There were a few who supported her locally – a handful of women and a couple of Quakers – and whenever a train halted she would attempt to rally support. The young subaltern had no trouble finding her.

A small crowd of onlookers had gathered on the train station platform. Evelyn Charteris, flanked by a couple of women supporters, stood on a makeshift dais and harangued the bemused passengers, who waited as the engine took on water.

'This war was instigated by British business interests to secure the goldmines of South Africa and force the Transvaal Republic to give the vote to outsiders. And once that vote had been secured the Afrikaners could be dislodged from power.'

One of the men in the crowd interrupted: 'Nothing wrong

with having a piece of gold in your pocket! God knows I could do with a bit myself.'

The crowd cheered.

'It is not unpatriotic to be compassionate to the women and children caught up in this conflict –' she said, raising her voice, but was interrupted.

'You take them in then!' another in the crowd called, causing more ribaldry and a surge towards the dais.

'They're the enemy!' someone shouted.

Evelyn pointed beyond the train towards the internment camp. '*They* are not our enemy. It is imperative we help them. Do you have no conscience about others' suffering?'

The antagonism was picked up by another: 'You people are nothing but a bunch of bleeding-heart suffragettes with those conscientious objectors, those conchies, hanging on your skirts!'

'Or up 'em!' cried one of the men.

'Conchies and whores!' a woman shouted from the back of the crowd.

Evelyn tried to shout over the belligerent heckling. 'We are doing whatever we can to help these homeless women and children. Are we so uncivilized we cannot offer them consolation?'

The crowd were having none of it and pushed forward, elbowing aside the two women who tried to shield her. Had it not been for the subaltern and his men forcing their way forward, she would have been thrown to the ground. The civilians soon yielded, beginning to filter away once the soldiers had reached her. The young officer was unfailingly polite, but equally determined to do his duty.

'Mrs Charteris, I have orders for you to accompany me to the camp commandant.' For a moment she was flustered and backed away, as if intending to resist. But he stepped quickly in front of her, blocking any chance she had of escaping. 'By any means necessary,' he said quietly.

There was no point in chastising a young officer doing his duty, so she nodded and fell into step as he accompanied her off the platform and along the street. They walked in silence until she reached her house, where she saw a bonfire was burning in the small picket-fenced garden. The two soldiers who had been left behind came out with armfuls of her books and papers and tossed them on to the fire.

'Am I that much of a danger, lieutenant?'

'Apparently more than you realize, ma'am.'

The thousand white dust-blown tents shimmered in the glaring sunlight. The women and children incarcerated in the sprawling internment camp huddled beneath the flapping canvas scoured by mountain winds that could bring heat, cold and wet in an unforgiving punishment. They were a hardy breed, the Boers, and their womenfolk were used to the harshness of the veld. It was God's country but there were times it felt as if the devil himself bore down on them. And God tested his people, said the church leaders of the Dutch Reformed Church, their Calvinistic stoicism entrenching their belief that the Almighty had predestined their journey through this vale of tears. Well and good, the women said among themselves, but their men were riding commando, their farms had been destroyed and their children were dying of disease and malnutrition. God's calloused hand struck them hard. A woman's bitterness would be ploughed deep and watered with her tears; the crop would yield a hatred for the English that would never be appeased.

Radcliffe and Pierce sat astride their horses gazing at the

tent city in the distance. Radcliffe traced his finger across the map case.

'This is Bergfontein,' he said, flapping the case closed. The dust cloud had swept from the far valley and across the plain, leaving the rail link and the scattered houses stark against the harsh landscape.

'You think that Charteris woman is still here?' said Pierce as they eased their horses from their vantage point and down the gentle slope.

'Maybe,' said Radcliffe. 'She wrote enough letters to me in Dublin and someone that determined isn't going to give up easily.'

Pierce scanned the inhospitable vista. 'The British found the perfect place to dump people. The Spanish set up camps like this to deal with the Cuban guerrillas. They kept some of the toughest bastards around in them, called them *reconcentrados*. But I never thought I'd see the day when women and children were fenced in such places.'

Radcliffe swirled his mouth from his canteen of water and spat. 'They call them concentration camps here.'

They urged their horses across the tracks where the stationary train hissed an occasional gasp of steam. The flatbed railcars behind it were empty and African levies sat idly by, backs against the wheels, seeking shade from the sun's glare. Radcliffe and Pierce rode along the dusty main street with its scattered houses. The barbed-wire encampment on the edge of town needed only a few soldiers to guard its perimeter, and were it not for the tents, Bergfontein would be no different to any other South African *dorp*, clinging to the lifeline of its rail link.

It was barely a hundred paces from the tracks to the first

house, where an African woman swept the front stoep of a house. She squinted up at them as they rode by, lowered her eyes as Radcliffe glanced her way, and then looked up again at the black man riding at his side. He was no servant. Not with saddle and clothes that matched the white man. And he was armed. Her mouth gaped in disbelief. The woman had heard that the British had given rifles to some of the Africans who scouted for them, but to her eyes it was plain to see that this man was no scout. And now he had reined in his horse and was looking at her.

'Mrs Charteris. You know where she is?' asked the black rider.

The woman stared, uncertainty making her dumb.

'You speak English?' the man said.

She nodded. But still no words came.

The rider's eyes widened in expectation of an answer. 'Mrs Charteris?' he said again.

The woman pointed and finally found her voice. 'The second street. Her house is there. You will see it.'

Pierce watched the woman quickly bend to her task again, shoulders hunched, as a white woman stepped on to the street with a disparaging look towards her servant and the man on horseback. She was about to say something to Pierce, an admonishment perhaps, but Pierce held her gaze until discomfort made her turn back into the house. He tongue-clicked a command for his horse to walk on.

'Thank you,' he said to the servant.

But she kept her gaze lowered.

Radcliffe and Pierce tethered their horses to a bungalow's picket fence.

'You think this is it?' asked Pierce. There were four other

tin-roofed dwellings along the dusty street.

Radcliffe nodded towards the charred bonfire where a few singed documents and book pages had survived. 'Who else would have their books burned?'

A woman appeared from the side garden carrying a basket of vegetables, a broad-brimmed hat shielding her face from the sun. She stopped when she saw the two rough-looking riders walking towards her front door.

'Yes?' she demanded.

They stopped and looked at her. The woman glared at them. But then: 'I know you,' she said quickly, her challenge softened as her sharp memory recalled a photograph in an English newspaper.

'We've never met, Mrs Charteris. I'm –'

'Joseph Radcliffe,' she whispered, hand to her mouth. 'Oh. Thank God,' she muttered. Her eyes closed as if she might faint.

Radcliffe's concern for her made him step towards her, but then she recovered and smiled, extending her hand in greeting.

'Mr Radcliffe from Dublin. And you must be Mr Pierce.'

Pierce had already removed his hat and took her hand in his own. She gripped it firmly.

'Benjamin Pierce, yes ma'am.'

'Of course you are. Of course. I remember your name so clearly from all the letters. Please forgive me, you took me completely by surprise. I had absolutely no idea that you would actually come. Come inside, come inside at once.'

The two men looked at each other. From what she'd said it seemed they had been expected. Perplexed, they followed her up the steps to her front door and into the cool, high-ceilinged room.

'We seem to have arrived at an inopportune moment, Mrs Charteris. You're moving house?' Radcliffe asked when he saw the sparsely furnished, untidy room. Books were stacked on the floor in front of half-empty shelves, an old leather-topped mahogany desk was laden with untidy piles of letters. A broken chair, one leg torn from its seat, was propped in a corner.

Evelyn Charteris put the basket down on the kitchen table, draping her hat on a chair. 'No, no. The authorities searched the house. It will take me an age to put it back together. Food, as scarce as it is, is more important than a tidy house. So it's all something of a mess,' she said, and cleared an armful of books and piano sheet music from a couch. 'They burned a lot of my papers and books. The soldiers have their orders, so one can't blame them, though they attend to their duties with zealousness.' She paused, pulling a hand through her short auburn hair. 'Please sit. You must be weary after your journey and I'm talking too much. Forgive me. I'm being ungracious. One forgets how to treat guests.'

They shuffled awkwardly further into the room and seated themselves on the edge of the small couch. There was barely any other furniture in the room, other than the broken chair which, Radcliffe guessed, would have seated Evelyn Charteris when it was whole.

'I can make tea,' she offered. And then apologetically, 'I don't have coffee – well, we do, chicory, but...'

The two men shared a glance like two schoolboys in the presence of a benevolent teacher. They both nodded and muttered their acceptance.

She smiled as if it was a small victory. 'Good.' She stepped to the kitchen and half turned. 'I have only tinned milk, by the way, there's no fresh milk... or fruit or vegetables come to that... which is why there is so much illness in the camp.'

'Black tea would be fine, thank you, Mrs Charteris,' said Pierce.

She gazed at them for a moment longer. 'It is an absolute

miracle you've come. And at exactly the right time. The conditions in the camps are deteriorating and we are sorely in need of a champion like yourself, Mr Radcliffe. I want to hear everything that you have planned, when the others are coming, what the government has said. I can't tell you what an enormous relief it is that you've responded to my letter. I knew that would do the trick.'

Radcliffe fingered his hat, uncertainty gnawing at him. 'What letter might that be?'

CHAPTER TWENTY

Benjamin Pierce sipped his tea as he sat in the shade of Evelyn Charteris's stoep. The verandah offered a view of the dusty street and in the distance the start of the barbed wire encampment. Best leave Joseph and the woman alone, he had decided when she learned that no delegation from England followed them. He shook his head and sighed. That woman had a temper. By God she did. She'd fair torn a strip off Joseph. Made it plain as day what she thought. Why in God's name had he come all this way if it was not in response to her letter begging him to reach out to those people of influence whose liberal thoughts and concerns needed to be expressed with action? If a delegation could not be brought from England to see the conditions in these camps then women and children would die in their thousands.

Pierce nursed the china cup and touched a finger to the moisture on his moustache. Mrs Charteris had calmed when Radcliffe told her about Edward, and the belief that he might have been wounded. The woman knew nothing of Radcliffe's son, but a father's pilgrimage had softened her temper. Pierce drank the cup dry. A warm sense of contentment settled momentarily on him. It was gratitude. Thank God he had never married.

*

Sallow-faced children peered across their fingertips beyond the barbed wire. Their dirt-streaked faces and imploring eyes cut into Radcliffe's heart as he and Evelyn walked past.

'Women and children shouldn't be treated like this. I'll do what I can, but I have to find my son first,' said Radcliffe.

The children obviously knew Evelyn and muttered words of respectful greeting to her. One of the women was bent over a washboard at the entrance of a bell tent and straightened to look at them as they passed. Radcliffe noticed that despite the dire conditions these women endured they showed no sign of being victims at the hands of their captors. The proud-looking woman faced them and gave an almost imperceptible nod to Evelyn.

Evelyn Charteris did not slow her pace or alter her stride; she wanted Radcliffe to walk the wire and see what could not be experienced in a letter, no matter how passionately it had been written.

'These people scraped a living from the land but they ate fresh food. They were healthy. Now they're given only tinned beef. There's no milk for the babies, no vegetables, no jam, a pound of corn meal and half a pound of meat a day. There was no meat at all to start with. Our Lord Kitchener has the ear of the British government; they like his proposals of using reduced-scale army rations. Not feeding these people properly saves the government money. Their diet is more restricted than that of soldiers in the barrack room; it leaves these people malnourished and allows the rapid spread of disease.'

'But there are civilians running the camps?' said Radcliffe. 'Or so I've heard. It's not all military, is it?'

'No, but who controls everything? The military, of course. We have one doctor and a few nurses for all these women and children. They are mostly *bywoners*. Sharecroppers, dirt-poor tenant farmers,' she said by way of explanation. 'Few of them knew any illness because they lived such remote lives but now there's a dozen or more to a tent, disease goes through the camp like wildfire. This is why I wrote to you.'

'I passed your letters on to the newspapers,' he answered. 'There was not much more I could do.'

'It wasn't enough,' she said.

Radcliffe offered no defence. There was little concern in Britain for the fate of farmers' wives. 'But I promise you, I will do anything I can to make them aware of what the high command is doing here. I will stop this,' he said.

A couple of soldiers guarding the perimeter fence walked by, rifles slung over their shoulders. They looked suspiciously at Radcliffe, but nodded to Evelyn.

'Mrs Charteris,' said one in greeting. 'Not planning any trouble today, I hope?'

'Not today, Albert,' she answered. She was obviously acquainted with the soldier. Once the men were out of earshot she glanced back at them. 'I've seen him give boiled sweets to the children. Even those who serve here don't necessarily like their duty.'

'Pierce and I have witnessed violence inflicted on women and children before now. Soldiers don't have the luxury of refusing to do their duty. Thank God these women and children are not flogged… or worse,' Radcliffe said. Rape was not unknown to armies at war but as far as he could see the British held their men in check. Despite these being harsh times he knew that soldiers guilty of violating their orders were dealt with by the severest punishments. Some soldiers had been hanged for looting, despite it being commonplace and almost considered a soldier's right – but more violent acts against women were perhaps held in check by the hatred the Boer women felt for the invaders and the fear of severe retribution by the military.

She glanced at him. She knew that he had been a cavalry officer. Had he been one of those who had ordered such violence in his time? If that was the case then her own judgement of the man was wrong. She quickly dismissed the thought. Joseph Radcliffe's reputation went before him.

'These women are not abused by their captors. I'm not saying the superintendents of the camps are bad people, they have no evil intent, but their incompetence is magnified by their lack of supplies. Their own soldiers are dying in their hundreds from disease… but women and children are suffering and dying needlessly.'

He waited patiently as she expressed her frustration and helplessness at the hollow-cheeked torment that stared at her from the other side of the barbed wire.

'There are times when enteric fever goes through them like a bushfire. It's malignant. If we had fresh milk that would help nourish them, give them strength. We have a few chickens which give us a meagre ration of eggs, for the really sick, and giving that with biscuits and rice helps. But when the fever grips they need ice packs and where would we get those? Sponge baths are the best we can do for the children, but when it turns to pneumonia we need poultices. We manage to get some supplies – not always legally. Codeine, beta-naphthol, zinc sulphocarbonate, tincture of capsicum, ergotine for haemorrhage.' She hesitated, a frown creasing her forehead. 'Some of the women use it to bring on abortion. I'm not sure I can blame them.'

She fell silent. Radcliffe knew that she did not have a child of her own. Perhaps a childless woman saw the purging of a baby from the womb as some kind of irretrievable loss.

As if the thought of the dying children triggered her desire to help, she remembered Radcliffe's torment. 'I'll ask about your son. There's a fairly decent officer here; he might know something and then –'

'Missus!' a voice called. They turned to see Sheenagh O'Connor rein in her horse. She was already clambering down from the buggy. 'Missus Charteris. Thank God I'm not too late.'

Evelyn stepped quickly to her and took her by the arm. 'Not here, Sheenagh. The house.'

Radcliffe took the horse's bridle and guided it after the women.

'But the train,' said Sheenagh. 'I've brought another sack of...' She glanced nervously at the stranger who held her horse. 'Y'know... for the women and kids, those on the train. They'll need it.'

'What train?' asked Evelyn.

'The one they're sending out today to Swartberg.' She glanced towards the railway siding and the idling steam engine. 'I was worried I'd be too late but I see they've not loaded them yet.'

'What are you talking about? There's no train leaving here today.'

Sheenagh suddenly looked frightened, eyes darting from the rail siding back to Evelyn.

'What is it?' Evelyn asked.

'Mother of God. It's a trap is what it is.'

Evelyn and Radcliffe escorted a flustered Sheenagh O'Connor into the house. Pierce, as requested by Evelyn, tipped a decent measure of brandy into a glass for the Irish girl.

'You gave favours to British officers to get medicines for the camp, and one of them told you that they were shipping women and children from here. Today?' said Radcliffe.

'Aye, the bastard… Oh!' She quickly looked in apology to Evelyn.

'You're not the only woman to hear rough language from soldiers,' said Evelyn as Radcliffe pulled up a chair to sit close to her and take one of her trembling hands in his own.

'Were the British testing you? Just wanting to see who it was that brought medicines to the camp?' he asked.

Sheenagh looked startled. 'I hadn't thought of that,' she said. 'Perhaps that's all it is. Do you think?'

Radcliffe tried to reason it out with her. 'You were fed a lie to bring you here today. If someone has followed you then they still have no proof against you unless they saw you with the army satchel.' He sensed that another piece of the story was missing.

So did Pierce. 'They would have wanted to catch you red-handed with the medical supplies because then you would have been forced to tell them where you got them from. Perhaps they're after one of their own for aiding and abetting the enemy.' Pierce eased the lace curtains aside. 'Well, there's no sign of anyone tailing you.'

Sheenagh clung to that hope for a few moments. 'That'd be fine. Worst they could do was put me away. That's what it must be.'

'It's an officer you know?' Evelyn asked.

'A friend… of sorts… if you see what I mean.'

'His name?' said Radcliffe.

'Ah, well, now, I'm asking m'self just how involved he is in this. Mebbe it's him they want to snare as well. If they nab me then I'll tell them who it was that gave me the stuff. Sometimes it's best to keep your trap shut until you need to spill the beans.' She looked to Radcliffe and Pierce. 'I don't know who you are, sir, but I thank you for your kindness and concern for my welfare.'

Evelyn pressed a hand against her arm. 'Forgive me. These gentlemen are from Dublin –'

'Dublin is it? That's the damnedest accent I've heard from those parts.'

'Mr Radcliffe and Mr Pierce are here looking for Mr Radcliffe's son,' Evelyn explained. 'There's a chance he's joined the irregulars.'

Sheenagh's hand went to her lips. 'Mary, Mother of God. Edward Radcliffe is your boy.'

Radcliffe pushed the chair back in surprise.

Sheenagh swallowed the brandy and looked at the startled faces around her. 'There's a story I have to tell you.'

She told them what little she knew of Edward being shot and how Liam Maguire had brought him to her. He was a brave enough lad, there was no doubt about that, but he certainly wasn't riding with the British. Radcliffe and Pierce listened without interruption until she had finished.

'Someone had to attend to his wound,' she said finally. 'The British would have been too suspicious and Maguire and the others couldn't risk that.'

'It's more than you they want,' Radcliffe said. 'There has to be another train leaving from somewhere else. They want to draw the commando into an ambush. Is my boy a part of Maguire's group?'

'No, the lad's just riding to tell them is all.'

'Then we have to get to them before they spring the trap. And you must make yourself scarce. I thank you for the risk you took in caring for Edward.'

'He's a stubborn lad, and I've no doubt he'll make himself useful. But, Mr Radcliffe, it's damned near a day's ride to the commando from here.'

'I'll find them,' Radcliffe said.

Evelyn took Sheenagh's hands in her own and brought her to her feet. 'The British must realize that you've been passing on medical supplies and perhaps even information. You need to get away. There's a train to Cape Town from Langfontein. That's a few hours down the line.'

'You're right. Time I made m'self scarce,' said Sheenagh as Pierce opened out the map case on the table.

'Don't go back to town. Stay away from any soldiers,' Radcliffe told her.

She thought of her hidden stash of money beneath the floorboard in her room. Hard-earned money. She'd need that if she was to escape. 'Difficult that, for a girl like myself, Mr Radcliffe, but under the circumstances I'll heed your advice,' she lied and added a smile.

There was little time for anything more to be said. They ushered the girl outside and with a wary eye for any suspicious activity from the garrison soldiers Radcliffe and Pierce tightened their saddle cinches as Evelyn helped Sheenagh on to the buggy. Radcliffe took Evelyn to one side.

'I promise you I will do whatever I can to help when I get home,' he said.

In the moment that she cupped his rough hands between her own, she felt something more than his warmth. In the brief time since they had met, his kindness and strength had caught her unawares, so marked was the contrast to the harsh world that surrounded her. Whatever this new feeling was, it caused a flush of colour to her neck. Had he noticed? she wondered.

'I wish the circumstances of our meeting had been different,' he said gently, and let his eyes settle on her longer than was necessary. His smile seemed one of regret.

She nodded. 'Do take care, Mr Radcliffe. And I will pray for your son's safety.'

'Thank you. I'll find him and take him home. I wish you well, Mrs Charteris, and hope that one day we may meet again.'

Sheenagh gathered the reins and released the handbrake. 'Mr Pierce,' she said, smiling at him. 'They say we Irish are the blacks of Europe, and I've known a few Irishmen in my time, but I'm not that well acquainted with American gentlemen of colour. Be sure to look me up when you have a chance.'

She slapped the reins and the buggy pulled away, leaving an embarrassed Pierce to look sheepishly at Radcliffe as he climbed into the saddle.

'Damned if you're not old enough to be her grandfather,' said Radcliffe.

'Damned if I care,' Pierce answered.

As Radcliffe and Pierce made their way through the town and out on to the open veld, their departure went unnoticed by the lone trooper who had been ordered to follow Sheenagh O'Connor. He waited patiently on the ridge line, chewing a strip of biltong, savouring the cured salted beef on his tongue. A man could live a while out here on the stuff, but it tasted like old boot leather when compared to a tin of bully beef made into a warm hash with peeled onions and some broken army biscuits to glue your guts together.

Trooper Marlowe wondered if his mates and Captain Belmont had snared the Dutchies yet. God knows where they were but the lads would take to killing with gusto. Their blood would be up and Belmont, the mad bastard, would be at the front, sabre in hand, cutting his way through the Boers. Lance and blade: the Dutchies hated it. Gunfire and artillery, some old *boojer* prisoner had told him, that they could deal with, but not the sabre or bayonet. Scared the bejeezus out of them, they did.

He kept his silhouette low, watching dutifully for the pretty whore to leave Bergfontein. Belmont had chosen him and that meant, in his eyes, that the captain trusted him to do his job as best as a man could do. His field telescope picked up the buggy. He kept it trained on her for a few moments, swinging the glass left and right, seeing if he could determine which direction she might go once she got to the crossroads outside the town. Straight ahead was his guess; that would take her right back to Verensberg. And then he'd have time for a beer and maybe a quick knee-trembler himself. Whores weren't cheap for ordinary troopers, but there would be one willing to give him a couple of minutes. He didn't need any longer. More than that you might as well marry them.

Marlowe waited. Sheenagh O'Connor had halted the buggy as if uncertain about which way to go. *Straight ahead, my lovely, c'mon now. Back where you belong.* He smiled as she whipped the horse on to the road to Verensberg. He gathered the reins and eased himself into the saddle. *All right then, m'darlin'. Soon be home.*

Radcliffe's plan was to ride towards the foothills of the mountains, cutting across the vast expanse of plain that would bring them to where the rail track meandered below the mountain slopes. Sheenagh had pinpointed the commando encampment on the map. The two men had traced their fingers along the dark line of the tracks and tried to determine where the commandos might stop the train to release what they thought to be captured Boer women and children. Both men knew that the odds were against them reaching the camp in time and that it was unlikely Pierce's horse would be able to keep up with the Irish stallion. They had agreed that if

Radcliffe went ahead then Pierce would keep going until he was in position – between five hundred yards and a mile away – to try and cover the rescue attempt as sniper with his .50-calibre Sharps. Now Pierce watched as Radcliffe's horse galloped two hundred yards ahead. His own horse was labouring, but he kept it to a steady rhythm, willing to ride his horse to death if need be. A bizarre twist of fate had brought Edward Radcliffe close to them. They would be unlikely to have such luck bless them again. He watched the shimmering figure of his friend gain even more ground ahead of him. Damn, that horse could run.

Pierce knew they had covered more miles than a man ought to over this punishing terrain. His body ached from the horse's efforts, his age telling on him, back muscles biting. Riding was as easy as breathing to him, but galloping across this hard, hot ground was like a slave-master whipping his back with an iron rod. He cursed the loss of his youth when he could stay in the saddle for days on end, chasing down the Sioux, the best horsemen he'd ever come across. They would ambush like a snake from beneath a log. Step too close and you'd feel their blade before you saw 'em. Was that how these Dutchmen fought? If they were hidden from view in any of those distant rocks he risked being seen for the black man he was. And an armed African in this war meant he'd be seen as their enemy. And one dead African amid the slaughter would ruffle nobody's feathers.

How long had they been riding now? He squinted at the sun, its ball of crimson flare settling behind the black-etched crags. There would be hours of daylight left on the other side of those mountains but here the plain was cooling: shadows draping the mountainsides. He reckoned it had been at least five hours of hard riding, easing the horse as best he could, but he could feel it was beginning to falter. It had nearly stumbled twice and its flanks were sheathed in milk-white sweat. Then, suddenly, he heard the crack of bone breaking seconds after the horse's front hoof caught a scrub-covered hole. The horse's head dipped as it tumbled and Pierce had no chance to stop himself falling forward. He instinctively half turned, hoping he would roll when he hit the ground. It happened so fast that the horse's momentum spun him and then a mighty fist slammed into his back, shafting pain through his lungs. The air was punched out of him and a sudden darkness fell over him. The sun's warmth fled from his body.

Pierce had no idea how long he had lain unconscious. He rolled on to one side, his mind telling him that nothing was broken, but his back muscles hurt like hell and he took some time to get on to his knees and then to stand upright. Yards away his horse stood shivering in pain, its left front leg lifted from the ground. Pierce looked around him: there was no sign of anyone, and no witness to his fall. He eased his aching body towards the horse, painfully at first, murmuring comforting words to keep it as calm as possible. Its head hung low, its own agony from the broken leg holding it still.

He let the animal snuffle his hand as he pressed his pistol against its head and pulled the trigger.

Its great body dropped to the ground, quivered for a few seconds and then lay still. Pierce scanned the horizon. If Radcliffe had managed to reach the ambush site then he would need Pierce and his marksmanship as cover to exfiltrate Edward. Pierce pulled his rifle free from the saddle and slipped his water canteen over his shoulder. Ignoring the persistent pain in his back he started off on a slow but determined jog towards the distant train line.

CHAPTER TWENTY-ONE

A day's ride to the south-east from where Radcliffe and Pierce had sipped tea, Liam's commando rested in the lee of the hillside that afforded them protection from a direct attack and an escape route should a British patrol stumble upon them. Jackson Lee, the American volunteer, lay below the skyline on lookout, watching as the approaching horseman kicked up dust. He was getting too close for comfort and if he veered his horse in the next four hundred yards then he would be riding directly into the commando's camp.

The American held his breath as the rider brought his horse to a halt and lifted his hat to shield his eyes from the sun. He looked left and right as if determining his course, and then spurred his horse towards the commando.

Jackson Lee instinctively ducked his head and scrambled backwards.

'Shit,' he muttered, and then called out to the men below: 'Rider coming in!'

Liam's men sprang into action. The hardship of living rough had made them quick to move in defence and they would kill any unwanted intruder rather than risk a trap being sprung on them.

'Any others?' Liam called to the lookout.

'No sign,' Lee answered.

Liam wondered if any of the British irregular troops had

managed to sneak closer during the night and were ready to ambush them. Only one person knew about this hiding place and that was Sheenagh O'Connor and if she had been taken then the British might have beaten it out of her.

'No shooting!' Liam commanded. 'Jackson! Stay there! Keep yer eyes peeled! Corin! Hertzog! Take him!'

Corin and the older Boer dropped their rifles and scrambled into position as the horseman slowed his mount to manoeuvre between rocky pillars that gave entry to a narrow gulley. Hertzog pulled a knife from his belt as Corin leaped forward, startling the horse which shied away, throwing its rider off balance as Hertzog reached up and pulled him down. Edward hit the ground hard. Pain shot through his back, and he was winded from the impact.

'It's the *rooinek*!' Hertzog shouted, knife in hand ready to kill.

Liam was already at his shoulder, pushing him aside. 'What the fuck is he doing here?' He reached down and grabbed Edward's shirtfront. 'Boy! On yer feet!'

Edward coughed dirt and staggered dazedly to his feet.

'What game is this? You got Englishmen following you?' Liam demanded.

'No, no,' Edward said quickly, seeing that the hard-looking men would need little excuse to rid themselves of an intruder. 'Sheenagh sent me to warn you. The British are shipping out a trainload of women and children from the camp.'

'Today?'

'Yes.'

'How many are there in their escort?' said Corin.

'There's only a light escort part of the way,' said Edward. 'Sheenagh said only as far as the refuelling depot.'

'There'll be the usual front and rear guard detail on the train,' said Hertzog.

'No, I don't think so,' Edward said. 'Sheenagh said it's just the women and children. That makes sense, doesn't it? Why guard them?'

'Aye, mebbe so,' said Maguire. 'Sick women and kids wouldn't need any kind of guarding.' He was considering his options but his look of doubt made it plain he did not wish to stop the train.

Hertzog pulled his fingers through his beard. 'Liam, *ons vrouens en kinders*, we can save them.'

'God in heaven,' said Liam. 'We can't be slowing ourselves down with women and children.'

The Boers gathered around their natural leader. These women and children might not be their own but they were their volk, their people. And any chance to rescue them from the hellish conditions of the camp should be taken.

'I will send a few men with them and have them taken to safety. The British are not everywhere. Not yet. They'll have a chance. We must give them that,' insisted Hertzog.

'We can't care for women and children if they're sick. You know that!' argued Liam.

Edward felt the surge of anxiety running through the Boers. 'Sheenagh has taken extra medicine, Liam. She's gone to Bergfontein and the Englishwoman.'

'There!' Hertzog said. 'We can do this and if you will not then I will take my people from the commando.'

The men voiced their support for Hertzog.

Liam knew he could not risk weakening the commando any further. 'Aye, right enough,' he said reluctantly. 'We'll use what supply wagons we have hidden for the women and children. But we'll split the group. Front and back of the train. Just in case they've posted guards. Edward, you've done good work. Get yourself away now.'

Edward grabbed Liam's arm as he turned away to organize the men who were already harnessing mules to the flatbed wagons. 'Liam. Let me help. I'm a good rider, and I'm fast.'

'You can't help the Crown's enemy, lad. They'll shoot you for it if they find out.'

'I can help rescue women and children though. I can be a courier between you two,' he said, looking from the Irishman to Hertzog. 'You'll need a messenger. Give me a chance – I won't let you down.'

'You don't have to prove anything to me, lad,' said Liam. He glanced at Hertzog, who nodded. 'All right. You ride with them.'

The day was long in its dying. And the Boer commando waited patiently as the heat baked into the rock face. They could endure the harshness of their own country but what they could not endure was that it should be taken from them. The late afternoon's sunbeams speared through crocodile-spine rocks a hundred feet high that sawtoothed their way less than a mile from the rail track, their deep black shadows offering refuge from the heat for Hertzog and his men, who were to provide protection for the escape route. Once the train was hit he and the others in the divided force would escort the wagons to safety. The rail line went south from Bergfontein and skirted thirty miles to the east of Verensberg; there it passed through a refuelling depot and siding where extra rolling stock was held. The track then edged along a low mountain range for several miles; embankments shielded its journey once it had cut through the low foothills. After that it would sweep in a clear run across the rock-strewn plain. In two days it could reach deep into the Cape Colony.

As if straining against the day's heat the slow-moving engine chugged laboriously along, hauling its carriages. Bonneted women held the open-topped boxcars' swaying walls as the wheels click-clacked across the heat-expanded rail joints. Hertzog wedged himself between two slabs of rock, steadied his elbows and held binoculars to his face. The jagged rocks gave him and his men good cover and he had taken the Radcliffe boy with him because his group were going to take the rear of the train: if anything were to go wrong he would rather risk the brave young horseman in getting word to Maguire than any of his own men.

They heard the engine first, its efforts echoing from the concealed rock face, and then it hove slowly into view. Hertzog stared intently, waiting for the smoke to clear so he could identify the number of soldiers stationed on the front of the train. It was still more than a mile away, and the binoculars against his eyes made his face sweat. He dropped the glasses quickly and dragged a sleeve across his face. '*Ja*,' he muttered to himself, satisfied at what he saw. He glanced down at the men's upturned faces as they waited for his command. He grinned. 'No guards at the front.'

The men tightened their grip on their reins; Mausers rested on their hips. They spoke to each other quickly in Afrikaans, which Edward did not understand. But their eagerness to attack needed no translation.

'Wait,' said Hertzog as he put the binoculars back to his eyes, searching out the rear flatbed that in any normal supply train would hold a half-dozen soldiers to guard the rear. There was no sign of any soldiers. Boer women and children were less important than horse fodder. This cargo was of no practical use to an enemy. No weapons or supplies were being carried. Hertzog turned to the others. 'When the train passes and Liam blows the track we take them. Be watchful, people. If the escort is still with them they will be further back along the track. I don't want any of those women and children caught in crossfire.'

Edward sat dumbly listening to the orders issued in the guttural language. All he could do was wait until he was ordered – in English – to do otherwise. His stomach knotted and his throat dried up, excitement churned with fear. He was glad he would take no part in the killing.

Hertzog was about to climb down from his vantage point when he stopped. His weather-creased face made it difficult to see him frown with doubt. He raised the binoculars again. Something was wrong. He watched the train. What was it that did not seem right? He cursed himself for not understanding what his instincts were trying to tell him. Keep looking! he told himself desperately. The steam puffed above the boxcars; the women's bonnets shielded their faces from wind and soot. And then he realized what was wrong. There were no children aboard the train. He pressed the binoculars tighter to his face, willing his old eyes to be as sharp as when he levelled a rifle against an enemy. As one of the women in a boxcar turned to face the direction of travel, her bonnet pulled back from her face. Hertzog gasped in realization and quickly turned to the men waiting below.

'They are not women! They're soldiers! Boy! Ride to Liam, tell him it's a trap! There'll be other soldiers somewhere. Tell Liam to retreat. Before they kill us all. You tell him!'

Even as the battle-hardened Boers digested the warning, Edward had already spurred his horse away.

Hertzog clambered down and mounted his horse. One of the men called: 'Hertzog? What now?'

'We retreat. We cannot help Maguire,' the old man commanded.

It was a grim fact. There could be no telling where the British had laid their ambush. Hertzog and the others must live and fight another day. The Irish girl had been used. The British knew everything. With a curse, Hertzog heeled his horse, leaving behind the sound of the puffing train and the disguised soldiers ready to kill Liam Maguire's commando. Unless the boy got there in time.

Belmont had studied the ground carefully before he gave Sheenagh the false information. He and his men had lived as did the commandos and knew the most likely place for a Boer ambush on the train. The Boers would need a quick escape route after their attack and that would mean a place where their wagons could be used for the women and children. Belmont knew his enemy; the Irishmen who had worked the goldfields were efficient with their explosives and were a boon to the Dutchies. They would do exactly as he expected. Dumb bastards. Blow the track before it reached the final bend and the safety of the mountainside, grind the train to a halt and then rush the boxcars. There'd be no embrace from the Dutchy women though – the only kiss they'd be getting was a twelve-inch shaft of steel if they got past the gunfire. He wished he could be on the train to see the look of surprise when they were cut down. And those that weren't would turn tail and run. Straight on to his men.

He and his troopers had followed the rail line until a depression in the land a couple of miles back allowed them to move south of its intended journey and to stay below the skyline. Further back still from this depression were boulders that could hide man and horse, allowing the troopers he had placed there to shoot any survivors who got past him and his ambush.

Belmont and his riders waited in the saddle, carbines at the ready. Horses shifted their weight; men tilted their bush hats above their eyes now that the sun had dipped. He wished he could light a cheroot, but denied himself the pleasure. A wisp of tobacco smoke might carry and could lose him his advantage. No one drank from their canteens; no sabres were yet drawn; there was no sound except for the occasional jangling of bridle as a horse shook flies from its eyes. He glanced down the extended line at his hard-bitten men. Common bastards, men who fought with their fists if no other weapon presented itself. Miners, boiler-makers and peasant-stock labourers. The army had given them shelter and food and a life to be proud of. And he had given their aggression full rein. They relished a good fight and if a wounded Boer needed dispatching there was none who would shirk his duty. Despite their impatience to engage their enemy no one moved or showed any sign of nervousness. They could beat the Boer at his own game. The harsh land held no surprises for them; they adapted and lived like their enemy. Meagre rations and hardship. The harder the better. Bread was only that in name; meat was either horse or trek ox and even those men who had lived with little more than army biscuits and salted beef found it difficult to get their teeth into that. It was a welcome comfort to relieve the Boer farms of milk, eggs and chickens. A low, indistinct rumble reached them. Saddle leather creaked as men braced themselves. Horses' ears pricked as the beasts felt their riders' tension. Now the rumble became the sound of a train. Its engine tooted. Three short blasts followed by two more told Belmont the train was about to enter the open plain.

He saw the impending events in his mind's eye. There would be an explosion, a nerve-jangling screech as the train's wheels were locked, cries of greeting from the Boers and then volley fire from the men on the train. Shouts, curses and screams followed by the thunder of hooves as the commando retreated. There was never a good day to die but today was as good as any – for the Boers.

The rail track erupted, showering the air with metal bolts and ripped timber sleepers. Liam Maguire grabbed the shoulder of his brother who was clambering over the rocks, eager to reach the slowing train, its wheels locked, metal on metal rending the air as the engineer desperately tried to halt his train.

'Wait! You wanna get your head ripped off!'

The debris clattered around them and then Liam rose from the shelter of the rocks, through the dust that was yet to settle. The American Jackson Lee was in reserve with half a dozen men, two wagons and the commando's horses. 'Us first! Wait 'til we get the women down! Then the wagons!' he shouted, swarming forward with forty others. 'We need those boxcars in the middle covered! Frenchie! See to it!'

'I'll do it!' said Corin, running from his brother's side.

'Corin!' Liam yelled in a vain attempt to stop the lad from running along the length of the track, eighty yards from the train. He watched as Frenchie and half a dozen other men peeled away to run with his brother towards the middle of the train. Uncertainty made Liam falter for a moment as he watched the commandos sprint ever closer to the boxcars. There was barely time to think about why the Boer women were not screaming. They would, wouldn't they? a voice demanded in his head.

Before he could answer his own question the Boer women levelled rifles at them. *Mother of Christ!*

'Take cover!' he screamed.

Too late. Gunfire raked the men. Disbelief and shock struck them as hard as the bullets that ripped into them. Men fell dead, wounded crawled, survivors threw themselves flat, desperately pressing their faces into the dirt, scrabbling to find the smallest rock that might give them cover. The rapid gunfire from the train raked across the open ground. Men lay writhing, gripping stomachs that spilled their innards into the dirt. No saviour of a bullet found them: the English were going to let them suffer. Bodies lay strewn the length of the train. Skulls smashed, brains splattered, limbs splintered. One man crawled with half his leg dragging behind him: multiple rounds had shattered the bones. He screamed in pain and half rose: an act of incredible bravery and defiance – or the death wish of a mutilated man. No sooner had he lifted his torso from the ground than more bullets tore into him.

Liam panicked. They had to get back to the rocks and the horses but that meant a retreat across the face of the train. Corin! A greater fear made him roll and clamber to his feet. He fired as rapidly as the bolt-action Mauser allowed, not caring where the shots fell, in a vain attempt to keep the soldiers' heads down. Bullets spat up dirt around him; one tugged at his coat, another ripped his boot leather. Miraculously he was untouched as he ran to where he had last seen his brother. Another fighter joined him but Liam heard the thwack of bullets crushing bone and flesh and the man went down head first, arms askew, dead before he hit the ground.

The commandos were pulling back, trying to give each other covering fire. Then rifle fire came from the kopje which hid Jackson Lee. It gave them a chance. Something hit his side. A searing tear that felt like a serrated knife blade. The bullet ripped flesh but missed bone. He twisted and fell, his rifle falling from his hands. Shock surged through him, his mouth suddenly more parched than it had been before the shooting started – if that were possible. Dizziness claimed him, and then strong hands grabbed him and hauled him to his feet. One of his men mouthed something. Shouting. Unheard. Gunfire crackling, the likes of which he'd never heard before. Not this close. Corin! He couldn't see him. A thought lodged in his mind behind the fear that gripped it. Hertzog would ride in once he heard the gunfire. He could already hear shooting coming from their rear. *Come on, you old bastard! We need you! Hurry, man!* In the distance a horseman led the way. One horseman.

Hertzog's riders galloped away from the train, feet pushed forward in stirrups, reins long in their hands, leaning back in the saddle as they crested the lip that would hurtle the horses down into the depression. The broad horizon that had lain before them a few heartbeats before changed to a line of mounted soldiers who levelled rifles at them. Terror and surprise made them cry out in helpless warning to each other. At least half fell from the volley. Hertzog felt and heard a bullet whip past his face. Horses screamed, tumbling as some of the rounds tore into them, throwing riders beneath hooves. He spurred his horse and saw that their momentum carried the survivors through the Englishmen's line, galloping hard to escape the ambush. He dared a backward glance, saw the fallen men, saw the wounded horses floundering, their distress and misery ignored as the English rode through them. They were going for the train! Thank God they did not pursue him. They were clear! His men's horses surged up the far bank of the depression. The etched line of the horizon beckoned. The men cried out to each other in exultation.

Belmont's hidden riflemen shot them all.

*

Edward reached the rear of the train, urging his horse away from the gunfire that shattered rocks as the soldiers sought him out. He pressed himself low across the horse's withers, shortening his grip on the reins, his face against the musky smell of its mane. He could see the remnants of the attack as the soldiers in the boxcars trained their rifles on the retreating commando, firing over the corpses littering the ground. Gunfire rattled back and forth as some of the men in the kopje helped give cover to the survivors of the failed attack. Somewhere off to the left he could see a line of horsemen fast approaching.

It was a tableau from a music hall. Men dressed as women kept up a sustained fire on Liam's commando. A smashed violin case lay open, its instrument intact, the strings taut, the wood polished. Corin crawled towards it, blood smeared across his jacket from a gunshot wound. Around him lay dead men, men that Edward recognized. The Frenchman stared, gaping at the blue sky, chest shattered, life wrenched from him. Edward yanked back on the reins and brought the horse to a sudden halt. Throwing himself off its back, he kept a grip on the reins, determined to reach Corin and get him to safety. The horse defied his strength and wrenched itself free, galloping away as soldiers cried out muffled warnings that Edward could barely hear. *Cease fire! Cease fire! Cavalry!*

Edward scrambled frantically towards the fallen Irishman. The ground trembled from the approaching cavalrymen, who were suddenly among them, sabres slashing down into the retreating men. Edward hauled Corin to his feet, and saw horsemen bearing down on him. There was a revolver tucked in Corin's belt. Edward snatched it, losing his grip on the young Irishman as he fumbled with the cumbersome Webley pistol. Grasping it in both trembling hands he pulled back the knurled hammer, pointed the barrel at the trooper who bore down on them, sword arm raised, chest exposed. He fired.

The heavy-calibre .45's recoil snapped through his wrists and forearm, almost making him drop the weapon – as did the sudden horror of killing a man. The horse had veered, and the rider smashed into the ground barely yards from them. Fear gave Edward strength as he tried to drag the groaning Corin away. The young Irishman staggered to his feet as Edward realized another horsemen was almost upon them. He twisted away but the horse struck him, and as he fell back he saw the sabre slash down, cut through Corin's neck from ear to shoulder, severing his head.

Edward screamed as the dead man staggered on for another yard, spurting blood splashing the ground. He turned and blindly fired again at the cavalrymen who wheeled their horses left and right. One of them fell as the bullet struck him in the face. Another trooper, seeing him standing defiantly, spurred his horse around, pulling the reins, wrenching the horse towards Edward. The man's bush hat had blown free. It was Belmont. There was no violence or rage in his face. His eyes locked on the boy, his body bent to urge on his horse. Tears stung Edward's eyes as terror took an even firmer grip on him. He was going to die. He pulled the trigger. And missed. The gun exploded two, three times more as he shot wildly at Belmont. One of the bullets tore the tunic of his sword arm, but no blossoming blood rose appeared. Sunlight caught the blade, making it shimmer in the glare. The horse whinnied; the swordsman grunted with effort. Blood pounded in Edward's ears as the muffled screams and cries of battle receded into a distant place in his mind. He half turned his body, arm extended, aiming directly at Belmont's chest, and felt the gun explode.

Edward's world fell silent.

The single gunshot echoed.

CHAPTER TWENTY-TWO

The lone trooper following Sheenagh O'Connor recoiled in shock. A gunshot's echo rolled back on itself as its sound bounced from the rock face. Far below him in the heat haze he saw the buggy's horse startle. The woman he had diligently followed slumped a second after her head whipped back.

'Fuck!' he muttered, and pulled his carbine from its sleeve. He urged his horse downhill, his eyes sweeping the tumbledown rocks to his left where the shot must have come from. The buggy's horse had momentarily spooked, started forward a few yards and then stopped, uncertain now that no one held its reins in check. Marlowe spurred his mount, laying himself low across its mane in case he became a target. As he reached the buggy the carriage horse took fright again, and he quickly grabbed the trailing rein, forcing his own mount alongside. Using the horses for cover he slid down, peered across his saddle to scan the broken hillside for the sniper. Nothing moved. Dutchies? Would they kill a woman who helped them? he wondered. A quick glance at the sprawled body and staring face of Sheenagh O'Connor told him she was dead. The bullet had smashed into her chest. He waited, letting his eyes catch any peripheral movement, and without looking down tugged free his field telescope from its pouch. The horses snuffled, their ears raised, heads turning towards the outcrop nearly five hundred yards away. He swung the glass and caught sight of the figure that clambered through the shadows, rifle in hand, to where a horse was tethered under cover of a thorn tree. He held the glass steady until he knew without doubt who the sniper was.

There was no point shouting a challenge. The rider had not looked back, most likely had not seen him. The doubt gnawed at him a moment longer. He was going to be questioned by the provost and the shit would get deeper. Captain Belmont had given him his orders and he'd rather go through the mill with stiff-arsed rear echelon officers than face Belmont's wrath. A breeze whispered a small devil wind across the plain, ruffling the girl's dress, exposing her petticoats. Trooper Marlowe tied his horse to the rear of the buggy and clambered up, lifting the slight girl in his arms. He laid her down and then cut a length from the rope each man carried to make a shelter from their groundsheet. He carefully bound her dress so that the breeze would not lift her skirts. She may have been a whore but now she was a dead whore and there was no need for anyone in town to be gawking at the poor girl's underclothes. He settled her body and straightened the bonnet so that her hair was tucked away. As his calloused fingers closed her eyes he felt a sense of regret. There'd be no beer or quick fuck now.

An hour later he guided the buggy back through the streets of Bergfontein. Passers-by stopped when they saw the girl's body and turned to follow. By the time he reached the camp commandant's office the corporal of the guard had summoned the young Lancashire regiment lieutenant, who in turn ordered that Sheenagh O'Connor's body be taken to the mortuary tent. He saw Evelyn Charteris pushing through the onlookers and quickly forced a path through to her.

'Mrs Charteris, there's no need for you to see this,' he said kindly.

'It's Sheenagh's carriage. Where is she?'

'She has been shot. Fatally, I'm sorry to say.'

'But… she was here, only a few hours ago. What happened? Who shot her?' Evelyn asked, unable to grasp that the girl was dead; then, as she strengthened her resolve: 'I want to see her,' she said.

The lieutenant hesitated for only a moment; there was no point in arguing with her. He ushered her through the crowd and followed the soldiers who carried the dead girl into the mortuary tent. There were a dozen other bodies in the tent, mostly women and children who had died in the camp, but also two soldiers who had succumbed to enteric fever. They lay in rough wooden coffins, ready for burial. Under the watchful eye of the lieutenant they laid Sheenagh's body down carefully. He nodded the soldiers away.

'Mrs Charteris, the trooper found her on the Verensberg road.'

She turned her gaze away from the dead girl. 'Verensberg? She was riding for the Cape Town train. Why would she go back there?' she said.

The lieutenant answered her with his own question. 'Why would she not? Why Cape Town? Was she on the run?'

Evelyn quickly covered the truth. 'No, she had had enough of the life she led. She wanted a fresh start.'

The lieutenant considered her answer. This was a dead whore, not the general's wife. There was little point in pursuing the matter. That would be up to his colonel.

'Colonel Thompson will question the man who found her. Do you wish to stay here with… the girl?'

She nodded. Death was already withering Sheenagh's face – a face that no longer showed blushed cheeks and that vibrant smile. Blood and vomit had spilled down from her half-open mouth. Her skin sagged and the crumpled body bore little resemblance to the young woman who had bravely helped those in need and who bore her own life of prostitution with resigned acceptance.

'I'll wash her,' Evelyn said.

The lieutenant turned and left the tent. Evelyn took a pail of water and cloth and began to wipe Sheenagh's face. Beyond the thousands of tents she knew there might have been a greater slaughter if the ambush had been successful, but for now this death was enough to bear.

Trooper Marlowe stood to attention in front of the ageing camp commandant, who perspired beneath his tight tunic. Colonel Reginald Thompson still regretted his regiment had been posted from India to help administer this war. India would have afforded him servants and a punkah-wallah to sit giving gentle, rhythmic tugs on a string attached to a fan, to keep the infernal heat moving. There were coolies in Natal, down in Durban, but not up here in this bloody hot basin of a wasteland, and as far as he was concerned the natives were only fit for lifting and carrying. And they stank. Wouldn't have one in the same building, let alone his office. And now this. A murder on his doorstep. Bad enough he was trying to do his best for the wretched Boer women and children, a task too great with insufficient resources.

The company sergeant major stood motionless at the door, shoulders braced as Colonel Thompson listened to Marlowe's account. The CSM had heard tall stories before but an officer killing a whore in broad daylight was a gem. A right bloody gem. Not that he'd blab in the sergeants' mess. Not until the news flashed around the army like a bloody veld fire. Then he could tell the others how he had been in the room when the murder was first reported.

'You are certain?' demanded the colonel.

'Sir,' answered Marlowe, affirming what he had witnessed, his eyes staring unwaveringly at the picture on the wall behind the colonel's head. A woven tapestry of a rose-covered thatched cottage. Not like the broken down hovel he'd been raised in. Bloody officers and their la-di-da wives who had nothing better to do than embroider pretty pictures for their husbands.

'You understand the seriousness of the matter?'

'Sir,' Marlowe answered again, thinking how bloody stupid it would be to think otherwise. He could have left the girl out there, said he'd seen nothing, and then had Belmont on his case. Sod that. He saw what he saw.

'I see. And Captain Belmont specifically ordered you on this detail?'

'That he did, sir. Told me to follow the whore . . . the girl . . . and to report everything that I saw to General Reece-Sullivan at HQ.'

Colonel Thompson thought it through. Somewhere in this mess might be a way of easing the situation in his own command.

'Quite. Well, that you will do. Captain Belmont obviously had his reasons for your orders. You will report to General Reece-Sullivan at Field HQ and I will send a telegraph advising him of the matter. You will accompany Mrs Charteris to him there.'

Marlowe dropped his gaze. He had not heard of this woman.

'She is a woman of conscience,' explained the colonel.

Marlowe's eyes snapped back to the embroidered illusion.

'And she knew the dead girl. Was visited often by her. A whore and a Christian lady. An unlikely combination, I grant you, but war brings the strangest of people together.' He nodded to the CSM. Enough was enough. He could wash his hands of this affair and rid himself of the troublesome Mrs Charteris at the same time.

It was a solemn, virtually silent journey as Marlowe guided the buggy across the harsh plain towards the British Army's Field Headquarters at Swartberg, Evelyn sitting at his side, staring at the seemingly endless wasteland. Few words had passed between the travellers: both wished they had not been ordered to undertake the journey and only the grinding iron-clad wheels broke the silence. Thoughts of Sheenagh being slain in that very seat chilled Evelyn. Soldiers had washed away the blood but for the first ten miles she could scarcely bear to let her back press against it. Fatigue and the relentless hush eventually rendered her as callous as the colonel, who had insisted that there was no choice about the buggy: there were no other carriages available to transport her to General Reece-Sullivan's HQ.

The good news was that Swartberg would be a fairly safe haven as the British were massing troops there for the push north, and if Marlowe were lucky Captain Belmont would be there after his attack on the train. He was keen to rejoin his troop but knew that he would have to face questioning from the stern, unyielding General Reece-Sullivan first. The sooner he got that over with the better but he wished he could whip the horses on faster. The slow speed of the uncomfortable buggy frustrated him. He preferred to spur a horse forward at a gallop, not proceed at this pedestrian, arse-aching pace, as though he were little more than a hansom-cab driver. The buggy's hood was up, which helped against the sun's glare. He spat dust unapologetically from his mouth. What a godforsaken country. Harsh, rock-strewn veld that could turn into a quagmire when heavy rains fell. He glowered at the shimmering mountains, eyes straining from the glare. Something moved, he thought, but he couldn't be sure. He eased back on the reins.

'What is it?' Evelyn asked, jolted from her reverie.

Trooper Marlow reached for his carbine. 'There,' he said, squinting even more, letting his instincts tell him whether danger lay ahead. Then she too saw the shimmer move. Evelyn stood up, despite Marlow's warning, shielding her eyes as she heard the man's voice plead for help, his arm raised, holding a rifle aloft to attract their attention.

'I know him,' she told Marlow, recognizing the dark figure.

Pierce was near exhaustion when the buggy reached him. They gave him water and wheeled the buggy around to retrieve his saddle from the dead horse. He made no mention of the intended ambush in front of the soldier, who was wary of having an armed African sitting on the luggage rack behind him, even though his back would be turned to them; he demanded Pierce hand over his weapons. Evelyn defended him, but Pierce was too weary to care and surrendered them, and then sat on the carriage's tailgate facing Trooper Marlowe's tethered horse as it trotted behind.

A battle had been fought miles away. He had heard no gunfire but the distant whistle of an engine had told him all he needed to know. Its triumphant tooting heralded success for the British and slaughter for their enemies. He had failed his friend by not reaching the rendezvous, but like any man used to the uncertainty of war he knew in his heart that in the end it would have made no difference.

CHAPTER TWENTY-THREE

Claude Belmont sat with his feet dangling over the edge of the flatbed railcar. The engine had been shifted into reverse and now sped along towards the British Army Field HQ. In the boxcars behind him the soldiers had cheered, releasing their exuberance at the victory over the Boers. Now he sat like the figurehead on a great ship rolling across an open sea, an unemotional expression chiselled on his features that showed no sense of satisfaction in a well-executed plan bearing fruition. He puffed his cheroot, savouring the sweet smoke in his lungs. Anything could happen in a close-quarter fight and some of his men lay dead in the boxcars behind those raucous soldiers. They'd quieten down soon enough, he knew that. For many of them it was their first big kill. They had fooled around when they were first ordered to don women's clothing, guffawing and uttering playful and crude comments – as one would expect – until the company NCOs shut them up. It was a damned pheasant shoot at the end of the day. And Sheenagh O'Connor had played right into his hands. It would be a shame to testify against her and see her dragged into prison – if she were that lucky.

Belmont leaned back and let the air cool him. It swept over him, brushing away the stench of death, but it also heralded a return to the garrison and the demands from those of higher rank that would bear down on him. Reports would be written and questions asked about the whore. And as far as the ambush was concerned there would be questions as to whether rules of war had been broken, whether the wounded had been cared for. Why shoot to kill and then nurse those who did not die immediately? he questioned privately. He was a field officer, a cavalryman who ate and slept with only one desire: to seek out and destroy his enemy. He tossed the cheroot's stub away. He had played this game as best he could. They had dispatched enough of those badly wounded and brought others back for treatment. He could play their game if he had to. Show willing. Anything to cover the cracks in officialdom and allow the staff officers to swear before the do-gooders in parliament that honour had been maintained in the field of conflict.

What had surprised him, though, was the Radcliffe boy being in the fray. How in God Almighty had the lad got himself there? A Fenian brat after all, perhaps? It would make a good story if it could be believed. The American's son far from home, fighting for the Foreign Brigade. Christ, that'd set the cat among the pigeons back in Dublin. The lad's father would be hauled away and that'd be that. Good riddance to those who helped his enemy. He swilled water from his canteen, spat it free into the slipstream and tipped the remainder over his head, pulling his fingers through his hair, wiping a hand across his stubbled, sunburned face.

Killing was the only reason to go to war and war was the only reason to live.

Several miles behind the train bodies lay scattered among the stones of the plain. Some were twisted in grotesque positions, a leg tucked under the body, an arm flung above the head as if shot down in a macabre dance of death. The heat had already dried their blood into the hard-baked ground as flies settled into their wounds and feasted on any moisture left in their blind eyes.

Radcliffe gazed across the scene. It was as if the hand of God had swept across the field of pain and flattened these men with one crippling blow. The great Irish horse that had borne him here so quickly stood quivering from exhaustion, chest heaving, nearly dead from fatigue. Radcliffe had spared neither his horse nor himself. He trembled as he walked, uncertainly picking his way through the carnage from body to body, searching for Edward.

As each corpse revealed itself to be that of a stranger, Radcliffe quickened his pace, daring to hope that his son was not among the fallen. He was blind to any movement and deaf to any sound as he prayed to an uncaring God to grant him mercy and the life of his boy. The slow metallic double-click of a bolt-action rifle touched a deeper instinct than that of prayer, and he spun on his heel, reaching for the pistol at his side. A big man stood casually aiming his rifle from the hip. His belly pressed against the rough woollen waistcoat and homespun jacket that hugged his muscled frame. Without taking his eyes off Radcliffe he spat a globule of chewing tobacco into the dirt.

'We've been watching you,' an American voice said.

Radcliffe felt a surge of relief as he heard an accent that took him back to a place far from the massacre. 'I'm Joseph Radcliffe, and I'm looking for my son.'

Jackson Lee lowered his rifle. 'We know who you are.' He turned and began walking towards the rocks at the foot of the kopje. Radcliffe followed him between a cleft in the rocks where he saw spent cartridge cases. Someone had fired from here into the killing ground. Boer or British? he wondered. Another twenty yards of edging around boulders brought the two men to an open, flat piece of ground that made a good encampment. Barely a dozen gaunt-faced men glared at him. He'd seen that look on men's faces before, when horror had pierced their souls and fear strangled their hearts. Horses were tethered and four wagons stood empty at the head of a track that Radcliffe realized was the way in and out from this rocky enclave.

'We can't bury our dead,' said one man from the corner of the camp as he laid a final stone on to a mound. His Irish accent was tinged with a matter-of-fact regret.

Radcliffe scanned the men. The Foreign Brigade. Irish and American, he knew that much at least. There'd be others. And Boers no doubt. This must have been a small commando. What? Two hundred men? Less? Before they got wiped out, that is.

The man at the grave hammered a crude cross made from ammunition box wood into the ground. 'Not out there. Kith and kin we can dig in here. The others stay for the scavengers.'

Radcliffe looked at the men who remained silent. They were a beaten bunch of fighters.

'How many did you lose?' he asked the man at the graveside.

Liam Maguire threw down the rock he had used to hammer in the cross. 'Sixty out there. Another forty-odd a mile from here. Dutchies mostly back there. Our own, some French, German and Boers out there by the rail line.'

'Seems your man here knows who I am,' said Radcliffe, looking towards Jackson Lee.

Liam ignored Radcliffe's comment. 'Jesus, they shot the hell out of us. Popped up they did. A terrible thing. Then they chased us like rabbits. We held our own for a bit. They weren't gonna risk losing men for a handful of us, were they?' he said, picking up his rifle and using it as a walking aid. Radcliffe noticed the bloody bandage strapped around his middle.

'Aye, I know who you are,' said the wounded Maguire, tugging a piece of folded paper from inside his jacket. He stepped closer and extended it to Radcliffe with a hand ingrained with dried blood and dirt.

Radcliffe half opened the old newspaper cutting by its crease. Most of the text was smudged from dirt and other dark stains but there was a clear enough photograph of him. The article's broken typeface peeked half-seen from the grubby folds: *AMERI LAWY DEFENDS FENIA*.

'Says there who y'are. And what ya did. I could recite the whole bloody thing if you asked me. Some nights out here ya get desperate enough to read a torn bit of paper from the *Dublin Evening Mail*. We passed it around. Me and the lads.'

'Where did you get this?' said Radcliffe.

'From yer boy. It was your name that saved him from us shooting him as a spy. Looked to be a year or two younger than my slip of a brother, who's buried back there,' said Liam, nodding towards the grave, seeing the light of hope in Radcliffe's eyes. 'You'd best prepare yourself for a shock, Mr Radcliffe. About your lad. I'm sorry. He tried to save my Corin. But he couldn't. God bless him for trying, mind.'

The skirl of bagpipes rent the air as a battalion from the Highland Division marched out of the Swartberg HQ encampment. The Scottish troops' swirling kilts were held in check by the khaki aprons they wore to subdue the bright colours of their tartans. As the pipes played 'Road to the Isles', troops cheered and waved the Jocks marching off to the front. In a less celebratory manner Radcliffe walked into the camp leading his exhausted and dust-laden horse. There was a five-foot-high wall that ran for several hundred yards – a defensive barrier between them and the open veld that soldiers patrolled. He was obliged to show his papers at the sentry post and was then allowed through as the rhythmic scuff of soldiers' boots marched past him. The camp was a cluster of tin buildings with criss-crossing boardwalks laid for the mud churned up by the violent rainstorms. There were stone-built stables that held grain and feed for the hundreds of horses that this war demanded and further up the track longhorn cattle were corralled – fresh meat for the troops. Radcliffe led his horse past field kitchens laboured in by Africans and army cooks while off-duty soldiers lazed in front of their tents: some smoked; others sat heads bowed writing letters or reading. From somewhere in the distance a concertina squeezed out the rousing notes of 'Soldiers of the Queen'. Radcliffe realized that these men were fresh troops, and were obviously being gathered for the next big push. Bell tents, rifles stacked in front of each entrance, spread out towards the rail track that cut through the camp.

Radcliffe headed for the stables, avoiding marching squads of men as work details unloaded supplies from the railhead yard. An African wearing a floppy broad-brimmed hat loped towards him carrying a pail of water that slopped as he ran. Mhlangana faltered when he saw the exhausted dust-caked man and horse, but quickly offered Radcliffe a ladle of water.

'*Inkosi*,' Mhlangana said. '*Sawubona*, I see you. Drink. Let me help you.'

Radcliffe gazed at the concerned African, for a moment not recognizing him from their previous encounter. Exhaustion had slowed his thoughts, but he quickly gulped the water as his horse dipped its head into the pail and slurped noisily. 'Thank you,' he said.

'*Inkosi*, you have seen more killing?' asked Mhlangana, sensing that it was more than tiredness etched on Radcliffe's face.

'Enough for a lifetime,' Radcliffe answered. 'And I wish never to see it again.' He smiled grimly.

Mhlangana nodded. 'There is an African proverb, *inkosi*: "Human blood is heavy, and the man who has shed it cannot run from it."' He looked with compassion at Pierce's friend.

The words rang true. Radcliffe had spilled enough blood in his time to know of such haunting.

'Take my horse. Find him a dark corner where it's cool and give him more water. Can you get him some feed?' Radcliffe asked.

'Yes, *inkosi*,' said Mhlangana.

'Is my friend here?'

'Mr Pierce? No. I have not seen him.'

Radcliffe nodded, and touched the horse's face with affection. 'Look after him well, Mhlangana. Where is the field hospital?'

Mhlangana took the horse's rein. 'Through the tents across there, into the old farm buildings and the sheds. That is where they have the wounded. I will take your horse to the stable and care for him. I will wait there and watch in case Mr Pierce comes here. Will he come, *inkosi*?'

'I don't know. I hope so.'

Radcliffe made his way wearily through the tented area towards the cluster of buildings. What had once been an old railway shed was now a vast hospital ward where orderlies and a handful of nurses attended to the wounded men who lay in four rows of palliasses, one each side and two head-to-head in the centre of the shed. Radcliffe watched as the handful of orderlies attended to the injured; then he stopped one who hurried past with a bundle of bloodied bandages.

'Where's the doctor in charge?'

The orderly hardly gave Radcliffe a second look. Despite his appearance his voice carried the authority of an officer. 'Through that door at the end. There's another small ward. He's in there.'

Radcliffe walked along the ranks of the sick. The fighting had been on various fronts, but this looked as though the British had taken a recent beating. Many of the men would never see war again, and some would not see the next day. He pushed through the door that led to a smaller room with no more than twenty-odd stretchers balanced on boxes, makeshift beds bolstered with a blanket beneath each man in a bid to offer some small comfort. An armed guard stood on the other side of the door. He was an older man, probably a non-combatant, but he turned quickly to face the intruder.

'No entry here, sir, if you please.'

Radcliffe looked past him to where a tall grey-haired man, pince-nez spectacles pinching the bridge of his hooked nose, studied the chart of a wounded man. A Boer. This was the prison ward.

'I'm here to see the doctor,' Radcliffe said, scanning the beds. 'I think my son's here.'

'Not here, sir. No, I think you're mistaken. This is for Dutchies, this room is. Prisoners of war.'

The doctor had raised his head at the intrusion and handed the chart back to the orderly. 'Who are you?' he asked.

Radcliffe removed his hat. 'My name is Joseph Radcliffe. I believe my son was brought here, perhaps by Captain Belmont's troops after a recent action. My boy is sixteen years old, dark hair, and he's tall for his age. Which might make people think he is older. His name is Edward.'

The older man extended his hand. 'I'm Amery. I know your name. Not too popular among some back home, Mr Radcliffe.'

'No.'

'It's not my business to ask of the circumstances but I have your boy under my care. Do you know of his injuries?'

'He's alive then?' said Radcliffe, hope pushing weariness aside.

The doctor scowled. 'You had better know, Mr Radcliffe, that he suffered a grievous wound. It's my opinion that infection and shock might still take him. He is unconscious. We are doing the best we can.'

'What kind of wound?' Radcliffe asked, swallowing hard, being no stranger to mutilation.

'Sabre. It took his arm between wrist and elbow.'

Radcliffe saw the blade in his mind's eye. He knew the viciousness of a sabre. How many times had he swung down his own into an enemy and seen the vicious cut inflicted? He nodded, understanding.

Amery took him by the arm and guided him. 'He's in the corner.'

Radcliffe stood at the foot of the makeshift bed and gazed down at the gaunt, unconscious Edward. He turned to Amery. 'May I stay?'

'Of course,' he said gently, and gestured to an orderly to bring a stool. 'For a short while only, I'm afraid.'

Radcliffe nodded. 'Thank you.'

As Amery turned away Radcliffe could restrain himself no longer. He bent forward and eased his son into his arms and held him, as he would a small child. Amery looked back and saw Radcliffe's shoulders tremble as he let every regret spill out.

Mhlangana brushed the dirt-laden horse with hard, long strokes that made the big Irish horse shiver. A nosebag full of oats contented the great beast. Across the horse's withers he saw a buggy carrying a white woman and a soldier come to a halt outside the building the British General Reece-Sullivan used as his headquarters. At the rear of the carriage, half-obscured by a trailing horse, Benjamin Pierce eased himself down on to the ground. Evelyn Charteris had told the sentry at the camp's gate that the African was a scout. Marlowe said nothing. He didn't care about an African friend of the conchie-loving woman, and had no desire to become more embroiled than he already was. So he kept his mouth shut. Let the darkie be whatever he wanted to be. The sooner he made his report, the sooner he could rejoin Captain Belmont.

Mhlangana could not help smiling when he saw Pierce, who said something to the woman and then strode into the street carrying his rifle and saddle, looking directly to where Radcliffe's horse was tethered. Mhlangana waited in the stable's shadows, uncertain whether to show that he knew this big man who carried his own weapon. Pierce grinned when he reached him, dropped the saddle and embraced the man who had helped them at Tugela. Mhlangana winced.

'My brother, I see you,' said Mhlangana.

The two men shook hands. 'I see you, Mhlangana.' Pierce saw the slight stoop of a man who's been beaten and is trying to ease the burden of the shirt on his back. 'You hurt?'

'It is nothing,' said Mhlangana.

Pierce turned him half around. He could see the top of the welts behind Mhlangana's collar. 'The British whip you?' he asked.

Mhlangana nodded. 'For helping you with the gun. I told you, we are not permitted to fight.'

'Then why help?'

'The English will beat us, but the Boer, he would shoot us. Blacks mean nothing to them. They are our real foe: we are blood enemies. The English are harsh but the Boers do not even see us. Who would you choose to help?'

'Damned if I know,' said Pierce. 'Is Joseph Radcliffe here?'

'He is already here, yes.'

'Is there anyone with him? A boy?'

'No, there is no one. But your friend, he came a long way and he has the eyes of a man who has seen a bad thing. A very bad thing. He has gone to the hospital.'

'Did the train bring in wounded?'

'Yes. But they were not English. They were Boers.'

Pierce sighed. Radcliffe must have ridden hard to no avail. Mhlangana had confirmed Pierce's realization of what had happened. The ambush had been successful but perhaps Edward was alive, otherwise Radcliffe would not be searching the hospital. 'Best I stay out of sight until I know what's happening. Can you get me some food?'

They had allowed Radcliffe less than an hour with his son, but there was little use in him staying while Amery and the nurses attended to the boy. There was nowhere for Radcliffe to sit and wait and despite his anxiety the reality of his hunger and thirst finally prompted him to seek out food. As he walked across the dusty street, now empty of marching soldiers, a small group of cavalry approached, their horses at an easy walk, cluttered, not in formation – a group of men going back up the line. Radcliffe stopped and turned in the middle of the street. He had recognized their leader. It was Belmont and his marauders.

Pierce took the last bite of an apple as he leaned against the stable door's rough wood and glanced down the street. He saw Radcliffe stop. Pierce tossed the apple core away and without taking his eyes from the unfolding scene called out softly to the African: 'Mhlangana, fetch my rifle. Quickly now.'

The horsemen came into view and then halted a dozen strides from where his friend stood.

Pierce ran his tongue over his teeth. There would be a shit storm if Radcliffe attacked Belmont. And both Radcliffe and Pierce could either be dead in the next few minutes or in front of a firing squad by next morning. Military justice would be swift. He took the weapon from a concerned Mhlangana and eased a round into its chamber. Outside, nothing seemed to move. Belmont sat at the head of the phalanx of his men watching Radcliffe. Neither man reached for a weapon. Flies buzzed and settled. Horses shook their heads, rattling bit and bridle. Belmont looked unconcerned as he studied the man he knew to be his enemy although, if the American was here in Swartberg, perhaps Radcliffe knew what had happened at the ambush.

'Your boy chose the wrong side,' Belmont said. 'Seems the puppy slipped its lead.'

Radcliffe realized in that moment that it had to have been Belmont who ambushed the train. He made no gesture or threat but neither did he move. Perhaps, Pierce thought, Radcliffe was daring Belmont to pass him. If such was the case then Pierce reasoned that Radcliffe would not let him. Radcliffe's hand moved slowly to the butt of his pistol, a small gesture that did not go unnoticed by Belmont. The edge of Belmont's mouth creased slightly in a restrained smile of understanding. So be it.

'The lad had a mind to kill me. He has courage – anyone can see that. I took his arm not his life. Consider him lucky.'

Radcliffe saw the man's eyes glint. Here and now. They would finish it in this street. He grasped Belmont's reins, pistol half cleared; Belmont wrenched them free, his fist curled around his sabre's hilt. For a few brief heartbeats it was as if each man sought the advantage. Radcliffe sidestepped and levelled the revolver, but Belmont's men pressed forward as their captain brought his horse back under control.

Pierce's thumb had already pulled back the rifle's hammer and tensioned the rear trigger when the door of the building across the street opened and General Reece-Sullivan's aide-de-camp came out and quickly took in the stand-off. Whatever was going on between these two men was not clear but it was apparent that violence would soon erupt. He clattered down the few steps to the street and stood a few paces from Radcliffe's shoulder.

'Mr Radcliffe, sir. General Reece-Sullivan's compliments.' He waited a moment but neither Belmont nor Radcliffe looked away from the other. Belmont's sabre was now in his hand; Radcliffe's gun hand did not waver. A cold-blooded killing in the main street would lead to a certain conviction. The aide-de-camp tried again with a more insistent tone. 'Sir. General Reece-Sullivan would very much appreciate it if you would join him in his office. Now, Mr Radcliffe.'

Radcliffe's aim and gaze stayed on Belmont. It was Evelyn Charteris's voice that broke the spell.

'Joseph.'

Radcliffe turned, surprised to see her, and then glanced at the aide-de-camp, as if registering his presence for the first time. The aide-de-camp dipped his head respectfully.

'*Major* Radcliffe. If you please, sir, would you accompany me?'

Radcliffe lowered his revolver. 'You've injured my son twice, Belmont. I will come for you and I will kill you for it.'

Without another word he stepped past the aide-de-camp and strode towards Evelyn, who waited at the door, her concern eased by his approach.

Pierce lowered his rifle. He had sighted on the man who rode behind Belmont, knowing Belmont would be Radcliffe's target. He sighed with relief. They had been a squeeze of a trigger away from sudden violence.

Belmont eased his horse forward at the walk past the aide-de-camp, who followed a respectful stride behind Radcliffe as he approached Evelyn. She took his hands in her own. Her warmth seeped into him and he felt a surge of gratitude for her presence. Evelyn held his eyes with her own, beseeching him to remain calm.

'Joseph. Thank God. We brought in Mr Pierce,' she said quietly.

'He's here? Is he hurt?'

'No. We've only just got here. His horse broke a leg. It was fortunate we saw him.'

Radcliffe looked around quickly. There was no obvious sign of Pierce. 'Why are you here?'

She grimaced and shook her head. 'Sheenagh O'Connor was shot and killed after she left us at Bergfontein. They've arrested an English officer. Captain Belmont had her followed and his trooper witnessed the killing.'

'Belmont? And the officer?'

'Major Taylor.'

Radcliffe tried to put a face to the name but could not.

'Did you find your son?' she asked.

'He's in the field hospital. Belmont's ambush was a success. My boy lost half his arm.'

Evelyn Charteris did not flinch. She saw Radcliffe's anxiety and squeezed his hands tighter still. 'You're wanted, inside. I'll stay with your son.'

Radcliffe pulled her to him instinctively, his lips touching her forehead. Despite the heat and dust he was aware of the scent of her and it gave him a longing for her. Embarrassed, he released her. Her smile told him there was no need for forgiveness. He nodded his thanks as the aide-de-camp held the door open.

As Radcliffe was escorted inside the building, Evelyn walked briskly across to the stables and was quickly concealed by its cool shadows. She looked vainly for Pierce, but saw another African who kept his head down as he cleaned a stall, only glancing up to watch she was not followed, and then signalled with his head that she should look to her left.

'Mrs Charteris,' Pierce said as he stepped from behind stacked bales of hay.

Evelyn whispered quickly: 'Mr Pierce, I heard orders given in the general's office that Mr Radcliffe is to be held under armed escort. More than that I do not know. Edward is badly injured. A sabre took his arm.' She saw the news of the injury register in his eyes. 'Stay here. Do not attempt to approach him, otherwise you too will be in jeopardy. I will do what I can.' She smiled in encouragement at Pierce's stern look of concern. 'Good luck to us all, Mr Pierce.'

She turned quickly and was soon out of sight.

Pierce felt his guts squirm. Edward was badly injured. Surely the British would send the boy home. And why would they hold Radcliffe?

CHAPTER TWENTY-FOUR

The general's room was large, with a broad desk straddling the centre of the room. Woven rugs added a blood-red warmth to the polished planks. Along one side of the wall trestle tables bore rolls of maps, and stretched across one wall was a large waxed map, broad enough for three men to stand in front of, and high enough to require a stick to point out details. It was a permanent fixture with small tagged flags positioned here and there: some clustered together, others spread out in lines of varying colours that clearly indicated different regiments in the field. It was a fine map, drawn and printed with skill by craftsmen in England. It showed shaded foothills of mountain ranges that curved from the bottom left corner of the map and snaked their way across the coloured landscape. The symbolic ladder lines of a railway track cut across the expansive plain through the foothills and disappeared off the edge. Oil lamps hung from the ceiling and were placed strategically around the room. The British high command were obliged to work through the hours of darkness as they planned their attack on the Boer army. There was electric light, but they could not afford to let a power failure hinder their planning.

General Reece-Sullivan stood in front of the wall map, a cigarette burning between his fingers. His back was to the door when Radcliffe entered the room. Three other staff officers were present, bent over an unfurled map on one of the trestle tables. They glanced in Radcliffe's direction and then went back to their studies.

'Sir,' said the aide-de-camp. 'Major Joseph Radcliffe.'

Reece-Sullivan ignored his officer for a moment longer, and then turned to face the man he had summoned. Reece-Sullivan was a dapper man, with a trimmed grey moustache and neatly parted hair. His slight frame suggested the body of a younger man but Radcliffe had read somewhere that Reece-Sullivan was an experienced officer and a favoured general of the commander-in-chief. For a moment Reece-Sullivan studied Radcliffe, before moving to the desk where he raised a china cup and saucer and took a sip of tea.

'A courtesy rank, Mr Radcliffe? Major?'

'The courtesy afforded by my friends in the British Army, general.'

'Former US Cavalry, so I'm told. A courtesy that is rightly earned,' he conceded.

Radcliffe knew there was every likelihood that he would be held in custody now that he had been allowed into the general's office and seen the deployment of troops indicated on the wall map. The British were moving north in a pincer movement. The Boer army in this theatre of war would be trapped.

Reece-Sullivan noticed him glance at the wall map. 'You came through the lines?'

'Yes.'

The general lifted the cup to his lips again, and then rolled them together to dry them so that he would not moisten the end of his cigarette. He drew in a lungful of smoke and turned to the map. 'The Boers are converging with thousands of men at the head of this valley. It's a desperate gamble on their part. We're hurting them badly now. But this' – he gestured with the cup towards the battle plan – 'will finish them. I believe you have already witnessed one of our minor successes. A train ambush. Near enough a hundred or so killed. An excellent result by one of our cavalry officers. Chap called Belmont. I think you might know him. From what I hear you had a bit of a run-in back in Dublin, before the Irish embarked.'

Radcliffe realized that his presence in South Africa had prompted the British to look into his background. It was not difficult to sense the veiled animosity here. A liberal American lawyer caught up in an imperial war was bound to raise some suspicions. He took another step closer to the desk and the man who might have the power of life and death over Edward.

'General, I'd like to speak to you about my son.'

Reece-Sullivan turned and faced the map again, admiring his own strategic skill. 'We have the Irish, reinforced by the Highland Division, across these mountains here. It'll be like a game drive. A pheasant shoot. We're beating them down towards us. Then they'll be under our guns. And Belmont's raiders will slash into their rear flank. Though their commando units are fluid. Moving quickly. We can't quite pin down their movements.' He looked at Radcliffe.

'I can't help you with intelligence reports from the field.'

Reece-Sullivan arched his eyebrows, the cup faltering before it reached his lips. 'I don't expect you to.'

'Then why tell me of your plans?' Radcliffe glanced at the armed guard who stood at the door. 'Am I under arrest?'

Reece-Sullivan replaced the empty cup and saucer on his desk. He fingered some documents into a neater line so they were perfectly parallel with the fountain pen to one side. 'Arrest? No. I doubt you'll wish to be anywhere else other than with your son. There's little danger of you escaping. You'll be held under escort. Until the battle is over. You can have access to your son, with supervision. Of course you will surrender your weapons.'

'I'm not your enemy, general,' said Radcliffe. 'I'm here for my son, that's all.'

'Radcliffe,' said the general, deliberately ignoring his honorary rank, 'as a lawyer you have known association with the Irish Fenians.'

'As a lawyer. Due process, general, the backbone of British law. I also helped the Irish Regiment of Foot take the hills at Tugela. Alex Baxter was my friend.'

'Duly noted. Lieutenant Baxter is now a brevet major, by the way. I'm sorry, Radcliffe, but your son's circumstances dictate my actions.'

'Circumstances? He's badly wounded.'

'So are twenty-four officers and more than two hundred and fifty of our men. Your son was lucky that we have the services of civilian surgeons who generously volunteer for months at a time. They give their service selflessly for a token payment of a pound a day. Sir George Amery is first rate.'

Radcliffe felt the weight of the general's power unsettle him. He lowered his voice and adopted a more conciliatory tone: 'General, I'd like to make arrangements for my son to return home.'

Reece-Sullivan tapped the edge of the piece of paper that was not quite tidy enough. 'Where is home?' he asked casually.

'I think you know the answer to that question. Dublin.'

The general nodded to the aide-de-camp, who poured two cut-glass snifters of brandy and then offered one of them to Radcliffe, who declined. Reece-Sullivan sat himself comfortably in the half-moon spindle-backed chair at his desk and accepted the crystal glass from his aide-de-camp. He raised it to his nose and sniffed appreciatively. He waited, watching Radcliffe.

'It's a fine brandy, Radcliffe. Not French. South African.

Damned decent it is too. And beggars can't be choosers in war, can they?'

Radcliffe knew the man had authority over him and his suggestion was little more than a taunt to make it clear who was in control. Radcliffe relented, took the brandy glass and sipped its warmth.

'This war has taught us enormously important lessons,' said the general. 'We have a great deal of respect for our enemy. We treat their wounded as we would our own. And they show the utmost courtesy to our casualties. War has rules.'

'Rules?' said Radcliffe.

'The discipline of war. You're an ex-cavalry officer, you understand that.'

'I understand you have men who shoot the wounded, who pillage farms and imprison women and children. There are few rules that are not broken in war, general. We both know that.'

'We deprive the enemy of home comfort, sanctuary and supplies. All within regulations.'

There was a sudden commotion outside the window as four soldiers manhandled a struggling Major Taylor. His top tunic button was missing, his face ruddy with exertion and humiliation.

'Get your hands off me! Leave me I say!' he shouted at his escort. His tunic was dusty; dirt clung to his cheeks and hair; his hands were manacled. It looked as though he had fallen or made an attempt at escape.

It was Sergeant McCory from the Royal Irish who barked an order at the officer: 'Behave yourself now, Major Taylor, sir! There's no escape to be had. Come along now, like a good gentleman!'

For a moment the officers in the room looked concerned as Taylor resisted and the men restraining him barely managed to keep him from breaking the window. Now Radcliffe remembered Taylor from the argument at the Dublin barracks. He was one of Belmont's cronies. Radcliffe saw that Private Mulraney was part of the detail and then Lawrence Baxter stepped into view and spoke quietly to the arrested man. Whatever he said calmed the situation and the escort hauled Taylor out of sight.

Radcliffe felt a brief surge of hope. If the Irish lads were here then perhaps Baxter might help him with Edward. At least put in a good word. The officers returned to their maps, their embarrassment at a fellow officer's untoward behaviour pushed from their minds. Best not discussed.

The incident didn't seem to ruffle Reece-Sullivan. 'You're wrong. No one under my command is immune from punishment... if those rules are broken. No favour is given. There can be no distinction between the ranks or a man's nationality when it comes to breaking those rules. None. If we lose discipline we yield to chaos and we peel away the veneer that separates man from beast.'

Radcliffe felt lightheaded from drinking the brandy on an empty stomach. For a moment he struggled to grasp any meaning from what had begun to sound like a lecture.

'I don't understand what this has to do with my son,' he said, pushing the glass and what was left of the brandy away from him on the desk.

'One of the fighters captured with your son wore a British Army tunic,' said the general.

Radcliffe felt the frustration of dealing with this prim officer. He barely managed to keep the contempt from his voice. 'They take them off dead soldiers. Most of the Boers are dirt farmers; their own clothes are threadbare.'

'The chief of staff, General Lord Kitchener, issued an order that any Boer caught wearing a British uniform was to be shot as a spy.'

Radcliffe pushed back the chair. 'For God's sake! Your high command issues an order that cannot possibly be known by the enemy in the field. How is a guerrilla fighter supposed to know that? They don't get newspapers in the wilderness. They are prisoners of war. Follow your own conscience, sir.' Radcliffe rapped the desktop with his knuckles, teeth gritted to cage the venom that threatened to spit out. 'My son was not wearing a uniform. I want to take him home.'

For the first time since Radcliffe had entered the room he saw colour seep up from the general's collar. His ill temper was under control, but he was quickly on his feet.

'His papers say he's English-born. An Englishman fighting his own kind. Even a noted lawyer like yourself would find that indefensible. It's treason.'

Chapter Twenty-Five

Pierce saw Radcliffe being escorted by an armed guard across the street. Radcliffe glanced quickly in his friend's direction. Two other soldiers were striding directly towards the stable.

'Goddammit,' Pierce muttered. He turned away from the door and stripped off his jacket and shirt so that he looked just like an African levy in undershirt and braces. He slid his rifle and sabre beneath the straw. Another twenty paces and the soldiers would be in the stable. Pierce went to the Irish horse, unhooked Radcliffe's sabre from the saddle and pulled free his rifle. He hesitated and slid the rifle back into its sleeve. If Radcliffe was under arrest then these soldiers were coming for his weapons; if they found none that would be suspicious. He quickly hid the sabre next to his own as the soldiers came inside.

'Oi!' one of the men said, pointing at Pierce, seeing him as nothing more than a native labourer. 'Where's the American's saddle?'

Pierce looked blank and, turning his back, hunched to his work of lifting straw bales. The soldier grabbed him, twisting him around. 'Kaffir! I'm talking to you.'

Mhlangana quickly stepped forward, putting aside the pitching fork he'd been using. '*Baas*, it's here. He doesn't speak English.' Then he turned to Pierce and spoke rapidly in Zulu. Pierce nodded as if in understanding. The soldier wrenched free Radcliffe's carbine and without another word left the stable.

The sun was already setting and the clear sky would bring a cold night with it. Mhlangana stood for a moment with Pierce and watched the soldiers cross the street.

'You will have to stay here tonight. You cannot go out among the soldiers; they will think you a thief and you will end up being tied to a gun wheel and flogged. You cannot help Mr Radcliffe until we find where they have taken him. I will ask my friends who work in the field kitchens. They will know.' There was nothing more to be said and the African turned back to the task at hand. Pierce went down on his haunches, pushing his back against the stable wall. He needed to watch the street and when the time came he would find Radcliffe and Edward.

General Reece-Sullivan watched Radcliffe being escorted to his quarters. Events had become untidy. An American lawyer whose name was known to the British public, hailed by the liberal press, often condemned by the rest, had stumbled upon his doorstep in search of a son who fought for the enemy. A damned fine mess, though no one would thank him for releasing anyone committing an act of treason. But a regular army officer committing murder and witnessed by a trooper: that could not be brushed under the carpet. Not now. Not with an eyewitness. The whole business was compounded by the Charteris woman. How much support did she have? Not much, but there was growing concern back home about the camps, and the army did not need bleeding-heart do-gooders raising their voices. Reece-Sullivan felt cursed by ill fortune at a time when he needed all the luck that Fate could muster. He was already deploying his forces to snare the Boers. His provost marshal was with another division and Major Taylor had been held by a sergeant major and two corporals of the Military Foot Police. In consideration of the accused man's rank he had ordered that an officer and detail from the Royal Irish should escort him into custody. The division was on the move and an act of murder had to be dealt with swiftly. A speedy resolution was vital. Military law dictated that a general court martial could be dispensed with if a major offensive was about to be launched, and that gave Reece-Sullivan the authority to convene a field court martial with himself as president and for two other officers of equal or senior rank to the accused to serve with him. Reece-Sullivan had put his decision into motion the moment he had received the cablegram from Bergfontein. Ill luck had seen to it that the telegraph lines were now down. Had the Boers cut the wires a day earlier then no such message explaining the details of the girl's death would have reached him and his hand would not have been forced: he would not have had to try a regular army officer. War was a cruel mistress.

Major Frederick Leslie Taylor had been brought into the general's office under escort. A corporal sat in the corner of the room to transcribe the events that would follow. A lieutenant colonel from a Scottish regiment and a major from the Lancers sat either side of Reece-Sullivan.

Taylor looked dishevelled. He had spent hours before his arrest poring over maps trying to determine how best to interpret what meagre intelligence he had gathered about the Boer forces. He had dedicated himself to providing the general with the best possible scenario prior to the major assault. Exhaustion had put him on edge and caused him to curse the escort from the Royal Irish. He had made a fool of himself when they restrained him. And when they had read the charges against him he had panicked. His throat had tightened and he'd found it difficult to breathe. In the turmoil of the impending attack to be suddenly accused of murdering Sheenagh O'Connor had come as a tremendous shock. He had been so careful. No one could know what had happened. Why had he been implicated? Had Sheenagh told someone about him giving her medical supplies? Was that the evidence they had against him? Finally he had brought himself under control and cleared his muddled thinking. A generous apology had been made to the field court martial for the way he had behaved when arrested. And now they had reached the point with their questioning where he was master of his own fate.

'I did my duty,' he said calmly. 'She was a spy. She could have compromised many of my fellow officers. When I approached her with the intention of arresting her she drew a revolver. I acted in self-defence. I did not know that I had killed her because her horse bolted and she escaped. My horse stumbled so I could not pursue her any further. I presumed she had sought out protection from those Irishmen she had been giving information to.'

Taylor fell silent, content that he had explained the circumstances in the simplest, most irrefutable terms.

General Reece-Sullivan remained silent. The lieutenant colonel at his side referred to a handwritten sheet of paper.

'Major, we have an eyewitness. Captain Claude Belmont of the 21st Dragoons baited a trap using the girl. He then had her followed by this witness.'

Taylor felt the breath driven out of him. He floundered for a moment. He had threatened Belmont and now the cavalryman had snared him.

'Belmont?' was all he could whisper.

'He was concerned you may have compromised yourself with the girl. That you had given her medical supplies in return for sexual favours.'

'Well... yes, yes, I admit that. The supplies. I did. Of course. I was gaining her trust. But it wasn't I who gave her any information. It was I who brought Belmont in. I told him he was the risk to our security. He threatened me.'

'And you reported this?' asked the lieutenant colonel.

'No. No, I didn't. It was a verbal threat. What could I do?'

'Behave as any officer should,' said the major next to the general. 'You could have made an official reprimand against him. There would have been a court of inquiry.'

'But he threatened to kill me,' Taylor pleaded, hearing the pathetic whine in his voice as soon as he had spoken.

General Reece-Sullivan placed a fingertip on a sheet of paper. 'Captain Belmont made a written statement under oath. He thought that you were a risk, and that it was you who was most likely responsible for passing on information to the girl. In his statement he wrote that your intimacy with this woman might also have compromised the security of the regiment's Dublin barracks, which came under attack.'

Taylor shook his head vigorously. 'No. No. Not at all. I swear it.'

'No matter. We do not have any evidence to corroborate that accusation but we do have evidence that you shot and killed the girl. His trooper witnessed everything. His man saw her shot. He saw you ride off. We have his sworn statement.'

Taylor was rendered speechless. His mind refused to co-operate. No matter how hard he thought no answer was forthcoming.

'No,' he muttered desperately. 'I... killed a spy. Yes, I admit that. She might have escaped had I not. I gave her medical supplies to draw her in, don't you see, general? To find out where the commando was hiding.'

He could see from the look on their faces that his words had no mitigating effect.

Reece-Sullivan's voice was dry. 'There are factors at play here that cannot be ignored. The girl's body was taken to Bergfontein where Mrs Charteris related how the girl regularly brought medical supplies given to her by an unnamed army major as payment for sexual favours. The Charteris woman would be an influential witness should this become public.' The general stared directly at Taylor. The man was coming apart; anyone could see that. 'Which must never happen,' said Reece-Sullivan. 'Major Taylor, you are an officer who was promoted beyond his capabilities and whose weakness of character should have been noted some time ago. And now you have committed murder.'

Reece-Sullivan looked to the officers either side. They nodded. It was a foregone decision.

'The army and your own family will cleanse themselves of your dishonour in the appropriate manner.'

Taylor understood what punishment would be pronounced. 'You have no right. Only the commander-in-chief can sanction the death sentence.'

Reece-Sullivan had passed the charge sheet to each of his fellow judges for their signatures. Now he penned his own.

'Military exigencies and circumstances have dictated that this field general court martial be convened. You have been found guilty as charged of premeditated murder without provocation. By reason of the nature of the country, the great distances involved, and the operations of the enemy, it is not practicable to relay the case to the commander-in-chief.

Telegraph lines have been cut and sentence is confirmed by me, the field officer commanding.'

Taylor tried to muster courage he'd never had. Thankfully shocked numbness made the doomed effort redundant.

'Guard!' the aide-de-camp called.

Darkness came quickly and hundreds of oil lamps were lit and hung outside bell tents – a glowing field of fireflies. Shadows fell across men's faces as they were partially caught in the lamps' glow. Pierce had not moved, watching to see where sentries patrolled and men came and went. By midnight the camp would be quiet. A cur dog could give him away but it might be less of a risk than trying to reach Radcliffe in daylight. He watched as African levies gathered in small groups around braziers, huddled against the cold night's air. No matter what hardship they endured, he realized, they sat and ate with a muted cheerfulness. They laughed, teeth shining in the firelight. There was no difference between these people and those at home who had been enslaved before Lincoln's war. He pulled his jacket back on and moved to the edge of a brazier where Mhlangana ladled out what looked to be a kind of porridge into a tin plate and handed it to Pierce and then passed him a piece of roughly torn bread.

'Your friend is near the railway line. There is a tin shed there. He is not in chains, but they have a guard watching him. One of the levies saw him. They have given him a blanket and food.'

'Near the soldiers' tents?'

'No. It is beyond them and past the buildings where the general works. It is closer to the supply yards where the train comes in.'

Pierce nodded. He dragged the piece of bread through the cloying food and pushed it into his mouth. Mhlangana watched, and smiled, as Pierce tested the blandness. It was hot, but it wouldn't fill him.

'*Putu*,' said Mhlangana.

'*Putu*,' Pierce repeated. 'We call this grits back home. Corn. We crush corn and boil it. Grits, though there's usually a piece of meat that comes with it.'

'We will have some meat, but not today,' said Mhlangana, and used his fingers to scoop the food.

As Pierce ate, his eyes followed the movement of shadows as soldiers went back and forth to their own field kitchens. There would be picket lines set and guards rotated through the night.

'You have fought in a war before?' said Mhlangana.

Pierce nodded. 'Oh yeah.'

'But not here?'

'No. A long way from here.'

'Did you win your war?'

Pierce scowled and then sighed. 'Well, they say we did. I think we won some of it.'

'Did many people die?'

'Sometimes there were dead as far as the eye could see.' He gazed into the firelight as his memory recalled the great slaughter.

Mhlangana let the words settle. 'Then you were hungry for war?'

Pierce dragged his fingers around the remains of the food on the plate and sucked them clean. 'No. Freedom.'

Neither man spoke for a moment. Mhlangana hugged his knees to his chest and began to speak quietly, as the other men settled into silence and listened. 'We work for the Boers and when the English took their women from the farms then our people were taken and put in other camps. Places only for blacks. But we work for the English now. We are crying out in our hunger. Our hearts are starving. We stand at the table of the white man and we look for crumbs of compassion, and we go hungry. We are beggars in our own land.'

A low, almost imperceptible murmur went around the gathered men.

Mhlangana continued and they remained silent and unmoving; his soft voice was meant only for them to hear. 'We are not even allowed to dream. For they say there can be no dream of freedom, they say they will come in the night and snatch that dream from our hearts so we will wake in darkness and see only the white shadows walking this land. But I say our dream is greater than anything a thief can carry away. We do not want the bitterness of revenge on our tongues, but the day must come when we will not let them starve us any longer.'

This time there was no response from the gathered men. Some of them nodded and went back to their food.

'I reckon that's about it,' said Pierce. He got to his feet and then stepped away into the darkness. There was little sense, Pierce decided, in trying to move through the shadows and risk being challenged. He lifted a pail of water and a lantern from a corner of the stables and made his way directly across the camp, his shoulders hunched in a subservient manner. If questioned he would pretend not to understand English. There were manned picket lines beyond in the darkness – a dull glow from a solitary lamp showed the soldier's post. Clouds occasionally obscured the night sky but any half-decent Boer sniper could have picked off the sentry and created havoc in the camp. One man and a rifle could cause hundreds of men to stand to, ready to repel an attack that need never come. They would lose a night's sleep and that gave an enemy the edge. The Boers, he decided, were far enough away not to pose a threat; the danger for him and Radcliffe lay within this camp. What seemed to be a parade ground loomed out of the darkness when he followed the boardwalk towards the rail yard. Tin huts boxed three sides of the large square; they had the look of an extended makeshift barracks, each corrugated hut joined to the other. This appeared to be where some of the fresh troops were quartered, and as he walked across the square he saw the field hospital with its Red Cross dark against the half-lit white canvas background.

He hesitated, thinking for a moment that he could try and see Edward, but caution stopped him. It would be too dangerous: the boy might recognize him and name him for who he was. But where was Radcliffe being held? He could not see any solitary hut. Then, moments before he turned away into the darkness, a door opened and a lantern lit the features of his friend as a guard escorted him in the direction of the hospital. Pierce fixed the hut in his mind's eye and watched as Radcliffe was taken into the hospital. Pierce knew he would not be able to linger in the vicinity of the hut to wait for Radcliffe's return. An African bearing a pail of water needed to be heading purposefully towards a destination.

He turned back to retrace his steps. Now that he knew where Radcliffe was being held, and how long it would take to reach the hut, he could plan how best to approach him in daylight. He would need Mhlangana to arrange for him to change places with whoever took Radcliffe's washing water. If he could get close enough then he would find out what his friend wanted to do. They would need to move quickly because he still had no idea how badly injured Edward might be. And if they could make a run for it then to where and how? The countryside would be swarming with British troops. A couple of months back a boy had run off to war and here they were, two ageing men trying to save his skin. Goddammit, war was a whore in the night that robbed a man blind.

Chapter Twenty-Six

Sir George Amery was looking forward to his bed after a long day of surgery and care for the soldiers. Treating the sick and wounded in this godforsaken war took its toll on everyone. He read the notes on one of the Boer prisoners, his eyes blurring with tiredness, willing himself to push on for a few more minutes to determine the man's chances of survival. Behind him in the corner of the room the kind-hearted soldier who guarded the ward was questioning a new prisoner, brought in an hour earlier with a leg wound. Amery's orderlies eased off his bloodied clothing, readying him for a hospital suit and then surgery. The guard's low murmuring voice was almost soporific as he checked in the Boer's personal items, writing down each item of his personal belongings in a heavy bound war book.

'Right we are then, now… the sooner we get this done the quicker that leg o' yours'll be seen to.'

A gold watch was passed from an orderly to the guard.

'That's a handsome piece, lad. Right, tuck that under his pillow,' said the guard, licking the tip of his pencil and noting it down.

'There you go, Dutchy,' said the orderly, 'safe and sound. Right where you can reach it.'

'Anything else?' asked the guard. 'Got any money, have you?'

The Boer seemed comforted by the fact that no one had stolen his watch. He nodded.

'All right, let's have it. You'll have it all back – Dutchy or Briton, we treat 'em all the same here.'

'A shilling,' said the Boer, pulling it from his tattered jacket, handing it over to the guard who added it to his list.

'Anything else?'

The Boer shook his head. The guard raised his eyes above the ward book. There was always something else. 'It goes in the book, lad. You see that, don't you? It all goes in the book, lad. You see that, don't you? Friend or foe – in the book it goes.'

The prisoner started to pull bits and pieces from every pocket. A small collection: a pipe, tobacco pouch, a matchbox, a bible, a silver snuffbox, a pot of beef essence and half a dozen Mauser bullets.

The guard watched as the men made a final foray through his pockets and then nodded that that was all.

'Right. There we are then,' said the guard.

Amery smiled, thankful for the kind voice of a decent man in this place of pain. A comfort of any kind was welcome. There were neither beds, nor sufficient linen, nor stretchers, nor nurses, and ambulances were often contributed by volunteers. The army seemed to have no concept of men's pain. Those with shattered limbs were bundled unceremoniously on to the back of flatbed wagons whose jolting across the stony veld caused them even more agony. They were brave men, barely uttering complaint, but he thanked God for the Indian stretcher-bearers whose compassion and fearlessness sent them out under fire to carry back the wounded. Medical supplies were at times life-threateningly scarce, especially for the treatment of typhoid. The field hospital overflowed into bell tents that were meant to hold six healthy men. But when sickness struck, then ten typhoid patients at a time had to lie in that same space day and night on the hard ground, or, when it rained, in inches of mud. A groundsheet if they were lucky, a blanket if they were blessed. He had tested the forbearance of the army generals with his continual demands for supplies. He had only three doctors and a handful of nurses to attend to more than three hundred sick and injured men. Amery was haunted by the lack of nourishing food for his patients. Beef broth and horse-meat stew were staples but were not enough. His practice in England was far removed in all manner from this primitive environment, but his determination to relieve the men's suffering was not diminished. He had scratched the scab of army callousness by dismissing half a dozen doctors whose ability to deal with the injured left a great deal to be desired. Reece-Sullivan had suppressed his irritation because of Amery's influence and standing within the medical community, and had quickly drafted the incompetent doctors to other units.

Amery spent another hour in the main ward and then returned to the prisoners of war to assure himself that the wounded Boer had been taken into the shed that served as the surgical unit. He saw Evelyn Charteris with the hospital guard. Amery knew he was a family man: a soldier who had a gentle enough nature to be in charge of the wounded enemy. He and Evelyn were lifting Edward into a better position.

'There you go now, son,' said the ward guard.

Evelyn smiled at him with gratitude; she would not have been able to lift Edward on her own. 'Thank you,' she said.

'Got a lad his age myself back home,' he said, and then saw Amery step closer. 'Good evening, Sir George.'

The surgeon nodded his acknowledgement. Evelyn was already attending to Edward's bandages.

'You can manage?' said Amery.

'I've done this before. There's no infection yet.'

He watched for a moment and saw that she was adept as a nurse. He peered at the discoloured and raw-looking stump. 'The dry air helps heal wounds. It's the only good thing about this place.'

The ward guard had returned to the chair by the room's rear door, which led out into the open space around the hospital. He settled himself with his rifle across his lap.

'He's a good man,' Amery told Evelyn, glancing at the guard. 'He will call an orderly and have him check the boy through the night. He'll have morphia. I'll see to that. Try to get the lad to sip some beef tea before you leave him.'

'I will. Thank you again, Sir George.'

He touched her shoulder. 'I know what you tried to do in the camps, Mrs Charteris, and I appreciate your distress at what happened to that poor girl. From what I have heard the officer who murdered her did so to protect himself. Occasionally in these frightful times justice will be done.' And with that he turned away and left Evelyn in the dim glow of the oil lamp as she put a new dressing on the rawness of Edward's arm. The boy's eyes half opened, the morphia still fogging his mind. His eyes widened as a figure appeared behind the woman who tended him.

'Father,' he whispered in disbelief.

Evelyn turned quickly and smiled warmly at Radcliffe, whose guard moved to the door and sat with the older soldier. 'Joseph, he's doing well,' she assured him. 'He has to get over the shock of the wound, and then he will gain his strength quickly.'

She stepped back so that Joseph could ease himself between the beds and sit next to his son. Radcliffe laid his hand on the boy's face and lent forward to kiss his forehead. Evelyn moved quietly away to give them privacy.

Edward's mouth was dry and he licked his parched lips, trying to form words to speak to his father. Radcliffe took a beaker of water from the top of the old ammunition box that served as a bedside table, and tilted the boy's head so he could drink.

'It's OK,' Radcliffe said.

The boy took a few sips and then nodded that he had had enough. He looked down at the stump of his arm. Radcliffe saw Edward grimly gather his courage and clench his jaw before smiling bravely at his father. 'You came after me. Just as well. Look at what happened to me.' Then, despite himself, his eyes welled with tears.

His father held the boy's good hand to his lips.

'I'm sorry, Father, truly I am.'

Radcliffe let Edward compose himself. He was aware that the guards were not that far away and might overhear anything he said. 'Liam told me what happened. You were very brave.'

'He's alive?' Edward whispered.

Radcliffe nodded. The boy sighed. 'Good. I tried to save his brother. I couldn't. It was Belmont's men...' His voice trailed away at the memory.

'Don't think about it now,' Radcliffe said, not wishing the wounded boy to become more distressed.

Edward's voice was husky with emotion. 'It was terrible, Father...'

'I know, son, I know. You will heal, you're young; it's something you will deal with. I promise you.'

Edward squeezed his father's hand. 'No. No... I don't mean my arm, I meant... I killed... two men. Shot them... It was the foulest thing. I feel... so ashamed.'

Radcliffe held back the tears that stung his eyes. The boy seemed settled for a moment. And then he began to whisper. Radcliffe lowered his head so he could hear.

> 'With sabres drawn and glistening, and carbines
> by their thighs – ah, my brave horsemen!
> My handsome, tan-faced horsemen! what life,
> what joy and pride...'

Radcliffe looked uncertainly at his son.

'It's a poem,' said Edward.

Radcliffe's voice was tinged with regret. 'I don't know any poetry.'

Edward looked at his father for a moment. 'I know.'

The boy's eyes closed as he drifted into sleep and, as his breathing settled, Radcliffe could no longer hold back his silent tears.

Ghostly outlines of bell tents squatted in their orderly rows as here and there a dull glow from an oil lamp softened the darkness. One of the braziers still offered warmth from its embers, its light half-obscured from Radcliffe's sight by Evelyn Charteris who stood beside it, arms folded, a shawl around her shoulders. She glanced in Radcliffe's direction as he left the field hospital, his escort behind him. The soldier kept a discreet distance between him and his charge: there was nowhere for his prisoner to run.

Radcliffe stepped closer to her. 'Thank you,' he said. 'A man forgets a woman's tenderness.'

They walked side by side towards Radcliffe's quarters. 'You're tender with your son.'

'It's not the same as coming from a woman.'

She gave an almost imperceptible sigh. 'I've seen women without it. Usually because of what men do.' She caught her breath, aware of the condemnation; and then smiled regretfully in the hope of softening her words. 'This war punishes so many.'

Radcliffe glanced back at his escort. The man was far enough away to be out of earshot. 'It occurs to me we could have met under different circumstances. One day I might have looked at your letters and seen the woman behind the words. I'd have been drawn to finding out more about you.'

She shook her head gently. 'What I do makes me self-centred. Which is not a particularly good thing.'

'Probably not when it comes to relationships. But it's a duty one has to others. Is that so self-centred?'

The uneven boardwalk made him take her arm to steady her, but he did not remove his hand when they passed the bumpy planking. She felt a slight pressure as he almost whispered to her: 'I have... responsibilities that I cannot neglect. There are parts of my life that cannot be brushed away.'

'I understand,' she said carefully, letting him know with her eyes what both of them sensed. Whatever this moment between them meant, despite its innocence, something more was trying to be expressed.

'All I'm saying is... if things were different...' Radcliffe said awkwardly.

How sad, she thought, that behind their words these unfledged feelings would never take flight.

'Things are what they are,' she said quietly.

They were getting closer to Radcliffe's hut. The urge to say more was undeniable, and who knew when they might have this time again. She let her hand rest on his. With no regard to the soldier a dozen paces behind them, she raised her face to his and kissed his cheek. They embraced gently, holding the moment for a few shuddering heartbeats.

'Sometimes I wonder which is the cruellest – what others do or what we do to ourselves,' she said.

He was glad of her tenderness and wished he could ease her

into the dull glow of his room and his bed. Instead, he nodded in understanding.

She stepped back from him. 'It's cold. I think I'll go back. Your son is strong. Don't worry about him.'

'I've seen men maimed before. Some can't live with it.'

'He will. Don't doubt him. He's got courage – the wounded men told me what he did. If you have that inside of you, I believe you can face anything. He'll come through it. I know he will.'

Radcliffe glanced back to the soldier and felt gratitude well up inside of him. The older man was a non-combatant and had kept a discreet distance, even half turning away, plunging his face into cupped hands to light a cigarette. He had given them as much privacy as his duties allowed. Radcliffe knew he had to take advantage and betray the man's trust. He held Evelyn close to him and whispered, 'The Boers are riding into a trap. I feel I owe them. Do you know anyone who can warn them?'

He felt her body stiffen. She was suddenly more nervous, and glanced back at the guard.

'I can't help the enemy. That's not why I'm here,' she answered quietly.

It was a gentle rebuke, and he knew the risk of asking her had failed. He nodded, knowing he had clumsily tested her loyalty to her own countrymen. 'You're right. I'm sorry.'

Yet in that moment she seemed to be his only chance to pass a warning to the commandos. How many times in a courtroom had he manipulated the emotions of a witness? To do so could risk resentment and hostility, but there were times when it touched the conscience of those being questioned.

'Why was Sheenagh O'Connor shot dead by a British Army officer? Because she smuggled medicines? You don't kill a woman for that. You arrest her. What was it she knew that threatened others and caused her to be shot in cold blood?

Whatever the answer is, the simple fact is that she tried to save women and children under your care. She didn't have to do that. She risked everything. Get a warning out and stop the slaughter.'

She hesitated, conflicted. 'I can't.'

Radcliffe knew he had lost his appeal, but then the gods of war gave him an unexpected opportunity to secure her support. Two stretcher-bearers carried out the young wounded Boer and took him towards the guardroom and the cells.

'What are they doing with that boy?' she asked.

'The guards tell me they're going to shoot him as a spy tomorrow morning, because he was wearing a British tunic.'

She held back the outrage that rose from her despair. 'If you need to go... to warn the commandos... I'll stay with Edward. I'll care for him. But I cannot do so myself.'

He had lost the gamble. There was no questioning her compassion, but, despite her own fight against the authorities, her loyalty to her own people could not be challenged.

He barely kept the fear from his voice. 'I understand. But there's something else. I think they're going to execute Edward for treason.'

CHAPTER TWENTY-SEVEN

Dawn.

Brevet Major Lawrence Baxter squinted across the purple mountains which had not yet felt the warmth of the sun. It was a cold morning and he shivered, reaching his fingers beneath his buttoned tunic to tug at his shirt and pull it closer to his throat. He had been ordered to hold his company to the rear and then go up the line to rejoin his regiment. He knew that Captain Belmont had led a successful operation against a Boer commando and the prisoners were being taken to prisoner-of-war camps, and that the troops in this camp, several thousand strong, would soon be taking part in the next, decisive assault against the enemy. However, he had no idea that Joseph Radcliffe and Benjamin Pierce were here. Nor did he know that his boyhood friend, Edward Radcliffe, lay wounded in the field hospital. Baxter had led the detail to arrest Major Taylor, and neither Sergeant McCory nor Private Mulraney had seen Radcliffe under escort in the general's office. The vagaries of war sometimes allowed men to find lost friends on a vast battlefield but could also keep apart men who were billeted within a few hundred yards of each other.

And now his duty demanded an act of random killing that neither he nor his Irish soldiers had any taste for.

He watched as Sergeant McCory marched out a dozen men. Mulraney and Flynn, now recovered from his wound, were among those chosen from a short-straw lottery. The open veld reached towards the mountains that now began to change colour. Golden light speared through the ragged-toothed peaks and Baxter closed his eyes for a moment and let the sun warm him. The slow, subdued *lef', right, lef', right* chant from Sergeant McCory as he brought the firing squad into position crept up behind Baxter. What soldier could want this duty? he thought. In the guardroom each man had been relieved of his personal weapon and issued with another. A round was already loaded in the chamber. One of the dozen rifles held a blank cartridge. This 'bullet of conscience' allowed each of the men chosen for the firing squad to believe that they had not fired a fatal shot.

McCory brought the men to a halt, and then spaced them by arm's distance, as if preparing for a parade-ground inspection. He stood them at ease and waited stoically. Thirty paces in front of their extended line was a chair. Carpenters had hammered in two stakes in front of each of the chair legs, and then bound chair leg and stake together, to stop the executed man from flying backwards from the impact of the firing squad's bullets.

Baxter clicked open his father's timepiece. *Sweet Jesus, let's get this over and done with. This is no way to kill a man, let alone a youngster.*

The guardroom door opened and an army padre led out the two stretcher-bearers who carried the wounded boy. He was moaning in between his tearful cries, in a language that none of the men who waited to kill him understood. He had been strapped on to the stretcher, but his head turned left and right, as if trying to see where he was being taken.

Out of the corner of his eye Mulraney saw that he was just a boy. 'Mother of God, Flynn. It's a lad we're doing away with this morning,' he whispered from the corner of his mouth.

'Fuck's sake,' said Flynn.

'Keep it down,' McCory's voice instructed under his breath. 'Steady now. The lad's fearful enough. No need for him to hear you cursing. See to it we do our job proper.'

Major Baxter waited as the solemn procession moved towards the execution chair. The priest and the stretcher-bearers were followed by the officer in charge of the detail, a fresh-faced new lieutenant, a recent replacement. Baxter watched him closely. The execution was not to be mishandled, which was why Baxter had been ordered to attend. The young officer stared intently at the chair, glancing nervously back and forth from it to the wounded boy. Most officers bore their family name like a medieval banner. Honour was all. How you behaved under duress was the mark of the man. Baxter glanced at the rank of men he had fought with these past months. Some were replacements; most were not. The rascal Flynn dared a glance in his direction. *Fecking hateful thing this is, major. The colonel, God rest his soul, would despise what it is we're doing.* Baxter imagined the words, and had they been spoken Flynn would have been correct. But Colonel Alex Baxter would have taken the duty just as seriously and seen to it that it was carried out in good order. Had he lived. Lawrence glared back at Flynn, forcing him to avert his eyes. Baxter strode forward. The boy was struggling and the young lieutenant was dithering.

'You,' Baxter said to one of the soldiers from the stretcher-bearer detail. 'Bind his ankles. You, hold him,' he ordered the second man. It seemed the padre was about to protest at Baxter's intrusion. His lips parted, but he held his peace now that they had control over the boy. Baxter wished to Christ they could gag him and stop him crying out. But they could not, of course, and thankfully when they got him into the chair he pressed his head into his chest and the fabric of his shirt muffled his sobs.

Baxter glanced at the lieutenant. Enough of a look to see that he could control the situation. The lieutenant nodded. The boy's hands were strapped to the arms of the chair, his chest secured by a broad strap. The lieutenant pinned a square piece of linen over his heart and then quickly placed a blindfold over his eyes. The moment the boy was plunged into darkness. He cried out again. '*Nee, asseblief… Waar is my moeder… my moeder…*'

'I'd be calling for my own mother an' all, poor bastard,' muttered Mulraney.

Before McCory could chastise him the lieutenant nodded his permission to proceed.

'Ready!' Sergeant McCory ordered.

The squad brought the rifles into their shoulders, butts pressed against cheeks.

'Aim.'

Eyes gazed down barrels at the squirming boy.

The boy wailed, thrashing his head.

Jesus. The damned chair was too short to secure his head.

Rifles wavered as his body bucked.

'Fire!'

The bullets tore through him.

The volley reverberated across the camp. Men faltered in whatever they were doing, and then carried on. The shots were a clarion call to them all. The Dutchy may have been an enemy but the same fate could await any man.

The firing squad began lowering their weapons, but their eyes were held by the boy who quivered and shook despite the bloodstains that blossomed on his shirtfront. His writhing had allowed the rounds to miss his heart. Blood coughed and spluttered from his shattered lungs.

The young lieutenant looked horror-struck.

Baxter barked a command. 'Lieutenant!'

The replacement officer looked aghast. This was the first time he had seen death close up. A death that he was responsible for, supposedly seeing it was done in the most humane manner.

'Finish it!' Baxter commanded, his own hand involuntarily reaching for the flap of his holster and the revolver at the end of its lanyard.

For a moment the fresh-faced lieutenant hesitated but then military discipline cut through his daze of uncertainty. He strode forward, placed his revolver's barrel close to the boy's temple and shot him.

Saliva thick on his tongue, the lieutenant turned away quickly to the side of a hut, where he leaned and vomited, his wretchedness witnessed by Evelyn Charteris through the hospital ward window. She could not see the execution site, which was concealed by the buildings between the hospital and the firing squad, but as the stretcher-bearers carried the boy's shattered body towards the mortuary tent her mind formed a graphic picture of his death. Only hours earlier he had lain in the bed next to Edward. The room was silent. Men stared at the ceiling, prayer or curse behind their lips. The guard got to his feet and tugged the calico curtain across.

'No need for anyone here to see that,' he said.

She nodded, thankful for his concern.

'You all right for a bit? I'll get these lads a brew, put a bit extra sugar in for them.'

She smiled in gratitude. Tea. The great British panacea for the ills of the world.

Pierce had watched them strap the boy to the chair and used the distraction of the execution to move closer to Radcliffe.

His friend was shaving in a bowl of water outside his hut. His guard stood some way off talking to another soldier as they both looked towards the execution site. At the sound of the rattling gunfire Pierce followed Radcliffe's gaze to where the general stood at his window, smoking a cigarette, seemingly unperturbed at the result of his orders. Radcliffe turned and saw Pierce, glanced at his distracted guard and threw out the waste water.

'I need more water,' he called.

The guard looked quickly, settled on Pierce and pointed in his direction. 'Boy! Water! *Amanzi!*'

Pierce hurriedly went to a hand pump and filled a pail of water, then carried it to Radcliffe. Satisfied that his order had been carried out, the guard shared a cigarette with the other soldier. As Pierce poured water into the bowl, Radcliffe stooped and swilled his face, being careful not to be seen talking by his guard.

'Mrs Charteris brought me in,' said Pierce.

'She told me.'

'Said she'd try and help Edward.'

'Yes, she is, thank God.'

'She told me he lost half his arm.'

'Belmont set the ambush. He did it.' Radcliffe smothered his concern and regret. 'Edward's strong. He'll pull through. I know he will.'

It was all Pierce could do not to extend a hand of comfort to his friend's shoulder. He kept a wary eye on the guard and made a fuss of cleaning Radcliffe's bowl. 'I saw you in the street with Belmont. I had you covered. I'm sorry, Joseph, I couldn't get to the rail line.'

'Made no difference. We were too late anyway. Listen, the Boer they shot was a wounded boy. I tried to save him but

Reece-Sullivan follows orders like a damned train on a track. He's notching up a reputation. They arrested an English officer for killing the Irish girl. Taylor. You remember him?'

'Taylor? The asshole captain from Dublin last Christmas?'

'He's a major now,' said Radcliffe as he towelled his face.

'A major asshole. I remember him. Gave me some bruised ribs that night. You reckon he did it?'

'Seems so. There was a witness. I saw him brought in and I heard my guard talking about it. Taylor's had a court martial. A quick one. And that means that Reece-Sullivan is wasting no time. He doesn't want any unfinished business before they advance. Have you seen Baxter and any of the Irish regiment?'

Pierce acted as if he were a servant, helping Radcliffe on with his jacket. 'Him and some of the others were in the firing-squad detail.'

'See if you can speak to him. I need help, Ben. I reckon Reece-Sullivan is going to order Edward's execution before too long.'

'Edward? He can't,' said Pierce, trying to grasp why the boy would be shot.

The guard began making his way towards them, grinding out the cigarette beneath his studded boot. Radcliffe turned his back to the approaching man. 'He will. I'll appeal to him but if he refuses then we have to get Edward out. I don't know how long they'll let me wander around here. Not much longer if they issue the order. Get to Edward in case I can't. Tell him we're going to make a run for it. He has to be ready.'

'How soon you plan on doing this?'

'Tonight.'

'With a wound like his?'

'No choice, Ben. I heard the soldiers talking; a supply train comes in at midnight. They leave it in the siding before offloading. Taylor will be shot at dawn tomorrow, and unless I can argue Edward's case with the general, they'll shoot my boy at the same time. They've got a war to win. We've seen this before. Field punishment barely gives pause to an army's advance.'

Pierce nodded. 'Midnight,' he agreed.

Chapter Twenty-Eight

Major Frederick Taylor pressed his face against the wooden door, desperate to stop himself from falling to the ground as fear sucked the strength from his legs. He fought back the tears that threatened to engulf him. His mind had painted a tableau of what had gone on outside as he heard every pitiful sound of the boy being taken to his death. The small window was too high to see out of even though he'd dragged the wooden cot with its riempie-laced base beneath it. The thought had even occurred to him that the provost was slack in his duties. A determined and desperate man could have fashioned a noose from the bed's leather cords. And do what with them? The one rafter supporting the tin roof was probably beetle-infested like every other piece of wood in the damned country. It would snap if any weight were brought to bear. Despite the slit of a window letting in the daylight the room already felt like a tomb. He had to control the panic otherwise he would die. There was always a chance for life and he had to seize it. Slowly but surely he regained control of his emotions, wiped the sweat from his face and calmed his breathing. He dried his palms on his tunic. This time when he put his face close to the door he sought out the crack in the heat-warped grain.

'Guard,' he whispered.

He could hear no sound outside in the passage. He gently tapped the door and raised his voice slightly. 'Guard, I need you. Are you there?'

He listened hard, cursing the pounding in his chest that filled his ears with his own terrified heartbeat. Nothing stirred on the other side of the door. The guard was elsewhere. Probably talking to others about how the army was going to kill one of its own chosen sons.

'Guard,' he called again.

He waited and moments later was relieved to hear the sounds of an army boot scuffing the dirt and the rattle of a rifle strap. Then there was the unmistakable sound of a man standing on the other side of the door.

'What is it, major?' said the guard.

'Please open the door,' said Taylor.

'And why would I do that?' answered the guard.

Taylor felt his mouth drying. He licked his lips. Now was the time to risk everything. 'You can help me.'

He heard the man grunt. 'I don't think anyone can help you, major, not unless they fire blanks.'

Taylor pressed his face closer to the crack and whispered urgently: 'I have gold. Sovereigns. Gold sovereigns. Help me and they're yours.'

Taylor held his breath. All the man had to do now was to go to the corporal of the guard and tell him that the prisoner had tried to bribe him. He waited. The silence meant the man was thinking about the proposition. Had he even seen a gold sovereign before? Taylor doubted it. The gamble was worth it. The very mention of gold touched every man's nerve.

'Step away from the door,' said the guard.

Taylor held back a gasp of relief. He did as he was told without hesitation.

'Tell me when your back is against the wall. No funny business, major. I'd as soon shoot you now as let you wait until the firing squad tomorrow.'

Taylor closed his eyes and let his breath ease from his chest. Was the man going to search him and take the hidden sovereigns or could he be bought? It only took three long backward paces for him to reach the cell wall.

'I've done as you asked,' he said, striving to keep his voice even.

He heard the jangle of keys and the grinding of a key in the lock. The door swung open and the guard stood with his rifle levelled at the hip. The two men stared at each other for a moment.

'What game you playing at?' asked the guard.

'No game. I swear,' Taylor said.

He had not thought about this man before now. He was as faceless as any of the soldiers who had crossed Taylor's path, but now he studied him. The man's coarse features reflected a working-class life and the scarred knuckles that gripped the rifle probably indicated a man who would use his fists to settle an argument. A rough-edged man then, not young, probably close to middle age, thirty-something, perhaps even forty. Signed up to take the Queen's shilling to keep himself out of prison. Or desperate not to end up in the workhouse. He was no front-line soldier. Unfit perhaps. Considered poor fighting material as far as soldiering was concerned. Better to be kept rear echelon. He would want as easy a life as he could get. Not unlike himself, Taylor acknowledged.

Taylor carefully bent and felt inside his boot.

'Careful now,' said the guard, an edge to his voice. 'If there's a knife coming out of there, I'll shoot you dead. Make no mistake.'

The man had not yet been bought or his silence guaranteed.

Taylor eased out a thin strap of leather from the inside of his boot that held a dozen gold half-sovereigns one below the other. Taylor held it in front of him. 'I can get more of these. Get me out of here, come with me and we will make for the gold- and diamond fields together.'

'You been in the sun too long before you murdered that whore, major? Is that what's happenin' in your brain box? Gone a bit queer in the head, have you?'

'Listen to me, I have friends who own parcels of land in the Transvaal goldfields and they will look after us. They know my family. They'll give us a stake. Once my family know I am free they'll send money. We can buy a stake of our own.'

'Aye and then I'll end up in a convenient accident down a bloody mine shaft.'

'No, no, you're wrong. I swear. We will be partners. I would not forget a man who helped me and neither would my family. The kaffirs do the work. You would be my mine manager. Don't you see there's gold ripe for the digging? Why in God's name do you think we're fighting this godforsaken war?'

He thumbed a couple of sovereigns free and extended them to the guard, who quickly looked over his shoulder although he was the only one on duty. He edged closer.

'No funny business,' he said and took the coins from Taylor's outstretched fingers. 'I'd want a paper signed by you so that I have my rights. I'll not be a part of this unless I have that guarantee.'

'Of course. And when you have that you can register it with a lawyer, any lawyer, anywhere. That protects you. Get me pencil and paper and I'll write whatever it is you want.'

The guard rubbed the coins together, and then raised one to his mouth and bit into it, as if that would give the fool any idea of its worth or quality. Then he backed away again. Taylor smiled as if he had pacified a threatening dog with a titbit.

'All right,' said the guard. 'I'll get us horses –'

'And supplies,' Taylor interrupted. 'Tonight.'

'Don't take me for a fool, major. I'll get what's needed.'

The guard backed out of the room. Taylor felt the warm gush of relief course through him.

He nodded, smiling at the man who would secure his freedom and give him life. 'We'll get out of this stinking war and we'll make more money than you dreamed of,' he said, knowing he would kill him at the first opportunity.

Pierce returned to the stables, but Mhlangana had gone. A field kitchen levy told him where. Pierce lifted a small sack of flour on to his shoulder, using the pretence of being an African labourer again, the only way he could move through the gathered troops as he searched for the Royal Irish Regiment of Foot. Soldiers were breaking camp and being gathered into marching formation. There was no sign of the small detachment that he had seen forming the firing squad, and no regimental flag or pennant proclaimed where they might be encamped. Frustratingly, his search was hampered because he knew he dare not ask their whereabouts as his accent would immediately give him away. The rail tracks passed close to the field hospital and he was torn between trying to get to see Edward and Evelyn Charteris or finding Lawrence Baxter to solicit his help. He spotted Mhlangana and a group of Africans unloading lengths of rail track from a flatbed. Mhlangana saw him skirt the work party and moved to where other Africans were heaving the weighty lengths of iron on to the criss-cross stack of stored railway lines.

'You have seen Mr Radcliffe?' asked Mhlangana.

Pierce nodded. 'I'm looking for the Royal Irish Regiment. Do you remember them from the battle for the hills?'

The African thought for a moment. He shook his head. 'There were so many soldiers. I do not remember.'

Pierce felt the edge of desperation creep into his voice. If anyone knew the Royal Irish's whereabouts this man who laboured for the army was his best hope. 'Think, Mhlangana. When we used the guns. Those men we helped. The infantry. They are the men I'm looking for.'

There was little time for further interrogation. The work party had to return to unloading the flatbed.

Mhlangana's brow creased as he tried to remember. 'Too many soldiers, my friend. They all look the same.'

Pierce turned and ignoring the flour sack strode quickly to where soldiers had begun marching from the camp. He quickened his pace along the railway line that ran parallel to the departing troops. Amid the body of marching ranks, each led by officers on horseback, he caught sight of the young lieutenant who had officiated at the firing squad, and the officer who rode next to him was Baxter. Pierce began to run, but now some of those who marched on the column's right flank glanced his way. Damned if his lungs weren't already burning. An old man's legs could buckle on this uneven ground. Pierce pumped his arms, forcing his legs to carry him faster. The sentry post was a few hundred yards away. The steady footfall of the hundreds of men scuffed the hard ground, a relentless whispering rhythm that smothered his own sharp pace. Pierce gasped for air. He had covered less than two hundred yards but he was hurting. He saw one of the sentries turn to face him. An African running alongside soldiers was not a normal sight. The soldier slipped his rifle from his shoulder and held it across his chest. If he cried out a challenge and Pierce failed to respond then it could earn him a bullet. Pierce stopped and leaned on his knees, sucking in the hot, dry air. He spat.

The soldiers' pace never faltered. *Scuff, scuff, scuff, scuff.* Dust rose, half obscuring the receding figures. Baxter was too far ahead now for Pierce to even make out his features. For a moment he thought Baxter's instinct had alerted him: he half turned in the saddle and glanced back – most likely at his own men, Pierce realized as he straightened and half raised his arm in forlorn hope.

The soldiers marched on.

Pierce cursed. It was still early in the day and already a boy had been shot to death and the reality was that another would soon die.

Time was running out.

He reached the field hospital in time to see three Africans carrying small pails of broth and bread for the sick and wounded. A fourth man carried a tray of freshly washed bandages. Pierce quickly grabbed a dozen rolls in the spread of his hands, ignoring the questioning African. Once inside it was too late for any complaint and Pierce followed one of the levies into the prisoners' ward.

Evelyn Charteris had her back to him as she carefully tended one of the men's wounds. Pierce placed the bandages on a small trolley that held dressings. The hospital guard didn't even look at him. Routine bred complacency. Pierce swiftly saw where Edward lay as the African levy spooned broth into tin plates. Pierce picked up a plate and spoon and went to Edward, who turned his face from the wall at the sound of the footsteps and saw him. A quick gesture for silence stopped the boy from calling out his name. Pierce knelt by the bed and put the food on the upturned ammunition box. Under the pretence of helping Edward sit up, he whispered urgently.

'We're getting out of here, near enough midnight. I'm gonna be coming through the door for you then.' Pierce reached under his shirt and pulled out the bone-handled knife. 'We found this along the way,' he said, pressing it into Edward's hand. The boy pushed it beneath the blanket.

Pierce gave him an encouraging smile. Edward's brow furrowed with uncertainty. Pierce placed a hand on the boy's chest. 'Save your questions for later.' He glanced back at the guard who had got to his feet and started to help hand out the plates to the patients. 'Is he here all night?'

Edward nodded.

'Come midnight you'll hear a train whistle coming in. You call him over, get him close... kill him. Go for his throat,' said Pierce. 'You'll only get one chance, son. Do it quick and do it right.'

The guard looked at the two Africans in his ward. 'All right, let's have you natives out of here. Come on now. Orderlies have to get these men washed once they've finished their grub.'

Pierce whispered quickly. He could see the boy was still uncertain. 'You have to, son. If you don't none of us is going to get out of here alive. Your father and me... we have to stop them hurting you...'

'No... Benjamin... they've been kind to me...'

'Son. Plain and simple. Unless I get a message to you telling you otherwise... these kind people are gonna put you in front of a firing squad. Now you fix on that thought and do what I told you.'

As Pierce turned for the door Evelyn looked up and saw him. She had the presence of mind to keep her surprise silent. With a glance at Edward she followed Pierce outside. She bundled soiled bedclothes into a laundry bag to make a conversation less suspicious to anyone who looked their way.

'Mr Pierce, what's going on? Is there any news of what they intend doing to Edward?'

Pierce took the bag from her. 'Mrs Charteris, shouldn't you be back in Bergfontein by now?'

'I am not allowed to travel until the general gives me permission. Please don't evade the question. Mr Radcliffe has already told me of the risk of Edward being executed.'

'The less you know the safer you will be,' he told her, but as soon as he had spoken he saw the anger flare in her eyes.

'Do not play me for a fool, Mr Pierce. I deal with lies and incompetence every day of my life while people die around me. I will not be kept in the dark about this boy's fate. Not after the murder that was committed this morning. Now, tell me, what it is you and Mr Radcliffe are planning – because if there is any way I can help I will.'

Pierce looked at the woman whose passion challenged the Empire-makers. She had a will of iron and a hide as tough as a plains buffalo, a toughness which could pass well camouflaged behind that mask of beauty. Only those who had dealt with her might know how determined she was.

'All right. Joseph is going to make a final appeal to the general today. If it is denied then we will take Edward from here tonight.'

This straightforward answer caused her to hesitate. The plan was madness. The wounded boy was still in need of care. How would they get him out of a guarded room, and then ride off to God-knows-where?

'You cannot. It's impossible. There's a guard day and night and the boy has yet to make sufficient progress from his wound. He could die in the saddle – assuming you even got past the picket line.'

'You asked; I told you. I suggest you get some sleep tonight, Mrs Charteris, you don't want to be around later.'

Pierce turned away. She reached out and grabbed his arm. 'Wait. You must understand that he is very weak and needs medical attention. Someone must treat the boy wherever it is you intend going. He needs medication and his wound needs dressing every day. If infection sets in he will die.'

'All right, you said you wanted to help: can you get bandages and dressings, whatever he needs, and medicine to give him a chance? I'm not asking you to take anything from those wounded men in there that would not be used on Edward. Make up a satchel of supplies you think he'll need for at least a week's ride. We'll do the rest. Can you do that?'

She sighed and shook her head, urgency making her eyes dart between him and the hospital. 'Only Sir George has the keys to the medicines we would need. Some fresh bandages perhaps. That's all – and perhaps a couple of field dressings.'

'OK. That's better than nothing.'

'I'll come with you,' she suddenly blurted out, taking both herself and Pierce by surprise. 'He'll need nursing.'

'Lady, I know you're tough but we'll be riding hard for the border, wherever the hell that is. It's no place for a woman – even one like you.'

'Don't patronize me, Mr Pierce. I shall nurse him. Tell me where I must be and I will be ready.'

'We're talking about riding a horse day in day out. This is no buggy ride.'

'I was brought up on a farm, Mr Pierce. I can ride as well as any man.'

Pierce smiled. 'I'm sure you can, Mrs Charteris, and God help any man who says you can't. I'll send word.'

Pierce put the laundry bag on his shoulder and strode off into the camp. If they were lucky enough to pull off this escape they would need a guide to get them away safely.

Chapter Twenty-Nine

Radcliffe was escorted to the general's office and as he entered the building he saw Sir George Amery standing with his hands clenched behind his back, staring through the window at the increasing bustle of activity in the camp. He turned to Radcliffe.

'Mr Radcliffe, it has been suggested to me that your son may be in danger. The general's aide-de-camp informed me that a decision has been made but would not tell me what that decision is. With your permission I would like to speak to General Reece-Sullivan on your and your son's behalf.'

'Sir George, I am most grateful,' said Radcliffe as the aide-de-camp opened the general's door.

'Gentlemen, the general will see you now.'

Radcliffe stepped back to allow the distinguished surgeon across the threshold. Once inside the aide-de-camp closed the door and remained in the room. There were two other officers who stood either side of the general.

'Sir George, Major Radcliffe,' the general said in a perfunctory greeting and gestured towards the two officers. 'Colonel McFarlane and Major Summers served on Major Taylor's field court martial. They have assisted me in my decision-making regarding Boer prisoners of war, and I have invited them to be here so that you will know that the decision reached is not mine alone. There will be no suggestion of prejudice on my part.'

Sir George took a purposeful stride towards the general.

It seemed for a moment that he was about to rap his knuckles on Reece-Sullivan's desk, but restraint won the moment. His tone was critical enough. 'Before this matter goes any further I protest most strongly against the execution of the wounded boy this morning. It was barbaric. He was my patient.'

General Reece-Sullivan balanced his fingers lightly on the desk in front of him. 'We value your services, Sir George, but military matters you really must leave to us.'

'You can be assured, general, that my protestations will be made known to the newspapers in England. We are not fighting savages; this is a war between two white nations, where a level of civilized decency must prevail.'

Neither man had been invited to sit in the general's presence, and Amery stood ramrod straight, his height obliging the general to crane his neck. The surgeon's eyes blazed behind the pince-nez spectacles.

Radcliffe quickly interrupted what he knew could soon become a war of words between two colonial die-hards.

'Black or white, Sir George, the general here doesn't distinguish between them. Caste, creed or rank, no one escapes military justice. Am I correct, general, isn't that what you told me?'

For a moment, Reece-Sullivan felt, surprisingly, that Radcliffe had leaped to his defence. 'Quite right, Radcliffe. Thank you.'

'You see, Sir George, the general knows he has the authority to commute a death sentence to penal servitude but that does not send out a strong enough message, does it, general?'

'Soldiers understand that. Radcliffe is correct, Sir George. We are fighting a guerrilla war. Our enemy does not face us man to man. We must inflict our superiority against them whenever, and however, is practicable.'

'My son came here to find his friend who served with the Royal Irish. He came as any boy seeking adventure would.

I had the opportunity of speaking to Lieutenant Baxter after the battle of Pieters Hill. He explained to me how my son was shot, mistakenly, by his soldiers as he rode towards them when they were clearing a Boer farmstead. They did not know his identity and his troops came under fire from a nearby commando. It was these men who took my son with them. He did not join the enemy forces; instead they helped him recover from his wound because they realized that I was his father. It is my name that causes you to think of him as a traitor. He's just a boy. Send him home.'

General Reece-Sullivan listened patiently. There was no need for him to act otherwise. A decision had already been reached. It made no difference what these non-combatants said; they were civilians in a fighting man's war.

The surgeon pressed his case. 'I would urge you to consider Mr Radcliffe's appeal quite seriously, general, otherwise should you authorize this boy's execution I will have no choice but to go directly to Lord Kitchener,' said Sir George.

Lieutenant Colonel McFarlane said, 'Our telegraph wires were cut two days ago by the Boers. Lord Kitchener had already instructed that each field commander has the right, under army regulations, to make appropriate decisions in these matters. I believe the general has followed the correct procedure, Sir George. It really is a military matter.'

Reece-Sullivan picked up the document from his desk. 'The surviving commandos under your care, Sir George, will be held as prisoners of war.' Radcliffe felt a brief surge of relief. Sir George Amery dipped his head in acknowledgement.

'Thank you, general. Thank you,' said the surgeon.

However,' said Reece-Sullivan, looking directly at Radcliffe, 'not your boy.'

Radcliffe and Sir George knew the decision had gone

against them.

'You cannot –' said Radcliffe.

Reece-Sullivan stood like a figurehead between the two officers. 'See the reality. An Englishman shot and killed two British soldiers while riding with Irish volunteers of the Foreign Brigade. He will be executed tomorrow morning.' He pointed to the sheet of paper on his desk. 'The field punishment has already been signed.'

Sir George Amery looked as distraught as Radcliffe.

'No,' said Radcliffe, his mind racing, searching for any vulnerability in the general's decision. 'No... you cannot execute him. His mother is Irish. Under Irish law he can claim citizenship from the maternal line. It's a law recognized even by the English courts. He has committed no act of treason.'

Reece-Sullivan and the officers could not hide their concern. Colonel McFarlane looked surprised, but Major Summers leaned forward and spoke quietly, shielding his mouth with his hand.

'General, as you know I served with the judge advocate's office before I transferred to my line regiment. He is correct. It's a point of law that cannot be ignored. If the boy claims the citizenship of his mother he is, strictly speaking, a prisoner of war.'

Neither Radcliffe nor Sir George could hear what was being said, but a spark of hope flared when Radcliffe saw Reece-Sullivan's scowl. But then the general shook his head and turned away from the two officers to face Radcliffe.

'Your father was English. You were born in England,' challenged Reece-Sullivan.

'I'm a naturalized American. My father took me there when I was barely two years old,' Radcliffe answered.

The general pushed a sheet of paper on his desk with his

forefinger, squaring it so that the desktop retained its order. 'As far as I am concerned, in English law the child takes the birthright of his father. Your son is English whichever way one looks at it.' He raised his eyes and looked directly at Radcliffe. 'You will be allowed to see your son before sentence is carried out. You are not deemed to be an enemy, Radcliffe, but you will remain under escort – and confined until after my troops have moved up the line and the offensive has begun.'

Mhlangana watched the black American stride towards the stables. He was a stranger in a country where he had no business to be. How, Mhlangana wondered, had a man who looked as strong as any warrior, and who would be a respected elder, an *umkhulu*, in any Zulu clan, come with the white man as a friend and not as a servant? Zulus had fought their wars. They had once slain Xhosas and taken their land, they had beaten the redcoat English in the past, but these new soldiers dressed in the colour of the dirt fought a white enemy. And when the black American went back to his land, wherever that was, then the war would go on until the Boer was brought to his knees. Would the defeated Boers be whipped with a sjambok? Would the English make them their servants? If they did, what would that do for the Africans? How much lower could they sink under the white men? Perhaps the day would come when the great African tribes, Zulu, Xhosa, Sotho, Pondo, Tswana, all of them and more, forgot their enmity towards each other and raised their spears together. He sighed. It would never happen. Too much had been lost in the past and the spirits of their forefathers wandered in a land ruled by white ghosts. Mhlangana went about his cleaning duties in the stall, deliberately ignoring Pierce who dumped the laundry bag.

Pierce savoured the comforting smell of horseflesh, a welcome relief from the stench of the soiled bandages in the bag. He quickly went to the corner stall and shoved his hands into the straw, feeling for his rifle and the two sabres that were hidden there. Satisfied that they were still safe he turned and gestured Mhlangana to him. The African checked carefully that no one saw him move away from where he was sweeping a stall.

'When the supply train comes in at midnight, we're going to escape with Mr Radcliffe's son,' Pierce told him.

The African showed no sign of surprise but Pierce knew that by telling him Mhlangana now shared the risk. If a native levy contravened any rule the least he could expect was a flogging. Mhlangana nodded. He was no fool – he knew Pierce would need help and if he became involved then he would most likely suffer the same fate as the Boer boy that morning. He barely hesitated in making his decision and scratched a shape in the dirt with the end of his pitchfork.

'Here, this is where the train will stop. They will unload the train at first light. We must go behind the sheds at the other side of the track and then you will have a chance. It's a long train and the boxcars and the buildings will shield you. I will help you with the horses and the boy.'

Pierce saw the layout of the rail track and the sheds in his mind's eye. There were cattle pens for the long-horned beef away from the soldiers' bivouacs, and if he and the others could use the length of the train to obscure their escape and move between the track and the shelter of the cattle pens they could reach the outskirts of the camp and slip past the pickets. Somehow.

'Which direction do we head?'

Mhlangana's voice was barely a whisper as one of the other levies came into sight carrying a bale of straw. 'You must go north and east across the mountains into Zululand and in a few days you will be in Delagoa Bay. There you will be able to get a Portuguese ship.'

Pierce nodded. That made sense. If they got into Portuguese-held territory they would be safe from the British.

'But it is very hard to get there,' said Mhlangana. 'The English are going to win this war and there is nothing anyone can do about that. So they will send men after you.'

'I see that – but we can't let them kill the boy.'

Mhlangana clicked his tongue and shook his head. 'Ai. That would be bad. Which is why I will take you through the mountains.'

'You know it won't matter if the Boers or the English catch us – they'll shoot you.'

'I am Zulu. A warrior does not fear death. And they will never catch me.'

Pierce matched Mhlangana's grin, and quickly retrieved his revolver from the straw. 'Have the horses ready, muffle their hooves and make sure we have enough supplies for a week. Can you do that?'

Mhlangana nodded. 'I will have four horses saddled and ready before the train arrives.'

'Make it five. Mrs Charteris is coming with us.'

Pierce stood in the lee of one of the storage sheds and watched as Radcliffe was escorted from his quarters. The general had obviously taken an extra precaution and ordered the American be placed in leg irons until the next morning's execution was over. Pierce lifted a pail of water and made his way to where Radcliffe stripped off his jacket, rolled up his shirt sleeves and turned back the collar on his shirt. He leaned into the tin bowl of water balanced on a makeshift stand and soaped and rinsed his neck and face. As Pierce got closer he hoped his approach would not make the guard suspicious. It was a different soldier, but one who was just as alert. The man stood with the butt of his rifle resting on the ground, but as soon as Pierce got within thirty paces the weapon came up to his waist and was levelled.

'Halt! What you doin' 'ere?'

Pierce drooped his shoulders in a gesture of submission. '*Baas*.'

The guard looked at the bucket. 'He's got water. Bugger off.'

'*Baas?*' Pierce said again.

'Fuck off. Go! *Hamba!*'

Pierce looked as dumb as he could.

'He doesn't understand English,' said Radcliffe.

'Everybody understands a boot up the arse,' said the guard, taking a threatening step towards Pierce.

'Look,' said Radcliffe in a conciliatory tone, 'let him bring the water. He's only following orders. The guard commander sent him yesterday. They'll only flog him if he doesn't and maybe you'll be the one to get a kick up the arse. The army does things its own way. Why risk antagonizing anyone? It's your guard commander who sent him. It's only water.'

The guard thought about it for a moment. 'All right. Hurry up,' he said.

Pierce remained dumb and stooped as if not understanding.

'Hurry up! Come on!' the guard said, raising his voice and gesturing for what he took to be an ignorant savage to get a move on.

Radcliffe tossed the soapy water from the bowl and allowed Pierce to refill it with the clean water, making sure he stood between Pierce and the guard a dozen paces behind him.

'Midnight train it is. The horses will be at the stables,' Pierce whispered as Radcliffe saw the revolver in the bottom of the bucket. He reached in and quickly tucked it into his waistband.

'Get Edward out, Ben. I'll get to the stables but I need to give the general something to think about. He needs a distraction otherwise they'll be all over us.'

Pierce had no time to question his friend. Whatever Radcliffe planned he knew each of them would find a way to secure Edward's release and escape. Pierce nodded and then Radcliffe deliberately tipped what was left in the bucket over his front.

'Damn!' he said and pushed his friend away. 'Clumsy bastard!'

Pierce staggered a few steps away in pretence as Radcliffe bemoaned his soaked front, which now concealed any chance of the wet pistol being seen. As Pierce scurried away he did not look over his shoulder and see the guard's smirk. His friend was armed and whether the guard lived or died that night meant nothing to Pierce.

Chapter Thirty

The sunset seeped into the blue of the night sky; the day's heat was sucked down behind the black mountain ridges. African darkness came suddenly, as if the scorched land was desperate for respite – to slumber before bracing itself for the dawn's arrival.

Pierce had waited patiently as the hours ticked by, seeing in his mind's eye the route he would take across the compound, using shadows and the dull-edged buildings for cover. The field hospital could be reached without him being noticed. The waiting was the worst part. A man's imagination could whip him into blind alleys of fear as the thoughts of what could go wrong gained prominence. But Pierce had spent a lifetime waiting patiently, from his boyhood escape to being a Buffalo Soldier and hiding for days on end, unmoving as a lethal enemy hunted him. The American West was little different to the South African veld, and soon he would be hunted again. He doubted that being an American would save him if he was captured. He and Mhlangana were brothers of colour. And no one would ever know that the old veteran had met his end face down in the African dirt. The irony made him smile. Dead in a place his own ancestors had been taken from.

In the darkness of the stables the big Irish horse's withers rippled as it dipped its head and champed on the bit. Pierce made final adjustments to the saddle's girth, lowered the stirrup and then securely strapped on Radcliffe's cavalry sabre. Four more horses were saddled and ready in the near darkness of the stalls. The flickering of oil lamps here and there among the camp's bivouacs cast sufficient light to show Mhlangana fixing a small sack of supplies on to one of the horses. They checked that the sacking around the horses' hooves was tied on firmly enough. It was almost time. Pierce and Mhlangana were dressed just like the Boer commandos or the African scouts who lived on the veld. Trouser legs were pulled over their boots and a buttoned woollen waistcoat over a shirt complemented their short rough-weave jackets. Their brimmed hats cast their faces even further into shadow. Each had a bandolier of ammunition on his saddle ready to be pulled across the chest. If there was a fight they would give a good account of themselves. Pierce tugged on his leather riding gloves.

'She will come?' whispered Mhlangana. 'Mrs Charteris?'

'She's at the hospital making sure I can get in. Don't worry, she'll be here.'

The horse snuffled at Pierce's hand as he looked towards the darkening rail yard. His eyes adjusted to the dimness as his gaze followed the dull glow of the railway tracks disappearing into the blackness. Every time in his life he had been prepared to face danger and commit violence a sliver of edginess had quivered in his belly. Only when he committed to what he had to do would it leave him. He was tempted to check the watch that nestled on the end of its chain in his waistcoat pocket – but it would be a useless exercise in this near darkness. Instead he waited patiently, listening for the distant approach of the supply train. He saw the shadows move as Mhlangana steadied the horses. Pierce nodded to himself. The man knew how to deal with them. Best to stay calm so they didn't pick up the men's nervousness. Years of conflict, of waiting for an enemy attack or striking through the night into an opponent's camp, keyed up the senses. A state of readiness that never left until the action began. Killing would be part of the night's work if it came to it – the how and the why did not matter. He just hoped that Edward did what was necessary. Pulling a man's face close to your own and plunging a knife into him meant ignoring the part of you that screamed out in disgust. It took something special to be able to do it. The first time, that is. After that it was easier. The distant train whistle interrupted his thoughts.

Time to go.

Five lives depended on each of their actions as the minutes ticked away until the moment when the distant train whistle signalled its approach. There would be little time before the train pulled into the rail siding. Radcliffe listened for the muted sound of his guard shuffling outside, until his dry cough, the cough so many soldiers had picked up from the extreme climate, signalled his whereabouts.

Radcliffe waited until he heard the man move closer to the door and then quickly sat down on the edge of the bed and spooned stew into his mouth. He had deliberately not eaten the evening meal the sentry had brought and now it was cold, the congealed watery gravy forming a greasy slick on the plate. The guard detail would be changed an hour after midnight if the previous night's sentry rotation was followed. The moment he heard the approaching train he began to heave and cough as if choking, which wasn't hard given the gristle that passed for meat and the oily slime that clung to it. By the time the guard peered through the barred window Radcliffe was writhing on the dirt floor. He heard the sentry curse and fumble for the keys in the lock. The soldier saw his prisoner grasping his throat, his face red, with spittle and stew spewing from his mouth. As the sentry knelt and reached forward Radcliffe pulled free the concealed revolver and struck him with the knurled butt.

It took him less than a minute to retrieve the leg-iron's key but he hesitated, undecided whether to tie the man up or not. Who knew how long he might remain unconscious? He had no desire to kill the man: all he'd done was stand the night watch and do his duty. Radcliffe dragged the unconscious guard to the old iron bedstead and fed the leg-iron chain through the metal crosspiece, then turned the man's back and bound his wrists. He quickly unwound the khaki puttee from the man's leg and gagged his mouth. That at least would buy some time. He locked the door behind him and tossed the keys into the night. The train whistle sounded closer. Radcliffe quickly got his bearings and, denying himself the urge to run, walked quickly towards the heavy shadow that he knew to be the general's headquarters.

As Pierce edged through the deepening shadows towards the field hospital he heard a scuffle from behind one of the tin buildings. A man grunted and then there was the thud of a body falling. The disturbance came directly from the route he needed to take. There was no way for him to avoid it. If he didn't carry on then he would have to cross a couple of hundred yards of open space where men slept in their bivouacs. He hesitated. What lay ahead? If there was a commotion those troops would be on their feet at once with rifles in hand. He darted quickly alongside the building and stepped into its shadow. The moon's glow came and went behind the clouds, but even in the half-light he could see Major Taylor bending over a soldier's unconscious body, ready to ram the man's bayonet into his back. Something glinted. It was not the blade on the end of the rifle but gold coins that Taylor hastily snatched from the dirt. The scuff of Pierce's boots alerted Taylor, who turned quickly, bringing up the rifle. For a second the men faced each other. Two horses were tethered twenty feet away, saddled and provisioned. Incomprehension creased Taylor's face. He wore no cap or helmet and his eyes widened once he knew who faced him.

'You!' he hissed in recognition and levered the rifle's bolt action.

'Pull that trigger and you'll wake the whole damned British Army. You won't be going nowhere except to that firing squad,' said Pierce, his voice deliberately low.

Taylor's reaction was sudden and silent. He lunged in a classic infantryman attack. Pierce jumped back and half turned, but Taylor was skilful enough to correct his own balance and slashed with the rifle. The bayonet caught Pierce's coat but failed to draw blood. Taylor's eyes stayed locked on the American's and he threw his weight forward again with two rapid strides, grunting with determination, choking back the urge to cry out aggressively as all soldiers were taught to when lunging with the bayonet for the kill.

Pierce tried to regain his balance, fell backwards and managed to throw his shoulder to one side as the bayonet rammed into a sack of grain next to him. He wished the old Comanche knife was still in his boot and the thought flashed through his mind, as he rolled fighting for his life, that Edward might at that moment be ramming it into the hospital guard's throat.

Taylor was fast. He sidestepped and pushed his weight down, aiming for Pierce's chest. There was nothing he could do other than to grasp the blade with his left hand, gasping in pain as the steel bit. Bile gorged his throat when Taylor yanked back the rifle, dragging the bayonet's edge across his palm. Despite the chill night air sweat streaked both men. Concentration creased their features as each sought to outmanoeuvre the other. Taylor was winning this fight and the older man knew it; his breath was coming harder than Taylor's, but the pain focused his mind. Pierce curled his lacerated hand in on itself and tucked it into his chest. Taylor took another two attacking steps and threw his weight down, but this time Pierce half rolled and kicked his legs against the back of Taylor's knees. As Taylor's face hit the dirt he twisted quickly but the rifle had gone from his hands and the heavy American quickly straddled him. Taylor bucked but Pierce's weight was the greater. The killer spat and flailed and did not see the bunched fist come out of the darkness to shatter his jaw. Eyes wide with pain he gurgled blood but then Pierce leaned forward, pressing his hand against Taylor's face, forcing it away into the dirt, feeling the broken jaw crack further, until he heard the sudden sharp snap of the man's breaking neck. Taylor was dead.

Heaving with effort Pierce rolled off the dead man, tugged free the sweat rag from his neck and bound it as tight as he could over the ugly wound. Pressing his back against the wall for a moment he sucked in air and bent to retrieve his hat. The silent fight to the death had gone unnoticed. Beyond his heaving breath the sound of iron wheels and steam could be heard in the distance from across the open veld.

Benjamin Pierce, the old Buffalo Soldier, took his pain with him as he strode towards the field hospital and Edward Radcliffe.

CHAPTER THIRTY-ONE

Hunched by the dull glow of an oil lamp on the small table next to him, the hospital guard sat reading a letter from home. His wife had been ill and the four children had depended on their older brother to help care for them each day. The childlike writing reminded him that this woman was barely educated yet had been faithful and hard-working since they had first met as children working in the shoe factory – long before he had taken the Queen's shilling. She was an uncomplaining creature but she worried that if her illness worsened then her children would be placed in the workhouse, and it was only that fear which had caused her to bother him with her anxieties. She then assured him in an uncomplicated way that she was certain all would be well and went on to express her concern for his wellbeing. Despite him being a garrison soldier who was not required to fight in the front line she still fretted about him. He was older than most of the men in his company and those years had taken the edge off any anger or disappointment he might have once felt for not having bettered himself in life. More than anything he was grateful that he was clothed and fed and could send his pay home to care for his family. In these times such simple basics of life were a blessing.

Edward watched the guard hold the crumpled letter close to his face, his lips moving as he silently repeated the written words. Edward had already heard the first distant whistle of the train and now it tooted twice more as it drew closer. His mouth dried and muscles tensed as his hand slid beneath the blanket and grasped the knife.

'Can you help me? I want to sit up. I need water,' he said quietly.

The guard raised his eyes and without any sign of disgruntlement at having his letter from home interrupted, got to his feet and went across to help the boy. He bent down, his face close to Edward's, and wrapped an arm beneath his chest, careful to avoid his wound.

'Hang on a bit, then... Here we go, easy now.'

Edward eased the knife from beneath a blanket, his eyes fixed on the spot where the man's neck joined his shoulder. He would have to ram the blade hard and deep.

The guard smiled as he settled the pillow behind the boy's head. 'How's that then?'

Edward nodded gratefully. 'Thank you,' he said as he pushed the knife out of sight. It was impossible to kill this man, or any other, in cold blood.

'Right you are, son. I'll get you some water,' the guard said and turned towards the hospital trolley that held the carafe of water.

Pierce had waited by the ward's rear door. Evelyn Charteris had said she would make sure it was unlocked when she left the room. Pierce heard voices inside. He prayed it was Edward talking to the guard, luring him to his death. He turned the door handle. As he stepped into the dimly lit room he saw the guard turn away from Edward who was propped against the bed's head rail. The man's surprise gave him no time to cry out in alarm before Pierce's fist felled him.

'Ben! Don't kill him!' Edward hissed.

There was no need; the man was out cold.

Pierce stepped across the body and tugged back the blankets. 'Gotta get you dressed in a hurry, boy,' he said, opening the footlocker that held Edward's clothes.

Edward handed him the knife. 'You take it. I couldn't do it,' he said apologetically.

Pierce nodded as he palmed the blade and tucked it into his boot. The boy needed a moment of comfort. 'No shame in that,' he said with a hand on the boy's shoulder. 'Come on now,' he added, tugging the boy's jacket on over his hospital shirt and then steadying him as he pulled on his trousers and boots. Others woke to watch the silent escape. No one called out and none tried to join this kaffir who was helping the condemned boy. Their own wounds would slow any man down and to be shot in the night was a far less enticing prospect than staying in the clean sheets of a hospital bed and then to be sent to a prisoner-of-war camp.

Edward was weak but Pierce's strength was enough for them both. With his uninjured arm across Pierce's shoulder the two fugitives shuffled for the door.

'Good luck, *Engelsman*,' one of the Boers whispered.

Pierce eased Edward into the night and hesitated as a shadow moved. Evelyn Charteris stepped closer. She wore culottes, boots and a short riding jacket. Her broad-brimmed straw hat was tied beneath her chin. 'I came in case you needed help with him,' she whispered.

He nodded and let her go ahead to make sure the way was clear. Steam hissed and plumed as iron wheels screeched to a slow halt at the railway siding. A rhythmic hum sounded from one of the sheds and a half-dozen electric lamps illuminated the railway siding. A transport officer and his men waited for the train driver and his fireman to climb down, and further along the carriages an NCO bellowed for the train guards to disembark and fall into ranks. Evelyn raised a hand to halt her companions. Pierce held Edward close, pressing his back to the hospital wall. The glare from the lights would cast deep shadows on the blind side of the carriages. They needed to take advantage of it. Edward's head drooped and Pierce failed to hear the footfall of Sir George Amery as he came up behind them.

'Mrs Charteris,' he said quietly. Evelyn gasped and Pierce spun around. Amery was alone. Goddammit, Pierce had let an old man creep up on him. To reach his boot knife he would have to drop Edward and that could have grave consequences for the one-armed boy whose wound was already seeping blood into the dressing.

'I'm not here to cause you harm or to raise the alarm,' said Amery. 'Unless you have killed the ward guard.'

'He'll have a headache and bruised jaw, but that's all,' said Pierce.

Amery's expression briefly showed surprise at Pierce's accent, but this was not the time for further questions. 'I saw Mrs Charteris unlock the door earlier. It was obvious what was being planned.'

'You didn't warn anyone,' said Pierce, suddenly aware that the distinguished man might have alerted those in authority and that an ambush could be waiting around the next corner.

'No one.' Amery nodded towards the distant siding and the lights. 'They'll be switched off once the soldiers disembark. The glare will stop men's night vision for a while. If I were making a run for it I would do it soon.'

'I intend to.'

Amery stepped closer and unslung a canvas satchel from his shoulder. It was marked with a red cross. He handed it to

Evelyn. 'Everything you need for the boy. I will attend to the guard and delay my report of the boy's escape for as long as I can. God speed.'

Sir George Amery turned away as Evelyn Charteris hoisted the satchel and followed Pierce as he half carried Edward towards the stables.

No one would dare violate the sanctity of General Reece-Sullivan's office. No door needed to be forced, no window broken. The picket was thirty yards away – two men pacing back and forth, slow, lazy strides because they knew there was no danger from any enemy this deep in the camp and it would be near enough another hour before two sleepy soldiers came to replace them. Two hours on, four off. A standard bone-aching night where no decent sleep was to be had. But it was safe and the guardroom was a pig of a place in the heat or the cold. The men paced and turned and Joseph Radcliffe practically strolled into the building as they turned their backs. Radcliffe stepped into the room where he had stood only hours earlier. It was dark but there was enough low light for him to know that the faint shimmer that spread across the wall was the waxed map that showed the locations of the enemy and the planned attack. He was going to create a diversion – he knew the English would scour the countryside for them if he and Pierce managed to get Edward beyond the camp's perimeter, and he had to try and make them head in a different direction. He reached out, letting his fingers find the frayed edge of woven cotton. He teased a rent in the material and then ripped off a section that marked the planned attack. It was a crude attempt to fool a bone-headed general – a long shot – but a soldier's life sometimes depended on such things.

As he eased back into the shadows men's voices drifted across the camp. In the yellow glow from the lights of the railway siding shimmered the image of the soldiers being marched away. And then, as regimented as the men themselves, the lights dulled and darkened. His eyes scanned the distance to the stable block. Four more buildings to use as cover and then the stables and the train behind them would shield him from most of the tented soldiers. He realized it would take too long to dodge across the shadows – he could already see the waiting horses in the stable's entrance and the figure of his friend standing next to a bent figure in the saddle. Edward. Dammit, he had to risk cutting across the open ground. Lack of time was going to snare them any minute now. They had been lucky so far. No gunshots, no cries of alarm. With a determined pace he strode forward, denying himself the urge to run. The closer he got the clearer he could see Pierce, who had spotted him and raised a hand as if signalling a beacon for him to navigate to.

Pierce finished tying Edward's leg on to the stirrup strap. The look between the two men was enough for Radcliffe to know that it would not take much for him to fall from the saddle. Even in the near darkness Radcliffe could see Edward's gaunt features and stooped posture. The boy smiled when he saw his father, who placed a comforting hand on his son's.

'Father, thank heavens you're here,' Edward said in a voice barely above a whisper.

'We've a way to go, son.'

'I'll be all right,' he answered, without a hint of self-pity.

'Good man. You hold on. You're one of the best horsemen I ever saw. We're going to get you home.'

Radcliffe saw Pierce struggling with his wounded hand.

'Major Taylor got between me and Edward. He damned near spoiled things,' he said by way of explanation.

If Pierce was cut then Taylor was dead. 'They gonna find his body any time soon?'

'First light. Sure as hell didn't have time to bury the son of a bitch.' He looked towards Evelyn Charteris, whose horse was tethered at the end of the line. She was securing the medical satchel into the saddle's pannier. She glanced at Radcliffe and then concentrated on the task at hand. 'She'll stitch it up when we get clear of this place. It's time, Joseph. Our luck can't hold much longer.'

Radcliffe reached for the revolver as a figure jogged from the darkness. There was no need. It was Mhlangana.

He nodded and smiled at Radcliffe and addressed the two men. 'We must go. The cattle kraal gate has been opened. They will block the other side of the tracks in case the soldiers are alerted.'

Radcliffe peered along the track. He could just make out a mass of brown beasts herding themselves beyond the train. He went along the horses to where Evelyn had pulled down her stirrup ready to mount. He cupped his hands so that she might use it to raise herself. For a moment she hesitated and then bent her leg, placing her knee in his grip. He pushed her up into the saddle. She gathered the reins and looked down at him.

'Thank you, Mr Radcliffe,' she said quietly, the longing to know him better barely concealed in her voice.

'It is I who owe you thanks,' he said, holding back the regret that threatened to tinge his words. 'Good luck to you, Mrs Charteris. It's been a privilege.'

Her eyes widened. He smiled and squeezed her hand. It was obvious – he was not going to ride with them. She nodded. 'I wish we could have met in better circumstances.'

'So do I,' he answered. There could have been a life to be lived with this woman.

Radcliffe pulled himself into his saddle and, as Mhlangana

led them into the darkness towards the side of the train, turned to Pierce. 'Ben, get him home.'

Pierce glared at him. 'What do you mean? I can't do this on my own,' he said, forcing his voice into a desperate whisper.

'How far would we get? One long hard gallop if they chase us will finish Edward. You and your rifle might take some of them but they'll ride us into the ground, Ben. I'll lead them away up the valley.'

'Jesus H. Christ, you've had some damned stupid ideas in the years I've known you. This is the worst of 'em.' He sighed and shook his head. 'Joseph, I'm aching and hurting in every piece of my body. I'm damned near at the end of the road and I bet you're not far behind me. You hear me? We're old men. You can't take them on. You can't.'

'Just get him home for me, Ben. I'll get there somehow. Might take me a while longer is all.'

They had reached halfway along the rolling stock and could hear the low bleating of the cattle. Radcliffe reined his horse close to Edward. 'Go with Ben. I intend to give them something to chase for a few hours.'

'Father…?'

'Edward, if my love is enough to keep you in that saddle then you'll make it with room to spare… but you're the one who has to be tough enough to do it… and I know you can.'

The boy was in pain but sat determinedly in the saddle. 'You'll come home? You'll be there?'

Radcliffe gave a reassuring smile and touched his son's face. He could not bring himself to make another promise that might be broken. He eased his horse away from the others.

'Portuguese East Africa,' Pierce said, stretching out his arm. 'A week.'

Radcliffe gripped the big man's hand. There was a lifetime

of friendship and understanding in it.

'Ben… this goes wrong… you tell him about his mother,' Radcliffe said and without waiting for Pierce's complaint spurred his horse towards where sentries manned their picket lines at the five-foot-high stone wall five hundred yards into the darkness.

Mhlangana led the others quietly along the length of the train. They heard shouts of alarm behind them as the herd of cattle began to low and trample tents. Moments later muzzle flashes and gunshots in the distance broke the darkness. Joseph Radcliffe had spurred the Irish horse into the pickets and leaned forward in the saddle to give it its head across the high wall. Like a night demon it flew silently, bearing its rider to safety. The sentries' cries of alarm carried through the night as they fired blindly.

'*Halt!*'

'*Stop him!*'

'*Boers! Commandos!*'

The alarm ricocheted like a bullet through the night but by the time soldiers ran from their bivouacs and faced the agitated herd of cows others ran blindly in panic, believing they were under attack. Orders were barked as floundering men were brought under control: '*Stand to arms! Stand to!*'

Pierce brought up the rear and turned in the saddle. There was no pursuit and the temporary chaos faded in sight and sound as the darkness engulfed them. Somewhere in the great expanse of the veld his friend rode alone.

Chapter Thirty-Two

General Reece-Sullivan and his officers stayed on alert throughout the night but by dawn the expected attack had not arrived. Unshaven and irritated, he had ordered a search of the camp to ensure no infiltrators had penetrated their defences. Sir George Amery had attended to the hospital guard. When the stricken man regained consciousness Amery found him unsteady on his feet; he therefore delayed the guard's recovery and the report of the escape by applying a dose of chloroform. An act of concern for the man's welfare, he told himself, so that he would not stumble and hurt himself further.

It was only when the bodies of Major Taylor and his jailer were found that a rapid search by soldiers alerted them to the fact that Radcliffe had escaped and Edward had been taken. One of the African levies was missing and Evelyn Charteris was not in her quarters. Reece-Sullivan almost ran to his office, a twist of fear forewarning him that Radcliffe had seen the plans for the impending attack. He stood in front of the ripped map. Every troop location for the advance was missing.

'Sir?' his aide-de-camp queried after the general had stood stock-still in front of the vandalized map for a full minute. Reece-Sullivan took another half-minute before he brought his scattered thoughts under control. He had jeopardized the advance and his commander-in-chief would be as unforgiving towards him as he had towards Major Taylor, the Boer and

Edward Radcliffe. He would be relieved of command. At the very least. Perhaps worse. Reece-Sullivan was beating thousands of the enemy but one man threatened to bring down everything. He needed as strong a case as he could muster to convince any inquiry that he had acted in an appropriate manner.

'I was right all along,' he said, forcing calm into his voice. 'And my report shall reflect that the American was obviously a spy here to aid the enemy. It's obvious to me that if one looks at the facts, as we now know them, that Radcliffe and Major Taylor most likely worked together and were complicit in the murder of the woman who threatened to expose them. Radcliffe, with the help of someone, who we will presume to be one of the natives, escaped and killed his accomplice and his guard. We were not to know that he had somehow bribed this missing African to help him. The record will show that Radcliffe was to be executed. As a spy. Him and the boy.' General Reece-Sullivan took refuge from the uncertainty of his thoughts and his future behind his tidy desk. 'Have the sentries who were on duty here last night charged with dereliction of duty.'

The aide-de-camp recognized the cover-up might work, but not all the pieces fitted.

'And the Charteris woman, sir? She has a public following back home – even among some politicians. Are you… are we… saying that she was involved?'

Reece-Sullivan hesitated, concealing his uncertainty for the moment by selecting a cigarette from the silver cigarette box. 'No, of course she was not involved. A woman like Mrs Charteris might be a nuisance to us, but her humanitarian efforts have garnered widespread support, as you say. No… she… she was obviously forced to accompany Radcliffe…'

He paused. There needed to be a sound reason for his report to be feasible and accepted with as few questions as possible.

'To care for the injured boy,' his aide-de-camp suggested.

Reece-Sullivan lit the cigarette. 'Yes. Exactly. Very well. Signal those concerned, tell them Radcliffe is going to warn the Boers. He'll have to go down the valley.'

'It's too early, general. The heliograph won't work. The mist hasn't lifted yet, sir.'

'Then when it does,' Reece-Sullivan retorted sharply. Then relented. 'Thank you.'

The valley was little more than a hard-baked swathe of scrub and anthills, like most of the battlefields the British had found themselves fighting across during this war. Broad enough for a battalion to march abreast, its twisting route cut north-west through the mountain ranges and their escarpments. Reece-Sullivan's commanders had been moving their troops along the left flank of the valley for days, using the high ground to set their infantry. The plan was for the artillery in the north to bombard the Boer positions. Some would try and escape northwards, that was expected, but there were cut-off battalions waiting for them, while here in the south the Scottish and Irish troops would have a day's sport firing down into the defenceless Boers as they were forced into the killing ground. They would have no cover and mass surrender would be their only option once the firepower cut into them. If these thousands of Boers were taken out of the war – one way or the other – Reece-Sullivan's regiments would have a clear route to march north and attack the rear flank of the massed Boer army. A decisive victory was close at hand.

Pierce and the others were on the opposite mountain range. Mhlangana had taken them safely through the night and put enough distance between them and the English troops. Pierce called a halt and eased Edward from the saddle, laying him in the coolness of the rocks as the sun rose behind them. It would soon bring all the force of its heat to bear. As Evelyn tended to the wounded boy and Mhlangana prepared cold food, Pierce, rifle in hand, backtracked the few hundred yards to where sawtooth peaks shielded them from the valley. It felt as though he were on the roof of the world. The river of mist curling below twisted sluggishly, evaporating in the sun's rays. Pierce pulled open his field telescope and studied the distant troop positions. He could see men behind the rocks spread right along the opposite ridge. Sweeping his eye along the escarpment, he saw that they were little more than three hundred feet above the valley floor, but this gave the soldiers a strong defensive position and an ideal place to set an ambush. His own safety and that of those with him was of constant concern and he scanned the ground behind them, left and right along the route Mhlangana had brought them – but there was no sign of pursuit. By nightfall they would be well clear, a day closer to Portuguese East Africa and a ship home.

The night ride had gone well. Their slow, unhurried pace helped the wounded boy and the morphia that the surgeon had given them would see him through. Pierce had no doubt that Edward would be strong enough to survive, but the old soldier's experience told him that his friend might not be so lucky. He scanned the valley again as the morning mist rose up like ghosts of the dead, disappearing into the rocks and sky. It laid its gossamer dampness over him, leaving a residue of moisture on his jacket. He wiped a hand across his face. This place would soon be a vale of tears.

He was careful to angle the eyeglass so that the sun's rays did not catch it and expose his position to those on the opposite ridge; now that the mist had lifted he saw the ranged troops more clearly in the sharp morning light. A sudden glint caught the corner of his eye. In the far distance a heliograph mirror flashed. He lowered the field telescope and saw the dark shape of man and horse below. They were motionless. He tightened the focus. It was Radcliffe on the Irish stallion.

Pierce's cry of recognition and fear caught in his throat. He was helpless. All he could do was watch.

Brevet Major Lawrence Baxter buttoned his tunic. It had been a long cold night and his mouth tasted of the staleness that came from cheap tobacco and rough, hip-flask brandy. There had been no hot food for the past twenty-four hours and he willed the distant guns to start their rumbling thunder so the poor bastards could be driven on to his riflemen's fire. He was grateful that the Royal Irish were at the end of the line. The Scottish regiment up the line to their left would have first go at the retreating Boers coming from the north and those that got through had Belmont's marauders to deal with. It seemed unlikely that anyone desperate enough to gallop down the valley would survive. The sooner the killing started the better, he reasoned. Kill and move on. Keep killing until someone cried enough and signed a peace treaty that would haunt a nation for eternity but would at least save his soldiers from mutilation and death. He banished the pessimism from his mind. He would get his men through as best he could.

'Will you look at him!' cried Mulraney. 'Jeezus, the man's a sight for sore eyes!'

Baxter looked towards Mulraney as Sergeant McCory quickly approached with a field pad's sheet of paper clenched in his fist. He handed it to Baxter.

'Heliograph message, sir. We're to stop Mr Radcliffe getting through the valley. Orders are to shoot him.'

Baxter checked the text. It confirmed what McCory had said.

'What in God's name is going on?' he said and strode quickly towards Mulraney and the others who gazed down from their positions onto the valley.

'You see him, major?' said Mulraney. 'Man's sitting like he's not a care in the world. Shouldn't we tell him the *boojers* are gonna come full bloody tilt down there once the guns start?'

Baxter shook his head. It didn't make sense. 'What the hell is he doing down there?'

He heard the creak of a saddle and a horse's hoof scuff the ground. He looked over his shoulder. Belmont was tying a sweat rag around his neck; a half-smoked cheroot drooped from his lips. 'I suspect he's waiting for me,' said the dragoon. He tossed the cheroot, settled his slouch bush hat on his head and without haste guided the horse towards the meandering track that led down to the valley.

'Sir?' said McCory, needing an answer.

Lawrence Baxter squinted through the sunlight at the horseman below. 'The men are to hold their fire. Send a message asking for confirmation.'

That confirmation came soon enough. The mirrors flashed back and forth. The direct order was to be obeyed without hesitation. By the time the final message was in Baxter's hand Belmont had navigated his horse down the rocky path and the Royal Irish soldiers were standing watching the two men below them. None knew why the dragoon captain had ridden down but barracks rumour from the time at the Dublin garrison was that the arrogant Belmont had insulted Radcliffe's dead wife and thrashed his son on the New Year horse race. Others said

Belmont had severed young Radcliffe's arm in the Boer ambush. Whatever the cause, there was a score about to be settled.

'Two to one your man Radcliffe will take him,' said Mulraney.

'I'd have a guinea on that if I had it,' said another.

'Five to one,' said Corporal Murphy. 'Major Radcliffe's an old hand.'

'Belmont's a mean bastard,' said Flynn, picking a lump of dust-clogged snot from his nose. 'I'd have a half-crown on him.'

'Shut the gab!' said Sergeant McCory, but stood behind his men, as interested as they were in what was going on.

Belmont settled his horse fifty yards from Radcliffe. He saw that the American had a fine mount, better than his own. But Belmont was the younger and stronger man by some years and that's what mattered.

'War changes everything,' said Belmont, watching Radcliffe, who seemed equally unconcerned about what was going to happen between them.

'Killing never changes,' said Radcliffe. 'And you damned near killed my son.'

'I did,' said Belmont, drawing his sabre, feeling the horse bristle as it sensed his tension. 'He would have shot me. It was fair.'

'I know, but I'm still going to kill you for it,' said Radcliffe. 'There's a meanness in you that needs to be stopped. You're a man that needs killing.' He slid the cavalry sabre from its scabbard.

Belmont gathered the reins in his left hand, the leather tight against his riding gloves. He saw Radcliffe do the same. The Irish horse tucked in its head, its haunches bunching, hooves back-pacing, coiling for the charge. Man and horse eager to attack.

A moment of realization broke into Belmont's concentration. 'You're buying time. That's what this is about. Did you get the boy away?' he said, letting his eyes sweep across the opposite mountains. 'Course you did.'

The horses scuffed the ground with anticipation, both riders controlling their fidgeting mounts.

'It's been a good war, Radcliffe, but it's changing... trench warfare, big guns... small-minded generals... I'll wager there'll be little use for cavalry when this is over... No one to test ourselves against.'

The rising sun behind Radcliffe cast a long shadow. He had the advantage and knew he needed it. 'You won't need to,' he said and spurred the horse on.

They charged, sword arm held forward, wrists half-turned, blades' cutting edge ready to strike. It took less than ten seconds for them to barge and clash. Radcliffe's horse was the stronger and he heeled it into Belmont's. Muscle met muscle and the impact slowed Belmont's blow but he had half expected the assault and blocked Radcliffe's sabre thrust. Blades clanged, both men tight-reining their horses to keep them close. Their grunting efforts forced the blades back and forth in a flurry of slash and block, lunge and parry. Glancing blows cut into the horses. Wild-eyed, they snorted and whinnied. Belmont yanked the reins hard, forcing his mount's head violently away while Radcliffe used his legs to urge the horse into the attack, saving its mouth from a vicious grinding of the bit. Their sabres locked; each man's strength was tested. Belmont's gritted teeth yielded a snarl. Radcliffe's left hand was suddenly free of the reins and his body twisted, keeping Belmont's sabre out of harm's way, but slamming his fist into the side of Belmont's head.

Had the morning breeze carried the mutterings from the Irish ranks, Radcliffe would have heard Mulraney swear that the American was a street-fighter. Radcliffe had once fought the Plains Indians hand to hand and that bitter experience gave him an edge. The dragoon rocked from the blow as Radcliffe drew back his sabre and slashed. The blade cut through Belmont's field jacket but the man's horse veered away, saving him from serious injury. Belmont hauled on the reins, spitting blood from the blow that had glanced down his face and split his lip. It was of no consequence to him: the taste of blood was good. He attacked.

Radcliffe barely had time to defend himself. Belmont was a seasoned fighter; he feinted and with a rapid turn of his wrist brought his blade down across Radcliffe's chest. The sabre's tip ripped cloth and cut skin; Radcliffe twisted but the blade's momentum bit into his left shoulder and he felt the burn as it seared his flesh. He was suddenly vulnerable. His defence exposed. He pulled his foot free from the stirrup and raked Belmont's thigh with his spur, an attack that made the dragoon curse and served to offset his expected blow, which slashed through the air inches from Radcliffe's head.

Dust churned and sweat stung their eyes, but Radcliffe had bought vital seconds and rained a flurry of blows on his opponent. Belmont reeled but kicked his horse free from the melee. Both men sucked the dry, gritty air into their lungs. A quickening breeze made dust scuttle across the valley floor as they repositioned themselves for another charge. Belmont had claimed first blood. Radcliffe's wound trickled stickily into his shirt, which clung to the wound. He took a second to check – it was a cut that he could staunch; no artery had been slashed. Despite the stinging pain he knew it to be superficial. A sabre's heavy blade could take a limb, but he had been lucky. For a moment he sagged in the saddle and let the pain's keenness hold him. The horse's wheeling meant the sun's glare was now against him and he squinted as Belmont turned his horse left and right, seeking the angle for his attack, assessing how best to deliver the killing blow to the wounded American.

Radcliffe heard a plaintive cry from a distant past. He and Pierce had once fought the Comanche, whose war-painted braves knew when death was about to take them. In his mind's eye he saw the outnumbered warriors that the Buffalo Soldiers were about to kill. They chanted their death song and then urged their ponies forward, right into their enemy. This South African valley now swirled with their ghosts as the devil winds twisted up little dust storms – desert phantoms. For a moment Belmont was obscured and then the breeze died again. Radcliffe looked into the shimmering light. Perhaps the wound was more serious than he had thought.

The dragoon called out: 'You should have stayed at home, Radcliffe. Your glory days are far behind you. Give it up.'

There was no need to spur the impatient Irish horse this time. It surged forward. Radcliffe raised himself in the stirrups, leaned forward, arm extended, sabre pointed towards his adversary. Belmont grinned and savagely kicked the sides of his blood-flecked horse. The American would be dead in seconds. Raising himself from the saddle like that was a mistake that would cost him his life. He had no defence below his chest. Eager for the kill Belmont urged his horse on. Even if Radcliffe struck downward Belmont knew the strike would take vital seconds too long. An arm's length from his kill and Belmont blinked in disbelief. Radcliffe was no longer out of the saddle but lying low across the wild horse's withers. He had lunged below Belmont's guard.

The horses surged past each other. Radcliffe leaned back

in the saddle and put pressure on the reins. The stallion pulled up, then turned under the leg kick and stopped, chest heaving, sweat-streaked flanks shuddering from exertion. Radcliffe watched Belmont, now thirty yards away. The dragoon was upright in the saddle but the reins were loose in his hands. He stared towards Radcliffe and then the bloodied sabre dropped to the ground. Radcliffe eased his horse forward at the walk. Belmont's head slumped; his bush hat fell into the pooling blood below his mount. When Radcliffe reached him the dragoon lifted his head to face him. Blood seeped between his teeth as he grinned at Radcliffe.

He tried to say something but Radcliffe's strike had cut deep into his chest. Radcliffe watched him unemotionally, waited until his head drooped again and then his body fell silently into the dirt.

Moments passed. Radcliffe peered into the heat haze that had settled across the valley's distant horizon. Ride on or backtrack? If Reece-Sullivan had any sense he would have scouting parties scouring the escape route, which meant that if he backtracked he would come up against them. If he went forward he would ride into the Boers. It had come down to a game of devil's dice. A moment of regret claimed him. He wished his friend Colonel Baxter were still alive, and that Baxter's son were with his own boy. Old soldiers watching their sons grow up.

He slid the sabre into its scabbard and patted the horse's neck. It was a fearless beast and he offered a silent word of gratitude to the Irishman who had gifted it to him. Benjamin Pierce would see Edward home – all he needed to do now was to reach the end of the valley and find his way into the mountains before the British artillery began its bombardment and forced their enemy down into this killing ground.

He shook the dizziness from his mind. Blood from his wound now soaked his jacket and was seeping down into the saddle.

He remembered an African proverb – had it been Mhlangana who had told him? It didn't matter. Only the words stayed lodged in his memory: *Human blood is heavy, and the man who has shed it cannot run from it.*

Radcliffe swilled water from the canteen round his mouth and spat the sourness away. It was a race worth running. He dug in his heels and eased the reins. He gave the stallion its head and let it run ahead of the dust devil that chased them.

Major Lawrence Baxter and his men had watched the unfolding contest. They had fallen into an uncommon silence when Radcliffe killed Captain Belmont because now the horseman was galloping beneath them and orders had been issued to stop him.

'Sergeant McCory! The men will set their sights at five hundred yards. Volley fire when ready,' Baxter ordered.

McCory hesitated.

'When you're ready,' Baxter said quietly.

McCory smiled grimly. It was the best they could do to give Radcliffe a chance.

'Enemy to your front! Five hundred yards! Ready!' McCory commanded.

Mulraney thumbed his sight's bevelled wheel and set the range. 'Five hundred yards, my arse. Seven more like. The major's letting him get through, God bless him.'

Flynn levelled his rifle. 'He might get past us, but those fucking Scottish Protestant bastards up the line won't let him through.'

'FIRE!' McCory shouted.

Rifle fire splintered the air. They watched as the horse ran, full stride, its rider hunched low as if he were racing for the finish line. As man and horse cut across the valley floor, the bullets struck the ground, keeping pace with the gallop but falling short. The volley fire echoed and then Mulraney could no longer keep the discipline expected. He clambered to his feet and cheered. 'Go on, man! Go on! Ride! Go on with you!'

The cry was taken up along the Royal Irish ranks. Men stood, waved and cheered, willing the horseman on.

McCory glanced uncertainly at Baxter, who shook his head. *Leave them be.*

Radcliffe saw the bullets fall short. They splattered the ground like a sudden hailstorm. He thought he heard men cheering once the echoing reverberations settled but all he was certain of was the heaving effort of the stallion as it ran for the horizon. The swirling dust chased them but the black horse's coat shimmered defiantly ahead of it like a flag of war. Pain bit into Radcliffe's chest. The blood from his wound soaked him further. He ignored it and pumped his arms rhythmically forward, urging the horse to go faster and then faster still. The way ahead seemed clear but then another volley of bullets danced before him, right in his path, and a second later came the ragged sound of gunfire. He pulled the horse wide, felt the snap of air as the bullets sought them out. He ducked low on to the flying mane and spoke to the horse, telling it they would make it, said that they were faster than the wind, that the bullets chasing them couldn't reach them. He felt the great horse shudder as bullets struck home; it faltered and then regained its pace. Something struck his leg, a vicious punch that numbed him. Another clipped his right arm. Wasps tugged at his jacket, stinging his skin. Tears blurred his vision for a moment as the wind nipped his eyes. Blood made the reins slippery. He curled a fist around the horse's mane. They were slowing. The devil wind had caught them and began to enshroud man and horse. The rifles from the ridge fell silent. He knew they could still make it home.

But then the luck a man always needs in war ran out.

A platoon of men from the Highland Division were on the valley floor. They saw the surging dust cloud racing towards them and a horseman emerging from it bearing down on them on a black stallion, nostrils flared, blood streaking its flanks. They knelt, levelled their weapons and fired.

The devil wind swept past them taking horse and rider with it into the rippling heat haze, leaving only the distant sound of hoof beats in the desolate valley.

And then silence.

High on the ridge Pierce lowered the telescope and turned away.

Epilogue

The insistent rapping of the rain against the window pane reminded Pierce of the stuttering gunfire those five years past in South Africa. His friend saved many a life when he took on the guns. The Boer commandos had heard the power of the gunfire in the valley and turned away, forcing the British to regroup, and later an army of several thousand Boers, realizing their cause was lost, surrendered. And finally everyone went home.

Pierce's finger marked the page in the book he was reading. He stood up and crossed to the slightly open window, allowing a few splattering drops of rain to touch his face before closing it. The coals in the grate glowed comfortingly against the Dublin winter chill. Below, in the street, a cab arrived and a frock-coated Edward stepped down, one sleeve of his coat neatly pinned, the other arm extended to help a pretty young woman step down.

Edward had become a fine scholar and this attractive young woman was likely to become his wife. No doubt, Pierce thought, a family would soon follow. Edward's success seemed assured and he was already showing signs of becoming an excellent lawyer. Pierce heard the front door open and close. The sound had a familiarity to it, something he welcomed. Voices were muted downstairs but he knew Mrs Lachlan would have helped the young couple ease out of their wet coats and that hot food would soon be offered and accepted. Perhaps he would have a brandy first with Edward. He hoped so. He delighted in talking to the boy, took solace in telling him about his father and the road they had travelled together. It was good to reminisce and Edward enjoyed listening; he never failed to ask questions about the Buffalo Soldier's life, and always wanted to hear what Pierce had seen that fateful day in South Africa.

And Pierce never tired of the telling.

Edward came bounding up the stairs, smiled and greeted Pierce, making a gesture of putting a glass to his lips as he opened the door of the room opposite. The girl always stayed below stairs for a few moments, making sure that Mrs Lachlan prepared a tray with the food that Edward preferred. Such conversations were a delicate balance between youthful enthusiasm and a stalwart woman of immense patience. Pierce poured two good measures of brandy, catching a glimpse of Eileen Radcliffe in the chamber that had been prepared for her when Edward and Pierce had returned from the war. Pierce had seen to it that her sitting-room fire was kept lit and that she and her companion nurse enjoyed the privacy that that part of the house offered. Edward kissed his mother and she smiled. She still did not know who her son was, only that the young man was kind and gentle with her. Edward returned to where Pierce waited, took the glass and warmed himself next to the coals. Pierce liked that Edward smiled a lot. He was a young man in a hurry. Hungry to get God-knew-where, but he'd succeed wherever it was, no doubt about that, Pierce thought, sipping the brandy.

Their escape from the South African War had been fraught with danger. Once they'd reached Portuguese East Africa, their trusted guide had returned to his own people in Zululand. Pierce never heard of him again. Evelyn's photograph appeared occasionally in English and Irish newspapers. She had returned to Bergfontein concentration camp and with Pierce's help raised awareness of the prisoners' plight back home. One such photograph showed her guiding a group of important men and women from England along the camp's barbed wire. It was not hatred that had caused such suffering but inexperience, administrative ignorance and a distasteful, ill-judged policy that waged a new kind of war against women and children. Her testimony about Radcliffe and his son was reluctantly accepted by the British Army, with the help of the politicians who knew Radcliffe to be anything but a spy and traitor. General Reece-Sullivan lost his command. A year and a half after their escape Evelyn Charteris died from disease caught in one of the camps. Even though the Boers lost their war they gave this Englishwoman the greatest honour they could bestow: they buried her at the foot of their Women and Children's Memorial.

Pierce had done as he had promised and brought Edward home. Pierce did not object to the rain so much any more but he always remembered the warmth of the African sun. The Royal Irish had recovered Radcliffe's body from beneath the dead horse and buried him atop a kopje above the valley where he had died, a place that saw the rising and the setting of the sun on each skyline. His mind's eye saw Radcliffe on his horse in the warmth of the darkening valley and a small devil wind blowing the memories along with it.

He eased his book open to a page on which a poet had written that when a great man dies, people explore the horizon for a successor, but none comes and none will come, for his likeness is extinguished with him. Yet, because of his greatness, love shall always follow him.

HISTORICAL NOTES

Like all great conflicts that can split communities and families there were Irishmen not only from the same country, city or town fighting each other in the Anglo-Boer War, but from the same neighbourhood. Echoes of the American Civil War.

At the outbreak of hostilities between the South African Republics and Great Britain, European countries adopted a strict neutrality, issuing instructions to their citizens that they should refrain from taking any part in the conflict. The German and Dutch governments gave direct warnings that no assistance was to be offered and that any vessel found to be taking supplies to aid South Africa against Great Britain would have its cargo impounded and the shipping line would be subjected to punitive fines. The German people might well have sympathized with the South Africans but Count Von Bülow, the German Imperial Chancellor, issued a statement that the policy of a great country should not at a critical moment be governed by the dictates of feeling, but should be guided solely in accordance with the interests of the country, calmly and deliberately calculated. French popular sympathy was clearly with the Boers but the Paris administration ordered the prefects throughout the country to remove from official minutes the resolutions of sympathy for the Boers which had been adopted by the provincial councils.

The Americans were fascinated by the South African/Boer

War of 1899–1902. It was a spectacle of a farmer militia taking on the might of the British Empire and their professional soldiers – a conflict that reflected American's own struggle for independence. They displayed as much interest in this colonial war as they did in their own fight against Spain a year earlier during the Spanish-American War. America was now a colonial power like Britain and the South African War created divisions within American society. In 1900 Theodore Roosevelt, then governor of New York, wrote: 'The trouble with the war is not that both sides are wrong, but that from their different standpoints both sides are right.' He insisted that the Republican administration remain neutral but felt that Britain was undertaking the same role of benevolent international policeman that he sought for the United States. He felt that the interests of the English-speaking peoples and civilization 'demand the success of the English army'.

Some church ministers were also vociferous in support for the British. Bishop Joseph C. Hartzell – responsible for the American Methodist missions in Africa – proclaimed that only the British were fit to bear the white man's burden in Africa and explained that the Boers considered the Africans to be children of Ham and treated them as slaves, but the British in the Cape Colony (to the south of the Boer Republics) gave Africans the franchise under the same conditions as their white neighbours.

Needless to say, the German-American Methodists heartily contested Hartzell's assertions, claiming he had been influenced by the grant of free land for his missions by Cecil Rhodes – the great instigator of imperial expansionism in Southern Africa.

Mark Twain was not pro-British but was forthright in his opinion. 'England must not fall,' he said. 'It would mean an inundation of Russian and German political degradations... a sort of Middle-Age night and slavery which would last until

Christ comes again. Even wrong – and she is wrong – England must be upheld.'

Irish Americans saw the conflict through their own eyes and very differently to those who might have seen support for the British in purely economic terms. Gold and diamonds were part of international trade and the Boers were considered too backward to be stewards of the world's resources. The arguments and passions raged – pro-British, pro-Boer. Irish, Dutch and German Americans raised support and money for the Boers while a group of American women married to Englishmen raised forty thousand pounds to charter, equip and staff a hospital ship, the SS *Maine*.

More Americans volunteered to fight with the British than with the Boers.

For Irish Americans the fact that Britain was at war meant it was their duty to oppose the nation that held their kinsmen in subjugation in Ireland. Irish Americans were prepared to strike against the hated Empire and even proposed to mount a raid by Fenians into Canada which was thwarted by Theodore Roosevelt who threatened to turn out the militia and throw them into jail.

Similar emotions as those experienced by the Americans – and also those in Britain who were against the war – swept the world. The Boer War of 1899–1902 was the second conflict between the British and the South African Boer Republics of the Orange Free State and the Transvaal. These notes are not the place to recount the historical seeds of unrest that had begun two and a half centuries earlier, but when the British abolished slavery in 1834 the immigrant Dutch Calvinists – known as Voortrekkers (pioneers) – who spoke a vernacular form of Dutch known as Afrikaans, and who had settled the harsh land, undertook an exodus that became known as the Great Trek to escape from the Cape and Natal colonies ruled by the British. The Boers were determined to deny political rights to Africans and Coloureds (people of mixed race).

The first war in 1880 – which lasted all of ten weeks – ended in political defeat for the British (following three major military reversals) and a treaty was signed in 1881. From then onwards British political power and economic interest in the vast mineral wealth that South Africa held virtually predetermined another war between the Boers and the British. This imperial war was known by various names – the Anglo-Boer War, the South African War, and the War of Independence by the Boers – but whatever label history has placed on it, it was the cause of enormous suffering. The military lessons learned and tactics employed proved to be a precursor to the First World War, which followed a few years later. Artillery and trench warfare signalled the end of the great cavalry charges favoured by many of the imperial generals.

In 1895 a failed uprising by British immigrants, volunteers and Rhodesian troops – a scheme instigated by Cecil Rhodes, Prime Minister of the Cape Colony – was considered by the South African general, Jan Smuts, as being the real declaration of war, but it was another four years before the Boer Republics themselves declared war against the British in October 1899. The might of the British Empire gave British politicians and generals a false sense that an easy victory would be achieved by Christmas. It is a perpetual mystery why politicians, in particular, seem never to learn the lessons of history.

The war caught the British unprepared. Troops were drafted from the Empire – India, Canada, New Zealand and Australia – and as tensions heightened volunteers joined the Boer Republics to fight in the Foreign Brigade. Irish, French, Scandinavians, Germans, Russians and, in at least one recorded incident, a

Scotsman fought for the Afrikaner cause. In the years before the war began, the rush for gold and diamonds in the Transvaal Republic brought men from across the world, and many of them were Irish, who not only brought their strength and dreams to the goldfields but also secured their escape from British rule in Ireland. It was one of the vagaries of war that brought Irishmen to bear arms against each other.

In the nineteenth and twentieth centuries Ireland was part of the British Empire. The Irish Republicans – known then as Fenians – had had little success in their bid for Home Rule. Their ranks were riddled with traitors and the British Army and Irish constabulary had little difficulty in keeping their activities under control. The Irish served in government posts: the civil service, the military and the navy. It was an inconvenient fact for the Irish Nationalists that more than fifty thousand of their fellow countrymen fought for the British Army during the Boer War and were often led by Irish generals. This constituted the greatest number of Irish troops in any campaign during Queen Victoria's reign and many of these men were at the forefront of a number of key engagements, serving in Ireland's thirteen infantry battalions and three cavalry regiments. These men forged a lasting reputation for courage and tenacity. It was this moment in history that I wanted to use in *The Last Horseman*.

It was never my intention to look over the shoulders of the towering figures who were the key players in this conflict: Cecil John Rhodes; General Sir Redvers Buller; and Field Marshal Frederick Lord Roberts, affectionately known as 'Uncle Bob', who had had resounding success in the campaigns in India. That Lord Roberts and Sir Redvers Buller were at loggerheads, and that military and political divisions between many of the commanders became entrenched during this conflict, had a negative impact on the execution of the war. Water and food was scarce – and in general terms so was the feeding of this vast army as supply lines were long and difficult to manage and often destroyed by the enemy.

The British Army were unprepared for guerrilla warfare. They were used to volley fire during their colonial wars, often against a poorly armed enemy; now they were faced by a determined group of men and women who fought for their homeland. The Boers were expert horsemen, accustomed to riding across vast tracts of countryside, and they often depended on their shooting skills to put food on the table. These 'dirt farmers', frontiersmen who scraped a living from the harsh land, formed themselves into commandos: groups of highly mobile fighters who could strike fast at the lumbering British. (The same term would be applied to shock troops used by the British in the Second World War.) During the South African conflict the British soldiers had no bush- or fieldcraft and the generals often insisted their men advance on their enemy in closed order – virtually shoulder to shoulder. Boer marksmen with their German Mauser rifles – which had an effective range of two thousand metres and a five-round magazine whose ammunition used smokeless powder making it difficult to spot – made short work of many a brave British Tommy who had never heard of, let alone trained in, fire and manoeuvre. Onward they went against the guns until they could fight hand to hand and deliver a terrifying death to the Boers entrenched on hillsides and the rock-strewn kopjes. Infantry bayonet attacks, and cavalry assaults with lance and sword, put the fear of God into the Afrikaners. The soldiers of the British Army took their poor conditions in good spirits, as cheerful and philosophical as soldiers often are in any campaign, despite exercising a soldier's right to moan. They looked out for each other and held regimental pride close to their hearts.

Irish regiments' and brigades' exploits can be explored by reading any of the excellent non-fiction publications available on the Boer War, but the Royal Irish Regiment of Foot is a fictional unit, as is Belmont's 21st Dragoons. The Royal Irish are an amalgam of different units, and I chose to pit them against the Boer Army and Liam Maguire's commando from the Foreign Brigade at the great battle at the Tugela Heights in Natal (more correctly named 'Thukela') in mid to late February 1900. Across the Tugela River lay the steep, undulating ground of Pieters Hill, Harts Hill and Railway Hill, and General Fitzroy Hart's (5th) Irish Brigade's assault, along with other British regiments, was an exhausting attack over rolling hills to dislodge an entrenched enemy. Wounded soldiers were often left unattended in the field, their injuries seen to by their comrades only if circumstances permitted. In the first half of the war medical evacuation was crude and badly organized, and so too were the attempts to instil field hygiene. Poor water supplies forced men to drink whatever water could be found and this made a significant contribution to bringing down soldiers with enteric fever, typhoid and dysentery. (As Mulraney said: Drink from the Tugela and you'll have the scutters.)

A field dressing was all the men possessed by way of medical supplies and they had to wait until they could be taken from the battle by Indian stretcher-bearers. Although my story does not directly relate the fighting done by colonial troops I learned from my research that India contributed more soldiers and ambulance workers than any of the other British colonies and that the largest number of Boer prisoners of war were held in camps in India. Unlike the British and colonial soldiers who fell in the Boer War the graves of Indian 'auxiliaries' who died in South Africa are not known, and the only memorial to them was erected by the Indian community. These soldiers' contribution is seldom recognized but the comfort they afforded the wounded men in the field was significant. The Natal Indian Ambulance Corps was formed by a twenty-eight-year-old Indian lawyer practising in Natal: Mohandas K. Gandhi.

Gandhi's sympathies lay with the Boers and he expressed great admiration for their leaders and for the heroism of the Boer women. He justified his action in organizing the ambulance corps on the grounds that Indians who claimed rights as subjects of the British Empire had an obligation to contribute to the war effort.

Any reader familiar with British rifle shooting will know that it was Sergeant J. H. Scott who won the Silver Medal at Bisley in 1897, and not Captain Frederick Taylor. I took some licence with the facts as I wanted to establish that Sheenagh O'Connor's killer was a crack shot. I hope, too, that any 'gunners' will forgive the very brief description of firing the Royal Field Artillery 12-pounder. Other than the mechanics of opening and closing the breech and setting the gun's elevation, there are other tasks to be performed in setting a gun, and the fuze on the top of the shell should be turned to accommodate the length of time before it explodes, but in the heat of the action I needed to have Pierce load and fire the gun as quickly as possible. I followed, as closely as my understanding allowed, the information given by the 1897 *Treatise on Ammunition*, which was very kindly offered to me by one of the forum members on the Anglo-Boer War website (AngloBoerWar.com). There are many enthusiasts who contribute to online forums, and I would urge anyone receiving assistance from them to make a donation to help keep them going. Much effort is put into these sites' development and were it not for the breadth of experience that the forum members offer some of the minutiae that we fiction writers are forever seeking out might never be discovered.

I also found personal accounts of the war from individual soldiers' recollections, as well as observations made by war correspondents and diaries kept by nurses in the field. I'm sure that any reader with knowledge of this conflict will recognize that Evelyn Charteris could, in part, be modelled on Miss Emily Hobhouse, the daughter of an Anglican rector. This Cornishwoman travelled to South Africa to do what she could to alleviate the suffering of the women and children in the concentration camps. These internment camps were set up to house the families whose farms had been burned out in order to disrupt the Boer fighters' supply lines. This was a badly conceived concept based on a strategic and logistical problem. The welfare of the women and children became a mark of shame for the political and military class; the poor hygienic conditions and lack of sufficient food in the camps caused between 18,000 and 28,000 deaths and left an embittered Afrikaner nation with a legacy of hatred for the English.

Hobhouse, a member of the South African Women and Children's Distress Fund, visited some of the camps in the Orange Free State between January and April 1901. Unlike Evelyn Charteris, who depended on someone at home – in this story Joseph Radcliffe – to publicize her reports, Hobhouse published her findings to a shocked public in England. Her report led to a government enquiry: the Fawcett Commission. In their report the commission criticized the camps and listed a number of recommendations for improvement. The British High Commissioner in the Cape Colony, Lord Arthur Milner, assumed direct control of the camps in November 1901. He improved the conditions and rations in the camps. Before he took over, the death rate was 344 per thousand per annum in

October 1901. Infant deaths, mainly due to measles, stood at 629 per thousand. By January 1902, the overall mortality rate had reduced to 160, and by February to 69, and by May to 20. By the end of the war the death rate had fallen below the peacetime rate. Few people know that there were also concentration camps for Africans. When the white women and children were taken into camps their black servants and labourers from the farms were also detained in one of the sixty-six camps that were set up specifically for them and which claimed the lives of twenty thousand. At one stage there were more than 115,000 Africans incarcerated in these camps and many were used by the British as a labour force. (It is worth pointing out that unlike later Nazi concentration camps these camps were not set up with the express intention of exterminating a section of the human race, but to deprive the Boer commandos of supplies and to induce the burghers to surrender.)

It should be noted that the concentration camp at Bergfontein is fictional, as are the towns of Verensberg and Swartberg and the railway line connecting them.

It is interesting that an American lobbyist on behalf of the Boers argued that condemnation of the concentration camps would rebound on Boer supporters because of the role played by American imperialism during the Filipino revolt: the United States authorities had established concentration camps to suppress the insurrection in the Philippines early in 1899 where 'the torture by water cure and pumping sea water into prisoners make it difficult to protest…' Waterboarding has been around a long time.

The Boer commandos were made up of farmers, clerks, lawyers and foreigners. I referred to the original 1929 edition of *Commando: A Boer Journal of the Boer War* by Deneys Reitz, who fought as a young seventeen-year-old in the conflict.

Thomas Pakenham's acclaimed scholarly work *The Boer War* (1979) is one of the first books I turned to; there is also a wonderful shortened but illustrated, large-format edition of this work published by Weidenfeld & Nicolson. I also consulted the collected studies of various academics in *The South African War* (1980), General Editor: Peter Warwick and Advisory Editor: Professor S. B. Spies.

The Manual of Military Law 1898 explains that an officer is placed in arrest by either a staff officer or adjutant on the command of the senior officer. Being in arrest does not mean being placed in confinement as would happen to an NCO or private soldier. However, given that Major Taylor had committed murder I felt it appropriate for the story that I confine him.

The National Army Museum Book of the Boer War by Field Marshal Lord Carver (1999) is a gem of a book and contains documents, photographs and information that I had not found elsewhere. Leo Amery's seven-volume work published between 1900 and 1909, *The Times History of the War in South Africa 1899–1902*, is comprehensive and also partisan. Amery was committed to reform in the British Army and he levels criticism at the high command.

On a personal note I came across one of my wife's ancestors, Lieutenant Nicholas William Chiazzari, who served with the Naval Brigade, Natal Naval Volunteers, who when the Royal Engineers failed to span the Tugela worked through the night to get the troops across. The events were described by W. K. L. Dickson in his book *The Biograph In Battle: Its Story in the South African War.*

> January 16th... Our soldiers looked wretchedly wet and bedraggled as they wound their way over and around the kopjes. We could see them slowly

> approach the river and test the crossing, two men going up to their middles and wading round to make sure that there were no entanglements for the feet. Then the troopers followed one by one, while others tried to engineer the ferry, which they ultimately abandoned to our naval men, the handy boys, who are signalled for from the valley. Soon a party of thirteen was made up under command of Lieutenant Chiazzari, with Chief Gunner Instructor Baldwin assisting. They managed to quickly repair the ferry and send the troops across, toiling all evening and throughout the night until dawn. General Buller sent word to Captain Jones next morning that his men were worth their weight in gold.

Baldwin's account of the feat is most entertaining. I abbreviate it somewhat for convenience sake:

> We got orders to repair and handle the ferry just as it was getting dark, so we nipped down the hill and were soon at work, the Colonel of the Engineers passing it over to us. Lieutenant Chiazzari took the ferry while I remained on this side, and soon had the thing going in good shape. It's a wonder what a bit of rope will do along with plenty of willing chaps. We were six from [HMS] *Terrible*, and seven Natal Volunteers, including Lieutenant Chiazzari... Before dawn we had taken nearly all over at the rate of 126 horses and three waggons in forty-two minutes...

In addition to the gratitude of General Buller, Lieutenant Chiazzari was thanked by Major General N. G. Lyttelton and was twice mentioned in despatches and awarded the Distinguished Service Order.

The lines quoted by Edward Radcliffe are taken from Walt Whitman's 'Ashes of Soldiers':

> With sabres drawn and glistening, and carbines
> by their thighs, (ah, my brave horsemen!
> My handsome, tan-faced horsemen! what life,
> what joy and pride…)

Old soldiers know the awfulness of war and I wanted such men, in the characters of Joseph Radcliffe and Benjamin Pierce, to be obliged to face their own history: older men going to war to save a young man from its terror. It seemed a better way to tell the story than to have a single, robust hero, who could take on the rigours and hardship of such a conflict. These were men who had fought in the Civil War and Indian Wars in the USA, and knew the viciousness of killing and the changes it brings about in a man. Despite any liberties I may have taken in the eyes of historical purists I hope these characters, who share the story with ordinary Irish infantrymen (and a war-hungry cavalryman), bring dramatic conflict to the tale and will foster in the reader an interest in a war that foreshadowed a greater contest to come.

David Gilman
Devonshire, 2015

www.davidgilman.com
www.facebook.com/davidgilman.author

FURTHER SOURCES

King's College London: King's Collections: The Serving Soldier, www.kingscollections.org/servingsoldier/home

The National Archives, British Army Operations up to 1913

Pope, Georgina Fane, C.N.R., *Nursing in South Africa during the Boer War 1899–1900* (1902)

Steevens, G. W., *From Cape Town to Ladysmith: An Unfinished Record of the South African War* (1900)

University of Cape Town, South Africa, Department of Historical Studies

The Wellcome Trust

There were also many internet sites – more than fifty – that I turned to for snippets of information but they are too many to list here. However, one in particular that has many interesting contributions is www.angloboerwar.com.

GLOSSARY

Asseblief:	(Afrikaans) please.
Donga:	(Nguni) dry, eroded watercourse.
Kaffir:	originally an Arabic term for 'unbeliever' and 'infidel'. Once a common prefix in names of fauna and flora (such as *kaffirboom*, now known as the coral tree): there are over sixty compounds and combinations. Also an insulting and contemptuous word for a black African, common (along with the American term 'nigger') at the period of the novel; both are now considered unacceptably offensive.
Kopje	(pronounced kop-ee): (Dutch) a hillock.
Inkosi:	(Zulu) boss; respectful term for one in authority.
Mhlangana:	Zulu name pronounced Muh-shlan-gana.
Riempie:	(Dutch) a strip of leather used as a rope or in making furniture.
Rooinek:	(Afrikaans) literally 'redneck'; an English person.
Sawubona	(pronounced: sa-born-a): (Zulu) hello.
Sjambok	(pronounced shambok): (Dutch) a rhinoceros hide whip.
Stoep:	(Afrikaans) verandah.

ACKNOWLEDGEMENTS

My thanks to the staff at the National Library of Ireland, Dublin, for their kind assistance during my research for this book. My gratitude to Nic Cheetham and staff at Head of Zeus for their ongoing enthusiasm; so too to all those beavering away on my behalf at Blake Friedmann Literary Agency. Isobel Dixon, my literary agent, is a constant source of encouragement and sound advice. Without the skill of my editor, Richenda Todd, there would be many more mistakes, and those that may remain are due to my endless tinkering with the narrative long after her generous and insightful editing.